CONTROLLED BY COMPUTERS
FAR AWAY IN WASHINGTON,
THE SKYHUNTERS WENT TO WAR . . .

Infrared patterns of human beings in frenzied action, concealed from optical vision by camouflage, meant division headquarters. Division headquarters meant float over target. Float over target meant select aimpoint. Aimpoint selected meant bomb release.

Captain Townsend impassively watched the Third Shock Army come out of the dawn. The clanking of treads and the roar of diesels murmured from far away. In an hour or so, the Soviets would circumvent the minefields and the barricades thrown up by British engineers in the wee hours. Then they would charge across Townsend's position. *Over my dead body,* Townsend swore to himself. He smiled for the first time that morning, recognizing the truth in his thoughts. His army was running out of ammunition and out of territory to fight across. They might retreat from here, but they would not find another place to make a stand.

A flicker in the corner of his eye made him look up. A spattering of fireworks smeared across the sky, falling. The projectiles that advanced along the fireworks' course could not be seen, but the captain could intuit their presence, as earlier he could sense the presence of the Soviet tanks. He had never heard of an artillery or aerial bombardment quite like this before, but he understood its purpose. He visualized the graceful arc of the bombs' flight paths. Even with small warheads they would do great damage.

Now explosions bellowed from the Soviet battle line, unmistakably the sound of tank ammunition erupting in flame. Captain Townsend's eyes widened with a feeling he had not known for days: the feeling of hope.

MARC STIEGLER

DAVID'S SLING

BAEN
BOOKS

DAVID'S SLING

Copyright © 1988 by Marc Stiegler

A Baen Books Original

Baen Publishing Enterprises
260 Fifth Avenue
New York, N.Y. 10001

First Baen printing, January 1988

ISBN: 0-671-65369-5

Cover art by David Mattingly

Printed in the United States of America

Distributed by
SIMON & SCHUSTER
1230 Avenue of the Americas
New York, N.Y. 10020

To those who never stop
seeking the third alternatives.

THE BUILDERS

April 18

All side effects are effects.
We can never do merely one thing.
　　　　　　　—First Law Of Ecology

Glare. Howling wind. A rope sliding upward in the
snow. Sharp-cut steps in the mountainside. His leg straining to take that next step. Hilan Forstil knew nothing
beyond that next step. He balanced on the dull edge of
unconsciousness, yet he took that next step. And the next.

He remembered this feeling from long ago. The feeling
was one of exhaustion—an exhaustion so deep that even
the thought of death did not bother him. The memory
came from a time over two decades in his past—from his
time in Nigeria, working among starving children.

Such exhaustion made one sloppy, he knew. And such
sloppiness was dangerous in struggles like this. The danger to himself didn't bother him—after all, he didn't care
if he died—but it disturbed him that an error here could
kill his rope partner.

On the other hand, it was her fault that they were here
at all. An image flashed in his mind of Jan's face at their
last rest stop. The flush of her cheeks, the brilliant fury of
her blue eyes . . . her energy seemed too intense to be
healthy. Dimly, he remembered having had such energy
himself, standing at the base of the mountain. But the
mountain and its vertical miles of glacial white had consumed him. It had not consumed her.

He wanted to curse her.

And he wanted to thank her. With every step he completed, he touched an inner power he had forgotten. He
had worked so hard the last two decades to forge the tools
of external power; such tools seemed fragile now.

The rope slackened. Hilan breathed a sigh of relief and
slowed to match the speed of the rope. *Keep the rope just
barely dragging the ground between us,* Jan had explained

3

the day before, *except during a*—the rope yanked taut, causing Hilan to stumble—*switchback!*

He peered up. Sure enough, the chiseled footprints went on to his left for a short time, then veered back sharply to the right. Jan was directly above, climbing to the right with a cougar's enthusiasm. He couldn't go all the way around the switchback even if he had the energy: but if he continued to the left, the taut rope would drag Jan back as well. He took one more pressure-breath and shakily climbed straight up the mountain, shortcutting through the switch.

Noticing the jerking motions of the rope, Jan stopped to look back. Her mouth dropped open. "Hilan," she called loudly, "you can't—"

Hilan looked up at her, just as the snow yielded beneath his foot. He plunged through the snow bridge into the crevasse beneath.

The rope snapped taut, bouncing him wildly on the end. The plunge halted only a moment before he plummeted again and the rope slid farther over the edge. He looked down into the shadowy cavern below, interested but not afraid. The all-crushing fatigue numbed his mind; he just didn't care. He contemplated his own emptiness, knowing that his lack of fear should be the greatest cause for fear.

His descent slowed, then stopped. He swung lazily in the endless, rocky fracture, listening to the sudden quiet. A wheezing cough echoed down from above. Hilan pictured Jan on the edge of the precipice, leaning into her ice axe with all her strength to stop the fall. Both their lives depended on her endurance.

The realization of *her* danger finally impelled him to action. Miraculously, his ice axe yet dangled from his right wrist. He pressed his lips together for an explosive series of breaths—the whistling sound seemed almost natural now—and wriggled his ice axe into his backpack straps. He grasped the rope. The fatigue yielded to a last buildup of adrenalin.

He climbed over halfway up the rope before the adrenalin failed.

He clung to the rope, thinking about the danger to Jan. If he could not complete this climb, he had to save her.

He still had his knife. He could cut the rope, freeing her from his own fate. He would save enough strength to complete that last act, if necessary. But he was not that lost yet, not quite yet.

Shadows. Deadly quiet. A rope anchored in the snow. His left arm stretching to grasp the next handhold. He balanced on the dull edge of unconsciousness, yet he took that next handhold. And the next.

The rope ended. Hilan reached over the lip of ice, heaving himself out of the crevasse into the glare and the howling wind.

The two-man celebration began with champagne. "A toast to the Soviet Union!" Jim Mayfield exclaimed, raising his glass.

Earl Semmens raised his as well; the glasses tinkled in midair. "A toast to peace," he offered.

"And above all, a toast to tomorrow's Gallup poll results." Mayfield sipped the champagne. His eyes slid across the floor, lingering on the emblem woven with rich blues and golds into the carpet. It was his, at least for now. The emblem was the official seal of the President of the United States. He sat back down; the Secretary of State followed his lead.

Earl sat on the edge of his chair, staring out the window. He spoke in rehearsal of his planned statement to the press. "Yes, this treaty is another potent lever against the arms race. Now that we've curtailed the space-based Ballistic Missile Defense work, all incentives for building new missiles will disappear." He turned back to Mayfield, and for a moment his pudgy features held lines of worry. He tapped a nervous finger on the president's desk. "I wish they hadn't instigated that . . . little incident in Honduras just before the signing. God, they know how to goad us!" He shivered, then resumed his nervous tapping. "Well, we couldn't have done anything about that anyway, regardless of treaties. And the treaty's more important." He nodded his head, and his voice again sounded press-ready. "Yes, the whole world can sleep more securely now that the arms race in space has stopped."

Sometimes the elegant power of the Oval Office gave Jim a sense of grandeur. Seated behind a desk of massive proportions, a desk to dwarf even giants, he felt the ramifications of his decisions pulsing through the world. "Not quite everybody will sleep more securely, Earl. Those goddam contractors working on space weapons will have to find an honest way to make a living." He rubbed his hands. "We may balance the budget yet, Earl." He breathed a sigh of exultation. "Wouldn't *that* make a hit on the polls!"

The door from the Rose Garden swept open with smooth, decisive authority. Even without looking, Mayfield knew who it had to be—though he could not prevent himself from shooting a frown toward the door.

Only one person other than himself entered this room as if she owned it: Mayfield's Vice President, Nell Carson. Mayfield smiled blandly, confident that his irritation remained hidden. Watching her look back at him, Jim saw that Nell had no intention of concealing *her* irritation. It poisoned the joy of his celebration.

Sometimes the elegant power of the Oval Office gave Jim a sense of claustrophobic choking. As Nell looked at him, he felt a brief desire to plead that it wasn't his fault, whatever had happened. His eyes returned involuntarily to the emblem in the carpet; it reassured him.

Nell stepped to the center of the room to address both men. She spoke with tight control that did not reveal her gentle South Carolina accent. "Congratulations, Jim. You have the record for the most treaties with the Soviet Union in the history of American presidents. I have one question."

Jim looked up into her face, searching for the Nell he had known during the campaign—the Nell with the patient smile who had charmed the crowds with her enthusiasm and warmth. She had been a terrific asset during the campaign. When she spoke, the voters believed.

Unfortunately, the charming Nell had faded under the weight of office. Now he could only see the Nell who had devastated opponents with her incisive criticisms. Jim's throat felt dry as he filled the silence. "Yes? What one question do you have?"

"Now that you have set the presidential record, I was wondering: Can you stop now?"

Mayfield's smile turned gray, and his heart missed a beat—something it did more often now than before, something he should check . . . He excised the thought from his mind, removing it with surgical perfection, and reluctantly met her gaze, contemplating her question, looking beyond it to her problem.

Nell Carson was the problem, he decided. She *never* took a moment to look at the bright side. Perhaps that explained the drawn lines in her face. During the campaign, the only objection the media had raised about Nell was that she was too young. She had *looked* too young. No one said that any longer. Mayfield sighed. "Why do you always complain about our successes? You know we needed that treaty. We *had* to get that treaty. Our position with the public was slipping." He shrugged. "We have to depend on treaties, not weapons, if we're going to have a chance of dealing with our domestic problems."

Nell looked into his eyes. It seemed Jim could hear his words echoing back to him, amplified and clarified by Nell's implicit interpretation. She asked, "Who are you trying to convince?"

Mayfield stared at her in amazement. "I'm convincing the public, of course." Her hawkish glare made him shiver. "If I didn't know better, I'd swear you were a Republican!"

A tight smile crossed her face. "Perhaps I should be." She leaned over Jim's desk. "Don't you see the problem with what you've done? Six months ago, you made the agreement on Global Consequences of Nuclear War. There you agreed that, above a certain level of nuclear war, the radiation and climate effects of a war would destroy the attacker, even if the defender didn't shoot back. Now you put a limit on Ballistic Missile Defense. Either one of these treaties, all by itself, is okay. But when combined, they form a terrible danger. Don't you see how these separate agreements interact?"

She paused in her speech. A stiff creak announced Earl's attempt to shift his chair away from her.

She did not relent. "*Winning an all out war now sounds believable.* Without any missile defenses, but with an agreed threshold for nuclear suicide, the first side to launch its missiles is protected from retaliation—because the first strike will deliver as many megatons of destruction as the Earth can absorb. If the victim shoots back, he's destroying whatever survivors remain *in his own country.*"

Mayfield waved the objection aside. "Don't be boring; we've discussed this a million times. The Russians don't think that way. That would be the attitude of a madman!"

"That would be the attitude of a terrorist," came Nell's curt reply. "With strategies based on terror, only terrorists have a chance of winning." Her eyes swept over both men. Jim shivered.

Nell's mouth softened into a sad smile. "And I don't see a single terrorist in this room. I don't even see anyone willing to speak out about clear violations of national boundaries—like the fiasco outside Yuscaran."

Jim looked speechlessly at Earl. He felt like cement cracking under the weight of a speeding truck. "How did you find out about that?"

Nell laughed joylessly. "You sent me to Texas to give Kurt McKenna his medal, remember? I have the clearances, Jim, and under the circumstances, I had sufficient need to know." She lifted her briefcase and thumped it against the polished mahogany surface, making Jim wince. With forceful snaps, she released the latches and removed a flat-screen television with a tiny video player. "I think you should see this for yourself, Jim."

He had no time to object before the tape rolled into action.

They were traveling down a twisting trail, cloaked in jungle growth. It looked like a sticky, humid day, which made Mayfield appreciate the cool comfort of the Oval Office. He could hear tracks clanking in the background, though the sound was muted. Ahead of them on the trail was an armored vehicle. Mayfield wasn't sure, but he thought it was probably a Bradley armored personnel carrier. He vaguely remembered authorizing a few for the Hondurans.

Nell acted as commentator. "We're watching through the gun cameras of a personnel carrier," she explained.

A dull explosion sounded, and the screen washed out in a searing white flame. A scream came from very close by. With a chill, Mayfield realized that there had been people inside the machine now turning into an inferno.

Nell spoke with dry, scientific precision. "They hit the Bradley with a shaped charge. The penetrating explosion hit the ammunition magazine. The brightness of the explosion severely damaged our gun camera; the rest of this tape has been computer enhanced."

The whiteout of the screen faded; a ghostly soft image replaced it. Men scurried into the jungle as the second Bradley disgorged its troops. The computer enhancement kept the soldiers visible to Mayfield's untrained eye, though he suspected that without the computer's intervention, they would have disappeared in the heavy foliage. They all looked like Honduran troops.

One Caucasian stood out by virtue of his uniform and his pale blue eyes. He took off with astonishing speed, loping over the fallen trees, hurrying away from the others. The camera lurched as another explosion sounded, muted, but somehow closer. A sound he had not noticed before stopped—the sound of an engine thrumming. He could not see it, but Mayfield realized that the Bradley from which they watched the scene had been hit, though the camera continued to roll.

The focus shifted to another ragged cluster of men with machine guns, beyond the burning Bradley. Their seemingly random pattern proved quite methodical. They engaged the scattered Honduran troops one handful at a time, overwhelming them piecemeal.

Something seemed wrong with this battle. Mayfield asked, "Where's our air cover?"

"Our helicopters are old and tired, Jim. They're too dangerous to use in battle."

"What about artillery support?"

"We were using our newest radios for communication. They're very delicate, it turns out—oh, the boxes are mil-spec and indestructible, but their frequencies wobble and they get out of tune all the time. So nobody heard about the ambush until it was over." She paused, then ended. "I asked Kurt about it at the reception. He didn't exactly answer me; I suspect he couldn't say what he wanted to in civilized company. Instead he very politely told me that he was getting out of the army—that he intended to get as far away from it as he could go."

Only a couple of Honduran troops remained, hunched in silent fear behind trees and rocks. Suddenly another explosion sounded and half the enemy force fell to the ground. The other half dived for cover. They started shooting in several different directions, though no targets were visible. The gunfire achieved a syncopated rhythm, and continued for a time. One by one, however, the enemy troops twitched as if kicked, then stopped firing.

When just a few enemy troops remained, a long, camouflaged blur leaped out of the brush. "Kurt McKenna?" Mayfield asked. Nell just nodded.

A scuffle followed, then shooting, and Kurt spun down, struck. One of the two surviving opponents lifted his pistol, but McKenna rolled again, and the enemy with the gun went down.

The computer enhancement zoomed in on this struggle between the last two men—the one with the pale blue eyes and the other with . . . the other one also had pale blue eyes!

"Who is that?" Mayfield demanded.

"That's the Russian who organized this little party. Didn't you know? You authorized classifying this skirmish, so that no one would find out about the Russian involvement."

"Oh my God." Mayfield had classified it because it was too embarrassing, not because of any Russian involvement. Perhaps he should have read the report after all.

"To my knowledge, this is the first time Americans and Soviets have met in combat in this decade."

It wasn't a fair fight—Kurt had lost the use of one arm when he was shot earlier. Yet a few seconds later, he was the only one left standing.

Nell shut off the tape. Her voice changed from analytical to commanding. "Jim, we can't sign any more treaties like this last one."

Mayfield shuddered. But he couldn't let Nell Carson, or even some incident in Central America, interfere with the main task. The next election was only a year and a half away. He leaned back in his chair. "Don't worry, Nell. Everything's under control."

For just a moment, Nell's shoulders sagged. Then she

straightened and headed for the door. "I'm counting on it," she said, leaving as abruptly as she had arrived.

After a long moment, President Mayfield turned back to the Secretary and spoke quietly. Each relaxed into a smile. Earl popped another mint in his mouth, and Mayfield accepted one as well. The celebration continued.

They reached the glory of the mountain's peak. Hilan reveled in the view; his joy seemed too great for a single person—it bordered on reverence.

Below, sunlight chased itself up glacier-white slopes. The streaks of brilliance followed his own path, up from the clouds that clung low to the mountain's side. Above, a single white wisp of cloud traced across deep blue skies. The blue had a sharpness that comes of air too thin to fill a man's lungs.

Earth lay across the horizon, beyond a pillowed carpet of clouds. Only the grandest features revealed themselves at this distance. The planet did not seem small, yet it seemed conquerable, as this mountain had been. Hilan realized with hope that indeed mankind had penetrated the most dangerous places the planet offered. Yet he despaired, remembering that now the descendants of those explorers were themselves the greatest remaining threat.

Hilan had changed in the years since his service in Nigeria. He had changed most during a trip there several years later. Starvation no longer occurred frequently enough to cause a global reaction, but it continued; malnutrition hid in every shadow. The population had grown. Hilan realized that for every ten children he had saved, eleven would now die. Yes, Hilan and the others had held famine at bay for a moment. But they had not changed the culture that made famine possible. In some final analysis, his efforts had ended in failure.

His friends had rejected his analysis. He had tried to reject it as well, but he could not.

He had entered politics, believing that better solutions to the problems of mankind would require the accurate application of power. He did not yet know how to apply that power. Probably no one did. But for the moment, he would work to consolidate the power, in preparation for the day when he, or someone, learned how to use it.

Jan led him down the slopes to a shallow depression. Short ridges ringed it on three sides, protecting them from a bitter wind as they made camp. She borrowed his swiss army knife to slice open their freeze-dried food pouches, then started pacing between the packs and the stove to prepare dinner. Her cheeks glowed with an energy that struck Hilan again as somehow too fierce, too burning for a healthy woman. "Believe me, it's much easier going down," she promised him. "If this hadn't been such a great campsite, we could have gone all the way down the mountain today with no problem."

Hilan groaned softly and lay on his sleeping bag. Only his eyes moved, watching Jan pace.

"So, are you happy you came along? I am." Jan turned away in a fit of coughing. When she turned back, the flush of her cheeks had faded. She handed him back his knife.

Holding it, Hilan remembered his earlier desperate thoughts to save Jan if he could not make it. "When I stepped into that crevasse, I almost killed you. I wonder whether it makes sense to rope people together—whether it wouldn't be smarter to sacrifice the one who falls to guarantee that *someone* survives."

"Nonsense. Falls like that remind us why we wear ropes and why we make everyone on the climbing team interdependent in the first place. I'm just glad we responded effectively to the crisis."

"Did we?" Hilan stared at the rips in his gloves, cut during his climb up the rope. "You know, I was so tired before we even reached that crevasse that I hardly noticed the fall." Thinking about it, he was there again. "It was really strange, just staring down at the rocks that would kill me." His eyes unfocused. "I didn't react correctly at all."

Jan laughed. "Hilan, you had the *perfect* reaction— no reaction at all. I wouldn't worry about it."

Hilan grunted. "You're probably right. I'll miss the switch-back over and over, each time reinforcing the lesson that I learned. In fact, I'll learn the lesson far better than if I'd

simply gotten scared when I fell. It'll make a great reinforced revelation. Sounds like a good example for you to
teach at your beloved Institute."

"Yes," Jan said softly, "an excellent example."

Hilan exhaled. The air rushed from his lungs with the
easy freedom that reminded him how high up they were.
He had never thought of breathing as an effort, or of the
friction of the air upon his throat; now, in their absence, he
knew them.

"Jan." His muscles still hung in limp exhaustion, but his
thoughts raced. "Thank you for bringing me here. In my
role at home, I've welded myself so deeply to my senato-
rial image that sometimes I wonder whether I'm still here,
or whether I'm only an image. Now I know."

"I thought you'd like my mountain." She coughed. Hilan
studied her for a moment. Her flush from the climb had
faded. Now she seemed pale—as much too pale as she had
earlier seemed too flush. "I have a favor to ask of you."

He sighed. "You know how to exploit even a moment's
weakness. What do you want me to do—help you save the
world?"

Jan gave him an expression of surprised pleasure that
would have fit well on an American in the Orient who
rounded a corner and ran headlong into an old high school
chum.

That reaction pleased Hilan immensely. Jan did not
understand him as well as he understood her.

Even among his old friends, Hilan had been surprised
by how rare and how out of place the people who personally sought ways to save the world were. Even Hilan's wife
did not understand this fixation of his on the problems of
huge scale—questions of famine, of economic collapse, of
nuclear war. Jan, like himself, was one of those very few
who thought in such terms on a daily basis.

But Jan was an even rarer breed of human being than
those who sought answers to the big questions—she had
found some answers.

She had not yet solved any of the *big* problems, but she
had begun to heal at least one medium-size one—she had
synthesized a therapy that could usually cure the most
common American addiction: cigarette smoking.

Jan continued. "I don't know whether the favor I'm asking you will help save the world or not. Perhaps it will. I wish I knew." Another cough punctuated the sentence. "What I want you to do is talk with Nathan about the Sling."

"The Sling?"

"Yes. It's a military research project."

Despite the exhaustion, and the stiffness of his skin from cold and exposure, Hilan managed to grimace. "God, I hate the military." Again, the air left his lungs too fast. "I wish we didn't need it."

Jan smothered a laugh. "Our mammoth military-industrial complex isn't very American, is it? You know, the first act of the American government after the Revolutionary War was to disband its standing army. They sold the navy's ships. America's forces were reduced to 80 men, none above the rank of captain."

She stretched out on the sleeping bag beside him. "Even today you can see the strength of the anti-military roots of our country. How else could America engage in fierce public debates over permission for advisers to carry side-arms? Even at the heights of our military adventurism, an astute observer can see that it's unnatural for us: we do it so badly. We make far better businessmen than soldiers."

Hilan had never thought of it in quite this light before. "Yet America wound up as the principal adversary of the most powerful military force in human history." He thought about the absurdity of the situation. "How did we get ourselves into this position?" He shook his head. "Even more important, how have we managed to pull it off for such a long time?"

"For decades, we succeeded as a superpower by holding the ultimate club. We succeeded because we had more, and better, nuclear weapons." She shook her head. "But that doesn't work anymore. How could we convince a cold-eyed political pragmatist like Sipyagin that America would use nuclear arms, knowing that the Soviets would destroy us in turn? The nuclear threat served us well for a long time, but its time has come to an end. No one believes we can use it anymore."

Hilan shifted on his bag, trying to burrow into it. The

chilled air made the goose down warmth precious. "It's impossible for anyone to believe that we'd use nukes as long as Mayfield is the decision maker. Some people have trouble believing he can use a letter opener, much less a nuke." Hilan tried to say it without passion. President Mayfield was a member of his own party, after all.

Jan nodded. "You know, both the Soviets and the Americans go through cycles of confrontational behavior. You might think the greatest danger looms when both countries reach the peak of their aggression cycles at the same time. But that's not true. The greatest danger occurs when the cycles go out of phase—when the United States reaches one of its lowest lows and the Soviet Union reaches one of its highest highs."

The cold of the glacial air reached Hilan's heart. "And we've come to that moment in the cycle."

Jan didn't answer.

"So what's the Sling Project?"

Jan laughed at the compound of despair and hope in his voice. "We make better businessmen than soldiers. We must fight, then, as businessmen."

Hilan tried to snort, but it took too much effort. "A division of businessmen wouldn't last very long against a division of soldiers."

"No, of course not. We'd still need soldiers. But we can do with a lot fewer soldiers than some countries because we have another strength: we have crossed the threshold from one form of society to another. Our opponents live in the Industrial Age. We stand on the brink of the Information Age. We must build an Information Age system to defend ourselves."

"And just how do we do that?"

Jan smiled at his limp form. "You look so exhausted—and so curious at the same time. I think I'll leave you in this state and let Nathan tell you the rest of the story."

Hilan groaned. "Very well. When would you like to introduce us?"

Jan closed her eyes. "That may not work," she said. She coughed again, and this time it racked her whole body. Blood spattered the soft snow, a dark obscenity in the evening sunlight. "Dammit," she muttered, "I better at least get off the mountain."

Hilan rose unsteadily to his knees. "What's wrong? What's happening?"

"I'm really sorry, Hilan. The climb down may be harder than I'd hoped."

"What!?"

Jan rose to her feet and put her hands on his shoulders. "Hilan, you're a born crusader. In some ways you remind me of Nathan." She looked away for a moment. "But I haven't always marched to a crusader's rhythm. I was quite content as a chain-smoking psychotherapist, until three years ago. Then I had *my* reinforced revelation." She coughed again. "I found out I had lung cancer."

Hilan had met Jan just a year ago, through another of his rare crusader friends, who had just discovered the Institute. He'd wondered briefly about her past, about why she molded the Institute into a national resource that did all the things it was famous for—from seminars on mass media, to job matching, to weapon systems development—but he hadn't thought about it enough. Now it was obvious.

"The chemotherapy they have these days is quite terrific. They can keep you alive and active, even while the cancer is eating you up inside. Then the end comes quite suddenly." She closed her eyes. "Leslie and Nathan both insisted I shouldn't challenge the mountain this last time. I guess they were right."

Hilan stared with helpless horror.

"We'll find a hospital in the morning. Better get some sleep—we'll start early."

The ache deep within his bones allowed him no other response. He slept, but his sleep roiled with odd images: images of Soviets, and cigarettes, and nuclear missiles. Woven through them all were images of a man, dangling in a crevasse, with only the strength of the rope and the taut determination of his partner's straining muscles to save him.

SNAP. In games of ball and racket, such as tennis, the racket must cease to be a separate external object. It must become one with the player—an extension of his arm. The arm and the eye must also meld through the mediation of the mind. And though the mind controls this connection, it too must submerge its separateness, its awareness of self, into the union. Only the racket connected directly to the eye plays outstanding tennis.

CLICK. With the acquisition of the flatcam video recorder, the news reporter develops a similar relationship with his camera. With the tape riding quietly on his hip, and the flat camera lens pinned on his lapel, individual virtuosos can replace the old-style news teams. The camera is almost invisible; the reporter is quite inconspicuous. As he becomes less conspicuous, he becomes less inhibiting to the people who are his targets. The reporter's eye and the reporter's camera become a single device with which to capture the images he will later clean and craft in the lab. The lab supplies the magic. It is a place where background noise and foreground lighting can be toned to highlight the message, all by using powerful techniques of Information Age filtering.

WHIR. Bill Hardie knows that he has been born in the right moment of history—the beginning of the era of flatcam journalism. He can *see* from the camera lens in his lapel—not merely the lighting and the people, but the action, the emotions, the sensations. He can zero in on those elements with the skill of an astronomer picking out galaxies on the edge of the universe. Sometimes he can sense the critical moment, allowing him to shift his attention *before* the event, to capture it's very beginnings, rather than its concluding passage.

JUMP. The only flaw in Bill's coverage is an occasional jerkiness to the image, a reflection of a certain anxious impatience with real life. His analysis is too important to wait on the sluggish motions of other men. Fortunately, the jitter of his camera, like the noise of murmured voices in the background, can be removed in the laboratory.

FOCUS. Bill recognizes the heavy burden his talent places on him. He understands his mission in life. He must broadcast truth in a pure form to all people. Just as his computer filters the background noise that blurs the conversation, he must filter out the foreground noise that blurs the fundamental reality.

BREAK. Bill frowns at the young geological engineer from the Zetetic Institute up on the stage. The engineer poses a serious problem for Bill. This engineer introduces blaring noise into the foreground, drowning out the truth. The truth is: The people of the State of Washington must not let the United States dump its radioactive wastes there. Nuclear power plants and radioactive wastes are bad; this is the truth. Bill focuses his attention on the nuances of the situation, to wring victory from every tiny image as it happens.

SHADE. Three men sit spotlighted on the stage facing a dimly lit auditorium. Cigarette smoke forms miniature weather inversions here and there in the audience. A puff of acrid blue haze blows across Bill's face; he shifts locations.

FOCUS. The spotlights create the mood of an interrogation, with unseen prosecutors and accusers contemplating the three men nearly blinded by the light. The Zetetic engineer sits in the middle of the three, flanked by two older men—directors from the Power Commission. These directors are the ones who had hired the Zetetic Institute to act as an impartial consultant, to assess the safety of a radioactive waste storage facility near Hanford, Washington.

Why had they hired the Institute? They had known that the Institute had a reputation for doing good engineering. Equally important, the Institute had a reputation for presenting that engineering smoothly in public.

Indeed, the opening of the discussion is dry and crisp, almost too civilized; the Zetetic engineer simply presents facts about the geological properties of the proposed waste site. With careful clarity, he shows why it is a safe place to put radioactives. Bill realizes the Power Commission has taken a risk in hiring the Institute: Zetetics search diligently for facts, and facts could go against the Power Commission as easily as they could go in its favor.

The men of the Power Commission, in their dark blue suits, with their tight, closed faces, mirror the audience's hostility. They perform as perfect Establishment objects of disdain. Had the engineer sat to the side rather than in the middle of the trio, Bill would zoom on them and construct a crisp image of Good versus Evil—the audience versus the Power Commission.

But the engineer sits in the middle, looking gentle, even friendly, in his light blue suit and solid red tie. He maintains an open smile and equally open eyes, apparently oblivious to the emotional tension that stews amidst the combatants. Only the careful precision of his words hints that his understanding of the situation goes deep. Bill will have to perform magic with the lighting and the shading of the stage to make him look sinister. Even then, Bill's success will be incomplete.

PAN. Ovals of pale white float in the darkness of the auditorium: the faces of the concerned citizens who live near Hanford. From here the questions spring, randomly, in sharp tones of frustration and anger. One oval bobs twice, then rises. It is a young woman with spiked hair and mottled jeans. She asks, "How can we make them shut those plants down if we let them dump their waste products on our land?"

When the engineer responds to the woman's question, his voice warms the room with its honesty. "The best way to eliminate nuclear power is, of course, to find a better form of power, such as fusion or solar power satellites. Remember, if you just tell the Power Commission that they can't build nuclear power plants, without telling them what would be better, they'll probably build a coal-burning plant. Is that really better?" The engineer shrugs. "That's a separate study, of course."

ZOOM. For just a moment, the young man frowns. Bill catches that expression, savoring it, knowing it will be useful. "This is the safest place we can find to put the wastes that already exist. In other words, if we put them someplace else, it's more dangerous. Many of you are concerned about how dangerous nuclear reactors are. Don't you see that if you won't let the power companies use the safest methods they can find, then you are creating a self-fulfilling prophecy? Do you believe that you should sabotage the reactors to show how dangerous they are? That is exactly what a person does when he prevents others from using safety precautions."

WHIR, WHIR, WHIR. This is beautiful! Bill can use that bit about sabotage: it will make the engineer sound hostile, despite the soft cheer of his voice.

PAN. A middle-aged man with a beard and a faded flannel shirt speaks, arms crossed, from a slouched position in his seat. "We have the right to decide what to put outside our town."

SLIDE. The engineer nods. "That's true." His smile freezes in position as he looks into the speaker's eyes. "You have the right to decide. But living in a democracy is not just a matter of rights and freedoms; it is also a matter of responsibilities and duties. You have the right to shout 'Fire!' in a crowded theater. You have a duty to *not* exercise that freedom.

"Similarly, here you have the right to decide. But you have a duty to make that decision based on the most careful, rational analysis of the facts that you can. You have a duty not to decide based on a general hatred for the Power Commission, as some people might. And you have a duty not to decide on the basis of a love of high technology, as other people might."

CLIP. A voice from the darkness shouts, "It's not fair that it all goes in *our* backyards."

ROLL. The engineer sighs. "Our society carries with it a number of undesirable features. The only fairness we can approach is to spread the unfairness as fairly as we can. Let them put the radioactives here; it's the best place. But make them put the missile silos and the strip mines elsewhere. If someone figures out another arrangement that's as safe as putting the radioactives here, but that's more fair, and that doesn't have any *other* even more serious consequences, let's do that instead."

ZOOM. Another middle-aged man stands. This one wears a suit that might have done justice to a member of the Power Commission. "What about our property values? When they put that radioactive dump in our backyards, we'll be destroyed."

SLIDE. Another nod comes from the engineer. "Of course, if the Power Commission handles the waste properly, the property values should not be affected. So to encourage them, we recommend that the Commission be required to pay the owner of a property the difference between the value of the land considering the presence of the site, and the value of the land if the site weren't here, when he sells. We've subcontracted with a real estate assessor to establish a set of baseline values." He glanced sideways at the Commission men with a hint of amusement. "This was not the recommendation that the Commission liked most."

PAN. An elderly lady rasps from the front, "What if they don't handle the wastes properly? What if they make a mistake?"

ZOOM. Sorrow masks the Zetetic's face for a moment. "That's what we must prevent. As I've shown, there are a wide variety of mistakes that the system can tolerate because the base rock of the area is fundamentally safe. And the shipping containers are also safe from a wide variety of human errors and natural calamities. But ultimately, even this system must rely on human beings to not invent new kinds of errors. So we asked ourselves the following question: What mechanism could we use to inspire the operators of the site to seek out and correct unforeseen problems before they become critical?"

The young man smiles as he contemplates the probing analysis he has done on this problem. "Do you know how the Romans guaranteed the quality of their bridges? In the opening ceremony, the man who designed the bridge floated on a raft underneath while the first carts passed over. If the bridge collapsed, the builder of the bridge went with it. This ritual guaranteed the construction of many good bridges."

CUT. This story gets a short, murmured chuckle from the audience, as if against their own will, they appreciate the justice of the system.

SLIDE. The Zetetic engineer waves an open hand. "We have a similar plan here, involving both a carrot and a stick. For the stick, we recommend that the chief operating engineer and the plant manager for the waste site be required to live within twenty miles of the site during their tenure.

"We also recommend protection for the chief operating engineer. If he finds grave hazards with the plant that he cannot fix because of expense or politics, then he can blow the whistle with security: The Power Commission will be required to pay him five years' salary. Thus, the man in the best position to know about new dangers has a 'parachute' to protect him from the people who have the most to lose in fixing the problem."

PAUSE. The audience seems struck by this approach to guaranteeing safety. They don't know if it will work or not, but it is at least different. Even Bill feels a stab of surprise. He clenches his teeth with resolve, remembering that even this novel idea does not change the basic truth.

FLASH. A woman in the back, with two children squirming beside her, speaks. "Are you telling us that the danger from these radioactive wastes is zero?"

PAN. "Of course not," the engineer replies, leaving Bill with a wave of relief. He can certainly use *that* reply for some mileage. "What I'm telling you is that the danger from the radioactive dump is less than the danger of driving your car home tonight."

CUT. The discussion goes on, but to no purpose in Bill's value system. Most of the people leave with the same opinions they held upon arrival. But Bill knows that the engineer, with his facts, has swayed some of those people away from the truth. Herein Bill sees the significance of his own life: He must bring those people back to the fold, and convert others—enough others to defeat the damned Zetetic Institute.

Indeed, the Institute, and its emphasis on facts represent a grave danger to more issues other than the Hanford waste storage debate. Bill sees a task of greater scope facing him. Perhaps part of his purpose is to destroy the purveyors of such facts, facts that by denying truth become a travesty of truth.

CUT. CUT. CUT. CUT. The size of the editing job he faces with this video shakes him; the Zetetic engineer has been smooth indeed. The engineer qualifies as a politician, despite his early recitations on ground water, earthquakes, and mining costs. However, that smoothness does not worry Bill unduly: after all, whoever gets the last word wins the argument. And in news reporting, the editing reporter *always* gets the last word.

WRAP.

Yuri Klimov decided that it was the ivory figurines that lent the cold formality to the room. The shiny figurines

glared at him from their perches in the shiny black bookcases. Despite their carefully kept luster, however, they
were old. Age had worn them to soft curves in a thousand
little places meant for sharply carved angles. Age had
worn them as age had worn the General Secretary himself,
seated across the mahogany table from Yurii.

General Secretary Sipyagin closed his eyes. Yurii feared
he might have dozed off, but his eyes opened again, in a
slow, blinking motion. His pallid skin folded into a smile.
"Delightful, Yurii. I am pleased you have found the Americans easy to deal with."

Yurii shrugged. "Mayfield has little choice but to yield.
His people practically advertise their need for paper assur-
ances. All we need do is squeeze," he closed his fist ever
so gently, "and concessions flow forth." He smiled. "Mayfield got into office by promising to relax worldwide tensions. He must sign, and sign, and sign again to maintain
his position."

"Nevertheless, you handle him like a master. Now, a few
years ago when we tried negotiating with Keefer and *his*
henchmen, things were very different."

"The secret is to be able to think as the Americans
think—without losing our Soviet pragmatism." He shook
his head, and spoke with just a hint of puzzlement. "They
do not think like us, you know."

Sipyagin coughed in a sound of disgust. "Yes. They
think like weak children."

Yurii opened his mouth to object, then closed it. "Yes,
often like children."

"We'll start a new missile program immediately. When
those crazy Americans were toying with space defenses it
was a bad investment to build missiles—who knew what
kind of countermeasures we might have to retrofit? At last,
we've been relieved of this burden of uncertainty."

Yurii smiled. "Yes, now we can sharpen our strategic
edge."

Sipyagin gurgled with laughter. "As if we needed to
sharpen it any more."

Yurii joined the laughter. It was wonderful, sharing a
joke with the General Secretary, despite his infirmities.
Or perhaps because of them. "With this treaty, it will be

easy to maintain our strategic advantage. It might make more sense at this point to start undermining their tactical forces. I'll see what my men can do in the next round of discussions."

Sipyagin nodded. "A marvelous idea." He turned away to look at a stack of wrinkled papers by his side.

Clearly the General Secretary had dismissed him, but Yurii had one more request. "Sir, there is one last thing I would like to investigate in the strategic realm."

"Yes?"

"I question this whole concept of global consequences for a nuclear war. I know that our modellers agree with their modellers: you can set off just so many megatons before the radiation releases and the climate effects are so massive that they span the planet, no matter where they get set off. But many of those modellers are soft civilians, who want us to avoid nuclear warfare for their own reasons. I can't help wondering if the threshold might be higher than these people think. Simulation is a soft science, as I'm sure you know. Its results should not be left in the hands of biased civilians. If we knew that the threshold were higher, we would have an enormous edge over the Americans: we could continue barraging them with nuclear weapons even after they had ceased fire. Living in their fantasy world of nuclear danger, they would fear killing their own survivors."

The General Secretary chuckled. "Control of a nuclear war would belong completely to us then, wouldn't it? Very well." He waved his hand—was it shaking?—toward the door. Yurii felt Sipyagin's weary eyes follow him as he swept through it.

Yurii breathed deeply. The air in the hall was stale, but he felt refreshed nonetheless. Interviews with the General Secretary always reminded him how wonderful it was to be young and healthy.

May 26

They held an early ceremony—early enough to discourage people from coming, early enough to complete quickly, early enough to catch the morning dew before it evaporated. Dampness still shimmered on the rocks and markers that dotted the cemetery.

"I am the resurrection and the life, saieth the Lord; he that believeth in me, though he were dead, yet shall he live . . ." the minister's voice droned on.

Leslie felt disconnected from the service, as though watching through a telescope the odd behavior of an alien culture. It left him calm—perhaps too calm. He had lost too many people to be overwhelmed by the loss of one more. He would not be overwhelmed this time, though this time he had lost the most wonderful woman he had ever known: his wife, Jan Evans.

His mind skipped briefly across the toll death had taken around him during the years. Leslie Evans had flown as an Air Force fighter pilot. Even in peacetime, one fourth of all fighter pilots never reached retirement age. How odd for him to be attending Jan's funeral, rather than the other way around. There had certainly been moments during the last agonizing days of her life that he wished he could have reversed their positions, if only to give her a few hours without pain.

Perhaps the crowning irony was that her impending death had caused her to save his life. He too had been a cigarette smoker, until Jan contracted lung cancer. Jan had used him as her first guinea pig in her efforts to develop better cures for smoking. His fingers twitched at the thought of the cigarettes he had not touched for two years.

". . . and whosoever liveth and believeth in me shall never die . . ."

He could not have thanked her or loved her enough, had she lived a thousand years.

He heard a sniffle to his right. From the corner of his eye he watched his daughter, Kira, as she stared off to the horizon. Despite her sniffle, she seemed more angry than sad. Leslie knew the focus of her anger. He had watched her carefully during these last few days. Her attitudes reminded him of Jan in her youth. Kira had graduated from Virginia Tech just in time to witness the last throes of Jan's battle; now her graduation ceremony would seem stale and pointless. Leslie reached out and took her hand in his. She did not look at him, but her grip held surprising strength. Her nails dug into his hand. The pain seemed more real, more in tune with the grief battering his mind, than the words of the minister.

". . . Death will be swallowed up in victory . . ."

He saw Kira's face tighten with renewed anger. She was not a person to sit on her emotions without acting; Leslie worried about what she might do. She had engaged in long sessions with the Zetetic computers since coming home, searching for something. She had not tried to alter any of the data bases, but two days ago, she had mentioned that she had accepted a job with a small advertising firm. When Leslie did his own data base search, he found that this particular firm had just won a big contract with the largest tobacco company in the country. Leslie felt tired every time he thought about what that might mean. And of course, it wouldn't do him any good to confront her about it.

". . . When I consider thy Heaven, the work of thy fingers, the moon and the stars, which thou hast ordained . . ."

Nathan might be able to talk to her about it. Kira and her uncle had always had a special understanding. Leslie shifted his head to look at Nathan Pilstrom.

Nathan gazed at the preacher with calm, clear eyes. Nathan had not seen so many deaths as Leslie; he did not share Leslie's numbness to human mortality. But Nathan had his own sort of protection, a way of accepting the immediate reality as the starting point for his thoughts. He never dwelled on might-have-beens.

Nathan himself seemed surprised at times by his own stolid acceptance of events gone by. Even more surprising, his acceptance did not dull his enthusiasm for changing things as they might be tomorrow—things over which he could still exercise control. He had a pragmatic, Zetetic way of thinking. Nathan himself attributed his perspective to Jan's influence, but Leslie knew that the seeds had always been there. It seemed natural for Nathan to devise new ways of viewing the world.

But it didn't seem quite as natural for him to run a world-famous Institute. Jan had thrust him into that position, her last and greatest effort. Leslie wondered if Nathan might not harbor a mild irritation with Jan for sticking him with that responsibility. Because of Jan, he now had to deal with politics, and with politicians.

". . . Almighty God, our Heavenly Father, in whose hands are the living and the dead: we give these thanks for all Thy servants who have laid down their lives in the service of our country . . ."

Leslie looked far to his right to see Senator Hilan Forstil. Forstil was the only politician he had met whom he hadn't disliked on sight. He didn't understand his own lack of hostility; Forstil seemed as phony as any of them. Jan had assured him that Forstil was a straight shooter. Leslie took her word for it as long as he didn't have to bet money.

In this moment, however, Leslie thought he saw what Jan had meant. Of all the people at this funeral, Forstil seemed most grief-stricken. He stood apart from the others, speaking to no one, grappling with some deep personal loss.

And another person he didn't know—a young, serious, clean-shaven man—also stood separate from the others. Leslie was pretty sure he was Kurt McKenna, a kid just out of Special Forces, recruited for the Institute by Jan. He wondered how the gung-ho attitude of a ranger would mesh with Zetetic philosophy; the Institute fought fanaticism with a zeal that itself bordered on the fanatical. Kurt would no doubt set off new kinds of fireworks within the ZI realm; Leslie hoped they would be healthy.

". . . grant to them Thy mercy, and the light of Thy presence; and give us such a lively sense of Thy righteous will, that the work which Thou hast begun in them may be perfected . . ."

The ceremony ended. Leslie hugged his daughter tightly. Nathan came up beside them, and Leslie and Kira opened their arms to him as well. For a while the three of them stood huddled by the grave. After an immeasurable time they separated, reluctantly, like the fibers of a rope being parted.

Until now, Leslie had kept his thoughts away from Jan with scrupulous success. But images of her, accumulated for almost twenty-five years, welled up in his mind. And despite all the funerals of friends and pilots he had attended, despite the calloused surface of his mind that should have been inured to the tragic losses, he turned away from everyone and slipped into the cemetery's groves to walk alone with his grief.

ROLL. He dashes past the Institute with a flurry of pleasure, confident in his strength. Bill is a runner, a marathoner. He understands the pain that accompanies an effort too great—a pain almost as great as the pleasure of making that effort. For now, there is only pleasure.

The air melts as he passes, carrying away his perspiration. A wind gusts against him, full in the face, twisting through the curls of his hair. He presses against it, exultant with the knowledge that the gust cannot obstruct his passage. He continues, several laps across the entrance to the Institute.

Thirty-five minutes. Five miles. A year before, he had made similar runs in 32 minutes. A year before that, he had made them in 30 minutes. The difference, he concludes, is statistically insignificant. He feels as strong as he has ever been. That is the truth, not to be confused with the fact.

Bill showers and dresses. Invigorated, he returns to the Institute.

The Institute building shares no architectural theme with the other structures in this industrial park. In the late morning light the building glows a soft salmon color, its gentle contours reaching out warmly to those who pass by. The soft-gray windows contrast with the glaring mirrored portals of other nearby buildings, suggesting that quality

can nonetheless be quiet. This building seems somehow
friendlier than the others. Bill shakes his head and remembers that this building houses his target.

To the left of the driveway stands a small bronze sign
with a curious emblem. An arrow points up at a 45 degree
angle, soaring over a pair of embellished steps. After a
moment of squinting in the brightness, Bill realizes the
two steps form the letters "ZI" in a script almost completely lost in the design.

A shadow falls across him. He is not yet psyched up for
confrontation; he steps to the side and looks at the man
who stopped next to him.

The man smiles and points at the sign. "The Zetetic
Institute invites you to take the next step."

Bill stares, his mouth suddenly dry. The man seems
familiar. He is tall, though not so tall as Bill. A relaxed
alertness sets the lines of his body, similar to the lines of
the building itself. The man's smile is sincere; his gray eyes
probe the wide-eyed awareness in Bill's own eyes. The
honesty in those eyes strikes a chord of guilt in Bill's mind.

The man raises an eyebrow. "Sorry if I surprised you.
It's just that you looked so unhappy, staring at our sign."

Bill frowns.

The man puts out his hand. "I'm Nathan Pilstrom."

Nathan Pilstrom—Bill knows the name. He knows he
will remember why in a moment. Nathan Pilstrom grips
his hand firmly. The man seems disgustingly *natural*, the
caricature that gives the term *nice* a bad reputation. Bill
has never encountered a better façade.

Nathan leads him down through the courtyard, where a
pair of earth-colored toy robots hum to and fro. They seem
silly, hovering among the well-trimmed trees and shrubs.
Then he realizes that the robots are doing the trimming.

"So what's your interest in the Institute?"

Bill snaps back to awareness of the man beside him. His
throat still feels parched. His cover story resembles his
news stories: at its heart lies a vague form of the facts,
richly articulated, with statements that are not false. "I
saw one of your Zetetic engineers at a meeting near Hanford
recently. He really carved the audience to shreds, and so I
figured I should come and see if I can learn how he did it."

Nathan stops; Bill turns to him. Nathan speaks with distress, "You say he carved up the audience? Who was it—do you remember?"

Bill stares, then shakes his head. A gust of wind sweeps the street, throwing grit in Bill's eyes. He squints. "No, I don't remember his name. But he sure won the argument."

"I'll have to find out who it was," Nathan mutters. "Believe me, carving people up and winning arguments is not what Zeteticism is all about. Zeteticism has more in common with the martial arts—the true master avoids confrontation; he does not seek it out."

Bill shrugs. "Well, the ZI guy seemed like a winner, anyway." He grins, adding, "And the way your cult is growing, I figure I'm better off on the inside than on the outside."

"Our cult, hm? You've gotten too much of your information from the television news people."

Bill's breathing halts—the bastard dares to defame Bill's own profession! It takes a moment to find words that are polite. He shakes his head. "Well, 'cult' might be the wrong term. But you *are* the people who run the no-smoking courses, right? And you're the ones who talk about how the cosmetic industry makes people think they need more specialized products just so they can sell more junk. Right?"

Nathan winces. "The press has a breathtaking capacity for oversimplifying. You know that, right? Everyone knows that. Then why does everyone forget it every time the press says something?" Nathan's voice suggests frustration. Yet his tone remains lighthearted. He accepts this oddity of human behavior without cynicism or anger. "In answer, we *do* run clinics on advertising and media manipulation, and we *do* discuss the cosmetics industry. As for the question of human wants and desires, we might ask a question like this: Do people want more cosmetics, which persuades the companies to invent more of them? Or do the companies invent more of them, and persuade the people they want more? Anyone who thinks the persuasions flow strictly one way or the other is not fully connected to reality. There's a feedback loop here, almost as delicately balanced as a regional ecology." His arms sweep

as he declares, "We teach people to deal with the best
approximations of reality they can construct—and reality is
always far more complicated than the press coverage
suggests."

Watching that theatrical sweep of the arms, Bill remembers why he knows the name Nathan Pilstrom. He stares
for a moment at the man smiling at him: Nathan Pilstrom
is the founder of the Zetetic Institute. Bill almost stumbles
as they step across the threshold into the Institute.

Meeting the founder so unexpectedly leaves him surprised, yet the surprise drowns in the shock of his view
in this entranceway. His thoughts of Nathan swirl away,
swept aside as the walls now surrounding him imprint
themselves upon him. Bill gasps.

He has seen pictures of the Jewel Hall, but no picture
can capture it. Clusters of the world's finest gems blaze
across the walls, forming starry galaxies beyond price.
Bill's mouth hangs wide as he traces a series of emerald
droplets across the arching ceiling.

Nathan leads him to a central section of the wall. "Take
one," he offers.

"What?!"

Nathan rubs his hand across the wall. "Take one."

Bill reaches for a black opal: could it be the Flame Queen?
His fingers close around it. He clutches it tight—and his
fingers close *through* the lustrous stone until they touch. A
faint sensation of electricity tingles through his hand.

Nathan chuckles. "As you apparently know, the Zetetic
Institute gives seminars and training on a wide variety of
topics. What you haven't seen yet is the connecting theme
behind all those topics." Nathan leads him forward again,
toward a far door. "The Zetetic theme is that in the
Information Age, correct information is the key resource.
Men must act in harmony with the best information they
have. We strive to develop ever better methods for coping
with the vast quantities of information that inundate us
every day." He spreads his arms to encompass the room.
"The Jewel Hall is encrusted not with jewels, but with
holograms. The holograms embody all the visual information, all the beauty, of the jewels they pretend to be." He
laughed the deep, pleasant laugh of a grandfather who has

just passed a secret down two generations. "And the information that describes those jewels is all that's really important about them, isn't it? Would this display be any more spectacular if the jewels contained minerals as well as information?"

Bill shakes his head. "I guess not. It's incredible." A thrill runs through his mind. This Zetetic comparison of truth and materials makes the deepest sense to him—the truth, as Bill creates it for his audiences, *is* more valuable than any possible jewel.

"Congratulations on passing your first Zetetic test. Many people feel tricked when we acquaint them with this room. Actually, we offer just the opposite of a trick. We offer a lesson—a lesson that does not hurt, that is valuable, and that is not too expensive."

"I guess so." Bill still feels on the defensive. Yet he begins to feel the thrill of the hunt as well. Nathan Pilstrom makes a challenging target for his next report.

But Nathan steps through another door. Bill follows, tense and excited. What lesson lies in the room beyond the Jewel Hall?

He breathes a sigh of relief. A comfortingly normal room greets him. Its shape suggests the gentle contours of the overall building. A receptionist looks up at them.

Nathan taps a terminal on the side. "Take a look through our catalog of offerings. I think you'll be surprised at the number of ways that discriminating information can alter your life. Do you smoke?"

Bill shakes his head.

"Perhaps you would be interested in . . . no, probably not. How about a seminar on separating fact from fluff in newscasting?"

Damn this man! Bill frowns. "I don't think I need it."

Nathan stops. "My apologies. I don't mean to be pushy." He shrugs. "Sometimes I'm as bad as the car salesman we use as an example."

The receptionist, fielding a buzz from the intercom, interrupts. "Nathan, Senator Forstil has arrived."

He smiles at her warmly. "Thanks." He turns back to Bill with a final comment. "If you don't have specific needs for Zetetic methods, you should take the Sampler.

It'll give you some idea of how we apply surprising ideas to everyday problems."

"That sounds great." Yes, this is what Bill needs. Only with a broad view of the Institute can he find the most striking defects of the organization. The Sampler will be perfect.

Bill watches Nathan depart with cruel amusement. So Senator Forstil is involved with the Institute! He'll get some mileage out of that.

Only an expert could have discerned the quiet struggle in the soft-lit office. Nathan leaned against the edge of his desk, his arms folded. His head drooped, as if he might nod off at any moment. He seemed so casual, so cool.

But the expert would have spotted his twitch every time a stray sound rattled down the hall. The expert would have seen Nathan's lips draw to a short smile following each twitch. It was a smile of forgiving laughter—Nathan laughed at himself. He was very, very nervous about this meeting with Senator Forstil.

How annoying Nathan found it, to be the founder and president of an Institute dedicated to helping people overcome unsanity, and *still* be subject himself to such irrational anxiety!

Still, denial of that anxiety would mark an even lower level of sanity. Nathan smiled at the anxiety and jumped at every sound.

He let his eyes roam across the walls of his office. People who associated him with the Information Age often felt surprise at his choice of decorations. A number of mementos seemed appropriate: a flow chart hung in one corner, describing the first PEP program developed by the Zetetic Corporation. The signatures of the PEP development team members filled one corner of the chart. A long, narrow, Escher print snaked across the wall behind his desk.

But the works that dominated the room were the maps. Age had broken off their edges, had yellowed the paper and cracked the ink, but they were still readable.

Worse than the mars of aging were the defects in their basic structure. All the maps had serious flaws; not one of

them accurately represented the terrain it tried to depict.
The maps always reminded Nathan to remain hopeful for,
flawed as the maps were, men had achieved numerous
victories using them. Those who used maps wisely always
remembered the differences between the maps and their
terrains.

The old maps held no more flaws than the internal maps
modern men used to navigate through life—maps of in-
ferred deductions about other people's motives and plans.
The differences between those internal maps and external
realities contained lethal potentialities; yet wisdom could
prevail now as in the past.

Nathan jerked at a new sound. A light tread paused
briefly just outside his office. Nathan shifted forward as
the senator entered the room, and stared for a moment in
surprise. The senator had been one of the silent mourners
at Jan's funeral that morning, but the grief and mourning
had peeled away, like a molted skin. His expression now
belonged to a completely different person.

First analysis: short but snappy. His silvery gray hair
was swept back in precise curves. His mustache was neatly
trimmed, and his mouth gave no hint of pleasure or pain.
His expressionless gray suit fit him with the precision of
custom tailoring. A sharp streak of yellow crossed the face
of an otherwise somber silk tie, and a tiny gold pin with a
single diamond chip glinted on his lapel.

He gazed calmly at Nathan, as he analyzed Nathan in
turn.

First synthesis: Forstil projected an image of controlled
power—a power channeled to sharply defined purposes.
The illusion carried through to each detail of his appearance with a perfection too great to be unintended—so
great it could partly fulfill its own prophecy.

The senator's meticulous illusion frustrated Nathan's need
for insight. What motivated this man? What were his
ethics? Would Nathan have to manipulate him, or would
education be enough? In this first meeting, Nathan didn't
have a choice: his own ethics demanded crisp honesty,
unless the senator himself revealed manipulative behavior.
Nathan had to try education.

Meanwhile, Nathan was sure the senator's calm blue

eyes had seen more of him than he had seen of the
senator. Hilan had seen that Nathan was a soft touch for
truth. He knew Nathan preferred simple, open dealings.
Nathan smiled, and though the smile felt foolish, he continued. "Senator," he greeted the projection of power with
an outstretched hand, "what do you think of the Institute?"

They shook hands: again, nothing revealed. Senator
Forstil's face broke into a half-smile. "The Zetetic Institute," he rolled the words off his tongue, toying with the
sounds. "I've seen your building. Jan and I have discussed
some parts of Zetetic philosophy. But I know nothing
about your organization. What is a Zetetic Institute?"

Was there sarcasm there? Forstil gave no hint. "A good
question," Nathan replied, "but it has a difficult answer."
He pointed to the low table across from his desk. "Chair?"

Four chairs encircled the smoke-gray glass table. Two of
the chairs slunk low into the carpet; the other two displayed more austere lines, encouraging one to lean forward into the conversation. The senator took one of these.

Nathan had at times taken a low seat when faced with
dangerous people, to give them a false sense of security.
He sighed, thinking about the number of times he had had
to use manipulative techniques, just to avoid being harmed
by other people's manipulations. He took the high seat
opposite the senator. Nathan suspected the senator was
not easily manipulated.

The senator's probable immunity was more surprising
than most people realized. The typical manipulator succeeds because he believes his own propaganda, and thus
becomes vulnerable to the propaganda of others. Jan's
analysis said this man doubted his own illusions.

Forstil watched him patiently. Nathan returned to the
senator's question: what is a Zetetic Institute? Jan had
surely described the Institute for him before, so this question undoubtedly had qualities of a test, as well as a
request for information. His only possible response was
indirect—as unsatisfying as the description Jan herself had
surely given. "Let me describe the Institute in terms of
what it is *not*," Nathan began. "First, it is not a building,
or a collection of buildings. Most of the people who work
with the Institute work at home, wherever home may

be—from a condo around the corner in the Hunter Woods complex in Reston, Virginia, to an earth shelter outside Bozeman, Montana.

"The Institute should not be viewed as a corporation, though legally it is incorporated in the state of Virginia. Only a handful of people work for the Institute full-time. The others come and go, depending on particular contracts and projects that interest them.

"The Institute is not a cult—" Nathan felt some deja vu, having discussed this with the tall, angry man on the way in "—though the people of the Institute share many attitudes, behaviors, and slang expressions. It would be more accurate to say we share a common meta-philosophy—a philosophy about building your own philosophies. We are eclectics, taking the best or most useful ideas we find, wherever we find them, and weaving them into cloths of many colors."

"Sounds like a quick way to mental breakdown," Forstil observed. "Grabbing bits and pieces of ideas and lifestyles without a consistent framework."

"Only if it becomes an obsession," Nathan replied easily. "Only if you grab bits and pieces indiscriminately. The term 'zetetic' comes from the Greek word for 'skeptic.' A healthy dose of skepticism is the first thing we teach people who come here." Nathan frowned. He had not yet communicated the ethos of the Institute. But what more could he say? The Zetetic Institute could not be described using Industrial Age terminology, any more than quantum mechanics could be described with Aristotle's concepts of waves and particles, or any more than the Tao could be defined in terms of Western civilization.

But he had to answer, quickly and succinctly, for this man. "If I were to be so foolish as to sum up what the Institute is, rather than what it is not, I would say it is an Information Age resource pool for solving Industrial Age problems. Once the country makes the transition to a full-fledged Information Age society, the Institute will hopefully become a place to solve Information Age problems. For the moment, however, the Industrial Age and its institutions represent the important dangers to human progress."

Forstil gave him a barely perceptible nod. "And Industrial Age problems include everything from cigarette smoke to nuclear weapons."

Nathan relaxed. "Exactly."

"Very well." Hilan seemed to accept the basic idea of the Zetetic Institute, despite the ambiguities. "Now, what is a Sling?"

Nathan smiled; Forstil had moved to the central topic with bracing efficiency. "The Sling is an Information Age weapon for defeating Industrial Age armies. It may be the only chance free societies have in a world where they must compete with leaders of subjugated societies—leaders who can be far more ruthless because they aren't shackled by fickle popular opinion."

"That's fine rhetoric, Mr. Pilstrom. But what does it mean?"

"Let me demonstrate." Nathan whirled out of his chair and retrieved a keyboard from his desk. A color display in the wall next to Hilan glowed with a three-dimensional, skeletal, layout of an airplane. Forstil squinted at it. "Is it a glider?"

"Almost." As Nathan spoke, a set of arrows highlighted critical features. "The overall design comes from glider technology, most distinctively in the wing shape. The frame is built with high-strength composite fibers.

"That's where the resemblance to gliders ends, however. The tops of the wings are covered with amorphous semiconductor solar cells for power, which drive the tail prop as well as the on-board electronics. By optimal use of wind currents and solar power, the SkyHunter can stay airborne for months—until it wears out, in fact." Nathan smiled, concentrating on his keyboard. The skeletal aircraft grew skin; the background clarified into a mountain-lined horizon; and the craft lifted into the air, until it disappeared. "The SkyHunter contains no metal, so it is radar-invisible. It has no engine flare, so it is infrared-invisible. Paint it sky blue and cruise it at 30,000 feet, and it is lightwave-invisible—a completely undetectable platform."

The senator's voice sounded strained. "Is this room a secure facility?"

Nathan looked baffled for a moment, then laughed. "None of this is classified, senator. This is a picture of the WeatherWatch recon plane. It was designed by Lightcraft Corporation and manufactured by Lockheed for meteorologists. They collect high-altitude weather data in the Arctic for forecasting climate."

"You mean they built a stealth patrol plane *by accident*?"

"Yes," Nathan chuckled. "More or less. We have made some substitutions to heighten the effect, such as the materials for the solar arrays. The important mods, however, are down here." The view changed again, to the underbelly, which sprouted clumps of thin fibers. "We replaced the normal weather sensors with down-looking optical and infrared detectors. And there is an anchor point for bombs."

"How many bombs can a glider carry—two or three? Hardly the killing power of a battleship." The senator turned away from the screen to critique Nathan. "I'd overlooked that problem. You'd need thousands of these to stop an armored division."

Nathan shook his head. "Actually, we think it'd take three or four SkyHunters to stop a division." As Forstil objected, Nathan held up his hand to interrupt. "Remember, this is an *Information Age* weapon. The most critical part of the weapon cannot be seen in any picture. The critical part is the *information processing,* the *intelligence.*"

The wall display changed again—to an aerial scene of forests, threaded by a delicate web of narrow roads. The picture changed hue. The forest became a ghostly orange, and bright dots of blue now stood out as they lumbered along the gray streaks of road. "This is an infrared image," Nathan explained. "The blue dots are tanks." The view zoomed in on a patch of green. Forms with the outlines of human beings hustled, or paused, or lay on the ground. "The division command post," Nathan explained. The view zoomed one more time, on a particular figure. He was surrounded by other figures that came, listened for a time, then hurried away again. The scene brought to mind a queen bee groomed by her court of drones. "The commanding general."

The brilliant oranges and yellows of an explosion obliterated the scene, making the senator jump back in his seat.

Nathan spoke quietly, confidently. "The SkyHunter will not drop its pitiful load of bombs on just anything, senator. It will cruise patiently in the sky, hunting only the choicest prey. It does not hunt for the frail creatures of blood and bone sent by the enemy to die in battle. It hunts for the minds that command them. Senator, what does a division do when it loses its commander?"

Hilan thought for a moment. "The soldiers continue on to meet their current objectives."

"And then?"

The senator pursed his lips grudgingly. "They stop. They wait for further instructions." He shook his head. "But eventually, someone will get them organized again."

"By which time other SkyHunters will have destroyed the regimental command posts that would receive the orders, and the army headquarters that sent orders to the division." Nathan leaned forward. "But you're right. One SkyHunter cannot *destroy* a division, but it can *stop* one. It can transform that division from a brutally effective offensive machine into a frightened clutch of defenders, who would be easy pickings for a conventional brigade one fourth their size." Nathan could see the recognition in Hilan's eyes. Hilan's own subcommittee had recently estimated the Russian advantage along the German border to be four to one.

After a long pause, Nathan continued. "We also have two other Hunter platforms—one a ground-effect vehicle, the other an orbital munitions dispenser. I can show you those as well."

The senator shook his head. "Another time perhaps." He frowned. "More important, I need to know why *you* have to be the developers. Why not use the normal military acquisition system?"

"Because the normal military acquisition system *wouldn't* just acquire one—they'd *build* one, from scratch. They'd use military contractors to build a customized system that might be twice as good, but which would take ten times as long to develop and cost ten times as much to produce. It would be so good that by the time they could field it, it would be obsolete. They would *not* use commercially available systems, like the WeatherWatch airplane."

As Nathan spoke, he grew more forceful. No matter how often he addressed this topic, he could never approach it with complete Zetetic composure. "Do you know the story of the TACFIRE computer? It was designed to control artillery barrages. Unfortunately, it took 25 years to build. When they finally deployed it in the late '70s and early '80s, TACFIRE computers cost six million dollars apiece. During those 25 years, the technology changed to the point where TACFIRE could hardly be called a computer: it had the processing power of a six hundred dollar Apple II computer. And TACFIRE could not even operate with some of the artillery systems that had evolved during its 25-year development period." Nathan felt his voice rising, took a deep breath for control. "Senator, the state of the world scares me. The United States is in the throes of confronting the end of the Industrial Age culture it created. Meanwhile, the Russians grow more aggressive. Senator, I don't think we can *wait* twenty years for the American military to catch up with the civilian revolution in technology. We need to be able to protect ourselves better *this year*." Nathan stopped speaking, filled with sudden futility. After all, Senator Forstil belonged to the same party as President Mayfield.

But a shadow of tense worry broke through the senator's projected image. "You're right," he replied quietly. A long pause ensued; Nathan wondered if he should speak.

At last, Forstil continued. "I think I know why you wanted to talk with me, why Jan wanted me to talk with you. You've heard that various powerful people in the military want this project taken away from the Defense Nuclear Agency because they've given you a free hand. They want the Sling put under FIREFORS, where it can be controlled more effectively."

Nathan nodded.

"I'll give it serious consideration. For the moment my subcommittee will recommend against a transition to FIREFORS control. But if the army decides to enforce such a move itself, I cannot stop them. However," he smiled, and for another moment his image of controlled power relaxed, this time because his shark's smile seemed uncontrolled, "if the army decides to move on its own, I shall counsel them."

Nathan chuckled. "Thank you." They stood up, shook hands, and Forstil turned to depart. As he reached the door, he turned, puzzled. "One last thing."

"Yes?"

"Why do you call it the Sling?"

"Because David of Israel was the forerunner of the Information Age warrior." Nathan leaned back against his desk, returning to the position from which he had started this encounter. "Senator, when David stood against the Philistines, he faced the most heavily armed and armored enemy of his day. David himself was unarmored, and virtually unarmed. Yet, by the application of just a tiny amount of force, precisely applied, he defeated Goliath."

"Defeated him with nothing but his sling," the senator finished the analogy. "Moreover, he defeated the enemy by striking at *his* command center." He touched his forehead, as if he could feel the blow of a slingshot stone against his temple. "May our Sling work as well," was Hilan's parting prayer.

"May we never need to test it," was Nathan's.

Far beneath Daniel Wilcox's office, the cherry blossoms along the George Washington Parkway fluttered in a frenzy of color. From here, high in the Wilcox-Morris Building that dominated Rosslyn, the view took panoramic proportions—two sheer walls of glass, floor to ceiling, enclosed half the office. The sweeping view overcame the sense of enclosure with the sense of open sky. Daniel's eyes crinkled with amusement as he watched the new advertising executive, Kira Evans. She tried to shift her chair to look across that panorama. Her efforts amused him because the room had been designed so that *he* had the pleasure of that view from his desk. Kira could turn her back on the view, or she could turn her back on him; she could not face both at the same time.

He considered shifting to the conference table to accommodate her, but it was more fun to watch her cope with the problem. Besides, she had not earned such a view yet. If she wanted the use of an office such as this, she would have to take command of a corporate empire, as he had done.

Even as he watched, Kira resolved the dilemma, leaning forward, focusing her whole concentration on the job at hand. Daniel returned his attention to the layouts she had brought him, shuffling through to his favorite advertisement. This one ad suggested that Kira might indeed get an office of her own with panoramic windows. The ad was a beautifully crafted full-page paste-up, carefully explaining why the tobacco industry wasn't at fault for the rising incidence of smoking among children. He took a drag off his cigarette, and blew the smoke into the faint blue haze that swirled around him on its way to the air conditioning vent. "This is great stuff," he congratulated her. "An excellent utilization of our reborn plain-talk advertising strategy at work." He smiled. "I particularly like your point about advertisements saying that cigarettes are strictly for grown-ups, not for kids."

Kira fumbled with her cigarette, showing the same skill a thirteen-year-old girl might show in handling a snake, but she continued gamely. Clearly, she had gotten the word: if you worked with the Wilcox-Morris Tobacco Company, you had to smoke with them as well. That policy was strictly, strictly unofficial, of course. It would have been technically legal to hire, fire, and promote on the basis of smoking habits, but Daniel knew the consequences if he started such a policy: the news media would flay him alive, and legislation would follow. It was better to leave it unstated. Kira was a good example of how effective such unstated policies could be. She would get used to the cigarette between her lips; she would get hooked on the rush; she would become a good member of the team.

But not yet. His compliment on her advertisement had not pleased her; she seemed disturbed with the explanation that cigarette advertisements were strictly for adults. "Thank you for the compliment," she said, with a sincere smile that turned quickly to a frown. "But I'm afraid this ad may not work the way we intended. Our adults-only advertising may be the most effective kind of children's advertising possible. After all, what could possibly be a better way to get children started than telling them it's for grown-ups?"

Daniel waved the objection aside. "Nonsense. We're

just being up-front and honest. Nobody can get angry at us for that." From time to time, similar thoughts disturbed Daniel himself. He would have to help Kira overcome the sense of guilt, as he had himself. He would have to help her look beyond the intellectual questions if she were to mold herself into a useful tool.

Kira leaned forward in her chair as if to refresh the argument, thought better of it, then sank glumly back. "I suppose you're right."

"Of course I'm right." Daniel sought for something to distract her from further contemplation of her guilt.

Kira had great talent, and, God knew, the tobacco companies needed to cultivate every ounce of talent they could find these days. The enemies were so numerous, the fields of opportunities from which they needed to clear opponents were so vast, he needed to find a way to get Kira involved as rapidly as possible. A little bit of quiet conspiracy might be just the ticket. People loved to work together in conspiracies, to strike against great enemies, and Daniel had need for a new conspiracy. "Do you fully understand why we've recruited your agency?"

As Kira gave him a blank stare, Daniel came around his desk to take a chair close to her. He sat inside the range of the air conditioner; dry, cool air swished against his face.

"We recruited you because we have such a continuing problem with the media. They're constantly accusing us of brainwashing people. We're looking to you, with your young organization, for new ideas to combat this. The media is very effective at brainwashing people into thinking that *we* are the ones who do the brainwashing." He shook his head. "How can we make people realize that the media is more dangerous than the tobacco industry could ever be?" He leaned closer. "The news media is a continuing problem, but we've been dealing with them successfully for decades. However, a new problem's come up, and this one could really destroy us."

He paused to let the tension build. Her eyes narrowed. Finally she responded, in a whisper that matched his own. "What?"

"The Zetetic Institute."

A dozen little shifts showed her surprise. He hand pressed

against the table top, her breathing paused. "What?" she asked for explanation in a low voice that pitched up in a final question mark.

"The Zetetic Institute is our new problem." He waved at a report sitting on his desk. "It's a network of project group organizers and information salesmen. They're more a cult than a corporation, but they've got their fingers in just about every pie in America. And two years ago they put their fingers into *our* pie."

Kira nodded. "I've heard of them. But I can't believe they're dangerous to the Wilcox-Morris Corporation."

"So you've heard of them. Excellent." Her reaction to the mention of the Institute didn't match up with just a passing familiarity. She must have friends there. That could be useful. "Do you know about the Zetetic anti-smoking clinics? Those information salesmen have collected all the anti-smoking techniques ever devised into a single, consistent framework. Individually, those techniques are all pretty ineffective. But the Institute developed a method for matching techniques with individual strengths and weaknesses. After the Institute gets done tailoring a set for a particular person . . ."

Kira had recovered her composure. She now seemed eager, though puzzled. "But the Institute is a tiny organization! How can they threaten Wilcox-Morris?"

"They can threaten us with their growth rate." Daniel turned to his computer work station, tapped rapidly across the keys, and spun the display so Kira could see it. "They've shown exponential growth in the number of smoking clinics they've run for the last two years. If we wait until they're big enough to be a noticeable force, they'll be within one year of destroying our cigarette sales in the United States."

"What makes you think their growth curve won't flatten out?"

Daniel took a last heady drag off his menthol, ground out the stub, and lit a new one. He rose and started pacing across the room. "Eventually it will. But we need to flatten out their growth curve *now*, while they're still just a wiggle in the market research. If we wait, they'll surely cut into our bottom line." He turned at the end of the room to come back. The glowing tip of his second smoke left a contrail that defined his previous path.

Kira pursed her lips. "Do you want to run an advertising campaign against them? I can't believe it would be effective. That would be like the Hershey Company running advertisements against dietitians who tell overweight people to give up chocolate."

"Exactly. We can't use straightforward advertising. A frontal confrontation is inappropriate in this situation. It's similar to our problem with beating referenda. We should probably build an organization like the Citizens For Freedom—we used them to beat down legislation on no smoking in public buildings. We need somebody who seems unbiased—somebody who can complain about those ZI kooks messing with the minds of our children."

Daniel saw from the look in Kira's eyes that he had been too blunt in his analysis. He was not surprised when she responded badly. "The Zetetics are a bit cultish, but they aren't exactly kooks."

He backed off. "We might not need to go all the way to building an organization to counter them. First, we should try to exploit the media; after all, that's cheaper, and it's at least as effective when it works."

Kira nodded. "Yes, that seems like a sensible approach." Daniel could see that she still held distaste for the idea of fighting the Zetetic Institute, but he could also see that she was challenged by the problems of manipulating the media. "First, we need to find sharp newsmen who already distrust the Institute. That shouldn't be a problem; there are newsmen who distrust everything. Then we need to cultivate them and make sure they're successful, without letting them know they're being helped."

Daniel gave her a satisfied clap of his hands. "Yes! And we have some great ways of helping them. We have inside information on just about every dark corner of society—politicians, in particular. Our selected reporters will receive leaks to help them build their careers. And, of course, the magazines and cable channels that depend on Wilcox-Morris for advertising support will be particularly eager to run their pieces."

These thoughts were obviously new to Kira; her eyes

looked beyond him at the broad ramifications. She had an open look, her face filled with an emotion he dimly recalled from his childhood. It was the emotion that came with a sense of wonder. "Of course. You have leverage all over the country." Her wonder turned into a moment's revelation, as she realized how much easier her job would be, working with the tobacco industry.

Daniel shrugged. "Well, for what it's worth, we have all the power that money can buy. There are limitations, of course, on the power that money can buy, but there aren't many things that can buy more power than money."

"So, would you like a list of candidate reporters?" Excitement filled her voice. She clearly relished the idea of using the media as much as Daniel did himself.

"Excellent." He stood up, concluding the meeting. "I think we can do lots of business together."

Kira also stood up. "I agree. I'm quite confident that both of our companies will profit from this link-up." She paused at the door, and turned to him. "I still can't believe you think the Zetetic Institute is worth *bothering* with."

Daniel's voice grew stern. "I've made my career out of seeing where trouble will appear before anyone else could see it. There're other sources of trouble for our business, too—plenty of them. But this is one we have to nip in the bud. Believe me." He watched her depart, then snuffed out the remains of his second cigarette with methodical care. The ventilation sucked away the odor of tobacco with equally methodical efficiency—at least, it sucked away enough of the odor so that a smoker could no longer detect its presence.

Daniel stepped up to the great wall of glass, to look outside and luxuriate in the gentle springtime. For a moment, his mind flashed over the years of his life—from his childhood on a tiny farm, to his first deals in the commodities market, to his successes in stocks, and finally, his takeover of one of the biggest companies in the world. At each step, he had been involved with the tobacco industry—first, because he had been born there; then, because tobacco was such a volatile commodity; and finally, because the companies that controlled the world's cigarette industry were such cash cows.

At each step he had lived the harrowing life of a man whose survival depends on his interpretation of tiny indicators of the future. He had lived that life brilliantly. Consequently, it did not surprise him that Kira failed to see inevitable dangers. Not even the corporate directors of the huge conglomerates had seen the future as clearly as he. Had they been able to, they would have prevented his conquest of their companies.

And now his alarms pounded with every new bit of information he received on the Zetetic Institute. Politicians, he could control. Crowds of voters, he could manipulate. News media, he could redirect. But an organization dedicated to enhancing human rationality might be beyond his influence.

He was playing with lightning here in other ways as well. Kira might hold divided loyalties if she had friends in the Institute. Even more frightening was the danger that his attack on the Institute could backfire. The Zetetic Institute was, as Kira had noted, a tiny thing today. By bringing media attention to bear on it, he could be fueling its growth, even if all the attention were directed at its oddities. A certain percentage of the people who enjoyed going against the conventional wisdom would seek the Institute out because of such notoriety. He frowned, wondering about Kira's failure to comment on this danger.

But he knew that inaction led down a short path to disaster. And whatever the truth or falsehood behind the allegations that cigarettes killed, Daniel knew a more important truth.

He remembered his mother, on her broken-down farm in West Virginia, discing the soil with her broken-down tractor. That tractor had already taken two of her fingers in payment during half-successful attempts at repair. He remembered the hardness of living poor. He remembered how old she had looked at the age of 35—older than Kira Evans would look when she was 50.

Cigarettes were a minor part of the dangers of life. Poverty was the real horror. Poverty killed. Looking down upon the world from his steel-and-glass fortress, Daniel swore that never again would one he loved suffer from that kind of poverty.

The Zetetic Institute would fall before him, as the others had fallen in the past. As for the uncertainties of Kira, he felt little concern. He had already set in motion some of the types of plans they had discussed. His reporters were already on the job.

As he watched, the snarl of traffic on the parkway broke free, and started to flow as easily as the gentle Potomac River that paralleled its course. The bright wall of cherry blossoms was all that divided the flow of belching metal from the flow of quiet water.

Major Vorontsov. The title sounded good when it preceded his name. It was quite a victory. *Major Ivan Vorontsov.*

Ivan wondered why his victory tasted like the bitter steel of a Kalashnikov; why his mood matched the gunmetal gray of the weather outside his window, rather than the bright sunshine that the weather bureau—*his* weather bureau—had predicted for this day a week ago.

He had just received the promotion to major, making him one of the youngest majors in the army. He had also received an assignment—one that might well end his career.

They had ordered him to re-evaluate the predictions of global consequences of a nuclear war. The purpose of the re-evaluation was to "perform an analysis that allows the Soviet Union to maintain an advantage in confrontations with the United States."

Ivan was a good Russian. He was also pure Russian, born in Kursk as the only child of wholly Russian parents. As often happened with single children, he had learned early how to talk with adults, though he had never quite learned how to play with other children his own age. Also like many single children, he believed his parents' beliefs even more fiercely than his parents did. He loved his homeland. He disliked Americans. And he hated Germans.

So when his time had come to serve in the army, to protect the children of Russia and of the whole Soviet Union from her enemies, he had accepted the duty proudly.

He stepped out of his office, quickly marched down the hallway of the Military Meteorology building, and pushed through the massive door into the streets of Novosibirsk.

Bitter wind swept around him. He clenched his teeth against the cold and headed for the officers' quarters.

The gunmetal sky showed no hint of sun. Would the climatic effects of a nuclear war even be noticed here? He could imagine that the sunbathers along the Black Sea would be most affected, though he knew better.

Certainly, radioactive fallout from a war would affect all the people he cared about. That included his childhood friend Anna, and her three children, living so close to the strategic targets in Sevastopol.

He remembered the day his parents had brought Anna to stay. Her mother, Ivan knew, was always drunk, and her father was . . . different. He remembered how helpless Anna had been, yet how hopeful, despite her helplessness. Ivan's parents loved her as they loved all children—almost as much as they loved Ivan himself. And though Ivan never did learn how to be friends with his peers, he had learned from his parents the love of children.

How wasted their efforts would prove if Ivan let some damn fool—either American or Russian—initiate a nuclear exchange. Though Ivan loved his country's children, he worried that Russia's leaders might not share that feeling.

He thought again of the sunny skies predicted for today. How could men be so foolish as to think they could *know* the impact of a nuclear war on the fragile atmosphere! The work of climatology contained too much magic and too little science for categorical assertions.

Within that guaranteed uncertainty lurked the great danger. Ivan knew he could *make* the outcome of his re-analysis match any result they wanted him to report.

With too-crisp clarity, he saw why they had chosen him for this job. He was bright, ambitious, patriotic, and impressionable. And he had a knack for technology—a knack that compensated for his loner's attitude. He had the credentials, and presumably, the malleability to give them what they wanted.

He felt like a scientist in the days before the telescope, instructed by the Church to prove that the Sun circled the Earth. The truth could not be changed. But without instruments, truth could be distorted whenever convenient for the leaders—or when necessary for the followers.

Still, none of these games of distortion could change the
truth. And in the nuclear age, distorting the truth about
nuclear war endangered all the children, including the
adult children playing the game.

Ivan squeezed his eyes closed. Another gust of wind
slapped his face. His nostrils flared as he inhaled; the deep
breath of sharp, chilled air helped him make his decision.

He would gather the best scientists he could find. They
would study the consequences of nuclear war again. If the
earlier analysis had been *provably* hysterical, wonderful.
But the new Major Vorontsov would introduce no bias to
force the decision.

Ivan tramped onward against the last gusts of Siberian
winter, unswerving in his purpose.

Kira stepped from the elevator into the antiseptic beauty
of the Oeschlager Art Museum. She forced herself to slow
down as her high heels clicked across the slippery marble
floor. She turned, to step into the quiet elegance of the
displays. Soon she was surrounded by works that cost
thousands of hours of loving labor to construct. She needed
these moments, in this museum, to remember why she
had come to Wilcox-Morris. She needed these moments to
fuel her anger.

Her whole body itched from the taint of the Wilcox-
Morris Corporation. She wanted to run home to the shower,
to cleanse herself of it; yet she knew that that would not
help. Only her anger enabled her to continue.

The Oeschlager Museum sprawled over the first two
floors of the Wilcox Building. All costs of maintaining it,
and for collecting new works, came out of the advertising
budget of Wilcox-Morris. Thousands of people had died of
lung cancer, emphysema, and heart disease to support this
museum.

Kira stopped before a sculpture in silver and gold. In
the curves of the reflection she saw her mother's face—her
own face. Older people sometimes called her by her mother's name, so strong was the resemblance. And despite her
fierce defense of herself as a separate person, Kira could
not deny the similarity. They shared the same cheekbones
when seen in profile, the same pout when angry, the same

quick smile that puzzled people who missed the subtler points of human comedy.

They had not shared the dark anger seething behind Kira's eyes as she watched her reflection snake across the surface of the silvery sculpture. Perhaps that was a difference in age more than anything else. Her mother had not blamed the tobacco companies for her own death. In keeping with her other views of human responsibility, Jan had blamed herself for taking chances that might lead to suicide. Kira had a different point of view.

Uncle Nathan had the most complex view of blame, though in some sense, it was also the simplest. Blame, Uncle Nathan contended, was a concept without value in either Industrial Age or Information Age societies. The key question was not whom to blame, but rather, whose behavior to modify so that the problem did not arise again.

All that analysis had led him to Jan's answer to smoking, however; they agreed that the best solution lay in educating people to the danger and in teaching them how to quit. Uncle Nathan further contended that this was the *only* solution a free society could tolerate. Kira still felt uncertain about whether he was right. Certainly, it would not hurt to investigate other possibilities. *Know your enemy; he probably does not know himself*, the Zetetic commentary went. People did not usually pursue evil purposes with thoughtful intent, though they might pursue evil purposes while fiercely avoiding thoughts about intentions. The key lay in cultural engineering. Non-Zetetic cultures were always designed to give men rationalizations for not thinking about the inconsistencies of that culture. Given the right cultural environment, you could shape the adaptable human being to profoundly unsane purposes.

Like other creators of evil, Daniel Wilcox was not an evil man. The tobacco culture had engineered him; now, he was himself the chief engineer for the tobacco culture. Still, he was not evil, though he was undoubtedly quite ruthless. He was not evil, though his hands were covered with blood.

Kira looked about the room at the works of inspired genius, at the painfully detailed craftsmanship, that were also now covered with blood.

And she looked back at her own reflection. She too was now covered with blood. She had used her own mind in the creation of advertising that would attract children to their deaths. She had done it in order to get close to the source of power that drove the tobacco companies, so that she might find some way of destroying them. She had done it for a good cause.

And she could rationalize that, had she not created those ads, someone else would have, and they probably would have done just as good a job. But rationalization was not her purpose. She accepted her share of responsibility for the deaths that might result from her action, as surely as she accepted responsibility for the lives that might be saved, if she found a way to destroy the cigarette empire. *That* was her purpose in coming to Wilcox-Morris—to find some weakness, or set of weaknesses, with which she could destroy the industry.

Based on her first meeting with Daniel Wilcox, she questioned her ability to destroy him. He was too insightful; surely he recognized her revulsion at cigarette smoking, and her shock at the idea of attacking the Institute. She had recovered fairly well at the end. She could even get excited about *using* the news media, after having watched them take periodic shots at her mother and her uncle for years. She would certainly have no trouble composing a list of potentially useful reporters—she could get them from the Institute data base. She allowed herself a small smile, thinking about how easily she could mold them with the subtle power Wilcox afforded her.

Better yet, she realized that Wilcox's attack could be turned to the Institute's benefit. Wilcox could give Uncle Nathan a level of notoriety that poor Uncle Nathan would never bring upon himself. Perhaps this was the key to Wilcox's downfall.

And perhaps it was the key to her own downfall. Should she have highlighted this possible backfire with Wilcox? On impulse, she had concealed the thought from him, for fear that he would then discard the whole plan. Now she wasn't sure that had been wise. Surely he would think of that on his own, and he would expect her to think of it as well. She would have to be careful the next time she saw him.

She stepped carefully across museum floors toward the exit; her feet hurt in her new shoes. Two kinds of people went by. Dawdlers drifted here, either for the art or for the excuse it offered for not getting back to work. And urgent men in business suits rushed by, heading for the upper floors of the skyscraper.

The similarities between the Wilcox Building here in Rosslyn and the ZI headquarters in Reston fascinated and repelled her. Both structures projected images carefully designed for public consumption—images of elegant respectability, trustworthiness. The only real difference was the ultimate purpose: the tobacco companies projected trustworthiness so that they could betray the believers. The Institute projected trustworthiness so that they could teach the more malleable people how to be less malleable, how to separate that image from the substance. One of the most gratifying revelations in a Zetetic education was the moment when you looked at the Institute itself and, clear-eyed and laughing, separated the Institute's internal facts from its projected fantasies. To achieve that moment of revelation, Uncle Nathan said, the end justified the means.

Did the end justify the means? Kira didn't know. Uncle Nathan had a pat answer to that, too, of course: the end justifies the means as long as the end is moral, and as long as you account for all the side effects as parts of that end. Somehow, the side effects in her efforts to penetrate the Wilcox-Morris Corporation seemed too complicated to calculate.

This was why she lingered in the museum. She could not tell if her purpose here was moral or not. Until she figured it out, her anger was all that could sustain her as she plunged her hands into her work, defending the salesmen of death.

June 11

History is a race between education and catastrophe.

—*H. G. Wells*

PAN. Bill Hardie enters a room of soft contours and padded chairs. He glides to the corner, where he commands a view of both participants and podium. He turns, and the flatcam on his lapel sweeps the room.

ZOOM. A group of people emerge through the doorway. The sizes and shapes vary, but all look like residents of Fairfax County. They come to the headquarters of the Zetetic Institute not because it is the headquarters, but because it is handy. It wouldn't make sense for people to come from great distances just for the Sampler. The curious investigator could find many places throughout the country offering this seminar. The skeptical investigator could obtain a condensed version of the Sampler on videotape for the cost of postage and handling.

FOCUS. A man of medium height in a medium blue suit separates himself from the ragged line of people and walks to the front of the room with a light step—confident yet quiet. He sits on the edge of the desk, relaxed, projecting that relaxation to his audience. Even Bill feels at ease.

CUT. Everyone is seated now except Bill himself. Noting a number of eyes upon him, including the lecturer's, Bill slides into a chair.

The lecturer stands and introduces himself. "Good evening, everyone. I am Dr. Hammond, and this is a quick introduction to the Zetetic educational system."

Dr. Hammond shifts toward the audience as he warms up. "The Zetetic educational system arose to fill a gap in American society. The public schools teach our children oceans of facts and ideas. The colleges bend more toward teaching the theories that lie behind the uncovering of those facts. Meanwhile, vocational schools teach how to create products of various flavors.

"But what do you do with all those facts? Worse, what do you do with all those theories? How do they apply to the everyday occurrences of life?"

Hammond's eyes harden; his voice booms. "How do you extract the truth from a used car salesman? How do you spot a lawyer whose interest is his own welfare, not yours?" He steps forward. "Those are communication skills that aren't well taught. Another class of skills that is left out of most people's eduction is real business skills. America is supposed to run on a free-enterprise system. But how many people know how to operate in a free-enterprise system? To start your own business, how do you identify a market, make a business plan, acquire capital, design an advertising campaign, write a contract? Does it really make sense to leave the answers to these questions—the heart of the American economic process—to students working on MBAs? If it does, then we don't have a system of free enterprise—we have a system of elite enterprise, because only a handful of people understand what's required." He smiles. "And there are other analytic skills that we see in action, but that people rarely learn how to apply. For example, there's a vast difference between *accuracy* and *precision*. How many people here know the difference?"

BACK OFF. Bill frowns. A difference between accuracy and precision? What difference could there be? Only a few people raise their hands to suggest that they know.

Hammond looks around, unsurprised by the apparent ignorance of the majority. "Usually only physicists pay attention to the difference. But the difference is important in everything from household budgets to airplane repairs. Human beings have wasted vast quantities of effort through the centuries, trying to increase their precision beyond the level of their accuracy."

Hammond takes a deep breath. "You can find numerous texts on subliminal cuing and impulse motivation—but very little on how this information is used against you in advertising. And no educational institution will tell you that it's important for you to know.

"And everyone learns statistics—but how many people

can tell the difference between newspaper articles that use statistics to illuminate the truth, and articles that use them to conceal it?"

CUT. Bill bristles with hostility. Bill finds it particularly unnerving because, as Hammond makes his last statement, he looks toward Bill himself with a slowly rising eyebrow.

Hammond continues. "Nathan Pilstrom founded the Institute over a decade ago. He started with the limited idea of developing software that could teach some fundamentals of Information Age problem-solving. The individual software modules were called PEPs, or Personal Enhancement Programs."

PAUSE. Bill shakes his head in surprise. He didn't know the Zetetic Institute had created the PEPs. He'd used a couple himself.

"Of course, the Zetetic movement didn't become widely known until Nathan's sister, Jan Evans, synthesized antismoking techniques from all over the world into a comprehensive package. That package could be adapted with a high degree of success to each individual's therapy needs. And that is perhaps the unique feature of Zeteticism: it focuses on the methods used for *customizing methods* for each individual set of needs and values. Zeteticism explores methods of method-selection."

PAN. Methods of method-selection indeed! Bill recognizes the sound of hokum.

"So tonight we have a sampler for you—short discussions of a number of aspects of life upon which Zetetic ideas offer different perspectives. We'll lead off with a little experiment—something that you can all participate in. We shall explore the meaning of rational thought, irrational thought, and superrational thought: we shall play the game of the Prisoner's Dilemma."

PAN. Men enter, wearing badges with the insignia of the Institute, and escort groups of people away from the lecture hall. Dr. Hammond walks over to Bill. "Let me show you the way," he offers. His eyes follow Bill's face like a biologist who has just spotted a delightfully rare but disgusting insect. "That's a beautiful button on your collar there. I've never seen one quite like it."

He knows about the flatcam!

"When the games are over, would you be interested in a copy of our videotape? It would probably be easier to edit."

CUT. Bill opens his mouth, then closes it. He shrugs. "I'll roll my own if you don't mind."

Hammond tilts his head. "Suit yourself."

He escorts Bill to a small, antiseptic cubicle, chatting constantly, probing occasionally into Bill's viewpoint. The cubicle contains a beige computer terminal, a chair, nothing else. Bill stops at the doorway. There is something odd here—he inhales sharply.

Is there a scent of pine trees here, ever so subtle? He looks hard at Hammond. "Is my reaction to this room a part of the test?" he asks.

Hammond chuckles. "No. Mr. Hardie, this isn't a test. We aren't interested in your reactions in any direct way. Our purpose here is to give you an *experience*, so you can see how theories apply to action, and so you can see firsthand the importance of superrational thinking. We think it's particularly important to introduce superrational thinking to people such as yourself."

FOCUS. Bill does not ask what Hammond means when he speaks of people "such as himself."

Hammond waves Bill into the single chair next to the terminal. He explains the rules. "Here's the situation. Every person from the class is sitting in a cubicle like this one. Now, we're going to pair you up with one of these people, and together you are going to be the Prisoners."

"Are you going to lock me in?"

Hammond shakes his head. "Of course not. But you are on your honor not to enter another person's room. Not that it matters; you won't have time to hunt for them all over the Institute anyway."

"I see." Bill feels too warm, though the room is comfortable.

"As prisoners, the two of you have been put in separate rooms for interrogation. You have two choices: you can confess to the crime, or you can deny involvement."

"Why would I want to confess?"

"Because when you confess, you turn state's evidence

against the other guy. It's a betrayal as well as a confession. Then you get off with a quick parole, and the other guy goes up the river.

"Of course, the other guy might decide to betray you as well. Indeed, the *worst* thing that can happen to you is that your partner confesses—betraying you—while you sit here denying involvement."

"Then why should I ever do anything but betray the other guy?"

"Because the only way either of you can get out scot free is if you both deny involvement. Denying involvement is a collaboration—a conspiracy as well as a denial. So your best outcome is if you both conspire—but your worst outcome is if you conspire while the other guy betrays."

"So you're stuck with trusting this guy in another room whom you can't trust."

"Yes, it's quite a dilemma, isn't it?"

Bill glares. "Why is this game part of the Sampler?"

Hammond shrugs. "The results of the Prisoner's Dilemma apply to many real-life situations. We'll discuss some of the applications after we've analyzed the results of the game. The game might seem silly now, but remember that even obvious ideas need to be exercised before you can truly own them. You can't get more out of this seminar than you're willing to put in."

"But I can get a lot less than I put in."

"True enough. Life is generally like that—you must put something in to get something out."

Bill growls, "Okay."

"Good. You'll play this game with ten randomly selected people from the class. Then you'll play with them all again. We'll play ten rounds with each player and then discuss the results. For every game, all you have to do is punch either the Conspire button or the Betray button." Hammond shoots him a quizzical look. "So how are you going to play?"

Bill thinks about it for a long moment. "The only rational thing to do is to betray the other guy," he states with confidence. "You just can't take a chance on some random human being."

"I see your point." Hammond's smile again makes him feel like a bug under a microscope. "We'll keep score by adding up the years in jail you accumulate. Good luck." The door swished softly behind him.

Bill looks at the terminal, annoyed by this pointless game that dooms all the players to lose. Surely, everyone here is as rational as he is; if so, there will be an endless series of betrayals.

The terminal comes to life, telling him he is matched with partner number one, and that they have never played together before. Bill stabs the Betray button.

In less than a minute Bill realizes that not everyone is rational. Several people offer to Conspire in that first round, and they take terrible punishments as Bill betrays them. Bill himself gets off lightly. In the second round, he finds that the terminal gives him a description of his history with his opponent. He stabs the Betray button with a moment's regret—and realizes that when he thinks of the other player as an *opponent*, he is creating a fundamental statement about his relationship.

Seeing himself paired with a player who had given him a valuable Conspiracy the last time, Bill generously offers a Conspiracy in return—but the bastard Betrays, leaving Bill holding the bag. After a few more plays, Bill realizes that these people don't trust him worth a damn. He admits—with considerable reluctance—that he has given them cause for suspicion. In self-defense, he reverts to a constant stream of Betrayals.

On the third round, the handful of people to whom he has offered Conspiracies in the second round come back with Conspiracies for him. Of course, he has given up any acts of mercy, zapping all players with Betrayals.

Meanwhile, two of the players have doggedly continued to give him Conspiracies. It matters not that he Betrays them again and again. On the fourth round he reciprocates, and they remain as solid partners till the last round of the game. He gives up on the ones with whom he seesaws back and forth from Betrayals to Conspiracies, and switches to permanent Betrayals. They do the same.

At the end of ten rounds, he has accumulated over a century in jail.

Hammond pokes his head in. "How'd you do?" he asks.
FOCUS. Bill shrugs. "As well as anybody, I guess."

Back in the discussion room, Hammond disproves that
assessment. Several people do substantially better than
Bill. Hammond points out key features of the "winners."

The winners had three distinctive characteristics: They
were *optimistic*, offering to Conspire with untested partners. They were *just*, never letting a Betrayal go without
response. And they were *predictable in their responses*, so
their partners knew what they would do at all times. With
sudden insight, Bill realizes that these people were the
ones with whom he had seesawed early in the game; his
stubborn Betrayals constituted a major part of their losses.
Of course he had shared their losses, since they soon
responded with Betrayals of their own.

"All in all, we have a very rational group here," Hammond says with airy cheer. "Fortunately, I think we can
improve on that."

He continues. "I always feel sorry for people encounter-
ing the Prisoner's Dilemma for the first time. The Prisoner's Dilemma hurts because there is no formula for success.
Intuitively, we suspect that the right answer is to Conspire, thus working together with the other prisoner for
mutual gain. And if we could talk with the other prisoner,
if we could communicate, we could make a good arrangement. But looking at the situation without that ability to
communicate, we conclude that we must protect ourselves.
The merely rational mind inevitably derives a losing
formula."

Hammond leans forward and whispers, as if conspiring
with the members of the class in a secret fight with a
vicious universe. "But if you can step beyond rationality to
superrationality, then you *can* derive a winning formula.
The formula only works if your partners are superrational,
too—but at least it's a winning formula sometimes. It's
better than what happened to all of you in the Dilemma
you just faced." Hammond points at Bill. "What's the sum
of four plus three?"

SNAP. Bill looks up, startled. "Seven," he answers without hesitation.

"If another person in a different room were asked the same question, would he give the same answer?"

Bill mutters. "Of course."

"So the two of you would be able to make that agreement without communicating?"

"Sure," Bill snaps. "There's a formula for calculating the right answer."

"And everybody knows the formula." Hammond looks around the class. Some look puzzled; others look expectant.

Hammond continues. "Suppose some of the people didn't know the formula. Then you couldn't guarantee that you and the other person would get the same answer, could you?" A shiver seems to sweep the room as many people shake their heads.

"Okay, now suppose there were a formula for deciding what to do in the Prisoner's Dilemma. No matter who you were, if you applied the formula, you would get the right answer, right? And if you knew that your partner knew the formula, you wouldn't have to worry about the outcome: you could both crank the formula and come out with the right answer."

Hammond raises his arm and points to every person in the class. "So the very assumption that there *is* a formula tells us what the formula must be, does it not? If there is a formula, the formula says to Conspire, to cooperate with the other prisoner." His arm descends in a human exclamation mark. "But the formula only works if *you* know the formula, *and* if you know that your *partner* knows the formula, *and* if your partner knows that *you* know the formula."

About a fourth of the faces in the class brighten immediately with understanding; others brighten more slowly as they grasp the concept. Hammond drawls, "So you and your partner must in some sense be superrational to succeed, for you must be not only rational enough to select rationally among your individual choices, you must also be rational enough to understand the meaning of rationality for the group."

Hammond's eyes shine with pleasure in revealing the key to the game. "So the big question is, how do you find out if the other guy is as superrational as you are? In the

Prisoner's Dilemma, there is one way to find out." He spreads his arms in a gesture of martyrdom. "Assume your partner knows the formula in the first round: Give him a Conspiracy. If he knows the formula, he will also give you a Conspiracy in that first round, and you will have found each other.

"But if he doesn't give you a Conspiracy in that first round, you know that he doesn't know the formula. He may be rational as an individual, but he hasn't succeeded in looking outside his own viewpoint—he hasn't achieved superrationality, so you have to treat him accordingly. In games where your partner is only rational, or worse yet, irrational, you must betray him, for he will betray you."

Bill slides backward in his chair, amazed at the short yet devious flow of this logic.

"Consequently, the only way to make games like the Prisoner's Dilemma safe is to educate all the people who might become your partners, so they can be as superrational as you are. Only superrational people working together can win the Prisoner's Dilemma." Hammond stands triumphant before his newly baptized members of the superrational. At least some of them are superrational, anyway; Bill sees doubt on many faces. From those expressions, he knows which ones he would prefer to have as partners.

Bill cheers for victorious superrational mind. He senses the same desire in other people around the room, but the thoughts are too deep to accept just yet. He, and the others, must chew on the idea of superrationality.

Hammond realizes this. "And with that, we'll take a break. Think about situations in which this kind of thinking might affect *your* life. We'll talk about applications in a few minutes—applications in areas as diverse as office politics and child-rearing." He paused. "And *then*, we'll show everyone how to engage in a decision duel."

Jet lag gave Nathan a tremendous business advantage when he flew west. He noted this with little pleasure, sitting outside the Pelmour complex waiting for MDS Software Associates to open its doors. Here in Mountain View, California, it was not quite 8 A.M. His internal body

clocks, still set on D.C. time, told him it was closer to 11
A.M. Everyone on this coast was still coping with morning,
injecting fresh caffeine into their bloodstreams. Nathan,
however, was almost ready for lunch.

The Pelmour complex was one of the dozens of office
clusters designed for the unique requirements of upstart
startup companies here in the heart of Silicon Valley. The
Silicon Valley entrepreneur could not begin life with merely
a great idea, a reasonable product, a decent business plan,
and a tight chunk of venture capital. The Silicon Valley
entrepreneur had to initiate his future corporate empire
with the right *style*.

Much of that style was embodied in the building where
the entrepreneur began his life. He could not tool up in an
old warehouse, tainted by vanished crates of fruit once
plucked from orchard groves that blossomed in the days
before silicon. No one would believe he could succeed
from such a decrepit location; certainly, his business plan
was inadequate in scope.

Nor could he start life in an opulent penthouse office
overlooking the ocean. Such ostentation was allowed only
to those who had succeeded. Anyone who started in this
manner was just a pretender; his great new idea could
only be vaporware.

The proper entrepreneur instinctively understood that
proper businesses started in two-story buildings: Ship-
ments came and went through the loading dock in back,
on the bottom floor. Customers came and went through
the door in front, on the top floor. Back in the '90s,
construction crews had built miles of ridges here in Mountain View, to create enough cliff edges in which to embed
such proper two-story buildings.

The Pelmour complex was a long chain of these startup
company buildings, the entrepreneurial equivalent of a
tenement row. Nathan couldn't help chuckling as he
squinted down the stretch of bland sandstone building
fronts. Though he had started the Zetetic Corporation
outside Seattle, not San Francisco, he too had worked out
of one of these tenements for a time. Indeed, for Nathan,
the move to a Seattle tenement had been a step up; he
had written the first Personal Enhancement Program—the

Advertising Immunity PEP—in the spare bedroom of a friend in San Antonio. No real entrepreneur would have considered working under such conditions. Only his friends in San Antonio, and his sister Jan, had supported his efforts at the time. Jan had always believed in him.

The doors of MDS Software Associates opened. Delilah Lottspeich, the woman he had come to see, had a subcontract with MDS Software. He walked along the curved sidewalk to the front door. Few employees or subcontractors had arrived during the minutes before 8 o'clock; either they arrived enthusiastically early, or they started randomly late.

When he entered, he found people hurrying along behind the receptionist; evidently, enthusiasm was the driver here. Nathan held a brief negotiation with the receptionist before he persuaded one of the passing young men to escort him back to Delilah's office.

Security was not as strict here as it usually was in fledgling companies: the man waved at Delilah's office, then disappeared behind a labyrinth of room dividers. The whole office had the unnatural quiet that follows after the discussions have worn down, when everyone can strive toward well-understood goals. Only the soft click of keys, and the softer sound of mouse buttons, broke the stillness. A weak aroma of coffee came from the brewing station in the corner.

Nathan stepped across the threshold of Delilah's office. He did not announce himself. The mental gymnastics of a programmer are too delicate to disturb lightly; he would wait for the right moment.

She sat facing away from the door, unmoving, absorbed in the computer display. Her hair spilled across her pale shoulders, then cascaded down her back in a golden wave—a frozen wave, like a waterfall turned to ice in mid-flight. Touch it, and it might break.

The golden wave shimmered. Delilah twisted in her seat, and Nathan knocked on the door. She swiveled to face him.

Nathan's sense of watching a frozen waterfall did not diminish. Her arms and neck were long and thin and delicate. Her face held a cold, closed expression—the expression of someone who expects to be struck at any moment.

Nathan gave her his warmest smile. "Delilah Lottspeich? I'm Nathan Pilstrom. I called yesterday about a project we need you on."

"I remember," she snapped, her voice sharp with tension. "You wouldn't tell me what it was over the phone." She smiled, moderating her tone. "But I bet it's something interesting. I've taken about half the Zetetic series on liars."

"Oh, no!" Nathan exclaimed, slapping his forehead with mock dismay. "Then I don't stand a chance of manipulating you—unless you missed the course on Lying at a Job Interview."

She didn't respond to the joke.

The Liars series included Lying with Statistics, a study of economists; Lying with Facts, a study of news reporters; Lying with Implications, covering advertising strategies; and Lying with Words, on the fine art of politics. She offered him the chair next to her work station. "Call me Lila." As he sat down, she asked, "What's the Institute working on?"

Nathan leaned forward on the edge of the seat. "Have you ever heard of the Sling project?"

"I don't think so."

"We're developing a way to limit the death and destruction caused by war."

"Really." For a moment she lit up with excitement. "What have you developed? A new method for negotiating treaties?" Suspicion closed around her once more. "Wait a minute. Why do you want a digital sensor specialist for something like this—to verify compliance or something? You don't need me for that."

"No, we don't need you for that." Nathan took a deep breath. Just listening to her combination of hope and suspicion, he could predict her reaction to the real project— she would be horrified. "The Sling is a defensive system. By using Information Age techniques, we can pick out key elements in an enemy attack. By destroying those key elements, we can stop the attack with a minimal cost of life."

Her strident voice took on a pleading tone, hoping he would yet allow her to disbelieve what she had just heard. "Are you telling me that the Zetetic Institute now develops *weapons*?"

Nathan felt like he had been slapped. He sat very straight, very open, as if offering the other cheek for yet another blow. "Yes. We also develop weapons, Lila. If we have to fight a war, it is terribly important that we fight it the best way we know how, to end it quickly."

"You build machines to kill people? I can't believe it!" But the vehemence in her voice suggested that she *did* believe it. And she hated it.

"We build machines that kill people, yes." Nathan continued to speak as if to a rational person, though he doubted that his mental map of rationality matched the terrain he now faced. He had entered the room as one of her heroes; he would leave as one of her enemies. "But that's not the whole story. Just as we must accept some of the responsibility for the men who die because of the machines we build, so must we accept responsibility for the men who *do not* die, who *would have died* had we not built those machines."

She wheeled away from him. He had run out of time for rational discussion.

He had one more avenue of approach available: he could try manipulation. "Lila! You're a smart and sane person. You don't make decisions because of slogans and peer group prejudices—you make decisions because they are *right* decisions, after fully examining the facts." He had started his speech rapidly, with her name, to get her attention. As he proceeded he slowed down, to let the words set up a cognitive dissonance in her mind.

She now had two views of herself warring within her. One view said that she must not listen, because she hated war regardless of arguments. The other view said that she must listen, because she believed in making right decisions after hearing all the arguments. This conflict, this cognitive dissonance, had to be resolved. If Nathan could enhance her view of herself as a thinking person, she would resolve the dissonance by listening to him objectively. She would *become*, for a short time, the smart and sane person Nathan had told her she was.

This tactic assumed her emotional reactions clouded her views. If reflexive emotions held her, then Nathan's new words would appeal to her emotional belief in rational self. Thus Nathan could manipulate her.

But if she were fully rational, the words he had just offered would have no effect. She would weigh his words about the Sling independently from his words about her as a person. And that, too, would be wonderful; his purpose was to get her to give him a fair hearing. Thus, his best hope for success was that she was immune to his manipulation.

Nathan's use of cognitive dissonance here presented the only ethical use of manipulation that Nathan knew—manipulation geared to making a person less easily manipulated.

Small twitches of doubt broke the brittle lines of her face; the cognitive dissonance held her in thrall, unresolved.

Nathan continued, "I'm glad you see as clearly as I do the importance of careful thought. The lives of thousands of people rest with your analysis of what I have to say." He watched her face carefully, but could not tell if he was winning. "The key to ending a war and saving lives is to prevent people from ever going onto a battlefield. To prevent that, we want to confuse the commanders who order men into battle, to remove them from the picture. Doesn't that make sense?"

"No!"

The intensity of her response had surprised her, Nathan could see. Of course, her exclamation had not been an answer to Nathan's question. It had been her answer to herself. She had resolved the dissonance. Nathan had failed.

Nathan watched her turn back to her work station, bringing up a page of test graphics. Having denied his thoughts and facts, she now denied his existence.

Nathan did not know which parts of the Zetetic series on liars Lila had taken, but he knew one part she had missed—Lying with Your Own Preconceptions. The toughest part of the series, it dealt with the lies people told to themselves.

PAN. They step into another room. The room has the contours of a small auditorium, though only the first two tiers support ordered rows of seats. At the focal point of the room, Bill confronts the largest computer display he has ever seen—larger than the one in Houston for controlling spacecraft launches.

Hammond speaks. "This is the main screen upon which the Institute carries out its largest and most important decision duels. It's not used too often for that purpose. What we're looking at now is one of our demonstration duels—a duel held over a decade ago to determine the merits of strategic defense."

PAN. Bill looks back at the display in fascination. The colorful splashes that streak through the wall resolve, as he approaches, into lines of text. With a few exceptions, the entire screen holds only words, arrows, and rectangles. The rectangles enclose and divide the text displays.

They stop at a console perched high above the audience: clearly it is the display master controller. Hammond continues. "As you can see, the overall dueling area is divided into three sections." He taps a track ball on the console, and a pointing arrow zips across the screen. It circles the left half of the screen, then the right, and finally runs up and down the center band of gray. "Each duel pits a pair of alternatives against one another. Often, the alternatives are negations—one position in favor of some action, and one position against that action. The left part of the screen belongs to the proponent for the action, and the right half belongs to the opponent. These two people are known as the *slant moderators*. They have slanted viewpoints, of course, and they actually act as moderators—anyone can suggest ideas to them for presentation. Of course, no one calls them slant moderators. The nickname for slant moderator is *decision duelist*."

The pointer continues to roam across the center band. "The center is the 'third alternatives' area, where ideas outside of for-or-against may be presented by either of the duelists, or by anyone in the audience. In the duel we have here, the third alternatives section remained closed—no one came up with any striking ways to finesse the question."

The arrow shifts upward. Above the colored swirl of text boxes stands a single line of text, a single phrase. It dominates the screen, with thick letters black as asphalt. The lettering seems so solid Bill wonders whether it is part of the display, or whether it has been etched into the surface in bas relief.

This one phrase running across the top overlaps all three sections of the screen. Bill presumes that top line describes the theme of the duel, the title of the topic under discussion. Reading it now, he sees it does not. Instead, this dark, ominous line—so striking and hypnotic, as if sucking the light from the air—reads:

LET ACCURACY TRIUMPH OVER VICTORY

Despite the hypnotic pull, Bill tears his eyes away from the words. They disturb him.

Hammond speaks. "It's easy to get wrapped up in one's own point of view on a topic. After much study of the matter, we've concluded that you can't overemphasize the need for objective search for *rightness*, as opposed to *victory*." He smiles. "As it happens, we keep records on the duels written by certified slant moderators. We do *not* keep our records based on who *wins* the duel. We keep them based on whether the decision that comes out of the duel is *correct*. Thus, a duelist can have a perfect record even if he 'loses' every time he moderates."

A dark-haired woman wearing a smart business suit asks, "How do you know who's right? Sometimes it takes years to find out, and sometimes you can never find out."

Hammond concurs. "You're quite right. We can't trace the correctness of all the duels, so not every duel yields a record. However, we don't lose things just because it takes a long time to determine the outcome. The memories of the Zetetic data bases are very long indeed. In fact, the Zetetic data bases have started to free those of us who work here from our own short-term concerns. Even if we forget events and decisions as quickly as the news media forget, the knowledge remains available for recall with only a slight effort. We have automated the tracking of all the predictions of duelists, stock-brokers, crystal ball readers, and economists. A couple of years of lucky hits do not impress us." He snorts. "We also keep records of the promises made by politicians. I'm sure no one would be surprised by the results of *that* comparison."

Hammond leads them halfway down to the audience area, where a pair of work stations sit in friendly proximity. The left work station display shows a section of the left half of the main display—the proponent's half. Some early duelist has scratched PRO into the edge of the desk top. The right station shows a part of the right half of the display—the opponent's half; another duelist long ago labeled it CON. Bill runs his finger over the rough cuts in the desk top, amazed by the presence of such graffiti.

The cloth-covered arms of the work station chairs show frays and dark stains. Bill wonders how many hundreds of anxious decision duelists have sat in these chairs, rubbing nervous hands over those arms.

"We also keep score on the development of third alternatives that are better than either of the listed alternatives. In general, duels that settle on third alternatives find the best answers of all."

The lecturer drones on, but his voice blends into the scene as Bill watches the cursor on the main display flicker from point to point.

Beneath the blinking warning are the titles: YES, A USEFUL STRATEGIC DEFENSE CAN BE BUILT. And NO, A USEFUL STRATEGIC DEFENSE CANNOT BE BUILT. Beneath the titles are the assumptions, written in cautionary amber. About a dozen assumptions show for the PRO side, and another dozen on the CON side. On the PRO side is the comment, "We assume we are discussing alternatives for getting high rates of kill against ICBMs. We are not discussing engineering absurdities such as 'perfect' defenses."

Next to this assumption lies a picture of a button. When the arrow touches the button, a further discussion of this assumption—why it is necessary—expands into view.

On the CON side, one three-part assumption stands out. "A strategic defense system must pass three feasibility tests: It must be technically feasible. It must be economically feasible. It must be politically feasible."

Beneath the yellow assumption boxes are the opening arguments. The first of these are the cute slogans with much cleverness but little content, much favored by the media. The duelists put them up even if they disagree with them, just to get them out of the way. Appropriately, here the coloration of the text seems playful—purples and oranges and reds splashing about as though written with a child's crayons.

A purple background marks off a quote on the PRO side:

BUILD WEAPONS THAT KILL WEAPONS, NOT WEAPONS THAT KILL PEOPLE.

The CON duelist colored it purple because the statement has no meaningful content, only emotional appeal: whether a weapon kills people directly or not is irrelevant; what matters is whether the weapon increases or decreases the odds that more or fewer people will die.

On the CON side, the PRO duelist had marked a statement in red: PREVENT THE MILITARIZATION OF SPACE. When Hammond's arrow touches this field, an explanation window blossoms to explain the fatal flaw in this reasoning. Space was already militarized: if a war started, 10,000 nuclear warheads could fall through space in the first half hour. Moreover, as with the purple comment on the pro side, the important issue was not whether a weapon was space-based—the question was its effect on human life. The PRO duelist had placed another purple, satirical statement on level with the PREVENT MILITARIZATION slogan, connecting them with a thin line indicating they were two different ways of saying the same thing. The satirical alternative to PREVENT THE MILITARIZATON OF SPACE was MAKE THE WORLD SAFE FOR NUCLEAR WARHEADS.

Beneath the opening comments the words shrank in size, becoming more densely packed as the two sides parried back and forth with increasing verbosity. Both sides agreed to the format described in the CON assumptions: first came discussion of technical feasibility, then economic, then political.

The technical feasibility debate ran to great lengths. PRO constructed alternative after alternative, only to see each one knocked down by CON. But PRO responded to the CON objections, refining the alternatives to overcome the objections one by one. Bill realizes that he sees the evolution of a high-level design for strategic defense outlined before him.

Two-thirds of the way down the screen, the discussion ends, the PRO side triumphant. They have constructed over a hundred different approaches. CON has marked up all but two with bright red fatal flaws, but those two approaches seem capable of defense against words, and maybe also missiles.

Then the debate on the economics begins. This is a short discussion, surprisingly. Both sides agree upon a single criterion for economic viability: Can the system knock a missile down for less money than it costs to put a missile up? If you can shoot them down for more than they cost, then the defense is cheap; if you cannot, then the whole thing is easily defeated by building more missiles. A small amber button glows next to this agreement, which expands to explain the underlying assumption that the defender is not so much wealthier than the attacker that he can afford an extravagant imbalance. A millionaire can spend thousands of dollars protecting himself from a ten-dollar pistol, for example, and easily afford it.

Here both sides invoke large windows filled with spreadsheet calculations. Again, the PRO side shows one possible way of keeping the costs within the economic limit, while CON shows the other approach would fail. Both sides note the inaccuracies in these forecasts, and the size of the ranges. But only one successful approach is needed. The strategic defense system has passed the economic test.

Hammond explains that the political feasibility test is where the CON duelist had focused his attention all along. It is here that the brilliant thrust took place, the insight that makes this a classic in decision dueling. For though there are several approaches that are technically feasible, and one of those is indeed economically feasible, there are thousands of approaches that would fail. With brutal clarity the CON duelist demonstrates, with one military program after another, that the American military development system cannot select a solution that is better than mediocre. With the wings of the C-5, with the computers of TACFIRE, with the armor of the Bradley, the CON duelist demonstrates mediocre solutions that cost factors of two and three times as much as good solutions should.

The PRO duelist concedes: given the American system of military research and development, strategic defense is a hopeless proposition.

"And as everyone here knows, this early decision duel predicted the future quite accurately." Hammond sighs. "This also demonstrates another fundamental consideration of the decision duel—one that engineers all too often forget: the critical importance of finding an approach that can succeed, not only technically and economically, but also politically. This engineering blind spot mirrors the politician's tendency to forget technical viability. Politicians live in a universe where reality seems to be controlled by the perceptions of other politicians. In the heat of finding an approach that he can get other politicians to agree to, he forgets that there are laws he has no control over."

They walk from the room. The warning in asphalt-black from the top of the dueling display continues to etch itself in Bill Hardie's mind.

CUT. After several more demonstrations of Zetetic networks and techniques, he shuts off his flatcam. There is nothing in the Sampler to help him humiliate the Zetetic Institute.

A man could easily starve, wandering the halls of the Pentagon in search of an exit. The faceless, endless corridors contain few distinguishing landmarks for the novice explorer. And the corridors are truly endless—once aligned on a ring, a person could veer gently at each pentagon-corner and return eventually to the place whence he had started. Of course, whether he recognized his starting point or not was another matter.

Sitting at his mahogany desk in the heart of the great building, Charles Somerset reflected on a story he had once heard about wild turkeys. A wild turkey, when confronted with a fence, would simply spread its wings and leap the fence. But when confronted with a thick tree trunk lying on its side, the turkey would run around the log, that being an easier scheme. So the clever farmer strung a low wire, the height of a tree trunk, in a large circle. Instead of leaping, the turkey would run around the edge of the wire to find its end. By the time it returned to its starting place, the turkey had quite forgotten it had been there before. It would run, around and around, till it collapsed in exhaustion.

Charles didn't know whether the system worked with turkeys, but it certainly did with people in the Pentagon. Dazed, dizzy, and defeated by the corridors, exhausted Pentagon commanders could easily have their wings clipped by the smart operator. For some projects, the clipping took a lot of time and gentle nudging, but it yielded results in the end.

For these reasons, Charles loved the Pentagon. The dingy corridors did not dismay him. The hollow echo of air conditioning, the sometimes painful squeal of old battered chairs, the pounding rhythm of remodeling never quite completed, the echoes of conversations that seemed to linger in the hallways long after the speakers had departed: all contributed to the sensation of fighting under hostile conditions. Such conditions made victories over the maze of circles that much sweeter. Charles seldom noticed that the endless circles had trapped even him. Only on days like today did he feel encircled himself.

Today, he felt like a wagon train struggling against a circle of Indian warriors. He had assembled a fine flock of generals, colonels, and majors for the FIREFORS projects, not to mention the gaggles of civil servants and defense contractors. But they had left a few stray turkeys beyond the fence. Strays did not present an abnormality, but when they started acting like an Indian war party, he had to do something about it. Billions of dollars in FIREFORS projects could be canceled if people started concluding that the Sling Project, with a few paltry millions of dollars, could provide more capabilities at ludicrously less cost. Rumors had started already; an intense new school of treaty-loving budget-butchers waited for an opening to storm the FIREFORS train. It was exhausting to think about.

His glasses had slid down his nose during the morning's toil. He pushed them back into place with a sigh.

Charles and his projects had met threats like the Sling before. For over two decades, he had maintained a string of perfect scores in political combat. No one had ever canceled one of his projects. *Why not?* his opponents often asked. For one thing, the projects were too important, he explained. For another, the Defense Department already had too much money invested in them to just throw them away. This case was no different: hundreds of important people had staked their reputations on FIREFORS by putting money into it; no one wanted a handful of Zetetic fanatics, funded with peanuts, to beat them.

Fortunately, enemies like the Sling Project had many vulnerabilities. Charles had merely to pick one and apply the right formula. The Sling's dependence on commercial hardware and software was such a vulnerability. Commercial stuff might be cheaper, but it did not match the military requirement. It could not be rugged enough, for example. It could not survive an EMP blast, or a salt fog. And cheaply built hodgepodges of commercial stuff were not *systems*: they did not consider the logistics, the training, or the maintenance that a full-scale development project had to consider.

All these other considerations made military equipment cost tens and hundreds of times as much as commercial equipment. Ruggedization, logistics, training—these problems were responsible for the one little mar in the FIREFORS record: in two decades of effort, not one FIREFORS project had been completed. And of course none had been canceled. So all continued on course to their ever-more-distant deliveries, a fleet of juggernauts on an endless but important voyage.

His desk remained neat throughout the voyage. A single folder of papers to one side suggested to visitors that Charles had concentrated all his efforts on a single important task, excommunicating all else to his filing cabinets, and to his conference table.

Charles did not keep the conference table nearly so clean. Too often, unfriendly visitors came with the intention of spreading their accusatory documents across its surface. So Charles kept a carefully disarrayed assortment of materials there, organized to seem important, slightly skewed to suggest that a disturbance would damage the arrangement. Charles had plenty of space on his desk for displays, *if* the displays showed favorable results.

A single sheet of paper now rested on the single folder on his desk. It was the draft of a backchannel message from General Curtis to General Hicks, explaining why the Sling Project represented a dangerous duplication of effort. It suggested that control of the Sling Project should move to the FIREFORS program office, where FIREFORS could manage it more effectively.

The backchannel suggested funneling the Sling Project money into the common pool of FIREFORS funds. Then FIREFORS could build a system that included all the good features of both the Sling and the FIREFORS systems—though frankly, General Curtis felt confident that FIREFORS projects already incorporated all the key features of the Sling system. After all, FIREFORS had been working on these problems for twenty years; they had experience. General Curtis recommended to General Hicks that he look at the latest revision of the requirements document describing the FIREFORS products—Version 14.7. Thus General Hicks could see for himself that FIREFORS had indeed covered all critical Sling elements.

Charles smiled, reading about Version 14.7. It had just come off the presses that morning, thicker than Version 14.6 because of a new chapter describing additional variants of FIREFORS systems. The variants looked astonishingly like the Sling Hunters. The only parts of the Sling specifications omitted from the FIREFORS plan were the parts on low cost and quick delivery.

Though the backchannel was from General Curtis, Curtis had not written it; indeed, he had not yet seen it. But Charles had spent the whole week warming him up to the idea of such a message. The general would sign with only a glance at the wording.

With a small hum of pleasure, Charles edited a few fine

points in the message. His sharpened pencil stabbed against the paper, slashing streaks of red across the words. It seemed like a modern form of voodoo, wherein the slashes could appear upon the spirits of the men working on the Sling.

Charles hummed more loudly as he considered the devastating potency of this form of black magic.

President Mayfield looked at his watch with eager anticipation. The next step along the path to the next election had been sealed. His heart skipped once in a while, but only when he watched Nell Carson's puzzled expression for too long.

She strode across the room, from the conference table to the bookcase. Her eyes wandered aimlessly across the rows of volumes. It seemed as though she believed the answers to all her questions could be found here, but for some reason she could not read.

Disdainful, Mayfield glanced at the books himself. First he saw only a few books. With a mental step back, he saw more: he saw all the shelves filled with books. Then he remembered that this tiny collection represented a window into the main room of the Library of Congress; he saw walls filled with shelves.

In a moment of grander vision, he saw the rooms filled with walls of shelves, beyond the main room in the Library of Congress. Then he saw the buildings filled with rooms of shelves of books, beyond the main building. And he saw how tiny a single human mind seemed, compared to this enormous swirl of knowledge.

He lurched mentally to a horrible realization. In some desperately important sense, both he and Nell were *illiterate*. The answers to their questions might well lie within the behemoth of human experience. Yet those answers might as well not exist. For though both he and Nell could read, they couldn't read fast enough.

They couldn't read fast enough! His heart skipped a beat. He needed to look away and think of something else, but Nell's expression held him. He felt sure that Nell had seen the rooms of walls of shelves as clearly as he had, yet the vision did not frighten her. Only sorrow, and longing,

and puzzlement touched her expression as her reaching
fingers touched the books at random. The gesture seemed
so hopeless, yet the mind behind the gesture seemed so
hopeful.

She paced back to the table, her dress swishing gracefully as she moved. She paused at the table, reluctant to
sit. Yet she had no other purpose in this room; she returned to her chair.

Elated, Mayfield saw that Nell Carson, the woman of
never-ending surety, was uncertain about their new treaty.
Mayfield shifted his gaze to Secretary of State Earl
Semmens, seated across the table from Nell. Earl's posture suggested that he expected Nell to strike him physically; he evidently did not recognize Nell's uncertainty.

Unable to resist this opportunity to gloat, Mayfield prod-
ded his vice president. "So, Ms. Carson, what do you
think of our new agreement?"

Hard nails clicked against smooth table top. She looked
up abruptly, straight into Mayfield's eyes. "I don't know."
Even now, though she was filled with doubts, she was
annoyingly certain of her uncertainty. "Normally, when
the Soviets sign a treaty, we already have indications of
their next plans. Of course, we always refuse to understand those indications, but they're there nonetheless."
She paused. "This time, I can't see any indications."

"I can see that you can't see." Mayfield's ironic tone
showed his enjoyment of this moment. "It couldn't be that
we've finally penetrated that impenetrable Soviet suspicion, could it? It couldn't be that they've learned that
treaties are better than wars, could it?"

Nell sat frozen, unable to accept this view, yet unable to
refute it. Finally, she confessed, "It's possible, Jim. I can't
prove you're wrong, though I can show that it's highly
unlikely. They may have learned that treaties are better
than wars, but that is not the lesson we've been teaching.
We've been teaching them that having treaties *and* having
wars, when convenient, is the best of both worlds." Her
head tilted, as if listening for a clue. "My best guess is that
they have some ulterior motive for withdrawing troops from
Eastern Europe, though I have no idea what it might be."

Mayfield glanced back at his watch again; it was almost time.

Earl swiveled out of his defensive posture to confront Nell for the first time. "Ulterior motive? I'll give you an ulterior motive. The Soviet economy is creaking like an old maid's vertebrae! They desperately need to put those men back to work in the factories and the fields. They have to become more productive—*that's* their motive! This arms race is hurting them even more than it's hurting us, and it's *killing* us! What more motive do you need?"

Nell looked ready to respond, but Mayfield interrupted hurriedly. "Let's see what the rest of the country has to say about my—our—new treaty." His finger stabbed the squishy plastic button on his remote. The dull glow of a television lit up amidst the bookshelves.

For a moment Mayfield thought he had turned on an old movie—one about the gods of ancient Greece. The man who smiled out at them from the TV screen could easily pass as Apollo.

Nell whistled. "Whew! Who is that guy?"

Mayfield shrugged. "He's a new reporter for ABN. Some of my constituents tell me he'll be the newscasting star of the decade. They asked me to watch his spots. They say he knows the nation's pulse better than anybody." Actually, Mayfield himself knew the nation's pulse best. That had been proven repeatedly. Jim had an uncanny knack for positioning himself within the public spotlight.

Nell asked, "What's this guy's name?"

"Uh, Bill Hardin, or something like that. He looks like Apollo, doesn't he?"

"I've never seen a more perfect Neanderthal animal in my life."

ZOOM. *The Neanderthal Apollo wears a suit and tie and speaks with the bland accent of the Midwest. "Tonight's top story, of course, is President Mayfield's latest treaty with the Soviet Union. The new treaty, a remarkable American coup at the negotiation table, is known as the Mutual Force Reduction Agreement. It leads immediately to the withdrawal of several divisions of troops, both American and Soviet, from the European theater. This*

*will mean an immediate relaxation of tensions, and may
lead to even more impressive long-term troop withdrawals."*

Nell commented drily, "At least no one can accuse him
of pessimism."

"Shush," Mayfield chided.

FOCUS. *"America may be witnessing the most significant transition in world history: the transition from a
world of tense, sometimes violent conflict, to a world of
peace. President Mayfield has single-handedly propelled
this transition with his clockwork-like invention of new
ways to lower tensions, while maintaining the security of
both the United States and the Soviet Union. Indeed,
rumors have started circulating that President Mayfield
could become the next Nobel Peace Prize winner."*

What an incredible idea! The Nobel Peace Prize! Again
he looked over at Nell, who stared fixedly at the screen.
He felt a certain compassion for her, thinking how difficult
it must be for her to acknowledge the rightness of his long,
determined drive to peace. He felt flush with warm belief
in himself.

CUT. *The scene shifts to a picture of angry civilians and
equally angry police, facing each other on a wide swath of
concrete. "What incredible methods of persuasion did the
president use to make the Soviets agree to the Mutual
Force Reduction Agreement? He was able to arrange this
withdrawal of troops* despite *the ongoing unrest in East
Germany."* Huddled groups of East Germans suddenly
break into motion. A few bricks fly, then the sound of
machine guns fills the air. The viewer can almost smell the
gunpowder. *"The only place in the world today where the
Soviets face worse trouble than here in East Germany is in
the city of Ashkhabad, near the Iranian border. Here
militant Muslim extremists press for religious and other
freedoms. The violence grows as Iranian smugglers continue supplying guns and training to militant protesters."*

CUT. *A diplomatic delegation comes into view. "Even
this conflict seems on the verge of resolution, however.
After years of reticence, the Iranian government has agreed
to work out a plan with the Soviet Union for controlling
these smugglers. We have reason to believe this negotiation may have been arranged by President Mayfield as*

well. We believe he used his influence with Saudi Arabia, which persuaded the King of Jordan to press the Ayatollah of Iran for resolution of the issue."

Mayfield started to shake his head in denial of this last twist in Hardie's analysis, then stopped. The rumor wasn't true, of course; he had had no involvement with the Soviet-Iran talks whatsoever. And though he would never suggest that he *had* had something to do with it, such rumors could thrust him even closer to the Peace Prize. For now, it seemed silly to deny them.

He saw Nell contemplating him with her too-wide, solemn blue eyes. Something about her demanded a reaction. He thrust his chin forward, proud of the events he had initiated. He wondered why she made him feel so uncomfortable, why she made his heart speed up like a rabbit's.

Nell rose to leave, having heard as much president-worship as she could stand. "Congratulations," she offered with apparent sincerity. She nodded at the news reporter on the screen, then at Mayfield. "I hope you're both right. I hope we don't regret this a month from now."

"Don't worry," Mayfield said as she left the White House library room. "Next month we'll do something even better."

July 29

significance.
These filters protect against advertising.
        —Zetetic Commentaries*

A long corridor connected the receptionist hub of the
Institute's main building to Leslie Evans's office. Nathan
walked that corridor often, but he never walked it without
a moment's pause near the beginning of the hall. Nathan
paused there now. He stood in the heart of the Sling
Project.

A tapestry of colorful lines and boxes filled the walls of
the corridor. For a child's eye the pattern would hold little
beauty, and less meaning. But to an engineer, this corridor-
filling PERT chart held as much truth as a man could bear
in a single encounter. And for an engineer, truth always
appeared intricately meshed with beauty. In some engineering sense, the chart was beautiful.

Every task in the Sling Project had a box on the wall.
Lines of interdependency jagged across the spaces between the boxes—from boxes that could be completed
early, to boxes that could not be started until those early
boxes yielded completed products. For example, they had
to design the prototype SkyHunter before they could build
it. They had to build it before they could test it.

No single human mind could understand all the com-
plexities of all the components of the Sling Project. But in
this hall a person could at least grasp the outline of the
system as he walked from the accomplished past into the
dreamed-of future. The colors of the chart which described
the relation between accomplishment and dream, rippled
in an elastic dance with the passage of time.

Green-marked tasks were already completed. Nathan
had entered the hall from the past, from the beginning of
the project. He walked through a forest of greens for a

long time, and his confidence grew. The Sling team had already accomplished so much. He reached out and touched a green box at random: SELECT BASE VEHICLE FOR THE HOPPERHUNTER. There had been three alternatives for the hopper—a commercial hovercraft and two experimental walking platforms. The hovercraft had won out in the selection because of its speed, despite its inferior stability.

Pink marked the tasks now falling behind schedule. A pink box was not necessarily a catastrophe. Pink tasks still had slack time before they were needed for the next step in the dance of interdependencies, but they were warnings of potential trouble.

Nathan proceeded down the hall. Soon a light scattering of pink mingled with the green. As Nathan walked closer to the present, the pinks clustered more thickly, but they did not yet dominate any part of the wall.

Simple black marked the tasks not yet started, not yet needed. These tasks were the future—challenging, but nevertheless achievable. Nathan stopped where the black boxes collided with the pinks and greens. He stood in the present. Reaching forward, he touched a tiny part of the near future, when they would complete the design for the Crowbar control surfaces. The Crowbar was the projectile dispensed from the HighHunter, a deceptively simple metal bar that would simply fall to Earth from orbit and hit the ground—or an enemy tank—with all the speed and energy it gained in its meteoric flight. Black boxes such as this one covered the rest of the corridor.

Red marked the results of a pink box that had festered too long. Red marked disaster: a task that should already have been completed—one that had to be completed *immediately*. Every day the red box remained red, every day its schedule slipped, the schedule for the whole wall of tasks slipped. A single red box would ultimately distort the whole wall—all the way out to the box for the completion date, itself so far down the hall it disappeared from Nathan's sight. Red boxes represented the blood and sweat of engineers who would work 24 hours a day to repair the damage. Red boxes marked open wounds on the body of the project.

A single red box glared under Nathan's appraising gaze. This box had triggered his meeting today with Leslie. He touched it. The words inside described his own personal failure. COMPLETE STAFFING OF THE SOFTWARE DEVELOPMENT TEAM, the box reminded him. With an abrupt turn, he hurried through the black future of the Sling to Leslie's office.

He found Leslie glaring at a paper on his desk, listening to his telephone in annoyed silence. When he spoke he sounded like a miserly grouch. "And I'm telling you that you've billed us twice and delivered the fracture analysis zero times. Send us a copy of the originals and we'll talk again." He listened a few more moments. "Right. Good-bye." He mashed the telephone into its receiver. With an abrupt change of tone to that of a comic straight man, he asked Nathan, "Okay, guru, where's our software development team?"

Nathan shook his head. "I'm sorry, Les. I hate giving excuses—and I'm not giving you one now. But I think you'll find the problem I've run into interesting, even though it sounds like I'm making excuses."

Leslie chuckled. "That's the best lead-in for an excuse I've ever heard. Did they teach you that here at the ZI?"

Nathan made a face. "I've found that the software engineers in the United States today fall into three broad categories." He started ticking them off on his fingers. "First, there are brilliant engineers who refuse to work on military projects. Second, there are brilliant engineers who can and will work on military projects. Unfortunately, as nearly as I can figure from the Jobnet data bases, all of them already *are* working on military projects. The country has sucked an awful lot of people into this kind of work." He waved his hand in a frustrated wipe at an imaginary slate.

"Third there are engineers who are not brilliant. I've got tabs on several solid pluggers who could do some of our work, but no one who can make the Sling fly on schedule."

Les brought his hand to his lips. Several years ago, the motion would have ended with a puff from a thin cigarillo. The cigarillo was gone—Jan had made him well—but his hand remembered. "I know the problem. I've fought it for years." He sighed. "Joel Barton, the first man I worked for after getting out of the Air Force, told me the real reason why the Soviet Union would beat us. 'Les,' he said, 'they have three times as many airplanes, four times as many tanks, and five times as many men. But that isn't the real problem. The real problem is that they have *eight* times as many *smart minds*—physicists and engineers and such—working on their military problems.' He clapped me on the shoulder. 'Les, for us to keep up with them, you and I and every other engineer in the United States who does defense work will have to be eight times as productive as one of theirs.'" He cleared his throat.

Nathan shook his head in mild disappointment. "For shame, Les, do you want me to get up on one of my soapboxes?" he asked. "There's another alternative. We don't have to work eight times as hard, if we can harness the strength of the commercial equipment that our non-military engineers build." He smiled. "That way, we'll only need to work twice as hard as their engineers." The smile dropped. "But even working only twice as hard, I fear we need star-quality people to complete the Sling."

"Unquestionably," Les agreed. "We'll need stars. The schedule is tight, and the software will be the most difficult part to develop and test—it's the only part that we need to develop from scratch. To make schedule we'll have to keep the software team small and fast. If the team's too big, we'll run out of fuel at test time, when we find out how many ways the team members misunderstood each other when they were building their individual pieces."

Nathan had arrived tense; now the tension subsided as he listened to Leslie's summation. Les understood the problem as well as he did. "We'll do it with no more than four people," Les continued. "We need one sensor expert—a person whose specialty is transforming raw signals into clean images. He shouldn't just know how to handle visual images, either. This person will need to know the whole electromagnetic spectrum. And he'll have some hellish signals to process—the Crowbars will need to identify and lock on targets within seconds of hitting terminal velocity, just after coming out from their own little clouds of superheated plasma."

Nathan plunked into the chair next to Leslie's desk. "Right. Next, we'll need an expert systems specialist—someone who can analyze those images to decide what the Hunter should do. For example, the SkyHunter needs to look at a random collection of radar sites, communication sites, and images of tents and vehicles. From that, it'll have to figure out where the headquarters is. That's where we need to make the machine think like a human military expert."

"Our military expert is Kurt, right?" Leslie asked. When Nathan nodded, Leslie continued with a frown. "Jan is still doing a better job of running this project than we are."

"Yes." The conversation paused. For the first time since Jan's death, Nathan took a close look around Leslie's office.

The little things had changed—the picture frames on his desk contained only images of Kira. The clutter had shifted, too. Antiquated microcomputers that Leslie had collected in the corners of the room had gone away, opening sections of wall that had not seen sunlight for years. Nathan's nose itched as he thought of the spumes of dust that must have risen from that machine graveyard.

Though the piles of computers had disappeared, the stacks of books had grown, filling a third large bookcase. The pictures on the walls remained the same—pictures of jet fighters, transports, and surveillance aircraft that Leslie had flown and developed before the Air Force had decided to make him a general. The promotion had taken him by surprise; he had not wanted it. He had rushed to get out before they made him a totally political beast, spending his life crafting ways to defeat the internal system rather than ways to meet the external threats.

Nathan continued the count of people they needed. "Third, we need a person who blends robotics and comm expertise—someone who can take the decisions made by the expert and put them into action, moving the vehicle, firing the gun, and so on."

"Sounds like a complete trio to me," Les replied. "Of course, it might be nice if they all had compatible personalities while we're hiring stars. It would certainly make life easier, anyway. But I still only count three. Who's the fourth person?"

Nathan laughed. "The fourth person is the vicious one, the one whose purpose is to ruin your group dynamics. He's the tester—by virtue of his creation of the simulations. We can't smash up 10,000 hovercraft and airplanes trying to test the software. Long before we ever put any of this stuff in a real Hunter, we'll have to work out the bugs by plugging into simulations. The sims will look, feel, and taste like real Hunters, as far as the software is concerned."

Leslie wrinkled his nose. "Of course." He looked Nathan in the eye. "So we need four people. How many of them do we have now? Besides Kurt, that is."

Nathan sighed. "None of them. Though I do have a couple of leads."

"So you found some candidates on the Jobnet after all."

"Not in the usual way." Nathan laughed. "I looked through listings of people who *used to* be looking for jobs. Out of those people, I looked for people who had found short-term jobs. Hence, instead of a list of available people, I have a list of people who will be available soon. I doubt that anyone else has searched Jobnet looking for people this way."

Les snorted. He looked stern, and Nathan knew the Air Force had taken a grievous loss when this man had refused his promotion to general. "No one searches Jobnet with the techniques you use, except the ones who take your own classes on data manipulation and information filtering. You, my friend, are creating a huge collection of competitors for yourself. The Zetetic Institute is bound and determined to destroy its own advantage."

Nathan chuckled. "I wish that were the biggest problem we faced."

"If you already have a list of prospects lined up, why'd you come here to bother me?" Leslie asked.

Nathan leaned across Leslie's desk. "I'm bothering you because one of my prospects is an old friend of yours. Currently, he has a job that's barely more than a hobby. He's networking the cash registers for a group of knitting and stitchery shops. He's our comm and robotics man, if you can win him over."

"If *I* can win him over, huh? Who is this guy?"

Nathan removed a microfloppy from his inner suit pocket and handed it to Leslie. "Amos Leung."

Leslie blinked. "Amos? Jesus, I haven't seen Amos in over a decade. How did you know he worked for me?"

Nathan clapped his hands. "I didn't, actually. But I suspected. He worked on the Version G modifications to the E-3 comm system while you were program manager. I just guessed you might know him."

"Hmph. Well, Nathan, if you wanted a star, you'll get one in Amos."

"If we can get him."

"Yeah." Leslie pursed his lips. "He's a great software developer. But Jesus, he'll be a hard sell."

Nathan patted him on the shoulder. "I have great faith in your powers of persuasion."

Leslie scowled.

"Is there anything else we should discuss before I go in search of my next crisis?" Nathan asked.

"No—though you should know about FIREFORS's latest attempt on our lives."

The grim humor of Leslie's voice told Nathan they'd had a close call. "What was it?"

Leslie told him about the backchannel message that General Curtis had intended to send to General Hicks. Fortunately, Curtis had mentioned the message to an old friend of Leslie's, who had tipped Leslie off. Leslie had discreetly arranged for other old friends to dissuade Curtis from sending the message.

"Was that really all that dangerous—just a message from one general to another?" Nathan asked in puzzlement.

"Well, it would have been a whole lot harder for us to stop if it had been sent, that's for sure. Nathan, we're gonna have to watch those guys like hawks. And we'd better keep our noses clean. If FIREFORS gets a whiff that something's going wrong, they'll be on us in a minute."

"Like a bad cost overrun or something?"

"Yeah. That, or a bad schedule delay." He pulled a miniature copy of the corridor PERT chart from deep inside the paper clutter of his desk, and stabbed the small dot of red amongst the greens and pinks. Nathan felt another shiver up his spine as he considered the possible consequences.

Ivan leaned forward in his seat—the unpadded wooden back hurt his spine—then realized how nervous he must look in that pose. He sank back in the chair, only to lean forward again.

As he fidgeted, he occasionally looked out the window to watch children playing in the warmth of the summer sun. Once in a while he yielded to the need to look back at his commander, who now had to double as his executioner.

He could no longer hope that Colonel Savchenko, the man who had given him the promotion and the project on the consequences of nuclear war, had come here for any other purpose.

He chided himself for ever hoping for anything else. He remembered the gunmetal gray of the weather the day this project had started, the unremitting clarity with which he had *known* that his plans would lead to disaster. Yet over the months, as the grays of Siberia yielded to white-specked blues, Ivan too had yielded to brighter visions. He had come to believe that his superiors would believe him; he had deceived himself with hope that they would be happy to have him disrupt their dangerous self-deceptions. His hope had peaked as he had framed the summation of the report.

It was the summation that Colonel Savchenko now re-read with weary gray eyes. Ivan could almost read it more easily in his own mind than the colonel could read it in wide bold type:

Thus we see that, despite the uncertainties, the best available analyses of the effects of nuclear war all drive to the same conclusion. Five gigatons of explosions would cause a global disaster that would challenge the lives of even the luckiest war survivors. Avoidance of such a nuclear exchange must be a primary goal of the Soviet Union, even if it means concessions to foreign powers. Only if our country faced certain extinction could we justify a strategic battle that pressed the limits of global catastrophe.

Ivan stared at the colonel. A sunbeam of light through the window threw his trenchantly wrinkled features into sharp relief. He gave Ivan a millimeter shake of his head. "The wording in this summation is too strong. Indeed, you overstep the bounds of analysis when you presume to discuss global politics. Neither you nor I is in a position to declare what the State must and must not do."

"Unfortunately, sir, the facts drive one to these conclusions. Only a madman could decide that it's in the State's best interest to destroy the entire human race. No matter where you were, a major nuclear assault would be a disaster of unprecedented proportions."

The colonel sighed. "This entire report is a disaster of unprecedented proportions."

Ivan's fidgeting stopped. He sat very straight, very still. "There is not a single false word in this report, sir. Every page, every sentence, every word, contains as much truth as science can currently produce."

"Yes, yes, I'm sure. It's a disaster nonetheless."

"I deeply regret that the truth contradicts the preconceived notions some people may have had."

Savchenko looked up swiftly from the paper, to puzzle over Ivan's expressionless face. "*Do* you regret it?" His voice acquired the hard evenness of glare ice. "It makes no difference. We have neither the time nor the money to redo this effort from scratch without explaining what happened. And I'm sure you're right about the rigor of the research. We would find it impossible to explain away this verification of the current forecasts.

"However, the summation is neither factual nor even logical. It must be rewritten. In fact, this whole document needs to be interpreted carefully, as regards its impact on global strategy. Your brief summation will be replaced by an entire additional chapter." Ivan opened his mouth to speak, but the colonel raised his hand for silence. "But you will not write this last chapter, major. The final chapter needs a more senior hand—someone with not only a keen eye for the facts of the physical world, but with a sensitivity for the intangibles of international relations as well."

Ivan's mouth drew in a thin line.

"You, major, have a new assignment. An assignment in Czechoslovakia." The colonel rolled his lips; his brow dark-

ened in a moment of melancholy. "We have a cell of
tactical nuclear weapons effects analysts in the city of
Plzen. You will take charge of them. Your first task is to
develop a plan for the nuclear decapitation of the American VII Corps in the event of a drive to Stuttgart from
Cheb."

"Yes, sir." What a delicately molded axe they used on
him! Many officers would have fought for the chance to
serve in a foreign country. But those officers fought for the
prestigious command of combat troops. For an officer whose
greatest contributions lay in research, reassignment to the
borderlands spelled intellectual death. Ivan faced the horror of his own mortality—he could not live long enough to
erase this blackness from his record. He was young, yet
his career was already quite doomed.

The last moments of the meeting blurred in irrele-
vance. He found himself outside, walking alone in the
sunny warmth. He walked slowly, keeping careful control
over the mix of emotions jangling in his mind.

The emotions separated out as he walked. Some floated
to the top; others sank away, perhaps to return later, but
gone for now. The emotion that rose to domination was a
feeling of deep happiness.

Happiness! His career had been destroyed. Still he felt
light—the lightness that comes with feeling your own power
when you know you are *right*. Had he protected his career
by producing something politically astute, but scientifi-
cally wrong, he would have regretted it forever. Instead,
he had done what was right. He had done his best. He
refused to apologize for it.

A second emotion floated there and increased the sensation of lightness. This was a feeling of relief—relief in
knowing he would not have to fight another political battle. They would never try to use him this way again. And
they would never again make him walk this treacherous
tightrope, trying to squeeze half-truths from the system.
He walked a broad avenue where honesty counted more.

As the last glimmers of horror dissolved in the warmth
of his happiness, Ivan realized how lucky he was. Most
men go through their whole lives uncertain of their own

strength, never knowing whether they are cowards or heroes. Ivan knew.

Two children sailed past on bright red bicycles, laughing into the wind. Ivan laughed too, a curiously mixed laughter, both triumphant and defiant. The triumph was internal—his personal victory in choosing to give his best. The defiance was external, directed at those who disdained his best, claiming it was not sufficient. His defiance was anchored firmly in his unfounded belief that, ultimately, the people who gave their best would prevail.

He suddenly saw how his superiors had made their mistake in choosing him. Bright, ambitious Ivan seemed like the perfect tool for twisting the truth. How could they have known that cool, aloof Ivan, the loner with no family and few friends, cared so much about children? In his mind, he watched Anna and her three girls running.

There was a great irony in the freedom he gained from his lack of family. Had he had children of his own, he would have had to worry about preserving his career so that he could give them a good home.

Instead, he had been the worst choice they could have made for their purposes. He laughed again, this time with pure defiance. The laughter, and the lightness of his own power, sustained him all the way home.

Kurt straightened from his console. This desk work challenged even *his* powers of discipline. He ran a hand through his thick blond hair and realized it needed cutting.

Meanwhile, outside the window of his office in the Institute, a gentle summer day confronted him. The bright, dry terrain reminded him that he should not be inside this building. He should be outside, fighting the enemy in the open. Dammit, this was no way to conduct a war.

He shook his head. No one else around here even conceded that it *was* a war. Jan had never acknowledged it, though she had come close; Leslie might think it now and again, but never out loud; and Nathan . . . Kurt shook his head thinking about Nathan. He was so philosophical, how could he ever get anything done?

So far, Nathan's help had been zip. Kurt worked in isolation from the world, almost isolated from the problem

Jan had given him to solve—the problem of building expert software to make decisions for the Hunters. The necessary decisions covered a wide range of difficulties from decisions as basic as, *Where do I go?*, to decisions as complex as, *How do I kill them before they kill me?*

Kurt knew a great deal about how to kill them before they killed him. The survival instincts needed by the Hunters bore a striking resemblance to the survival skills needed by a lone Ranger behind enemy lines.

But the details differed in important ways. Kurt needed more information to complete his mission. He, like the combat expert system he was supposed to build, needed to know what kinds of data he would get from the sensors to make decisions. He also needed to know what kinds of orders he could give to the Hunter's controls to carry them out. At the moment, Kurt and his software were commanders without either recon patrols or assault teams.

Nathan had agreed that Kurt had problems he couldn't solve alone. Nathan was running as fast as he could, so he said, to gather the rest of the men for the development team. In the meantime, Nathan suggested that Kurt start with the simplest of the three combat expert systems.

Of the HopperHunter, the SkyHunter, and the High-Hunter, by far the simplest decision-making problem rested with the HighHunter. The HighHunter consisted of two parts—the container and the Crowbar. The container was a tin can mounted on rockets, which carried the Hunter into space, where it orbited until someone on the ground needed close fire support. Then the tin can popped open.

Within the tin can, dozens of Crowbars lay packed together. The Crowbars were the weapons of the High-Hunter. Each Crowbar had a sensor tab near the tip, four stubbed fins at the tail, and a tiny computer in the middle, all built into a long shaft of solid steel. When the Hunter canister popped open, the Crowbars fell. They fell twenty miles, with violent velocity, torturing the air as they screamed by.

As they fell, the sensor tab watched for targets—typically, enemy tanks. The computer selected one. The fins touched the air, twisting the Crowbar, guiding it to a final contact with the target.

The Crowbar contained no explosives—it didn't need them. After falling twenty miles, the steel shaft could crush any tank armor ever devised.

Kurt loved the concept of the Crowbar. It was simple— simple enough to be brutally rugged—yet it was effective.

So Kurt had started with the Crowbar's decision-making problem. At first it seemed so simple as to be unworthy of solving: pick a tank at random and head for it. But that was not quite so straightforward. It would be better to pick the lead tank, to block the passage of the others. What if he saw both tanks and personnel carriers—which should he select? Should he just take one at random? Random selection had several advantages besides simplicity. And Lordy, it was tricky figuring out how to fall at terminal velocity to assure the Crowbar would slam into the vehicle you had picked out.

Kurt understood why they needed him to carry out this mission. They needed someone who could identify and prioritize high-value targets. They also needed someone who could identify and translate high-speed images.

They needed someone with a background like his, with four years in Army Special Forces. And they needed someone with a background like his, with degrees in software engineering and artificial intelligence.

He also understood why it might be difficult to enlist the other people needed for the Sling Project. The Sling required unusual combinations of talents.

A polite knock on his open door made Kurt whirl to his feet. "Yes, sir, what can I do for you, sir?" he asked of Nathan.

Nathan moved from the back-lighting of the corridor to the front-lighting of the window. He looked uncomfortable. Kurt suspected he didn't like being called "sir," though Kurt didn't understand why. It was just a form of respect.

Nathan asked, "How would you like to join a discussion about sensors? I have a sales team down the hall trying to convince me that *their* near-infrared sensing fibers are the best invention since the eyeball."

"I'd be happy to join your meeting if you think I'd be useful."

Nathan shrugged. "It'll impact your life more directly than it'll impact mine," he said. "I can't help thinking you'd have an interest in the outcome."

Kurt followed him down the corridor, keeping his eyes straight ahead. The ceiling in this place still made him uncomfortable: it curved smoothly, seamlessly, to become the corridor walls—an absence of sharp edges that disturbed him. He'd never worked in a building that seemed so soft.

As they entered the room, three men rose to greet them. Two of them could have been twins, in their crisp white shirts and maroon ties; the third wore a powder-blue shirt and sat away from the others. "Jack Arbor," "Gary Celenza," the twins offered. "Howdy, I'm Gene Pickford, and I'm glad you gave us this opportunity to talk with you," the third burst out.

A shiver rippled down Kurt's spine as he formally introduced himself. He could almost smell them, they were so clearly marked as contractor marketeers. The marketeers from federal contractors represented one of the lowest forms of life he had met while in the Army. The contractors with their magic potions, and the officers who *believed* in the potions—these people endangered the field soldier as much as any enemy.

Only one kind of man endangered the field soldier more: the officer who demanded magic potions from the contractors. Such officers rejected ideas based on what was possible. They showed interest only in ideas based on what was improbable. In their blind desire for something better, they twisted the occasional honest contractor into a marketeer. Anyone foolish enough to offer simple facts found himself cast aside. And though those officers were a minority, somehow they dominated the others: their tales of hoped-for magic enthralled otherwise level-headed men.

Yet none of these kinds of men had first inspired Kurt to start thinking about leaving the Army. Another group— another derivative of this self-destroying game—made life so unbearable that the insane battle by Yuscaran could break him.

This group that had most upset him contained the men who had seen too many magic potions evaporate. They were the jaded cynics who no longer believed in any magic. The cynics stolidly performed their jobs today the way they had performed them yesterday; they could not be turned from their dead-end path by any force smaller than a kilo of detonating cyclonite. Kurt had finally left the Army to find a place where men judged new ideas on the merits of the ideas themselves—a place where men could be skeptical without being cynical.

After a lot of talk with no purpose, the loud man in powder blue shoved his hand deep in his pocket and tossed a shiny button on the table, where it skipped across the surface like a flat stone on a still pool of water. As it skittered toward the edge, Kurt clamped it to the table top.

A thread trailed from the button. Kurt recognized the connector through which the sensor transmitted its raw readings. On close examination, the head of the button resolved into thousands of circles, the tips of optical fibers. The loud man spoke. "That's it. A whole infrared sensor the size of a postage stamp."

Kurt saw Nathan raise an eyebrow. "Is the image processing done right there in the sensor bundle?"

"A significant amount of the processing is done right there."

Nathan's eyes moved from one marketeer to the next. "What about the rest of the processing?"

One of the twins placed a gray box the size of a cigarette pack on the table. "The rest is done here."

"Ah, that's more like it," Nathan said in soothing tones.

With adroit conversational fencing, Nathan coaxed from them the sensor's specification. Kurt admired Nathan's skill with the detached disinterest that an aerospace engineer might have for the improvisations of a jazz musician. These verbal fencing games were another part of the contracting world Kurt didn't like and didn't understand. He had always given other people straight answers; he expected them to reciprocate.

Nathan asked in the smooth tones of a potion seller, "What kinds of enhancements are you planning in the future?"

The powder blue shirt answered, "We're looking into

adding some extra synch bits on the transmitter to increase reliability. So far, that's the only enhancement we've heard more than one of our customers ask for. Of course, we do custom work, too. Frankly, we make almost nothing on the basic sensor; most of our profits come from the customizations that our customers need. For a project like yours, where you're planning to buy lots of basic units off the shelf, that would work to your advantage." He tapped the table next to the button. "And for the new Version D, we have a special introductory price that undercuts even our normal prices." For the first time in the conversation, he turned from Nathan to look at Kurt. "What do you think of our package here, Kurt?"

Kurt looked him in the eye. "If it meets its own spec, it sounds like it might be a good choice for the SkyHunter. Could we borrow one for testing?"

The man's smile turned to sorrow. "I'm afraid we're having awful trouble just keeping that one to show around. We're shipping as fast as they come off the line. But I'll see what I can do."

Nathan thanked them, rising to show them to the door. The marketeers took the hint, scooping up their samples and departing with much fanfare. Nathan turned back to Kurt. "So what did you think of their psychology?" he asked.

Walking back to his chair, Kurt looked at Nathan with puzzlement. He almost stumbled as he realized that he had just seen, in real life, one of the maneuvers he had just learned about here at the Institute. The man in powder blue had intentionally set up psychological distance between himself and the others. His job was to create ideas and alternatives for customers such as Nathan and Kurt to consider. If the customers rejected an idea out of hand, the other two marketeers would also reject it. If Nathan or Kurt seemed interested, however, the twins in crisp white would take it over as their own, adding their weight of authority and numbers.

Kurt cradled his arm as if to protect it from another bullet. "That psychological maneuvering is silly," he snorted in disgust. "That kind of stuff never persuades people to buy things."

Nathan looked at him with pleasure. "It certainly never makes *you* buy things. But the technique does help them push other people over the threshold."

Kurt made a faint motion of acceptance of his boss's words, though he didn't believe it for a moment. "Yes, sir."

"I understand why you're skeptical, but I think I can prove it to you. And you know what I like about that? Kurt, if I prove it to you, you'll believe me."

"Of course."

"Have you ever noticed how many people *aren't* convinced by proof?" Nathan switched back to talking about the meeting. "Did anything else about those guys and their sensor strike you?"

Kurt shrugged. "It seemed like a reasonable box to me."

"Yes, especially if they fix the comm problem."

"The comm problem?" Kurt shook his head. Had he fallen asleep in the meeting?

"Yes, the comm problem that they're planning to fix with their enhancement to the synch bits." His voice fell off, as if talking to himself. "And we'll wait a bit for the price to fall."

"What about the introductory offer?"

"Oh," Nathan waved his hand as if warding off a mosquito. "They always have introductory offers when they're afraid the first production run won't sell out at the initial high price." He laughed. "Of course, we'll have to figure out what options we need to build in. I'm sure that, if they make their money on the customizations, there's something fundamental missing from the basic box that needs to be added. But we'll see."

Kurt shook his head again. "I didn't sleep through that meeting, but I get the feeling I didn't hear the same words you did."

Nathan nodded. "Though the guys with the suits didn't fool you, Kurt, you are not immune to all forms of marketing."

Kurt pulled away in disbelief. Nathan chuckled. "You don't believe me. I'm not sure I want you to believe me, actually. But ask yourself the following question, sometime when you have an idle hour or two. Kurt, how did

Jan persuade you to come to work on the Sling Project?
What compelling reason did she give to make you accept a
position where you'd once again have to deal with all the
things in the Army that you quit to escape from? How'd
she do it?"

Kurt left, but Nathan's questions went with him. Like
droplets leaking from a pipe that no one can fix, the
questions struck him gently, again and again, all afternoon.

Again the blue haze swirled about Daniel, clinging to
him in short strands before it disappeared. Physicists often
visualized the electron as an incompressible point, surrounded by a cloud of probabilities. At moments like this,
Daniel thought of himself as the incarnation of that vision.
His cloud of probabilities was the set of paths to success,
combined with the set of paths to failure. His incompressible point was his purpose. His purpose at the moment
was to destroy the Zetetic Institute.

He spoke to Kira, setting the contrails of smoke to
spinning. "Hey, you've done a great job. I appreciate your
efforts. But it's clear that we missed a key point somewhere. Despite all your great efforts, the bottom line on
our campaign is a big null. It just isn't working."

Daniel watched Kira with admiration. She had not taken
the failure too personally. Her expression suggested a
more scientific astonishment—the puzzlement that comes
when an experiment invalidates previous research.

The failure had not been her fault. She had collected an
outstanding stable of usable newsmen. One had already
been lifted to national prominence in his crusade against
Zetetic quackery robbing people who want to give up
smoking, who are instead sold a barrel of worn and petty
philosophy. It was particularly nice since that reporter had
earlier spent his days defiling the tobacco industry. Sweet.

But all the work had been in vain. Despite Kira's best
efforts, despite his own best efforts, the Zetetic Institute
continued growing unreasonably. "We need a new approach. Or at least we need to figure out why our standard
approach isn't working. Frankly, I can't understand it."

Kira smiled in consolation, though she was as baffled as

he was. "I don't understand it either. You can't pick up a paper without seeing an article about some bizarre Zetetic ritual. Market research shows that half the people who have heard of them think they're born-again witches; the other half think they're meditating pacifists." She shook her head. When she spoke again, the lines of surprise around her mouth had softened to a look of awe. "How can the Institute get so much bad press and still thrive?"

Daniel inhaled through his mouth, tasting the hot cigarette smoke as it rushed into his lungs. He offered his most recent thoughts. "Could our attack have enhanced their fame? Could such fame have counterbalanced the success of our attack?"

Daniel watched her for a reaction of guilt. But she was all business, from the concentration of her eyes to the glowing tip of her cigarette. With some amusement, Daniel noted that she had developed some skill in holding her cigarette, though she had not yet developed grace. She nodded. "I thought about the dangers of making them famous, of course. We tried to place our attacks in strategic media centers. Our criticism appeared in places where favorable things were already being said, so we could cut off positive impressions near the root. So our campaign shouldn't have increased the Institute's visibility much at all." Kira looked out the window, across the landscape, where thick green leaves shrouded the trees hugging the Potomac. "Of course, we made the ZIs a *little* more famous. We can only point the journalists in a direction; we can't quite control them, so they always try to get wider coverage for their stories than we need." She nodded to the terminal on his desk. "If you're interested, we can download a complete description of our actions and results."

Daniel retrieved a cordless terminal from his desk and placed it on the conference table. "By all means, show me the facts. Though maybe we should concentrate on the background material, if you've got that: somewhere, there *must* be a clue to what has gone wrong."

"Easier done than said."

Together, they studied the fact bases on the Zetetic Institute. There were about 2,000 core Zetetics scattered across the globe, and another 15,000 who were frequently

connected with Zetetic projects. About 200,000 people had
had some significant contact with them, through educational seminars or therapy sessions such as the anti-smoking
clinics. "They're really a tiny organization," Kira commented.

"True," Daniel replied, "but look at all the things they
do." The Zetetic projects showed incomprehensible diversity of purpose. They had commercial software programs,
educational seminars, consulting, and engineering and government contracting. The one thing all the projects had in
common was a kind of information-intensiveness—projects
for which the most important commodity was *expertise*.

Daniel shook his head. "I must confess that I can't see
anything about their diversity that could protect them
from a media attack. One of the few things they *don't* get
into is the media business."

"That's right," Kira said, almost with pride. "Even though
they're hip-deep in communication, they don't operate
any of the classical commercial broadcasting systems." She
paused. "My research suggests that they reject the philosophy behind *broadcast* systems. Broadcasting treats its
viewers like empty cups; the broadcast sets out to fill the
empty cup. There's no give and take, no way of involving
the intellect, or the rationality, of the watcher." She chuckled. "From what I know of the Institute, that would never
do. The Institute's whole view of life is dynamic; they're as
interactively energetic as the conferencing networks they
operate."

Daniel stared at her with wide, delighted eyes. "I think
you've hit it!" He exhaled a puff of smoke, savoring the
tobacco aroma. "Their *conferencing networks* are the problem!" With the satisfaction of a physicist who has just
solved a particularly difficult equation, he brought up statistics on the Institute's communication networks. The
number of people who used these products far exceeded
the number who had had face-to-face contact with the
Institute and its philosophies. "Don't you see? The Zetetics
operate some of the largest commnets in the world—Jobnet,
among others." Jobnet was universally used for finding
people who could quickly plug into difficult or unusual
jobs. "Anybody who contacted the Institute through something as practical and mundane as Jobnet would surely

discount media blasts as sensationalism. In a sense, the Zetetic Institute uses word of mouth for all its important contacts—but the word of mouth is multiplied a thousand-fold by automation. Jesus!"

Kira's bright eyes acknowledged the accuracy of this analysis. "I'm sure you're right." Again she disturbed him; she didn't seem quite as pleased as she should have been. "Though I'm not entirely sure what to do with the idea."

Daniel paused for a moment, to give Kira's creativity a chance to flourish.

She sighed. "I suppose we could flood the networks with the same kind of criticisms that we're flooding the broadcasts with."

"Excellent."

Kira shrugged. "I'm not sure that it's excellent. We could have a lot of trouble keeping an effective level of pressure in the system, particularly if they find out that there *is* pressure. Are you familiar with the Zetetic specialty known as conference pruning?"

"No." Daniel sidled closer to Kira; she shifted her chair slightly away. "Tell me about it."

"A conference pruner is a professional editor of network bulletin boards and conferences. The Institute runs a certification system for pruners. A certified pruner sweeps the texts on the net and categorizes all the statements into three categories: opinion, fact, and falsehood. They label the opinions with their implicit assumptions, circumscribe the globality of the facts, and purge the falsehoods."

"Sounds like the kind of subjective decision-making that we should be able to manipulate."

Kira sighed again. "I don't know. They take their certification pretty seriously."

"I see. Perhaps a bit of outright bribery will do the trick."

The idea of bribery shocked her, but only for a moment. The shock faded into a look similar to the look of awe she had had earlier, pondering the Institute's immunity to media attack. "Of course. Surely some of them can be bought." She looked at Daniel with bemusement. "I have trouble remembering the sizes and kinds of resources available to the Wilcox-Morris Corporation."

Kira's attitude toward unethical maneuvers matched his own quite nicely. Interesting. "I understand your problem. Wilcox-Morris has so many resources that even I lose track at times. But you'd better get comfortable with all of them, Kira. We're in a fight for our lives with the people who hate us, and we need to fight with every resource available."

He started to rise, to terminate the meeting, but Kira held up her hand. "What should we do with the media blitz? Cancel it?"

"Not at all. It can't hurt, after all, as long as we're discreet." He rubbed his hands together. "I almost wish I could face off against Nathan Pilstrom myself, in public. It would be great to pit my world view against his in a showdown. I've read some of his writings; there are a lot of inconsistencies in his philosophy. I just know I could take him apart if I had the chance."

"Really?" Kira studied his face cautiously. "Are you sure?"

His heart leaped into his throat for just a moment before answering, "Quite sure."

"I might be able to arrange it."

"Excellent!" he cried. "We wouldn't want to try this undertaking just yet, of course; that would *certainly* increase his national visibility, as well as mine, and that's dangerous to us from both directions." A good tobacco baron needed to keep himself invisible if at all possible; he wanted his opposition to stay the same way. "But if the Institute keeps on growing, despite our sabotaging the net, it may be an appropriate risk."

"I'll start laying the groundwork," Kira promised. With that she left.

Daniel crushed out his cigarette as he looked across the landscape. A jet wobbled down its landing path toward National Airport. This airplane, like so many others that had traveled the same path, seemed to scrape its belly against the pointed tip of the Washington Monument. Of course, this was just an illusion of the angle and the distance; in reality, the plane never came near the monument.

The Institute's dependency on networking raised several inspirational opportunities. Jobnet was the lynchpin. As the controller of Jobnet, the Institute was eminently qualified for quickly assembling teams of people with diverse specialties. Those specialists could be scattered all over the country, or they could all live in the same condo complex. It didn't make any difference; they could *telecommute*, in any case.

With succulent joy, Daniel realized that the entire Zetetic organization was built around telecommuting. This information gave him the power to totally destroy the Institute.

The unions had been lobbying for years to ban telecommuting; it made it damn difficult to unionize workers. Until now, the tobacco companies had fought in favor of telecommuting, more because the unions opposed it than for any other reason. If it weakened the unions, it was fine with Wilcox-Morris.

Daniel returned to his desk and ran his hand across the smooth teak finish of the plaque hanging there. "I came, I saw, I conquered," the plaque played back his motto. Daniel had swallowed whole corporations that held to this same belief. Could the Zetetic philosophy stop him?

Ah, how surprised the unions would be when the entire tobacco industry tossed its support behind the ban on telecommuting. Many organizations would fight them, of course, not just the Institute. Other people telecommuted as well. But the telecommuters had not formed the kind of potent power blocks that the unions and tobacco industry had. History would repeat. The unions had succeeded in outlawing the sale of homemade clothing decades earlier, when the invention of the personal sewing machine threatened the textile factories. Now, with Daniel's help, the unions should be able to crush personal computer owners the way they had crushed personal sewing machine owners in that earlier era. Daniel could not imagine the unions and the tobacco corporations failing in a joint political enterprise.

How stunned the Institute would be when drawn and quartered by the collaboration! How sweet.

President Mayfield could not focus his attention on any one part of the nightmare. He winced every time his heart started racing too hard. Sometimes the thumping ended in a twisting spasm that made him want to clutch his chest. He looked down at the Presidential Seal woven into the carpet, but even that inspirational sight did not help calm him. They faced the greatest crisis of public confidence in his career.

His eyes shifted to Nell Carson, sitting in her usual position in the far corner, wearing her usual look of distant concern. She seemed relieved, almost happy, now that she knew what form the Soviet deception would take. He'd desperately wanted to exclude her from this meeting, this moment of terrible embarrassment, but he couldn't. Not only would she not let herself be excluded, but in some sense, her rigid strength of character gave him a secure feeling. She always disagreed with him, but she never stabbed him in the back.

His eyes flickered to the television. He'd never before let televisions into the Oval Office, but now he couldn't bear to see the news without the reassurance this room gave him. On the television his nightmare became vividly real, yet manageable and bearable, because the terror remained confined to the tiny screen. He thought about the millions of other viewers watching this broadcast and shuddered at the opinions they were certainly forming.

CUT. The scene shifts to a lone town on a wide, rolling plain. Wheat grows in fields tended by men and women wearing oddly assorted garments. The clothing is typical of the styles of Iranian farmers.

Mayfield looked back at Nell, who continued to watch the screen impassively. Desperate to see an expression he understood, he turned next to Earl Semmens, seated near the window with the pinched look of a poker player whose bluff has been called. At least Earl showed the proper level of shock and dismay. At least Earl shared the president's outrage and indignation.

ZOOM. The camera soars over the fields to view gray metal boxes against the horizon. Zooming still closer, the gray boxes resolve into battle tanks: Russian T-70s. In their wake, mashed pulp that was once wheat twists through the tortured soil. Bill Hardie's voice speaks with studied anger. "This is the most blatant use of brute force ever made in our time. Despite all his long speeches about peace, Soviet leader Sipyagin has once again shown us his lust for war.

Nell looked over at Mayfield for the first time. The corners of her mouth curled in a sad smile. "Now we know what they planned to gain from mutual force reduction."

CUT. FOCUS. Hardie's eyes seem to leap from the camera, to look directly at Mayfield. "But not all the fault for this new aggression should be placed at the doorstep of Sipyagin. It was *our* leadership that made it easy for the Soviet army to amass sufficient forces for this attack." *He paused for effect, and his anger grew more apparent.* "Our sources tell us that this invasion is being carried out with the divisions released from Europe by the recent Mutual Force Reduction Agreement. If we had not rushed so foolishly into that agreement, this invasion could never have taken place."

Mayfield clenched his teeth to keep from crying out at the distant announcer. Still, he could not help trying to defend himself. "Liar," he growled, "it's not true. I am *not* responsible for that invasion." He turned to look at the other people in the room. "How can he say that? A month ago he thought the agreement was the best treaty we'd ever made." Another image came to Mayfield: the image of the Nobel Peace Prize that should have been his. The image evaporated as he clung to it wistfully.

SOFTEN. The camera remains in the news room, fixed on Bill Hardie's sober expression. "The Russian justification for the attack is Iran's support for terrorists and rebels in the southwestern provinces of the Soviet Union. The Soviet invasion at dawn today started with the destruction of rebel bases within Iran. A Soviet spokesman has assured the president officially that this is just a minor police action, and the advance will terminate as soon as Iran has been purged of militant anti-Soviet groups. Since making the announcement, the fighting has spread rapidly." *Hardie purses his lips.* "It would seem that the longer the Soviets fight, the more anti-Soviet groups they encounter."

Nell spoke softly, almost gently, as if she were on Mayfield's side. He looked at her with startled eyes. "I'm sorry I didn't see it coming. I should have. You know, we could have learned this from history. This is exactly how they prepared for their Afghanistan invasion decades ago. They made a big fanfare about pulling their troops out of Europe—just to move them into position for an invasion."

The president shook his head helplessly. "What can we say to the people?"

Nell sat very still for a moment, then nodded her head as she said, "I don't know what to say, but I know what to do. We should stop."

"Stop what?"

"Stop making dangerous treaties."

Mayfield's voice rose defensively. "That wasn't a dangerous treaty. We needed to reduce the number of soldiers pointing guns at each other in Europe. It was a good idea. It still is!" He leaned forward with a shrewd look. "And besides, they didn't violate the treaty, did they? The treaty worked. People should keep that in mind."

With an exhausted sigh, Nell agreed. "Yes, your treaty worked. Frankly, I imagine they would have invaded Iran even without the treaty. But, Jim, even though your treaty worked, *it didn't work the way you wanted it to*. It didn't make the world any safer. Did it?" Her mouth twisted in distaste. "More to the point, it didn't make us any more popular, either."

Mayfield shook his head. "I don't get it. I know you don't care about the next election. I don't understand that, but I know it's true. All you care about is whether we set them up to attack Iran. Yet, if you think they would have attacked Iran anyway, why complain about our treaty?"

Nell blinked. "I'm not complaining about *that* treaty, Jim. I'm worried about the next one."

The president's heart skipped again. He saw Earl looking at Nell with the same shock he felt. "What do you know about the next treaty?"

Nell laughed. "Only that you're working on one, Jim. You're an addict." Her frustration came to the fore, spotlighted. "But don't you see that we have to be careful about what we sign?"

"Of course we have to be careful. But we don't have to be paranoid!"

Nell slumped back in her chair. Only the motion of her foot swaying rhythmically suggested the energy still waiting inside for a chance to act. "No, Jim, we don't dare be paranoid either. That would be as bad as being naive."

"What do you want me to do?" Mayfield almost screamed.

Her foot stopped moving. "I'd like you to let Senator Hilan Forstil review your next treaty before you sign it."

"What? That man's a warmonger!"

Nell leaned forward, speaking with carefully controlled anger. "No, Jim. Hilan is not a warmonger. He's a hawk."

"What's the difference?"

"A warmonger is someone who wants to start wars. A hawk is someone who hates war, who will avoid war with fierce energy—but if forced into a war despite his best efforts, knows that he has to win."

Mayfield felt his stomach tighten with revulsion. "That's just what we don't need working our negotiations—someone who has a vested interest in wrecking the treaty process. Forstil would give the media the biggest leaks since Arken published the radar signatures for Stealth bombers." He rolled his eyes. "One little leak, and he turned billions of dollars of airplanes into museum pieces. That was an important factor in our getting into office in the first place. We can't let our treaty process be handled that way."

Nell stared at him in disbelief. "Jim, Hilan is on your side. Believe me."

He couldn't believe her. Forstil made him feel as uncomfortable as Nell Carson did. He had no intention of letting them gang up on him. "Let me think about it," he said to put her off. He shifted in his leather chair, unsticking himself. He'd been sweating, despite the cool air that bathed him from the air ducts behind his desk.

"I thought you might say that." Nell rose from her chair. For a moment her shoulders drooped, but with another effort, she stood straight, a radiant vice president. "Think about Hilan, Jim. He can help you." She departed.

Mayfield buried his face in his hands. Why couldn't he have been president during a simpler time? He had completed a longstanding presidential task during his second year of office, yet no one had noticed: he had the collection of portraits of president's wives. This task had been underway since the days of Kennedy. That could have been his crowning achievement, if he'd lived in a reasonable world.

Well, just as he'd gotten the news media to love him yesterday, he'd get them to love him again tomorrow. A few more treaties, and he'd see that Peace Prize once more on the horizon.

A sonic boom and a crashing explosion made him open his eyes; it was just the sound from the television.

The muggy July heat faded slowly in the twilight as Kira bicycled down South Lakes Drive toward home. Only the heat faded, however; the muggy humidity remained. It did not help her think, and she had some thinking to do. Uncle Nathan was coming to dinner. They would surely play the game of wonders, and *this* time Kira intended to win. It was about time she won: today was her twenty-second birthday.

She shook her head to throw the stinging perspiration away from her eyes, regretting her choice of the bicycle for the day's commute to the Institute. At last she turned left on Cabot and plunged downhill.

This section of the ride did not last long, but it was the exhilarating part. Kira dropped low in the saddle, building up speed. The cool wind whipped across her face.

She veered right onto the uphill road spur that led to her townhouse. She continued to coast, though her speed dropped alarmingly. It was a matter of honor, to get all the way home from here without any more pedaling.

The bicycle bumped into the driveway, and Kira dismounted just before it started to wobble. The humidity closed in around her, displacing the cool wind. In that moment, as the tropical heat returned, Kira had a small revelation—she knew a winning strategy for Uncle Nathan's game.

She hurried to the bathroom and took a quick, cool shower, humming all the while at the thought of her upcoming victory. As she returned to the living room, however, her father interrupted her thoughts by thrusting a shiny, gift-wrapped package in her arms. "Happy birthday," he bellowed, hugging her.

Another package plopped on top of the first one. "Happy birthday," Uncle Nathan echoed with a softer smile.

Wonderful aromas circulated from the kitchen. Even as her nostrils flared, however, a pot lid clattered against a muffled explosion of air. Her father's face took on the expression of a chemist who has just heard his carefully prepared solution pop from its test tube and spatter against the ceiling. He ran for the kitchen. "Hurry!" her uncle called to him. Then, with a wink at Kira, he walked in the same direction.

Putting her presents down, Kira went to watch the hysteria. The kitchen looked like a child's playroom. Pots and pans teetered precariously on every inch of table space, and a fine film of flour coated the vertical surfaces. Her father muttered curses as he twisted dials and punched buttons. Uncle Nathan offered soothing sounds and gently stirred the biggest pot—the one full of chili. Kira could see, amidst the carnage, the makings of a gigantic chili-cheese pizza, a beautiful work of careful engineering.

Her father and uncle always cooked together for special occasions, and they always left a mess best cleaned up with a fire hose. Kira could remember her mother leaning against the door at the edge of the inferno, shaking her head, just as Kira leaned against the door now. At the memory, Kira jerked away from the kitchen and went to set the table. That, too, her mother had always done.

The game of wonders started without warning, as usual. While her father sliced the pizza, her uncle held up his fork for examination. Too casually, he turned it in the air and said, "You know, this fork is made of stainless steel. Do you realize how amazing it is for us to use stainless steel for dinner this evening?"

Kira smiled as her father asked, "Why is it amazing?"

"You need chromium to make stainless steel. But chromium is a rare metal. One of the few places left on Earth where there's an abundance of chromium is on the ocean floor, locked inside metallic nodules coughed up from cracks deep inside the earth. So we send down special robot submarines to scoop up the nodules, to extract the chromium, to make the stainless steel, so that we can use these forks to eat tonight."

Her father had finished serving; he held his pizza in the air and tapped the crust. "That's pretty amazing all right. There's another amazing thing here, too. Did you know that there was almost a terrible blight on the wheat fields this year? If the blight had taken hold, we might not have had the flour to make this pizza." He pointed at his glass of water. "And we needed water to solve the problem."

Kira frowned. Her father had never really liked the game, it seemed to her; his efforts always seemed half-hearted. But this wonder seemed unusually weak, even for him. "So by watering the fields, the plants stayed healthy enough to fight the disease, right?" she asked.

Her father reluctantly nodded. "That, too, but that wasn't what I had in mind." He smiled. "We first spotted the blight through satellite photos. Because the photos showed the problem before it spread, we were able to protect most of the fields. Well, the satellite got into position to take those pictures by firing its rockets. And the rockets used hydrogen for fuel. And of course we got the hydrogen for the fuel from water. And *that's* how we needed the water to make it possible to have pizza tonight."

Kira laughed. "That's pretty amazing," she conceded. "But there's another wonder here tonight as well. It's amazing that we're living here at all. You know, Washington D.C. was built on a swamp. They had terrible trouble with mosquitoes and yellow fever when they first put the Capitol here. It's unfit for human habitation."

Uncle Nathan wet his finger and held it in the air. "Doesn't feel too uncomfortable to me."

Kira smirked. "Of course not, silly. Our house is air conditioned. If air conditioning hadn't been invented, we wouldn't be here."

Nathan raised an eyebrow. "We'd certainly be less comfy, anyway."

"No, we wouldn't be here by D.C. at all. Do you think you could get so many bureaucrats to live in a swamp without air conditioning? Certainly not. And if you couldn't get that many bureaucrats together, the government couldn't have grown into the big, powerful monstrosity it now is. And if the government hadn't become an oversized dino-saur, we wouldn't have had to move the Institute's headquarters here. We'd live close to a center of business, like Los Angeles or Houston, instead of living close to the center of politics. Right?"

Her father whooped with laughter. Uncle Nathan shook his head. "I think you've hit on the answer to the nation's problems, Kira. If we ban the use of air conditioning in America's capital, we can substantially reduce the burden of government. I like it. And you're right: that's truly amazing. Without air conditioning, we wouldn't be here."

Kira flushed with the glow of victory. For as long as she could remember, she had been trying to come up with a more amazing wonder than her uncle. Yet the glow faded, and Kira felt oddly disappointed. It took her a minute's introspection to realize what was missing. Uncle Nathan hadn't acknowledged that she had beaten him.

The glow returned as her understanding reached an even deeper level. She hadn't really beaten her uncle. He had never really beaten her.

The game of wonders was a cooperative one. It wasn't a zero-sum game like baseball or football, wherein for every winner there had to be a loser. Nobody had to lose in the game of wonders. Everybody who felt the amazement, who ceased to take the little things for granted, was a winner. As Nathan had said before, *"It's not how you play the game, but whether everybody wins or everybody loses."* Cooperative games made human beings more human; often, zero-sum games made them brutes.

The spicy flavor of the chili pizza filled her mouth; she started listening to the ongoing conversation.

Nathan was speaking. "So our reputation seems to be growing even faster than our seminars."

"What happened?" Kira asked.

Nathan turned to her. "I've been invited to the reception announcing a new book, *Statesmanship and Politics.* It was written by Senator Larry Obata, a friend of Hilan Forstil's. The announcement takes place at the Capitol, on September 30."

"That's neat," Kira said. "Can I come, too?"

"I'll get you an invitation," Nathan promised. He sipped at his orange juice, then continued, "So now you all know my plans for the next couple of months. What're *you* up to, Kira?" His tone was even more casual than when he had begun the game earlier.

Kira swallowed hard; her stomach turned into a cold lump. "I'm doing some public relations work," she explained. "After all, that's what I got my degree in."

"Yes, I remember. You were going to develop advanced Information Age advertising concepts—ads that could compete with Madison Avenue without being misleading."

"Yeah. Well, I have some things to take care of first."

"Such as?"

Kira flushed, but she looked back at her uncle angrily. "I have to protect you from the cigarette industry, for one thing. And while I'm at it, I have to avenge my mother's murder."

"I see." He watched her with the cautious disapproval that was his strongest rebuke.

The sarcastic anger of her father's voice was a stronger rebuke. "So you think you can waltz in as an advertising agent and destroy one of the biggest, most powerful organizations on Earth?"

Kira shrugged. "I don't know. But I do know that they might destroy you if I don't." She told them about Wilcox's plans to flood the network conferences with anti-Zetetic propaganda.

"Very clever," Nathan said. "What a brilliant ally Daniel Wilcox would make if we could coax him into the Institute."

She shook her head. "Not very likely. Believe me, he's ruthless."

"That doesn't necessarily make him bad. But you're right." He sighed. "We must think of him in many ways as an enemy."

"And he's talking about having a debate with you, Uncle Nathan. He thinks he can take you apart."

"Really?" Nathan's eyes lit up.

Kira held up a cautionary finger. "He might not beat you in the debate itself, but he might win in the news coverage that followed." She told them about the way Wilcox was pulling the strings of the media. As she spoke, she remembered her suspicions that Wilcox had other anti-Zetetic plans that she didn't know about. She had been building relationships with some of the programmers at

Wilcox-Morris, trying to get access to more of the proprietary data bases, but she hadn't yet succeeded. As she thought about it, her anxiety increased; she had to work more quickly on those computers, and yet, she didn't dare.

Summing up Wilcox's plans, she added a final desperate warning to her uncle while her father was out of the room. "So you've got to be careful of what you say in public, because you never know how he'll twist it."

Nathan shook his head. "You're right, of course. Anything I say can be used against me. But you're wrong, too. I can't stop speaking. I can't stop trying to get people to think about their worlds in different ways. You see that, don't you?"

"I guess so." Kira slumped in her chair. "Well, be careful, anyway."

"Of course."

Suddenly the lights went down, and her father came in with a huge cake. Kira could tell they weren't too angry about her work with Wilcox-Morris; they obeyed her when she begged them to spare her their terrible, off-key rendition of "Happy Birthday."

August 6

"Your two-color morality is pathetic," sneered the Sophisticate. "The world isn't black and white. No one does pure good or pure bad. It's all gray. Therefore, no one is better than anyone else."

"I'm glad you see the flaws in two-color morality," replied the Zetet. "But knowing only gray, you conclude that all grays are the same shade. You mock the simplicity of the two-color view, yet you replace it with a one-color view. Can we not find a third, better alternative?"

— *Zetetic Commentaries*

A gentle voice full of wistful humor sang to Leslie as he stopped at the door to Amos Leung's house. "Good day," the disembodied voice of Amos Leung said. "What is the purpose of your visit?"

Leslie looked around the delicately articulated door frame in search of the speaker. No electronics of any kind presented themselves. He saw fine lines that might have been random scratches above the doorway arch. A casual observer would have seen nothing else, but Leslie knew Amos and his wife Florence well enough to know that random scratchings would not have been permitted here. He studied the lines, and they came together in patterns, in tracings of birds and flowers. The subtle crafting could only be Flo's handiwork.

"I came to see an old friend," Leslie said to the empty air, wondering whether the voice was really Amos's, or a very good imitation rigged in the house computer circuits.

"An old friend," the voice repeated. "What is your name, old friend?"

115

The r's were too harsh, Leslie realized, for it to be Amos's voice. Amos spoke with no trace of an accent, though he softly rounded off all his consonants. The voice belonged to the house, not the man. "Tell Amos that Leslie Evans is looking for him."

"Of course."

When Nathan had recommended Amos for the Sling Project, Leslie had been quite astonished. He had never met anyone quite like Amos, before or since. He remembered a conversation they had held while flying together to McChord Airfield, perhaps fifteen years ago.

The plane had been dark; they had turned down the lights for the movie watchers. "What do you do when you're not building comm systems, Amos?" Leslie had asked of this new fellow on the E-3 team, taking a short puff on his cigarillo.

Amos was sitting quite still and erect in his chair; he had made Leslie feel tall and awkward. Amos's Oriental features remained impassive no matter what Leslie said, and Leslie felt a periodic urge to grab him and shake him. He knew that somewhere underneath Amos's masklike expression a laughing observer looked back.

A tiny crack appeared in the mask, and the beginnings of a smile played at the corners of Amos's mouth. "Oh, when I'm not building comm systems, I guess mostly I build comm systems." He turned to Leslie and looked up into his eyes. "You know the echoes people used to get on MCI long-distance circuits? I became tired of these echoes, so I called the company and told them how to fix them."

"Really." Leslie smiled, too, unsure of whether Amos was pulling his leg.

"Yes." He held up his hand with the thumb and forefinger spread apart. "All it takes is a component about this size. It costs 75 cents in quantity."

"If it's so cheap to fix, why didn't MCI fix it without your help? How could they not have known about it?"

"Because they thought they needed the same kind of equipment Bell Telephone used." He spread his arms. "Bell used huge devices to solve the same problem. They cost thousands of dollars."

Leslie feared that Amos wasn't joking. "Did they use your recommendation?"

The tiniest lift of an eyebrow suggested a mental shrug. "Perhaps. At least, I no longer hear the echoes."

Leslie sat for a long time thinking about that. He reached the end of his cigarillo and crushed it in the ashtray.

Amos spoke again—the first time he had initiated a step in their conversation. "They called me several months later to offer me a job, with a sizable increase in salary." He paused, then added with peculiar emphasis, "Sizable."

"Why didn't you take it?"

"My job at present is satisfactory. I would not take another position unless it took me nearer to my ideal."

"Which is?"

"I should like to teach, and do research, and create products, all at the same time. Perhaps a part-time job as a professor, and a part-time job as a consultant would work well."

"I see. Well, good luck in finding your ideal." And that had been the end of the matter as far as Amos was concerned.

As the door to Amos's house opened, Leslie found himself hoping that Amos had not yet found his ideal.

Amos stood before him, bare-chested, breathing slightly harder than normal. No doubt he had been working his way through his exercises. "Hello," his soft voice sang between breaths.

Again Leslie felt like a clumsy giant, just as he had felt in the old days. He smiled at his old friend.

Was Amos an old friend? Leslie had always thought of Amos as a friend, but he had never been quite sure how Amos felt in return. Leslie held out his hand, with a warm, "Howdy, Amos. You've got a beautiful house here."

Amos did not take his hand, so Leslie pointed up at the tracings. "I particularly appreciate the artwork."

A shadow smile played at Amos's lips. "Come in. Let me assure you the interior of our house is more beautiful than the exterior."

"Thanks." He followed Amos to the living room; the door closed automatically.

This room was all sloping contours, accented with patches

of fine golden tapestry on cushions and drapes. The room relaxed him; it reminded him in some ways of the furnishings at the Institute. But the absence of chairs reminded him of the differences. "How are the girls in your *kung fu* classes, Amos?" Years ago, Amos had taught self-defense for young women; he refused to work with boys. Leslie remembered Amos's comment on the boys. "In America, they all feel a need to be macho. They become dangerous if taught advanced techniques."

"Quite well. I have a class of seven students now; three are excellent beginners. They may become good one day, if they have the interest."

A tiny woman appeared at the partition separating this room from what looked like a breakfast nook. "Colonel Evans!" she exclaimed. "How nice to see you."

Leslie turned to her with his broadest smile. "Flo." He half-bowed. "It is truly wonderful to see you." If Amos made Leslie feel like a giant, Flo made him feel like a mountain. She came up to his waist and stopped there, with a puckish smile and wide, happy eyes. But whereas Amos made him feel like an obtuse goat that might chew on the velvet coverings at any moment, Flo made him feel graceful. At least if he chewed on the covers, he would do so with dignity.

"Would you like Shanghai tea, colonel?" she asked.

"Wonderful, Flo. Thanks." She slipped softly out of view.

He turned to Amos, who pointed at a cushion. "Please sit down, old friend," he offered, coiling onto a cushion himself. Leslie could not tell if Amos mocked him with the phrase 'old friend' or not. "I presume you came on business."

Leslie collapsed into a sitting position. "Quite right. You've always known me too well, Amos. I need your help."

Amos watched him impassively.

"Have you heard of the Sling Project?"

"No."

"Um. Well, let me tell you about it." Leslie launched into an enthusiastic rendition about the Sling. He told of the seed of Information Age understanding that Nathan had begun with, and the gleam in the eye of a colonel in the Defense Nuclear Agency who had no charter to develop such a non-nuclear system. He described how the colonel had stretched the rules, then stretched them again and again, until he could fund the development of Nathan's idea. He told of his own involvement as the system's integrator, and his desperate search for the people who could make the software come together. He described his need for an additional, special person, a person who could ". . . make the heart and the mind of the system come together. That's you, Amos, if it's anyone in the world."

"Only if I accept the position."

"Well, yeah." The scent of warm tea reached him; Leslie turned his head to see Flo kneeling next to him, a cup held out. He accepted with a jerky motion, feeling like the clumsy giant despite Flo's gentle presence. "Amos, this is important stuff we're working on. Don't you see that?"

"Yes, I suppose it is."

Leslie felt again the desire to shake Amos, to make him come alive in the way of life that Leslie understood. For Leslie, if something was important, then it was *of course* a good thing to do. He had known that Amos didn't share his values, but he didn't know what values Amos had instead. "Listen, I don't know to what extent you achieved your lifestyle and job goals. I remember you wanted an arrangement that would let you spend one third of your time teaching, one third doing research, and one third creating products. Well, I can sort of offer you two of the three. You'll be creating a product, but the product needs you to incorporate a lot more current research ideas than you'd usually see in a military development effort. And you'll be working with other good people. You'll have to meet Nathan; I think you'll like him."

"Yes, I believe he might be an interesting person." Amos splayed his fingers in a gesture Leslie remembered from years ago: a gesture that forewarned the listener of an upcoming disappointment. "But I have already achieved my goal. I am living it now."

Leslie clenched his teeth. How could he impose his will on this man who epitomized the idea of an immovable object? He certainly couldn't do it through force. "How have you achieved your goal? I know about your consulting, but where do you do research? And who do you teach, besides the girls and boys in your kung fu class?"

"I do my research here at home. I have a reasonably sophisticated assemblage of equipment—better than many universities." Remembering the equipment that Amos used to have, Leslie could well believe it. "As for my teaching, I have acquired a most apt pupil." He smiled sideways at Flo with a surprising look of mischief. "Florence is fascinated by computers, we have discovered. I believe she is becoming a hacker."

Florence made a sound like a kitten laughing.

Leslie spread his arms to encompass both of them. "That's terrific! We'll hire both of you! You can work as a team right here at home. We'll run the whole show through the Zetetic Institute's DevelopNet—you've telecommuted on team projects before, right?—and you'll have all three parts of your life in place."

Amos shook his head. "I have the parts of my life in place already. All you have offered me is an opportunity to introduce chaos. You want to bring all the chaos of development panic, integration hysteria, and debugging terror into my life. What can you offer me so valuable that I should break my tranquility?"

Now it was Leslie's turn to sit impassively for a moment. "Do you have grandchildren, Amos?"

"Yes. Two."

"Do you keep up with world events at all? You know, one of the main reasons I had to come back to you is that so many people in our country now refuse to have anything to do with the ever-so-unpopular military-industrial complex. How long do you think we can live our tranquil lives in a place where the people consider the job of defending themselves to be dirty?"

"I do not know."

"If our project succeeds, we may make it." He held up his thumb and forefinger close together, the way Amos had once held them to describe a 75-cent circuit. "We're that close to entering the Information Age, and to developing a whole different concept of what it means to be a society, and what it means to defend yourself. That close—but not close enough, not yet." He clenched his fist. "I think it's important for your grandchildren to make it all the way into the Information Age, don't you?"

Amos sighed. "I suppose so."

Silence closed around them; Leslie was out of words.

Flo spoke. "Excuse me, Colonel Evans. Did you say earlier that you were using the WeatherWatcher airplane?"

Leslie felt his neck muscles relax as he looked into Flo's eyes. Her calming effect on him made him think of Jan . . . no, this was Flo, a person whose beauty was profoundly different from Jan's. "Yes, we're using the Weather-Watcher as the underlying platform for the SkyHunter. We modify it, of course."

"I see." She turned to Amos, and they exploded into rapid conversation in Mandarin, which Leslie could not follow.

Amos frowned. The mischievous look returned to his face, then a look bordering on anger came and went. "Yes, I suppose so." He turned to Leslie. "We will handle it strictly with telecommuting? Flo and I can work here all the time?"

Leslie straightened up on his cushion. He had thought he was beaten, but apparently he had been wrong. "Yeah, certainly. We'll work through telecommuting." He frowned. "Well, almost certainly. I hate being so honest, but I'll want to pull the team together into one location for testing."

"Time compression," Amos said. "I understand. Well, we shall deal with that problem when the time comes." He uncoiled from the cushion and slid out of the room.

Leslie sat dazed. Flo giggled, and he smiled at her. "How did you manage that, Flo?"

"I told him it might help him talk to our daughter if he accepted your job. He almost never gets to speak with her; they have grown apart."

"What? How will working on the Sling help him with his daughter?"

"Theresa is vice president of LightCraft Corporation. She is responsible for the development of the Weather-Watcher airplane."

Leslie laughed, then stopped abruptly, for it sounded loud in the quiet of the house.

                    *   *   *

The doorbell rang promptly at ten o'clock; the guy with the satellite photos had arrived. Lila stuffed her feet into a pair of old sandals and plodded to the door. She steeled herself for this contact, wishing he would leave the passwords to the data bases at the door and just leave her alone. But the guy had insisted on seeing her. He had been almost as mysterious as Nathan Pilstrom had been a month ago.

Nathan Pilstrom. She shuddered at the memory. Nathan had tainted her view of the Zetetic Institute. She had thought of Nathan Pilstrom and the Zetetic Institute as visionaries, leading to a better world, not as reactionary warmongers.

She peered through the peephole at the visitor. The visitor was a man, as she expected. The messages on Jobnet had been signed with the name Kurt, though with electronic mail, that didn't always guarantee the gender. Her hand hesitated on the doorknob. She hated to deal with men. Somehow, she always seemed to disappoint them; certainly, they always disappointed her.

She jerked on the doorknob and faced Kurt McKenna.

Her face flushed with a first small shock of dislike. He displayed all the features she found most unattractive in men. He had a sternly chiseled face, with the beauty of a sculpture. He held himself with a military straightness that bespoke an inbred arrogance. His eyes were direct and abrupt—eyes that wrote people off easily, never giving them a second chance. Her dislike grew rapidly.

Her skin prickled as she felt her dislike reflected by him; her vision wavered with the intensity of their resonating emotion. She was sure she would soon hate him.

She didn't want to hate him. She hated hate. How had this man done this to her? Why didn't he go away?

He stepped forward; she held her ground. "Ms. Lottspeich. I have a job for you."

The words seemed normal, except for the forced precision of his speech. She considered closing the door on him, but that would not be civilized. Unwilling to turn her back on him, she stepped back and pointed to the chairs in the corner of the living room that served as her office. "Sit down."

He did not share her fear of turning away; he swept across the room and sat in *her* chair. Lila pursed her lips, then realized he had not done it intentionally: he had no way of telling from the careless way she had left the chairs, which was which. Normally she made the choice clear for people by escorting them.

The other chair had no arms. She twisted it around so its back was to McKenna and sat down facing him, her arms draped across the top of it. In this position she had the solid mass of the chair between her and McKenna, which made her feel better.

"Here." He dropped a packet on the table. "These are pictures of northern Iran."

"Iran!" She tore the packet open and riffled the photos with a practiced eye. They were fresh shots from the new full-spectrum, high-resolution French Spot IV satellite. She smiled at the crisp detail, both optical and infrared. She didn't get to handle good stuff like this too often, though she was one of the best image analysts in the world. Her genius paid off most effectively when reconstructing the damaged pictures.

"Great photos, aren't they?"

The certainty in his voice made her recoil from his arrogance, but he was right. Lila remained silent.

"Ten years ago those photos would have been so classified that the name of the classification would have been classified. Today any schmuck can pick them up for the price of a post card."

"A post card?" She cast him a look of disgust. Hyperbole didn't impress her.

"Well, the price of a book of post cards. Anyway, photos like these sometimes mess things up for the men who defend our country."

She looked back at the pictures with a deeper appreciation. She smiled at the thought of the hawks in the military-industrial complex bubbling with impotent anger. "What do you want me to do with them?"

"We have indications that the Soviet army invading Iran is destroying the wheat fields, as well as most of the other crops. We need to know how extensive the damage is, and how fast the damage is spreading."

"You have several series of these photos, taken on different days?"

"Of course."

She pursed her lips at his quick dismissal of her question, but he continued.

"We also need to know *what* the Soviets are doing that's making such a mess, so that when we send relief, we can send something to straighten it out. Otherwise, people will starve." Kurt paused. "*That's* why we came to you. It'll be tough figuring out the cause of the problem, even with these photos. I understand you're the best."

Ordinarily Lila would have demurred, but this McKenna provoked her. "Yes, I guess I am," she said with a too-casual wave of the hand. She carefully replaced the photos in their envelope. "I presume you have these stored digitally somewhere that I can get at them, right? Certainly you didn't overlook such a critical yet tiny detail."

"I didn't." He reached into his pocket, pulling out a credit card. "Use this. We'll pay for the time directly, and all the photos are there. You can find their sort order in the main directory." He rose to leave; she rose, too. She didn't want to let him look down at her.

"We haven't discussed the fee yet," she said.

He stopped. "I know how expensive you are. I'll give you a ten percent bonus, for having to work with me."

She opened her mouth, closed it in stunned silence. He felt the jarring hostility as strongly as she did.

She considered throwing the photos at him. Why had she let him into her apartment? Why hadn't she refused his job? Knowing that people might starve if she failed, she couldn't just throw him out. As much as she hated this man, those people were more important. She vowed to rise above him in this moral sense.

He stopped at the door. He seemed more relaxed, now that he was leaving. "I take off tomorrow for D.C. The card contains my phone number. If you have any questions today, I'm at Rickey's Hyatt."

"When do you need my results?"

"Yesterday," he responded as he left.

She turned to her work station, to unlock the digitized versions of McKenna's photos. A brief, suspicious baffle-

ment crossed her mind. Why did this man care about
wheat fields in Iran? He belonged to the military-industrial
complex; she could smell it. He might care about the
Soviet tanks, finding ways to destroy them, but she was
sure he didn't care about those people. She should have
asked him while he was there, but she had been so eager
to get him out of her apartment she hadn't asked all her
questions. What did he really want from her? She would
ask him when she had to speak to him again.

With a shrug she opened the main directory McKenna
had given her on the new account.

Nathan stood outside Bair Drug and Hardware, watching the occasional car cruise down the main street of
Steilacoom. Here in the state of Washington, God had
ordained five months of deep blue skies to be shrouded by
seven months of slate gray clouds. The gray clouds kept
out the tourists who did not understand. The gray clouds
made the blue skies special for those who did understand:
Steilacoom was a bright jewel placed in a dull metal setting. No one took the blue skies for granted in Steilacoom.
This month was a blue sky month.

Nathan walked down Lafayette Street to its intersection
with Wilkes. To his left he could see the haunted restaurant E.R. Rogers, facing away toward the water. A soft
breeze, made damp by the Sound, carried a message of
tranquility. Every corner of Steilacoom held this peaceful
tranquility, a tranquility that was hard to find in the frenetic Zetetic headquarters just outside the nation's capital.
Fortunately, Nathan carried his own tranquility within
him. He had held that inner tranquility ever since Jan first
taught him to feel relaxation, to always remember what it
feels like to be calm.

But an earlier Nathan Pilstrom had not found tranquility
so easily. In past decades, that earlier Nathan had sought
out the Steilacooms of the world, desperately trying to
internalize their calming influence. That Steilacoom seren-
ity always seemed so beautiful, like the still waters of
Puget Sound he could see now below the edge of the road.
Sometimes that earlier Nathan had succeeded in grasp-

ing tranquility for a time, but always he had lost it again.
Finally, Jan and the Institute and he himself had developed new ways to train the mind to make those images more permanent.

Remembering those earlier, anxiety-ridden days, he realized how much he had in common with Juan Dante-Cortez. Nathan leaned against Bair's clean siding and waited.

A battered blue Chevy swung by him into a parking slot. The car door creaked open. A man Nathan barely recognized stood up.

Nathan had met Juan once, a decade ago in the software exhibition hall in Austin. Those had been heady times, when the computer software industry exploded across the world with the same flare that microcomputers had carried just a few years earlier. Nathan had been on the crest of that wave with the first educational software from the Zetetic Corporation. Juan had been there, too, a kid fresh out of college with a copter flight simulation that left experts gasping, wondering how he had cranked so much detail out of such a small machine. Juan had never even flown in a helicopter.

In those bygone days Juan had burned with the fever of the industry. But his fever had burned deep inside, almost invisible. He released that energy upon the world only through the rapid, continuous movement of his eyes and his hands. The rest of his body had seemed to be an insulator, a soft fleshy covering to protect everything he touched from the flame-hot temperatures inside himself.

Looking at Juan as he stepped from the old car, Nathan could see that the fever had burned through. It had cooked through his whole body, stripping the insulation, leaving a lean, leathery remnant. His eyes watched Nathan calmly, even carefully; his hands no longer swept in an unceasing dance, but moved with care to close the door and sweep back his thinning hair. Nathan wondered if he himself looked so dramatically changed when Juan looked back at him.

Slouched, Juan hardly seemed taller than Nathan himself. He maneuvered around the parked cars with long strides. "Nathan," he said, with a shallow smile, "it's been a long time."

Nathan nodded his head. "Too long." He crooked his head. "Hungry?"

"Of course." Juan straightened up. "Bair's Drugstore is a pretty strange place for a business meeting. It's perfect."

"I figured that most of your prospective employers might not think of taking you to Bair's for lunch. That just shows what fools they are—as you and I know, the best way to soften up a programmer is to fill him with chocolate-chocolate malted sodas before you lay on the Big Nasty." He pushed on the old-fashioned drugstore door handle, jiggling it in the middle of the motion to catch the jam properly, and opened the door. Nathan and Juan may have changed with time, but Bair's Drugstore had not. This permanence was key to Steilacoom's tranquility.

"I hope you don't tell anybody else the secret of the chocolate-chocolate malted soda," Juan replied with more pep. "You could get me into a lot of trouble." After they both chuckled, Juan continued, "And I hope you don't have a Big Nasty for me with dessert."

"I don't know, Juan. *You* must tell *me* if it's nasty." They sat at the round table across from the soda fountain, next to the Franklin stove, and ordered turkey sandwiches and chili. Apple pie would follow for dessert. And of course they ordered chocolate-chocolate malted sodas.

The conversation drifted across the missing years. They talked about the slump in the software market that had followed the boom, the growth of the Zetetic Institute, and the growth of Juan's company—Inferno, Inc. They talked about the breakup of Inferno, and about Jan's death and Juan's divorce. They did not talk about what either of them had done personally in the past year. They finished the apple pie.

"How did you find your way to Steilacoom?" Nathan asked as a first serious probe.

Juan answered by turning away, to squint into the sunshine pouring through Bair's front window. "I came here to find my soul again."

Yes, Juan had a great deal in common with that earlier Nathan Pilstrom. "Have you found it?"

Juan continued to stare into the sunshine with an expression of yearning, as if he clung to the sunshine, but it pushed him remorselessly away. "I don't know."

"Are you happy here?"

The leathery face relaxed into a wry smile. "I am content. Is that happiness?"

"If you ask the question, you know the answer. There's more to happiness than being content. You have to have a purpose, too—a worthwhile purpose."

A spasm rocked Juan's whole body. He turned back to Nathan, and for the first time his eyes held some of their old volcanic fire. "Do you know *why* I came to Steilacoom, Nathan?"

Nathan knew, but he didn't dare explain how he knew. "Tell me."

"It broke me, Nathan. Computer programming broke me. You see, I'm a Method programmer."

"You're a what?"

"I'm a Method programmer." He paused. "You know what a Method actor is, don't you? A Method actor lives the part he plays—he *becomes* the person he is portraying." A mellow note entered his discussion. "A Method programmer lives the program he writes—he *becomes* the program he is creating." He shrugged. "One day I was debugging ParaPower, a tool for running parallel simulations of world economics. We could have used it for comparing alternative agricultural policies, and banking policies, and military policies. It was going to revolutionize the job of politics and statesmanship. It was . . ." His eyes drifted; another spasm shook him, until he focused again on the sunshine. "I was tracing a fatal error through the simulation's concurrencies." Again he looked hard at Nathan. "The next thing I remember was a pillow on a hospital bed. Six weeks had passed." He shrugged. "The medical community finds me quite fascinating. They studied me at great length. I seem to have a unique form of epilepsy, triggered by the kind of creative, meticulous thinking I do when I'm programming. It's different from any other kind of thinking I've experienced. Do you know what I mean?"

Nathan nodded. "And yet, you're programming now. And my friends at 9ID tell me you're doing a super job with their budgeting system."

Juan snorted. "Yeah. It's so boring I can hardly keep my eyes open when I think about it." He closed his eyes as if to prove the point. "You might think of me as an alcoholic who, after going through a long period as a teetotaler, now makes his living as a wine taster." He opened his eyes again. "But you have to be careful not to like the wine too much."

"I see." Nathan clenched his teeth. How important was the Sling Project? He thought about the Information Age that might yet be stillborn if the governments of the world played their cards badly enough; he thought about the vast destructiveness of Industrial Age weapons and about the people who would die for no rational reason if another war began. "Juan, I've come here to offer you a very fine wine. But it has a purpose. Maybe the most important purpose we've ever encountered."

Juan nodded. "Yeah."

"You can stay here in Steilacoom, in communion with your soul, if you prefer. We'll run the project through telecomm, of course."

"Of course we'll run telecomm—until the crunch at the end, of course."

"Probably. The timelines are nasty, but we'll more than likely stretch them." Nathan smiled innocently. "Who knows? We might even make schedule."

"Nathan, only project managers believe those kinds of fantasies." Juan sighed. "I suppose contentment would kill me eventually, too. Just how much purpose have you got this time?"

Nathan told him the purpose, and the method, of the Sling.

Too often in the past months, Nathan had felt foolish describing the plan, explaining why this could be the most important project in the world, even though it was so tiny. He knew he sounded like a crusader when he spoke of it: he *was* a crusader. The sense of foolishness came whenever he talked to people who didn't care. It didn't upset Nathan too much that they didn't care about the Sling; it upset him that they didn't care about *anything* the way Nathan cared about the Sling.

Despite all the mechanisms the Zetetic Institute had

developed to help people cope with the Information Age world—mechanisms to reduce stress, to adapt to contexts, to reduce ego-involvement—the Institute had never found a way to help people to *care*. Life without caring was a shadow; the great moments of exhilaration came amidst the battles that only a crusader could know. Yet so few people accepted the risks, and those who did not care came closest to caring only when telling the rare crusaders that they were fools.

But Juan shared his crusader blood, fearful though he must be of this particular mission. So Nathan shared his vision freely, and found answers in Juan's sunken eyes.

He finished speaking, drained but excited, and waited for Juan's response.

At last Juan answered. "So you want me to build the simulations for the three Hunters. Every time someone gets a module written and ready to test, I'll already have the simulation tools on-line, ready to help them debug. Every time I fail, they'll miss their deadlines."

Nathan started to agree, but Juan continued.

"And we can't miss the deadlines because *they* will be the critical path. Somehow, that makes me the supercritical path, if there is such a thing." He bared his teeth as he stared into the now-fading sunshine. His face held a defiant look. It was not the expression of an animal that has been cornered, but of a man who understands the choices, knows the risks, and still accepts his purpose. "That's a real screamer, Nathan." His eyes glistened for a moment, looking at something only he could see. He blinked. When he looked back at Nathan his eyes had the steady, smoldering look of a controlled fire. "I guess you know that I'll do it."

"I guess I do. You know, the Institute has done a lot of work to help people deal more effectively with reality. We might have something that can help you travel from Steilacoom without leaving your soul here. I'll send you some info."

"Better do that, Nathan. Even if I never leave my house, I'll still be traveling for you—inside the Sling, inside every Hunter in the sky. Find a way for me to land without crashing."

A cloud crossed the sun, casting a brooding shadow across the town of Steilacoom.

Daniel sat at his desk and watched the wide-panel television display. He hummed a human purr.

FOCUS. "In addition to the con game the Zetetic Institute plays with people who need help fighting their tobacco habits, the Institute has become a major force in the military-industrial complex." Bill Hardie's eyes cloud with anger. "They've initiated the 'Sling Project,' a project to sell cheap trinkets to the Army, pretending that these trinkets have value for defending the nation. How useful are the Institute's machines?"

CUT. A gaunt hovercraft appears on the screen; something about the light makes it glitter like a fragile Christmas tree ornament. "This is the so-called 'HopperHunter,' designed to kill tanks. You can imagine how long it would survive on a battlefield where the tanks were allowed to shoot back."

Daniel nodded his head in tribute to the newscaster. How did he get that video footage? It was terrific. It delighted him that Bill Hardie was one of his own creations, one of the delicately ripened fruits that now burst with sweetness. If Bill ever found out that Wilcox-Morris arranged the flurries of intense coverage whenever he reported on the Zetetic Institute, it would make him hysterical.

Daniel had certainly expended a lot of tender care to ripen this fruit, particularly after Hardie's first visits to the ZI headquarters. The damned Institute had poisoned all of Daniel's nurturance, manipulating the reporter as skillfully as Daniel himself. Wilcox-Morris had suddenly had to prune Hardie's popularity back. His syndications had dwindled dramatically, almost fatally. Daniel himself had arranged new opportunities for Hardie in remote places, just to get him out of the Institute before the Zetetic rot penetrated to his core.

If Bill found out how hard Wilcox-Morris had worked to get him back on track, that, too, would make him hysterical. But Hardie didn't know. That, too, was sweet.

ZOOM. The television whines with the sound of turbine engines. The HopperHunter rises, wobbles, then crumples on its side. "You can see how long it survives when it just has to fight gravity."

CUT. Bill comes back into focus. "The greatest absurdity of this is that the Army already has similar systems— better systems—in development, under the auspices of the FIREFORS agency. The Zetetic Institute has inspired the Defense Department to another crude, inefficient duplication of effort."

Whew! Daniel loved this guy's fire; even he half-believed the golden boy on the screen. Maybe he *was* doing the whole world a service in destroying the Institute.

CUT. "In other news, the Senate finally passed a new law banning many major forms of telecommuting. The nation's unions have been fighting for this protection for their workers for decades. They finally put together a coalition of forces capable of pushing the ban through against loud opposition."

Daniel chuckled. Did Hardie really believe that the *unions* had put together that coalition? Daniel had had a devil of a time persuading them to accept his support! They didn't trust the Wilcox-Morris Corporation any more than Daniel trusted the news media.

FOCUS. "Union leaders, and some corporate leaders as well, have hailed this as a return to sanity for the economy. By forcing employers to offer a workplace, employees will now be able to get government inspections that assure fair and safe treatment. Thus, these workers will at last receive the same protection that textile workers have received since home manufacture of clothing for sale was banned half a century ago."

Daniel added to the message a second part: the workers will also be protected by the quick destruction of the Zetetic Institute.

CUT. "This historic telecommuting ban starts on October 2."

Daniel heard a knock at the door. He flicked off the television and said loudly, "Come on in, Kira."

Kira opened the door and strode quickly to her usual place at the conference table. The weekly meetings had become a tradition; Daniel looked forward to them more than he cared to admit. Bright minds were a rare and precious commodity. For the most part, the tobacco industry needed obedience, not creativity, from its employees.

Daniel started the conversation. "Judging from the figures, our campaign to smear the Institute through their own networks isn't working any better than our media campaign."

"Yes." Kira lowered her eyes briefly in acknowledgement of her failure. "We set up a series of 'artificial people' —software agents—to log on to the Zetetic nets and enter comments directed against the Institute. They dropped quite a bit of stuff on the system in the first two weeks of operation." She hesitated.

"And then?"

She frowned. "And then the Institute must have realized that something odd was happening. The pruning rate has gone up dramatically. And as nearly as we can tell, the pruning is directed at our comments. I suspect the Institute has come up with a set of software agents whose purpose is to recognize and box off anything written by our software agents."

"I see." What a clever game this had become—the battle between Wilcox-Morris and the Zetetic Institute for control of the nets, for control of the soul of the country. Point met counterpoint. "What if we release more agents— just drown the Institute in our cash flow?"

"I can't believe that will work. Remember, the Institute *owns* those conferencing nets. Every time we log on, they make money. We can try it, but it's more likely to increase their profits than anything else." She held up her hands helplessly. "What surprises me a little bit is how fast they caught on. I've ordered a quiet investigation downstairs with our computer people. A frightening number of software engineers and computer architects have close ties with the Institute. Someone might have leaked the word." She shrugged. "Or maybe not. The Zetetics are known for a lot of things, but not for their stupidity in information processing."

"Don't sweat it. We'll find another way." Daniel reached

inside his coat for a cigarette, then stopped. He had stopped smoking during these meetings.

Kira had followed his lead. He regretted the loss of amusement watching Kira handle tobacco, but he did not regret the loss of the opportunity to smoke.

Daniel smoked whenever he appeared in public, except when he had to deal persuasively with anti-smoking fanatics. Sometimes he smoked then, too, if he could afford the pleasure of aggravating his enemies. But he never smoked in private. Ironically, he had stopped smoking in private shortly after buying up his first tobacco company for the Wilcox empire. When he had acquired the company, he had also acquired their private research documents on the health hazards of smoking.

Tobacco companies had spent millions of dollars trying to find favorable scientific ways to describe tobacco's effects. They had given up only after being struck in the face, again and again, with proof that went far beyond simple statistical correlations. The proof was still statistical, —but the statistics were of the caliber of the physicist's wave equations. They were statistics that allowed the researcher to predict, for any given population, how many people would die of cancer in a given year. All the researcher needed was a base rate of death, and a description of how many people had been smoking for how long. Cigarette smoking so strongly outweighed other variances that additional factors merely put wiggles in the line. If you knew how many people smoked, you knew how many people died.

So Daniel no longer smoked in private. And with Kira, he felt a bond. He counted his time with her as private time. He enjoyed her company.

They talked at length about many other aspects of the business, but Daniel's mind drifted. The Zetetic Institute seemed determined not to go away; more drastic measures were in order. The telecommuting ban should provide the focal point.

As they finished, he said, "Do you remember saying you could arrange a meeting for me with Nathan Pilstrom, the president of the Institute?"

Kira froze in the act of packing her briefcase. "I said I might be able to arrange it. Why?"

"I think the time has come. Any idea where he'll be during the last week of September—someplace where I could talk with him?"

Kira nodded very cautiously. "I might be able to get you his schedule for the week. If I remember correctly, he's supposed to attend a reception at the Capitol that week. You could get invited as well. Or are you thinking of arranging a broadcast debate? That'll be harder."

"No," he replied, perhaps more sharply than he should have. Kira perked up at the intensity of his response. "I just want to meet the fellow. Maybe we can cut a deal."

Kira's head bounced with a light laugh. "Optimist."

"Yes. Cockeyed, incurable, and romantic," Daniel agreed gravely as he watched her leave.

Lila drove through the night, blind to the falling rain and the danger of her reckless speed. She had uncovered the lies in McKenna's words; she had uncovered them faster than he could have anticipated. He was still within striking distance.

Despite his arrogant attitude, or because of it, she had buried herself in his satellite photos moments after he left. What was happening in northeastern Iran? At first McKenna's claims seemed overblown. Some of the fields were decaying, true enough. Some had been destroyed. But considering the normal horror of war it was not unusual; in some macabre sense, it was even mild.

When she had turned to rates of destruction, she had found that the decay was spreading faster than the destruction. These fields didn't suffer from artillery bombardments or the crushing brutality of armored vehicles; rather, they suffered from lack of attention. The decay struck, oddly enough, around the small villages nestled in the Elburz Mountains and diminished near the major cities like Meshed. Near Meshed, the outright destruction of fields dominated.

Why were the fields unattended? This was the question she and her computer had sought through image processing. She had stretched the image contrasts. She had run series upon series of density slices across the multiple images. She had wrung hints of knowledge from each operation, but no understanding. She felt as though she were trying to reconstruct a jigsaw puzzle while viewing the pieces through a microscope; her perspective had been wrong.

The understanding came as a flash of Zetetic revelation—a flash that had little to do with the images she was processing. She had stopped, sick at the conclusion she had drawn.

She could be wrong—she had prayed she was wrong—but she had had few doubts. Why had the fields decayed? Because no one was tending them. Why was no one tending them? Because all the people had been killed. All of them.

It had taken her a long time to build up the fortitude to investigate why, and how, they had been murdered. She would have preferred not to know. She had considered logging off and forgetting everything. At the last, she had been driven forward by the taunting image of McKenna's sneer. With a cold, violent concentration, she had analyzed the photos with a whole different set of tools.

The satellite images did not just show Lila the colors of the rainbow; they showed the whole spectrum from low HF radio to high UV. She could not run full spectroscopic analyses—the atmosphere blocked too much energy for that—but she could run approximations. First she identified fluorine in the atmosphere—fluorine bundled in compounds with carbon. With oxygen. With hydrogen. With growing horror, she matched the spectrum against known molecules until, late at night, she hit the tag.

The match had not been perfect, but it had been too close for coincidence. The villages had been sprayed with some derivative of Soman, a persistent nerve gas.

Why hadn't anybody reported this in the newspapers? With more cold analysis, she understood that silence, too. The murderers had been thorough in destroying those isolated villages where rebels might breed, far from the brutal controls imposed on the cities. The Soviets had carefully left no witnesses.

And Kurt McKenna had thrust this atrocity into her face. Hating even the touch of the photos, she had scooped them back into the envelope. And now she drove with them to the Hyatt, to throw them back in his face as he had thrown them at her.

Standing outside his hotel room, she realized she had never felt true anger before. Nothing compared with this feeling of anger, the surge of fury's power as she pounded on his door. Her arm seemed a mere tool of force, to be used to break anything that blocked her way.

The door opened slowly. She pushed on it with the seemingly irresistible force of her anger, but the slow motion of the door seemed barely perturbed. A balancing force controlled its motion, mocking her: Kurt McKenna.

She stepped across the threshold, invading his private space, closing on him so she could feel his breath as she screamed, "You bastard! You don't care about those people! You *knew* what I'd find!"

A slight motion of his jawline suggested the control he exercised over his own feelings. "Three points, only one correct. Yes, I am a bastard. But I do care about those people—perhaps more than you do. And no, I didn't know with certainty what you'd find. But you've told me, just by being here. You found something even more terrible and evil than me."

She stood with her fists clenched, not quite able to pound on him as she had pounded on the door.

He glanced down, saw her stance, and smiled viciously. "Violence? You wouldn't want to reduce yourself to my level, would you? Or are you afraid that I would hit back? You'd be right. I use violence against anyone who uses it against me. Wouldn't you?"

"You bastard! You're as bad as they are!"

Now, in a flickering movement of his eyes, she saw an anger even greater than hers, though not so hot: a cold, killing anger. His anger consumed hers, sucking the fury from her arms, turning it back with the slow pressure of his breath on her face. Involuntarily, she stepped back.

His mouth worked a moment before he spoke, but his voice remained steady. "You know better. I don't kill civilians. I kill people who kill civilians." He paused, a pause that shouted with anger. "*You* are the one who's as bad as the people you hate. You don't really hate them. You don't even hate what they do. What you hate, Ms. Lottspeich, is *knowing* about what they do. If they would just leave you out of it, so you didn't have to know, you wouldn't hate anyone or anything."

She held her breath. That was ridiculous. And yet—she felt her hands clenching and unclenching—was it true?

"And most of the people like you in America can get away with it. After all, those soldiers can only touch you *over my dead body*, and the dead bodies of all the other fools like me who volunteer for the job. But you won't lift a finger to help us. You're too good for us, aren't you?"

She wondered what he was referring to, in his peculiar accusation. Then she realized: "Did Nathan Pilstrom send you?"

McKenna snorted. "Not on your life. Nathan never forces people to listen him, the way I forced you to listen to me. He has a vision that he offers to everybody, but you have to choose it of your own free will." His voice softened for a moment. "Perhaps he's right. Perhaps you shouldn't force ideas down other people's throats." Then the anger returned. "Or perhaps I'm right, instead."

"Why didn't you take this thing—what was it, the Sling Project—to one of your normal military contractors?"

Again Lila saw his jaws tighten. "They aren't *my* contractors."

"My father told me stories about Vietnam. The way the guns we were using—the M-16s—would jam in the middle of a fight and leave our troops unarmed. Do you know why the M-16s jammed in Vietnam? Do you know why people like me died because they couldn't shoot back? The original, commercial gun they modified into the M-16 didn't jam. But the Army's ordnance bureaucracy wouldn't allow a simple gun developed by someone else to become the standard. Oh, no. They had to improve it. They improved it enough so that it didn't work anymore." His nostrils flared. "To prove the goodness of their goddam bureaucracy, they crippled the men who had to fight—the men who had enough people trying to kill them.

"Those people in that bureaucracy had forgotten as thoroughly as you have. For too many of them, their contracts are more important than any results they might produce." He stopped speaking.

After a silence, Lila asked, "Why did you do this to *me*?"

"Because you're the best. And right now, right here on the Sling Project, we need the best." He pointed to the packet of photos, the packet filled with atrocities. "We need you, we need the best, because as ruthless as I am, I am not as ruthless as they are."

She shuddered, threw the packet aside. And as it thudded against the carpet, she saw how right he was. She feared the knowledge of evil, not the evil itself.

A fear of knowledge did not mesh with her self-image. Reluctantly, she reclaimed the packet from the floor.

Kurt continued. "Without your help, I'll have to kill civilians, too. Maybe I won't kill civilians as efficiently as they do, but I'll still kill them. When I shoot at soldiers like the ones in Iran, I'll have to use such massive weapons that the innocent bystanders won't have a chance."

"You said you don't kill civilians," she jeered.

"I lied," he said. "But you can change me into a person who's telling the truth."

They stood in rigid intensity, staring at one another, as McKenna explained how to stop wholesale murder—not by committing wholesale murder in return, but by committing selective murder of the men who gave the orders to commit wholesale murder. It was still murder, of course. But did it not count for something, that the number of casualties might decrease a hundredfold?

As McKenna spoke, Lila felt her anger shift, ever so slightly. Her anger no longer vented against McKenna's harsh personality. Somehow, in his own distorted way, he cared about people. Her anger now focused beyond him, at those even worse than McKenna. Her anger struck at the faceless creatures, certainly not men, who called down the rain of death upon the helpless villagers in the photos.

"Will you help me?" McKenna asked at last.

Her focus returned to McKenna, her immediate enemy. "Certainly not," she spat. With that she left. She ran through the rain to her car, realizing as she struggled with her keys that she still had McKenna's packet. With a grunt, she flung it into the car.

She drove almost blindly, trapped between the pitch-black night and her own black thoughts. The road vanished, except within the narrow, gleaming spots of her own headlights. Only occasionally could she glimpse the white road markers that inscribed a safe path.

She would not, could not help McKenna. He stood for everything she hated. No, not quite, she remembered. There was something even more hateful beyond him.

She remembered Nathan sitting next to her a month ago. He had been so open, his intentions naked to her, as he tried to explain his purpose. She had cut him off too abruptly. She had known that she was being unfair even at the time; now she thought she understood why. She had been afraid to listen, for fear that she might agree. She had slapped him verbally and conceptually, but unlike McKenna, he had not struck back. Yet she felt sure that his conviction ran as deep as McKenna's.

She would not, could not help McKenna. But she could certainly help Nathan.

She arrived home shaking from the fatigue of the stressful drive and from the anger that still had no physical outlet. She glanced at her watch; it was almost midnight. She felt feverishly awake.

She dialed the phone. A voice gasped blearily, "Pilstrom speaking," which reminded her that in D.C. it was close to 3 A.M. She felt a perverse pleasure in waking him.

"Nathan, this is Lila Lottspeich. Do you still need an image analyst on the Sling Project? Well, the next time you're awake, mail me a contract." She heard him muttering from the other end of the continent. She said loudly, "What? Yeah, I'm on the team. Goodnight." She smiled as she hung up, though she now regretted zapping Nathan in the middle of the night.

She smiled, thinking of the power she had to strike back against the creatures who killed indiscriminately. *Revenge.*

The feeling repelled her even as she reveled in it. Was she now as bad as they were? Her friends would certainly think so. They hated the military as much as she did.

Were those creatures as bad as she now thought? Doubt flickered in her mind, but it could not stand against her new conviction. She had uncovered their cruelty with her own mind; she saw the blood staining their hands.

Another new sensation scared her even more deeply. In all her years of passive objection to the military and all its works, she had never felt so thrust into the center of a conflict, so able to make a difference, so isolated in her strength, yet so willing to fight with all that strength. She had never felt so valiant.

As Lila lay down, to sleep with the secure joy of that valor, she wondered how long the feeling would last. She knew that if it wore off, this would be her last peaceful sleep for a long time.

THE RULE-MAKERS

September 14

Filter third for reliability. This filter protects against politicians.
                      —*Zetetic Commentaries*

Nathan stewed quietly in the waiting room outside Charles Somerset's office. The clatter of obsolete typewriters echoed down the cold, plaster-cast hallways of the Pentagon. Nathan wondered how people could work here, and how they could think clearly in such a hostile environment. One answer chilled him: perhaps they *couldn't* think clearly here. Perhaps they couldn't think here at all.

He closed his eyes, washing out the sounds and the distractions, trying to wash the irritation from his mind as well. He knew he would need his greatest powers of perception for this meeting. Each of his few other attempts to talk with FIREFORS people had met with either curt civility or expansive emptiness, both well-designed to prevent outsiders like Nathan from acquiring useful information. Yet now the program manager of FIREFORS had asked to see him. That could only mean an ambush. What was the PM of FIREFORS planning?

He heard a door squeak on its hinges and opened his eyes.

At first Nathan thought he was looking at a successful, cultured street beggar. Charles wore a brown suit that might have been slept in; clearly, it had been cut to hang limply on its owner. His striped red tie sagged in a sloppy knot near the collar. His eyeglasses had slid far down his nose, and his hairline had receded far up his forehead.

Charles continued to open the door. His lethargic care with the task kept pace with the slow slide of his eyeglasses; his smile of greeting brightened in harmonic time with both.

His every movement seemed soggy except that of his eyes. Beneath heavy lids, they darted across Nathan's face and posture. "Welcome," Charles said with a voice of

144

dispassionate amusement. With a moment's energetic effort, he raised his eyebrows. "Welcome to the team."

"Welcome to what team?" Nathan asked as he followed the program manager through the door.

"Why, the FIREFORS team, of course."

Nathan studied the schizophrenic arrangement of books and papers in the office while Charles's words sank in. "What do you mean by that?"

"You're a member of the team now. *My* team." After showing Nathan a chair next to the conference table, Charles retrieved a single sheet of paper from his desk. "This is a letter from General Hicks to General Curtis, authorizing transfer of Sling Project oversight to FIREFORS. It was mailed yesterday."

Charles Somerset had gained the power to destroy the Sling. Nathan sensed Charles's condescending gaze upon him. He realized that in some drab yet hideous fashion, this moment qualified as a great victory for Charles.

"Of course, the letter probably won't penetrate the bureaucracy to your contracting officer until tomorrow. But I thought you should know about it as soon as possible. We need to get a jump on the changes we'll have to make in the Sling. We need to get it into line with the rest of our projects."

Nathan looked up at him for a painful moment, then accepted a copy of the letter—both to read it and to take a moment to collect his thoughts.

There has been too much national coverage—the words jumped at Nathan from a middle paragraph—*of supposed FIREFORS competition with the Sling Project. I agree with you: it makes no difference whether the competition is real or not. We must consolidate.*

Nathan stared at the letter for a long time, to recover for continuing the psychological game now underway. He knew who he needed here: he needed Leslie. Leslie, with his years of maneuvering through military politics, would have known how to respond. But he would be out of town all week.

It probably didn't make any difference. The letter, the change in organization, each was now a *fait accompli*. Had it been possible for the Institute to do anything about it, Somerset surely would not have offered the information.

What Nathan really wanted to do was cut and run—just leave the room and the Pentagon and Charles's smiling face behind. But Charles was now in some sense both his boss and his customer; however dangerous that might be, he would only aggravate the danger by being nasty.

Charles scraped a chair across the floor to join him. "You all right?" he asked with too much pleasure and too little concern.

"Of course," Nathan said, straightening to look Charles in the eye. "You realize that just because this letter has been mailed, this isn't official yet. Since I share your concerns about following proper procedures, I can't make any commitments without authorization from my contracting officer."

Charles seemed taken aback by the astuteness of this response, but he recovered quickly. "No problem, it will be official soon enough. I was just planning to give you some general guidance now, anyway. We'll have a more detailed discussion of the new directions after you talk with DNA. And we'll get really explicit, down to the nitty gritty, after a complete project review." Charles looked wistful for a moment. "If we had our way, we would put a stop work on the project temporarily, until our re-evaluation is complete." He paused, a look of distaste crossing his face. "But we haven't been authorized to do that."

Nathan suppressed a smile; Charles's victory had not been unconditional, anyway.

Charles waited for Nathan to respond. When no words came forth, he continued on his own, more than willing to handle the discussion solo. "As for our new general guidance, I'd like to start with a little thing. We've read the reports on the Sling. It looks like a fine piece of work, although a little primitive, compared to what we've been doing. One of the things we haven't seen anywhere is a discussion of how the warheads in the HighHunter—you call them Crowbars, I think—pick their targets."

Nathan frowned. "We're still working on the algorithm for selecting important objects, such as commanders' tanks. Is that what you mean?"

Charles mumbled something. From the uncertain sound in his voice, Nathan suspected that Charles might not know what he meant himself. "What I'm driving at is, do your Crowbars talk to each other, so they can guarantee that they fall on different tanks? How do they know they won't all hit the same one?"

"Ah, I see." Nathan nodded; Kurt had worried at that question for a long time. "We thought about it, but we decided we couldn't do that. There's not enough space in the Crowbar for the comm and not enough time to figure it out anyway. Each Crowbar will have a slightly different set of parameters, so they are likely to pick different targets."

Charles shook his head, a slow pendulum with a catch in it. "That isn't acceptable. The warheads must communicate and guarantee that they don't conflict."

Nathan just stared for a moment. "But that would be silly." He explained with a tone that softened the bluntness of the words, "It's not only expensive, it's unnecessary as well. The idea is to put a lot of Crowbars up there, and have a pile of them come down together, like hailstones. If we get ten percent of them hitting the same thing, all we have to do is launch ten percent more to start with."

The pendulum swung again. A grave look touched Somerset's darting eyes. "Listen. I know you're new to this contracting business, but there're some serious things you need to learn. First of all, we've got to deal with the Bill Hardies of the world. Think what it would sound like if *he* reported on this: 'The Army is building a weapon that hits itself almost as often as it hits the enemy.'" Charles looked concerned, like a teacher speaking privately to a slow student. "We aren't talking here about technical necessity, or economic sanity—we're talking about political survival in case the news media get excited about us. Do you understand?"

Nathan considered that the last news campaign had resulted in the letter he had just read, and he felt a surge of understanding for Somerset's game. "Yes, I see your point," he conceded. "You want to create a more workable political design. But I still disagree with your conclusion— because your political design is completely unworkable as an engineering design. The problem you're addressing is not a valid one upon which to make a political decision, because as engineers, we know a right answer."

Charles grunted. "Maybe so, but I want to keep the FIREFORS team funded." Getting no answer again, he pointed out the corollary. "I want to keep *you* funded."

Nathan sighed. "What is your next point of general guidance?"

"Since you're going to need a comm processor for the new Crowbar-to-Crowbar communication, I'd like to recommend—and frankly, we'll probably demand when the time comes—that you use the AN/UYK 93 computer for the job."

Nathan looked at him with puzzlement. "Isn't that computer still under development?"

Charles smiled. "I'm glad you've heard of it. We've been trying to get word around about it for some time. This is my first indication that we've succeeded. Yes, it's almost ready."

Disbelieving horror dried Nathan's throat. "How can you expect us to use something that doesn't exist yet?"

Charles waved a hand, dismissing Nathan's concern. "The spec's available."

"What if it doesn't meet our needs?"

The hand waved again. "No problem. We'll just change the spec."

Nathan could think of no retorts that were sufficiently irrational.

"And I hope that, for all your communication systems in all these different Hunter platforms, you're using our JANEP protocol family."

Nathan shook his head violently. "That would be crazy. No one uses those protocols anymore. They're obsolete."

A stern expression molded Somerset's pliant features. Nathan would not have guessed it would look so natural there. "*We* use those protocols in all our products. You *must* use them to stay compatible."

A stillness settled across the room—the stillness of a battlefield after the carnage. "How can you expect to succeed when half your system is 15 years obsolete, and the other half is five years short of being born?" With a stab of insight—the stab of a nail—Nathan remembered Leslie's story of the Maneuver Control System.

MCS, as it was known to friends and enemies, was a

computer system built for the Army back in the '70s and '80s. The contractor had been required to use a computer that was over ten years old, and a software toolkit that was still under development—and wouldn't be ready for years. The contract had been a great success: millions of dollars had been spent on old hardware and futuristic software. Only the less important third priority—the job of building a Maneuver Control System—had failed, slipping its schedule year after year.

Somehow, the Defense Department always had deep passions for the technologies of yesterday and the technologies of tomorrow. But they never tolerated the technologies of *today*. And tragically, the technologies of today were the only technologies worth using—the only ones a sane person would use to protect his society.

Charles removed his glasses. While he wiped them, he delivered the final guideline. "One last thing. This business of using commercial equipment has got to stop. Military equipment has to be survivable. So every component of the Sling Hunters has to be militarized."

Only the slightest move forward betrayed Nathan's desire to leap across the conference table and strangle the murderer of his child. "We can't do that! We haven't anywhere near the resources for that kind of undertaking, even if it made sense. The whole idea of the Sling is to build a family of disposable systems, like Dixie cups or TOW missiles."

Charles nodded. "I think I see your confusion. Of course you've never been able to think of militarizing your Hunters, because you didn't have the resources. That's where FIREFORS can help you, even as you are helping us. If the Sling Project is sufficiently important, we can get you the money."

"But the Project would be doomed from the start! It would be far too expensive to build in large quantities."

"That's for someone else to decide. We're only responsible for designing products to meet the military requirement. The financial problems with deployment are handled elsewhere. Mr. Pilstrom, even if we *wanted* to worry about the production cost, *we aren't allowed to*."

Nathan heard a hint of exhaustion in Somerset's voice—

the exhaustion of a man who had once in his life worried about problems beyond his current battle. He saw in Charles the end product of bureaucracy: a basically good man with one terrible fault. He had learned how to succeed in the distorted reality that bureaucracies create.

Charles continued, again willing to carry the conversation alone. "There's a second alternative. We do have permission to use commercial components for subsystems that aren't mission-critical."

Nathan listened with suspicion. "What does that mean, not mission-critical?"

"A subsystem is mission-critical if the troops would be unable to continue fighting without that subsystem. If the subsystem is that critical, it must meet mil spec. Doesn't that make sense? Something that critical must work correctly."

Something didn't seem to fit quite right in that analysis, but Nathan couldn't see the flaw at the moment. "I guess it makes sense."

"But if the troops can continue to fight effectively without it, then it's not mission-critical. Then you can make it less rugged. You still have to make it more rugged than average commercial stuff, of course, but you can bend the spec." Charles looked eager—almost too eager—to help solve this problem. "We could just declare the entire Sling Project to be non-mission-critical, thus allowing us to make it commercial. Considering your hostility to militarizing the Hunters, that's probably our best bet."

How sincere Charles sounded when he used the term "we"! Did Charles actually believe his statements about "our" team? He might. Nathan shrugged. "That sounds like an interesting alternative. But as I said earlier, I won't make any commitments until this transfer of control is official."

"Of course." Charles sighed, not angry, but perhaps saddened by the vision of a lengthy educational process. "No commitments," he agreed.

Kira's knuckles whitened on the steering wheel of her car as she cursed the traffic jammed up before her. To her left, through the blazing colors of the autumn leaves, she could see the Potomac: a muddy soup with puddles of rock jutting randomly into the gray air. To her right, above the line of the trees, she could see a skyscraper jutting into the equally gray skies. Even in the dull shadow of this autumn twilight, the Wilcox-Morris Building had not lost its silvery sheen. She could see Daniel's office perched like an aerie at the pinnacle. She remembered looking down from that office onto the Parkway, and feeling a mixed sense of sympathy and superiority toward the men and women trapped there.

Trapped! She was trapped by the Parkway, just as Daniel would soon have the Zetetic Institute trapped. She had finally penetrated the murky complexity of the Wilcox-Morris data bases, and she knew why Daniel wanted to meet Uncle Nathan. She knew who else would be there when Daniel met him, and she knew the inevitable consequences of that meeting.

She had to warn Uncle Nathan before he got to the Capitol for Senator Obata's book announcement. If she didn't—

Her leg drove against the clutch pedal as if that forward pressure could somehow be translated into motion. But neither her fury nor her determination could budge the megatons of steel blocking her way.

Charles slid his glasses along his nose as he leaned back in his judge's chair, stretching his legs beneath his desk. He contemplated the amusing possibilities for his future relationships with the Zetetic Institute.

He saw three potential futures. One, the most absurd, was that the Institute would simply come back and tell him that the Sling Project could not be run the way Charles demanded. In that case, he could simply cancel the project for cause and move the funding associated with it to one of his other projects. Of course, the sums of money he had picked up with the Sling Project were mere niblets compared with the fortunes already invested in FIREFORS, but every little bit helped.

The second possible future was that Nathan would agree to militarize the Sling's Hunters. That might generate some very interesting results. The Sling was popular in some circles, and Charles might well be able to soak up considerable quantities of next year's Federal budget working on such a modified project. And though he had enjoyed defeating the Institute in this small campaign, he held no grudges against them. If they played along with his goals as program manager of FIREFORS, he would be delighted to hand them a few contracts.

Frankly, he didn't understand Nathan's hostility to building a bigger, more expensive system. How could you grow a reputation in defense except by working on big projects? And big projects, by definition, spent big sums of money. Charles was not merely protecting and enriching his own empire by changing the course of the Sling Project: he was helping the Zetetic Institute as well! Certainly this second possibility was most profitable to both the Institute and to the FIREFORS office.

The third possible future was that Nathan would opt for the commercial approach by declaring the Sling systems nonmission-critical. This third possibility was most dangerous. The Sling Hunters fulfilled many of the same functions as other FIREFORS products, yet they would cost less than a tenth as much. The budget-watchers could conclude that the fully militarized systems weren't necessary, and then the FIREFORS budget would be slashed to the bone.

Fortunately, Charles had a solution to that problem, made possible by the very nature of the rules governing non-mission-critical development. Since the commercial version of the Sling would be non-mission-critical, that meant it was less important than mission-critical projects. So the next time Congress came sniffing around for budget cuts, Charles would naturally supply the non-mission-critical project—namely, the Sling—for the axe. By sacrificing this tiny project to the blood suckers, he would be able to protect his larger projects from the knife and could maintain his spending rates unimpaired.

So though the second possible future was most profitable, the third was most ironic: the Sling Project would destroy itself to protect his comprehensive FIREFORS projects—the very projects that the Sling had been designed to destroy.

He almost hoped the third future would prevail.

*   *   *

PAN. His eyes and his camera capture the overblown beauty of the men and women arriving in the Mansfield room of the Capitol. The sweep of the high, ornately carved walls enters his flatcam with sharp clarity; the room's narrow width and length are lost in the growing density of the crowd. Bill understands the purpose of this room, so well suited to optical illusion: with just a handful of people, Senator Obata's press men create the atmosphere of a vast, tightly packed throng.

CUT. Bill catches a short glimpse of himself in a gold-framed mirror above a brass serving table. He blends in perfectly with the crowd. He watches his own smirk as it reflects back from the mirror. No one could guess his intentions. His flatcam, decorated in a simple gold design that neatly camouflages its intricacy, nestles against a small carnation in his lapel.

ZOOM. Senator Hilan Forstil arrives: at last, someone of interest. With casual grace Bill follows as Forstil weaves through the crowd. He stops to talk. Bill recognizes Forstil's companion and smiles seeing his prey: Nathan Pilstrom.

FOCUS. Forstil says, "Nathan Pilstrom. I'm glad to see you. How is the Sling Project?"

CLOSE AND HOLD. Pilstrom grimaces. "Things were fine until early this afternoon. We finally solved all our staffing problems a few weeks ago, and we'd started to catch up our schedule.

"But an hour ago I met Charles Somerset, the program manager of FIREFORS, for the first time." He describes the takeover of the Sling by FIREFORS with fatigued anger. "We'll probably declare the project non-mission-critical, so we can continue with our current design."

Forstil nods. "You know, the FIREFORS position sounds reasonable, as far as militarizing mission-critical items. The essential systems need to be survivable."

"It sounded reasonable to me, too, until I discussed it with Leslie Evans, who's in charge of the systems integration. He pointed out the flaw quite clearly." Pilstrom settles himself into a professor's posture. "Suppose a function is mission-critical. But now suppose that the mil-spec box for this function is so expensive that we can't build

enough of them. Then, by definition, the more critical the
function is, the less likely we are to get it." Nathan rolls
his eyes. "The Sling, in its unmilitarized form, can eliminate the need for tactical nuclear weapons. Isn't that somehow mission-critical?"

SLIDE. A short man standing nearby perks up. He
turns to Pilstrom. "Eliminate nuclear weapons? How?"

ROLL. Pilstrom assesses the man as he would assess a
delicate goblet, deciding how much information he may
pour into this container before it overflows. "There's a
long answer and a short answer. The short answer—an
answer so short that it's misleading—is that, if we want to
eliminate nuclear weapons, all we have to do is build a
better weapon."

FOCUS. The man's face falls.

ROLL. Pilstrom continues. "But that's not as horrible as
it sounds. Something few people understand is that nuclear bombs make lousy weapons."

The man's expression turns to curiosity, matching Senator Forstil's.

"Remember, the purpose of a weapon is not to obliter-
ate the countryside. The purpose is to stop the enemy.
But that's exactly the opposite of the effect of a nuclear
blast. Nukes are great for killing farmers for miles around.
But do you have any idea how difficult it is to kill a guy
driving a tank?"

The short man sputters. "But surely if you drop nukes
on a bunch of soldiers you kill a lot of them."

Pilstrom nods. "But fewer than you might think. A nuke
is better than ordinary bombs. But if you plant ordinary
bombs very carefully—if you increase the informational
content of those bombs, and nothing else—only a handful
of those ordinary bombs would make a better weapon than
a nuclear bomb."

CUT. The gathering crowd around Pilstrom forces Bill
to shift position. The room is crammed with people, yet
somehow, the densest crowd rings around a small breathing space occupied by Senator Forstil and Nathan Pilstrom.

Forstil speaks. "I grant all that. But I still don't see why
we couldn't make the Sling systems mil-spec."

"We shouldn't make the Sling systems mil-spec primarily because that's not the right path to survivability for this system. There are at least two paths to making a system survivable. One is to make it very tough: make it mil-spec. The other alternative is to make it very cheap, so you can make lots of copies. Though every case is different, American history suggests that the second alternative is as viable as the first; indeed, the triumph of America has often rested on the second alternative. Look at our tanks in World War II. The Germans had better tanks, but the American commercial economy had developed mass production methods so powerful that we could pour tanks into the field until we overwhelmed them. Similarly, the German submarines sank four hundred ships in the last year of the war—but America *built* seven hundred! We *buried* them in our productivity."

BACK OFF. Nathan's voice breaks across the room with a forceful confidence that damps out other voices. An eerie silence hushes even the tinkling of the champagne glasses. Bill feels suddenly conspicuous. He accepts a small hors d'oeuvre sprinkled with caviar from the passing waiter. He is not hungry, but he chews it drily and swallows. The caviar leaves a salty aftertaste in his mouth.

ZOOM. "This power of the economy to work for America's defense is the unique strength that made us inconquerable. It's the power that we've lost sight of. It is the power that the Zetetic Institute is trying to restore with the Sling Project—the vitality, the creativity, the effectiveness of the best of our industry." His voice falls to the level of a personal vow. "Societies built around the principles of war have great difficulty learning to turn their swords into plowshares. America, a society built around peace, must always remember how to turn its plowshares into swords."

Another man in the crowd shifts forward just an inch —the distance of a thrust jaw. "If you're so much in love with our free enterprise system, why are you trying to destroy it?"

Pilstrom turns in astonishment. "What do you mean?"

"The Zetetic Institute's the bunch of weirdos who're trying to destroy advertising, isn't it?"

TURN. Bill suppresses a laugh. The man is repeating words from one of his newscasts.

ZOOM. Pilstrom gives a gentle rebuttal that twists Bill's internal laughter to dismay. He replies, "You've heard too many newscasters distorting the truth. We don't want to destroy advertising. We want to destroy *manipulative* advertising. We want to eliminate the kind of advertising that persuades the listener to buy *in spite* of the best information, rather than because of it. We want people to filter the informational content from commercial advertising—and all too often, when an advertisement is run through an informational filter, nothing is left.

"But there are many useful forms of advertising. Come to the Institute, and we'll show you some examples. Good advertising doesn't get enough good advertising these days."

PAUSE. The conversation stops. The crowd seems suspended—not quite ready to abandon the play of strong convictions, but not willing to wait for the conversation to pick up again.

PAN. A tall, immaculately dressed man steps out of the crowd, quickly, gracefully—a silent, defiant presence.

Bill studies the man. His camera captures the charm, but his mind does not quite grasp its source. The man stands with a relaxed straightness, as though looking down from a great height. He is not as handsome as Bill himself; the face is too narrow, the eyes too calculating for that. But only the senator comes close to projecting so much *presence*, and even for the senator, the projection is not effortless. For this man it is inevitable, as natural as breathing.

The intruder speaks. "What you're doing to advertisers isn't half as bad as what you're doing to our civil liberties."

ZOOM. Nathan looks completely baffled. "What do you think we've done to your civil liberties?"

"For one thing, you're attacking our right to smoke."

Nathan laughs, though a nervous catch suggests he wonders if both the criticism and the response are too obvious. "That would be an amazingly inaccurate analysis. Our relationship to liberty is quite the opposite: we're *restoring* people's rights. Two-thirds of the people who smoke don't want to. We help them regain their right to choose. Everyone who comes to our clinics volunteers."

The tall man's eyes hold steady, filled with accusation. "I'm speaking of the tens of thousands of men and women

who depend upon the tobacco industry for their liveli-
hoods. You're depriving them of their freedom to earn a
living doing what they do best."

"People do their best when creating better ways to live,
and better ways to earn livings. Creating something better
takes some ingenuity, and a lot of hard work. But the
search for better ways to live has been a part of our society
since the beginning of the Industrial Age. We don't deprive anyone of their ability to create something better;
we enhance it."

"But you can't deny that the end of the tobacco industry
would devastate the economy of North Carolina."

"Yes, it would devastate North Carolina—but only if
every smoker quit smoking at the same time. No matter
what the Zetetic Institute does, that's an unlikely outcome. We couldn't destroy North Carolina even if we
wanted to, which we don't."

"I know exactly how you'd do it. You'd destroy us exactly the way you *are* destroying us. You would encourage
other anti-smoking groups to attack us more violently,
with laws that restrict our freedom."

PAN. Something about the stranger has seemed wrong
to Bill since the beginning of the conversation. The stranger
speaks of the people who smoke as his own people, yet
Bill cannot imagine this graceful, commanding man with a
cigarette in his hand. The collision of his mind's image and
the camera's image gives Bill a moment of internal discord.

"Only people who don't hear the whole Zetetic message
react in that manner."

"But some of them do. Your lectures often fail—and
that's your fault as much as the listener's. So the vicious-
ness of the attacks on smokers rises every time your Institute speaks. Or do you deny your responsibility for inciting
those attacks?"

ZOOM. Bill realizes that the stranger has made a brilliant jab. Zetetics have a complex concept of responsibility—so complex that it plays out as confusion in short
newscasts.

Nathan lowers his head. "No. We know that we can
never do just one thing. We accept partial responsibility
for creating the tension that promotes those attacks—just

as we accept partial responsibility for the extra years of life
people earn when they stop smoking."

SPLAT. A bright pink liquid smacks against Bill's face,
blinding him. Gasping, he inhales the fragrance and tastes
the sweetness of the champagne punch.

WHUFF. Another rainburst of champagne plasters his
chest. It strikes his camera, drenching it with a short-
circuiting, rose-colored tint. Bill is crippled—rendered as
helpless as a quarterback struck in the gut by a hurtling
lineman. He can no longer pan or zoom or focus.

THUNK. A woman's head and shoulders press against
him. He blinks his eyes, clearing them so that he can see
the tackler. She leans against him, her face and hair buried against his chest. Her perfume has a subtle scent, yet
it reaches Bill despite the overpowering effervescence of
the champagne.

She lurches against him again, then straightens and
looks up at his astonished face. He sees blue eyes, too
beautiful to ignore; they remind Bill of the quiet blue of
the deep waters of Puget Sound. She steps back unsteadily. Her hand rises to cover her mouth in embarrassment; her other hand holds an empty glass. "I'm so sorry,"
the tipsy beauty apologizes. "Let me clean you off." She
closes on him again and commences to suck the champagne from his shirt.

He grabs her by the shoulders to thrust her away, but she
buries her nose deeper in his chest, close to his throat; he
weakens under the caress. Under the force of her forward
motion, Bill steps backward, clinging to her awkwardly.

The confrontation continues between Nathan Pilstrom
and the tall stranger. But it is beyond Bill's reach, now
that this woman has ruined his flatcam. He looks around; a
new crowd grows around him, deciding that the Zetetic
Institute is not as interesting as a drunken woman and a
champagne-spattered man. With a sweeping glare he
strengthens his grip on the girl, turns, and half-carries her
from the room. Without his camera, there is no point in
staying anyway.

As they cross the entranceway, she utters a wicked
laugh. Her hands run around his waist, burrow deep in his
back pockets. "Did I get your attention?" she asks.

Bill flushes; the air in the hall cools his forehead, but he burns with heat from the woman's hands, from her mouth upon his throat. He mutters incoherently. She replies with a murmur that tingles against the delicate skin beneath his ear lobe.

Who the hell is this person, anyway? Many women have thrown themselves at him before, with his handsome face and famous name; many more women would beg a night with him in the future.

Some have been even more beautiful than this one, though she is quite striking. He pushes her away; she caresses his hands, running her fingertips lightly up his forearm, bringing his fingers in contact with her neck, her cheeks.

He shakes himself, determined to master the situation. Though other lovers have been more beautiful, this one is . . . *special.* Her wide green eyes beckon to him from beneath lightly colored eyelids, a touch of makeup that is perfect, as though this woman has studied him, has analyzed his desires, has created psychometric charts of his behavior and now has come to lure him—but lure him where? Away from the confrontation brewing inside? It's too late to prevent the destruction of the Zetetic Institute—he has all the footage he needs. Besides, the woman has already succeeded if that is her purpose—he remembers with a small wrenching feeling the destruction of his flatcam.

Does she just want to lure him back to his apartment? He asks her; she answers yes.

He takes her, with her maddening eyes and teasing hands, back to his home. In the living room, her attack upon his shirt renews; he is half-unbuttoned before he can disengage to retreat to his bedroom and remove his flatcam. He slips the tape into his video system, a vast complex of the best equipment in the world.

He returns to her. Again the wrestling begins—but this time the girl struggles with an opponent who is free to respond to her every movement.

Now she weakens in turn. She escapes his arms and hurries to the bedroom, promising a quick return. He waits; the door opens; she strides out with a new and

sober awareness. Her dress covers her again with full
propriety; her eyes hold a cold glare. She utters a single
furious epithet, swings the front door of the apartment
wide, and leaves in a shattering slam of wooden door
against metal frame.

Bill lies still a moment, then, leaping to his feet, howls
in hopeless, helpless, furious frustration.

He calms himself. His life, his soul are not enmeshed
with the intricate peculiarities of the female mind. His
heart is in his flatcam. He returns to his bedroom to see
the material he has collected, with which to destroy the
Zetetic Institute.

The tape begins. Nothing. Nothing. Nothing. He howls
again and wrenches the tape from its drive. Yes, it is the
original.

With disbelief he replaces the tape and skips, faster and
faster, across its surface. It is blank. She has destroyed it.
She has cut out his heart.

His backup! Always upon returning home with fresh
video, he starts the backup recorder to cut a dupe. He
reaches for it now. With trembling fingers, he jabs the
buttons to begin its replay.

Words and images flow to him: the Mansfield room and
the debates of Nathan Pilstrom.

The woman destroyed his tape, but she did not destroy
his newscast. He turns from the video player; the tape's
contents burn brightly in his brain without amplification.
Playing it in its entirety, the Zetetic Institute sounds heroic. But there are moments of value.

"To eliminate nuclear weapons, all we have to do is
build better weapons"—the words of a world-destroyer.

"Turn plowshares into swords"—the words of a warmonger.

"Yes, it would devastate North Carolina"—the words of
an unfeeling theorizer.

"We accept partial responsibility for the attacks on
smokers"—the words of a fanatic.

Bill clenches his fist. He feels the harsh strength of the
crushing motion and smiles in satisfaction.

October 2

How emotionally entangled are you with your point of view? Test yourself— defend an opposing view, believing your life depends upon it.

—Zetetic Commentaries

Leslie paused at the beginning of the corridor. Nathan, he knew, never walked this hall without taking a moment to gaze at the PERT chart. The Sling Project's PERT chart dominated the walls, burying the oak veneer beneath thousands of modern hieroglyphics. Often Leslie passed it by without a glance; but then, Leslie traveled the hall far more often than Nathan.

When Leslie did pause amid the colorful lines and boxes, he did so to study the individual branches, to prune and tend and nurture them; the PERT chart was the incarnation of his part of the project. He gave the chart the same intense concentration that programmers gave to their software. In such a manner, he concentrated upon the branches this morning.

The green forest had grown with stately decorum, overrunning many of the boxes that had once glared pink or even red with danger. The pink had settled into a thin band creeping up one wall and down the other, separating the green past from the uncolored, black-lined boxes of future. The whole project raced against that pink band, trying to turn it to green before it could reach farther into the black. A program manager considered his forest's growth acceptable as long as the band of pink did not thicken, as long as it did not grow faster than the trailing green, and as long as it did not turn red. For a moment, he postponed his considerations of the meaning of the red.

The black future had become clearer: the first order of business for the software team had been to break up the major software tasks into exhaustive lists of carefully cir-

161

cumscribed, well-defined subtasks. *To define is to limit.*
Leslie could hear Jan telling him the Zetetic comment, a
phrase stolen from Oscar Wilde. In the initial steps of a
project, when flights of creative fancy supplied the ideas
critical to success, you needed to be careful not to define
the problem too well, lest it limit the creative process. But
once those initial concepts had sparked together, fusing at
last into a clear vision, it became equally critical to define,
to limit, with ruthless vigor. You did not want to be
surprised halfway through the engineering that transformed
ideas into products.

Amos, Juan, Kurt, and Lila had done an excellent job in
defining the Sling Project's transformation path. They had
completed the details for the PERT chart. Sadly, this
brought to bear another Zetetic commentary on the
lightning-speed Information Age: *If it is complete, it must
be obsolete.* Obsolescence occurred when the PERT chart's
unbendingly factual description of the present offered no
hope of reaching the planned future. On the Sling, a
handful of urgent tasks already burned with the heat of a
forest fire, threatening to consume that future.

The red boxes told this story. The single red box that
had driven him and Nathan so hard to find Amos and Juan
and Lila now lay in tranquil green, but before its transmu-
tation, it had ignited speckles of new, bright fires.

Since Amos had started, he had put out many fires,
healing a number of the newer red boxes to forest green.
Other green boxes, representing the work of so many
people, might grow toward the pink in an impersonal race,
but the reds and pinks that dominated the software team's
future represented personal battles. Those battles would
take everything they had to give. They didn't have time to
fight the absurd political battles that FIREFORS now
demanded of them. They didn't have time to play absurd
games because of a ban on telecommuting.

Leslie couldn't believe that the politicians had really
pulled such a stupid stunt. Nathan had pointed out the
analogy to the home-based sewing industry and its destruction by the textile mills, but Leslie didn't buy it at
first. There were surely more telecommuters to fight this
ban today than there had been clothing makers to fight

that earlier law. On the other hand, the telecommuters were not organized as a political force. Sanity had no effect on politicians unless it was concentrated in a power bloc. The organized power blocs belonged to the older, Industrial Age institutions, such as the tobacco companies.

Kira had uncovered the tobacco industry's sudden support for the ban only days before the congressional voting. Hilan Forstil had called to alert them to the same problem on the same day, furious and apologetic that he had been kept in the dark so effectively by other members of Congress up on the Hill. Leslie found it unbelievable that the tobacco companies could wield so much power, but Kira had described lists of senators, representatives, regulators, newsmen, and others of influence whom the tobacco industry could in turn influence.

Of course, the tobacco industry had not implemented this attack alone. The Institute had stepped on a surprising number of toes, considering its tiny size. Nathan saw a deeper meaning in the new attack: the Zetetic Institute was the first power structure of the Information Age. It had grown just large enough to attract the notice of the Industrial Age power structures. The corporate oligarchies, the unions, the news media, the government bureaucracies—all the old institutions that held power—could see the dark glimmers of their fading importance in a new society. Their survival depended on the destruction of the Institute. Only extraordinary forces could deflect their opposition to the Information Age.

Too late, the Institute itself had become the rallying point for the telecommuters. Kira had started organizing opposition, with Hilan's help. A quick analysis had shown that they could not prevent the ban from going into effect: they could only hope to revoke the law before it dismembered the telecommuting work force. With a chill, Leslie understood why the laws against selling homemade clothing had never been reversed: when the unions broke the home manufacturers in the first battle, they left no one able to fight. Struggling to make a new livelihood, the losers had no strength left over with which to fight the politicians.

Now the Institute had to battle with the union/tobacco

coalition, the FIREFORS bureaucracy, and the sheer technical difficulty of making the Sling work, all at the same
time. These simultaneous campaigns demanded more than
the Institute had to give.

In turn, Leslie and the Institute were demanding more
of Amos than he would agree to give. Amos had been testy
when Leslie had explained to him that he couldn't
telecommute on this first day of the ban. He had dismissed Leslie's careful explanations of how important it
was for Amos to drive to the Institute. He had complained
that the primitive nature of the Institute's equipment would
hideously impair his productivity, compared with what he
could achieve at home.

Finally, Amos had surrendered under the unrelenting
stream of Leslie's combination of apologies and pointed
reminders. The harshest point was that, if Amos did not
come in for work, there would soon be no Institute to
work for.

The Institute was the most closely scrutinized corporation in the country: over a dozen government regulators
would roam the halls to ensure that all the Zetetic workers
in the city were working on-site. Authorities throughout
the nation supervised Institute projects, ready to make
arrests and pass incredible fines for the least infraction of
the new laws. If they carried out the maximum legal
penalties, they could destroy the Institute in a few days.
Apparently, as the Institute grew stronger as the rallying
point for the telecommuters, it also grew more important as
a target for the opposition. Nathan's analysis seemed correct: the Institute now lay at the heart of the maelstrom.

As Leslie walked past the last of the red boxes on the
PERT chart, he thought again about Amos.

Amos had been as close to anger as Leslie had ever seen
him. The idea of driving through rush-hour traffic did not
suit him. "Amos, stay cool," Leslie had said. "In a couple
of weeks, this whole thing will calm down. When that
happens, you can call in sick every damn day of the week,
and work on 'hobbies' all the time. Then, when you complete a program module, you come in for one day, and we
pay you a huge amount of money for that day's work. Your
'hobbies' will coincidentally look a great deal like stuff we

need, but so what? We'll fight it in court." Amos offered to be sick immediately, but Leslie answered, "I'm sorry, Amos, we can't do it yet. Just hang in there for a couple of weeks. Or rather, hang out here for a couple of weeks."

Leslie hurried to his office to watch for Amos's arrival. When he reached his window, the view filled him with horror.

Many people had spoken of the increase in traffic that the ban on telecommuting would create. The intersection at Sunrise Valley and South Lakes Drive had been a nightmare for years, even in light traffic. In heavy traffic, with ex-telecommuters who hadn't driven in rush hour for years, the intersection filled with a swirling mob of crazies.

But this was not the ugliness on the scene that most terrified Leslie. A mob of protesters packed the sidewalk in front of the Institute's driveway. Had Leslie not come in at an ungodly early hour of the morning, he would have had to confront this mob himself. Reading the signs they carried, he saw that they had come as a result of Bill Hardie's news broadcast the night before. Hardie had used clips from Senator Obata's reception—a series of Nathan's statements ripped from context, like obscene entrails ripped from the guts of a beautiful animal. Leslie had seen only part of it; he could not stand to see facts twisted with such expert malevolence.

Staring out the window, he felt overwhelmed by the effect of that broadcast. What a tragic coincidence, that the mob should block the entrance to the Institute on the very day that the government inspectors started demanding their presence! He called the police even though he realized how futile it was: how could even the police penetrate the tortured jam of steaming automobiles?

One of the cars ensnared in the traffic—a bright yellow Toyota—dodged around the barriers and broke through the throng, turned down the quiet lane toward the Institute, then slowed as it approached the Institute's driveway, as if planning to enter. But the mob apparently dissuaded the driver; he accelerated past the crowd as several fists shook after him.

By the time he disappeared around the corner, he had accelerated to an insane speed. Whoever he was, he had superb reflexes, unbounded confidence, and a total disregard for other drivers and legal restraints. Nuts like that fellow made the road dangerous for everybody. It took Leslie a moment to realize that the nut behind the wheel was Amos Leung.

Leslie watched the crest of the hill over which the Toyota had gone with odd confidence. Amos would surely return.

A few moments later his solitary figure, small and dark, eased over the hill with a fluid swiftness that blended with the windblown movement of the bushes. His direction shifted off to the right. Leslie realized that Amos was heading for the rear doors of the Institute, away from the mob. He almost made it, before someone in the mob spotted him.

Part of the mob hurried to block his path. The speed and efficiency of this small group surprised Leslie; then he noticed that the hurrying men seemed different from the main body of protesters. They were huskier, and they moved more purposefully.

The combination of the ban and the mob didn't seem like a coincidence anymore. Someone had planted thugs here to ensure that the Institute couldn't meet the requirements of the law.

What could he do? The building was mostly empty; he could not assemble his own mob to counter the one outside.

But Kurt was here. He might qualify as a mob all by himself. Leslie ran through the building yelling for him.

It took only a few gasping words to propel McKenna into action. Leslie trailed after him and considered the possible foolishness of this rescue effort. Of all the people he knew, Amos was the one most capable of taking care of himself.

Amos had grown up the son of a quiet, retired Chinese master of arms. His training had started when he had learned to stand. He had practiced every day with the diligence and discipline of a Soviet gymnast—with shuriken, with swords, with his bare hands. Leslie remembered a story Amos had once told of a confrontation in a New York subway. Three teenagers had encircled him. With his back to the wall, he had offered them his wallet, but they were not interested. They drew knives.

Amos had considered disarming them, but their combination of numbers and weapons introduced a small risk to himself. He had therefore decided to disable them. Several minutes later, he had called the ambulance for them.

But outside the Institute he faced more than three assailants. As Leslie burst out of the door, he saw that Amos stood backed against a tree. He seemed impassive and quiet; only the odd way he held himself suggested danger to the knowing watcher. Someone reached for him.

Amos seemed to disappear. An invisibly fast force leaped from where he had stood, a force that touched one thug after another. You could see the progression of the force by the roll of violent jerking across the crowd. The thugs dropped in stunning succession. Leslie heard the soft, soggy sound of human bodies falling.

The violent force paused for a moment; Amos appeared where it had left off, reorienting himself. The remaining thugs held their ground, but seemed dazed by the attack. Amos disappeared again.

A gunshot barked. Amos reappeared, sliding across the green grass. When the sliding stopped, Amos lay unmoving, his face filled with the impassive calm Leslie had known so often. Now, however, his calmness seemed unnatural.

Leslie returned to the building and called the police again. A helicopter came to the rescue, filled with paramedics. They arrived too late.

Kira stood before the flat dullness of the apartment door and stared into the peephole. Of course, from her side of the door, she could see nothing. But she had come for a confrontation; let it start even now, before the door opened. With an angry swing of her wrist, she raised the knocker and struck home once, twice, three times.

She waited. Dull thudding suggested the motion of a large man. When the sound stopped, she knew he had come to the peephole, and that his confusion mounted with every passing moment. She smiled disarmingly, and wondered whether the smile confused him even more.

Click. The door sprang open in response to the strength
of a forceful man, a determined man. Bill Hardie stared
down at her with an astonishing display of teeth, halfway
between a smile of greeting and a snap of fangs. Though
he spoke softly, his voice blurred with the intensity of his
emotion. "You wiped my tape," he said.

"Yes." They stared at each other, fencers seeking an
opening. "Let me in," she said.

His eyes widened with amazement, then amusement.
His arms spanned the distance from the door to the door-
frame, blocking her entry. He crossed his legs into a more
casual stance. With this simple motion he declared how
little of his power he needed to deny her demand.

Kira stepped forward, crossing the threshold. Now, to
close the door, he would have to physically push her away.
Her eyes drew down from his half-mocking eyes, across
the dark tan of his throat, slightly mottled in color, to his
open shirt collar. She could see the lean lines of muscles
spreading across the exposed part of his chest; she could
sense their extension under the cotton of his shirt, down
his arms to the massive strength of his hands. He had
large hands—hands meant to lift great weights, to hold
and control the flight of a ballerina.

She stepped forward again, a small step. She could feel
the slow, steady surge of his breath as he exhaled.

Her smile widened as she reached forward to press her
hands against him, to force him to accept her arrival. With
his arms spread wide, he was completely vulnerable, even
though he stood unyielding before her.

He did not let her touch him. With the snap of an
uncoiling spring, Bill whirled away. One hand still held
the door. His other hand turned up, offering her the
sweep of the living room. "Please, the apartment is yours,"
he said with a mocking lilt in his voice. "You can go
anywhere but the bedroom."

"I'm flattered. I doubt that you make that offer to other
women who come here." She flipped her hair behind her
head and strode into the living room. He followed at a
distance, the hint of a swagger in his step.

She tossed her briefcase on one end of the couch and
turned to face him. She caught him watching her legs, the

firmness of her calves. For a moment, she allowed him to enjoy the sight of her body. "I came to tell you what a jerk you are."

His eyes flew up to her face in contempt. "What a jerk *I* am? Should I remind you that *you* are the one who destroyed *my* property?"

Kira pushed his comment aside with a wave of her hand. "The way I deceived you is nothing compared to the way you've deceived people all over the world."

"Really." He was mocking her again. He crossed his arms. One shoulder dropped as he leaned toward her. He made Kira think of a tree bowing into the wind. "I've given them the truth!"

"You've given them perversions of the truth." Kira warmed with anger at his sarcastic attitude. "You've twisted the language from a means of helping people think, to a weapon to shut the mind off. You've denied them the undistorted facts needed to form intelligent opinions."

"Undistorted facts!" His arms broke apart, then slapped against his legs as he snorted. "A newscast doesn't have the time for undistorted facts, little girl. But that's okay, because I give my audience something better: undistorted truth. I collect all those facts of yours together and distill them to find the truth. And then I select the facts that best present the truth, and give the people *those* facts. That's the problem with you Zetetics—you are Zetetic, right? You have this cockeyed idea that facts are more important than truth."

"Unfortunately, there's a massive flaw in your definition of truth. You don't understand that you can only extract the truth from the facts by using an unbiased mind."

"An unbiased mind?" Bill rolled his eyeballs. "Your Zetetics are biased all the time. Every one of your experts wears his biases like a collar on a dog. You can't describe a problem to them without hearing about their lists of starting prejudices."

"But of course. A Zetetic expert is trained to recognize his own biases, and state the assumptions that form the basis of his arguments. And he is trained to know the one form of bias that can be tolerated. It is the one form of bias that *must* be tolerated—the bias that makes good thinking possible."

Kira watched Bill squeeze his lips together as if he knew that she was waiting for his cue, as if he knew that he should not give it to her, as if he knew that he would give it to her anyway. "And what is this one oh-so-important bias?"

"The bias of extensive knowledge. The man who has detailed knowledge about the ten alternatives under consideration has the right—has the *duty*—to bias his opinion based on that knowledge. The legitimate expert always has a bias based on his information."

"Sure, little girl. Just how do you tell whether he's biased by his information or by his emotion?"

"There are at least two ways." She ticked the alternatives off with her fingers. "The first way is to have him tell you all his information and to make your own decision based on that. The second is to watch him as he gathers new information. If his bias is based on information, it will change as the information arrives. If his bias is based on emotion, it won't change until he's faced with personal destruction."

"And that's how you think I am, right? I won't change my opinion until I'm faced with personal destruction?" Mockingly he held his hands forward, clenched in the fists of a boxer. "Do you plan to destroy me?"

"I don't know." She turned from him to open her briefcase, and riffled through it for papers. The pause gave her a chance to reflect on the meaning of her upcoming actions. Softly, sympathetically, she continued, "I came to tell you that in addition to being a jerk, you're a stupid jerk."

"Oh ho." Bob. Weave. "You almost got me that time. You have a great vocabulary, did you know that?"

"Yes." Her moment of weakness, her sympathy, passed easily. "And you're a dupe as well. A puppet. A puppet of the Wilcox-Morris Corporation—the biggest tobacco company in the world."

Bill stopped waving his hands in the air. "What?"

She turned to the first page of a thick folder and started reading. It was merely a list of undistorted facts; she left the truth to Bill to determine. The facts listed were the names and positions of people who were invited to parties and sporting events and special art exhibitions. People from magazines and advertising agencies and television stations—all the people who had even the least chance of influencing decisions to give a special newscaster a special chance.

The facts included a list of the special-interest groups supported by Wilcox-Morris donations, with their newsletters that suggested which newscasters might be most interesting to listen to. It described pep talks with employees of tobacco companies, in which certain programs and articles received glowing praise, and where the employees heard that writing to the owners of those magazines and TV stations to praise certain editorials might be helpful to the survival of their companies, and the survival, therefore, of their jobs.

The facts included the dates when these campaigns of hidden persuasion peaked: they matched the dates of Bill's strongest attacks against the Zetetic Institute. The correspondence formed a fascinating nonfactual but possibly true study in coincidence.

Bill tore the folder from her hands and stared at the mere facts for himself. His proud face took on the lines of tortured anguish. She knew he wanted to tear the folder to pieces and fling it in her face, but he could not quite do it. His disrespect for facts did not run quite deep enough.

He spoke with the tense strength of a violin string snapping. "None of this could make the difference. I had to be able to make it without them; they didn't force anybody to cover me."

"Yes, you poor fool." Kira shook her head. "You *could* have made it on your own. That's what made you the perfect dupe. They had to find someone with the talent to become a great newscaster. Then all they had to do was give him the chance—and make sure that he learned, indirectly, that his chances came fastest when he did the work *they* wanted done. They needed someone to attack the Zetetic Institute. They found him."

She watched his jaw muscles swell and subside. She softened again. She knew that she herself had played loose with the difference between fact and truth in this encounter. "Let me point out that I have lied several times since I arrived here." He jumped, as if afraid of the touch of her words. "As a Zetetic scholar, I must point out the inaccuracies of my statements. It is not true that you are a jerk; it is only true that you have *acted* like a jerk many times. Nor is it true that you are stupid; you have only *acted* stupid repeatedly. Nor is it true that you are a dupe; you have the power to stop being a dupe, or an idiot, or a jerk, any time you desire. All you have to do is choose to think."

His eyes were upon her face, yet he did not see her. For the first time, she noticed the scars on his knuckles, and wondered what fights he had fought, what walls he had beaten to take such hurts.

When she left, he still stood in the center of the room, a tree that has been cracked in the middle, but that has not quite broken.

December 8

*America never remembers the past. The
Soviet Union never forgets.*
> —*Industrial Age Societies:
> A Historical Perspective*

Leslie stood outside the intricately etched doorway, reluctant even to make his presence known. He felt the eyes
of the kid behind him, and the eyes of the house in front
of him. None of it felt good.

This time the house did not sing to him with Amos
Leung's voice. He searched the porch for a doorbell,
found none. As he finished searching, the door opened.

Flo—beautiful, graceful Flo—appeared as a wraith. "Colonel Evans. You are quite punctual." She spoke with the
same melodious precision as always, but with little animation. "Please come in."

Les stepped to the side, motioning to Ronnie. "Thanks.
But first let me introduce Ronnie Dwyer. Ronnie just
finished his MS in computer science from RPI. We're
hoping he can help you with the comm problems."

Squeezing his hands together nervously, Ronnie stepped
forward and shook hands with Flo.

Flo smiled with good grace, saying, "I am pleased to
meet you."

Ronnie offered her a smile in return and mumbled
hello.

The living room in red and gold had not changed; only
the encompassing presence of Amos Leung was absent.
Leslie kicked one of the beautiful cushions accidentally.
The feeling of goatlike awkwardness that Amos always
brought upon him returned. He snorted.

"What did you say, Colonel Evans?" Flo asked.

"Nothing," Les replied. In some sense, Amos Leung's
presence remained.

"Would you care for some tea?"

173

Les nodded, but Ronnie spoke rapidly. "No thanks. I don't drink caffeine."

Les rolled his eyes; Flo just smiled at the boy. "I see. Do you drink water?"

"Uh, yeah."

Flo disappeared into the kitchen.

They sat in the quiet peace of Amos's living room for a while. At length Ronnie whispered, "She's beautiful."

"She certainly is. She's also old enough to be your mother."

"I guess so. Man, I wish I were here for some reason other than because her husband . . ."

The cup of tea appeared beside Leslie's cheek, giving off a warm and luscious aroma. "Because my husband died?" Flo finished the sentence.

Ronnie choked; Flo handed him his water.

"My husband was a wonderful man. It will be a great challenge for us to complete our small project without him." She turned away for a moment, then turned back. "But we shall."

Ronnie jumped into the work at hand. "What exactly was Dr. Leung working on at the end?"

"We had submitted part of the HopperHunter's obstacle-dodging software to Mr. Dante-Cortez for testing."

"Have you gotten the results back?"

"Yes. It worked quite well." Flo did not notice the look of shock on Ronnie's face; that kind of software could not possibly work well on first test. Leslie easily guessed the thoughts behind Ronnie's expression: *No one writes code that good.* Flo continued, "Of course, we had planned to make a few optimizations. The responsiveness of the simulated Hopper lagged when approaching a ridge crest."

Ronnie sipped his water. "What kind of documentation do you have for this stuff?"

"I am the documentation," Flo sang. She pointed at her head. "It is all here. That is why we will work together." She turned to Leslie. "I am sorry I cannot complete this task on my own. I did not . . . quite . . . learn enough to create new software by myself."

Leslie shook his head. "Of all the things to worry about,

Flo, that's not one of them. I think Ronnie'll fill the missing part of this team quite effectively."

Leslie listened to the two new partners as they spoke together. The contrast struck him as garish—perhaps similar to the one Amos might have seen when Leslie himself spoke with Florence.

They agreed that they would continue to work there in Flo's home, since the development system Amos had built was unique. Leslie shook his head in amazement. Ronnie didn't belong here, in this house filled with Amos's presence, and surely Flo knew it. Her pain at the thought must be terrific, yet it remained submerged when she spoke. Only her gauntness and a heaviness in her walk that few would notice revealed her sorrow.

Les yearned to take Flo into another room, to talk with her, to reach inside and caress her mind. Her loss in Amos paralleled his own loss in Jan.

He did not attempt to console her. He knew he could not reach behind her smile and her bright eyes, for an unyielding *differentness* sheltered her. Les realized that the house *could* yield to Ronnie's strange presence. Flo might even redecorate, an affirmation of the reality of her loss. She would adapt, brilliantly, outside that inner differentness.

In the meantime, Les saw hope that this unlikely collaboration would work. For the Sling's sake, it had to: on the PERT chart outside his office, a blood-red stream of boxes carved a grim scar across the body of the Sling.

Yurii smiled. Despite the harsh snow outside, despite the gentle crumbling of the General Secretary across the table, he felt at peace with the world. "We've been so successful negotiating with the Americans, I can't think of anything else we would want to take away from them."

Sipyagin wheezed, then commended him. "Yurii, you have outdone yourself this time. I can hardly believe what you've wrought myself, even though I have always firmly believed the Americans had the desire to commit suicide. How did you talk them into this incredible agreement?"

Yurii shrugged; when one's victory was as stupendous as this, one could afford humility. "I confess it hardly took

any effort on my part other than the suggestion. They
wanted to surrender the one area in which they have
always had the ability to overwhelm us."

"Can it be that, deep within their souls, the Americans
are afraid of their own technology? They must be, despite
their endless parade of shiny new gadgets."

"Perhaps." Yurii frowned. "And yet, I cannot quite believe it. Perhaps the American *politicians* are afraid of
technology. In some important sense, American technology does *not* belong to them. It belongs to the engineers
who create it, and the businessmen who sell it." He shook
his head. "Or their attitude could simply be pragmatic.
For the past several decades, the American power to
create technical wonders has not helped their military
machine. Why, even in the late 1980s, they were using
radios from the Korean war—radios with vacuum tubes in
them! I heard reports about American attempts to build
computerized command and control systems, while they
were depending on those radios for communications. It
was laughable."

The General Secretary chuckled deep in his throat.

Yurii shrugged. "Despite their technical wizardry, the
Americans make clumsy weapons."

"Except for their airplanes."

Yurii nodded. "Yes, their airplanes and their submarines are very good indeed. But even in those areas they
manage to hurt themselves. They build machines so expensive that even the Americans, wealthy as they are,
cannot afford many of them." He paused, refocusing on
the question of why the Americans had made their latest
agreement. "Perhaps this treaty reflects a new American
understanding of how poorly their technology has served
them. Perhaps they have recognized this ongoing failure,
and have resigned themselves to it. Perhaps they would
have carried out the terms of the treaty even without our
signing it." He smiled. "Well, our signing certainly hastened the process."

"Soon we'll have no strong enemies. It's time for us to
start identifying targets of opportunity."

Yurii gestured a warning. "I agree that we should identify some targets. But remember that from this time for-

ward, the longer we wait, the weaker the Americans will become. Why spend blood when patience will achieve the same goals?"

Sipyagin rolled his lips impatiently. "I suppose you're right. And yet it would be beautiful to conclude this struggle in my lifetime." He paused. "And I guess I'm still suspicious. Will the Americans really follow through on this treaty? Even now I can't believe that they could act so foolishly."

"I'd fear they were up to something myself, were it not for the effectiveness of our information-gathering system. We've already received confirmation of massive dismantlings in the American military effort."

"Really? What juicy tidbit has the KGB found for us now?"

Yurii laughed. "The KGB is not our best information-gathering system, my comrade. The American news media have found out for us."

"Ah, of course."

Yurii rose to push the American video cassette home inside a Japanese VCR. How wonderfully thoughtful their enemies were, to supply these delightful machines!

Up came the image of a popular TV newsman. Yurii asked, "How's your English these days? I can play it direct or in translation."

Sipyagin waved a languid hand. "I'll manage," he said.

ZOOM. *The camera closes in on Bill Hardie's nut-brown face. This newscaster had amused Yurii a number of times before. This time, however, something seems different; the wild fire in Hardie's wide eyes has cooled. "President Mayfield claims to have pulled off yet another coup in the frenetic realm of global negotiations. Restating his devotion to American-Soviet harmony, today he announced his latest treaty, the Smart Weapons Ban."*

"This man is popular in the United States?" the General Secretary asked.

"He was tremendously popular several months ago. He seems to have lost some of his following recently."

"He doesn't quite have the glitter I expected."

Yurii nodded. "Don't worry, I'm sure they'll replace him shortly. They always do."

CUT. The scene shifts to East Berlin. A line of pickets encounters a line of East German soldiers—soldiers who supposedly aren't allowed in East Berlin because of the Allied Accords signed after World War II, but who operate there nonetheless. Bill's voice takes a note of foreboding. "The signing of the Smart Weapons Ban strikes an odd note, considering the accusations streaming between East and West. The clashes between rioters and soldiers in East Germany reached a new height today. In a major demonstration in East Berlin, two people are reported dead and several others wounded. The Soviet Union has denounced West Germany and the United States for supporting the riots. All NATO countries have denied any involvement or assistance to the protesters whatsoever."

The General Secretary grumbled, "We're going to have to take sterner measures with those Germans."

CUT. "Despite the growing unrest, however, Soviet and American diplomats agreed that smart weapons should be banned from Europe and from other areas of likely American/Soviet conflict. In this context, smart weapons are defined to be weapons that use wholly internal guidance systems to find their targets. Retired Air Force Strategist Leslie Evans noted that this definition lets most of the Soviet smart systems deploy anyway, since their computers are too bulky and expensive to be placed inside the weapons themselves. However, Secretary of State Semmens hailed the treaty as 'an extraordinary victory, which will freeze another expensive and counterproductive arms race in its tracks.'"

Yurii shook his head again in wonder. The only conclusion he could draw was that the United States had given up. Though they retained their ICBMs, their bombers and their subs, they had chosen to give up their superpower status.

ZOOM. "Though the treaty does not explicitly ban the research and development of smart weapons, the Administration sees the treaty as an opportunity to close down numerous military R&D projects. At the top of the hit list is the largest and least productive R&D agency in the country, an agency that has spent over a billion dollars in the past decade without ever bringing a weapon system successfully through an operational test. The FIREFORS program office, and the twenty major programs controlled by it, will be dismantled as quickly as federal lawyers can cancel the contracts. For various technical and legal reasons, this process will not be completed until mid-January. Economic Advisor Pelino has stated that 'the Smart Weapons Ban has made possible extraordinary savings in the defense budget. These savings significantly improve our chances of seeing our deficit reduced in this decade.'" Bill pauses. "There are many ways to view the gains and losses implicit in the Smart Weapons Treaty. A representative of the Zetetic Institute has also pointed out that—"

The stereo speakers hissed with static; the tape contained just a short clip from a longer discussion.

The General Secretary gazed at the monitor with wonder. "They're really doing it, aren't they?"

"Yes, they really are."

Kira stepped to the threshold of Hilan Forstil's office and paused there, reluctant to disturb the senator. Then, annoyed with herself for her timidity, she set her shoulders and crossed the room to stand by Hilan's conference table.

He rose as she entered, nodded abruptly, and stepped around the desk to greet her. "Please come in, Ms. Evans," he offered with a wave of his hand. "I'm pleased to meet you."

"You, too," Kira replied, though she wasn't sure she meant it. As far as Kira was concerned, this man had betrayed them. She had come here only because Uncle Nathan had assured her that Senator Forstil was their key man in Congress, and Kira couldn't deny that they needed congressional help.

As they sat down together at the deeply polished mahogany table, Kira searched for clues to Forstil's makeup. She felt a small shock at the barrenness of the room; it seemed politically unreasonable. No coffee mugs from contractors rested on his desk, no personal mottos adorned the walls. Even the books on the shelves were studiously neutral: encyclopedias, dictionaries, and the works of Greek philosophers gave no clue as to his religious preferences, or his attitude toward technology, or his thoughts on telecommuting. Kira wondered if all senators had offices so carefully devoid of opinion.

Hilan sat patiently while she completed this inspection of his life. When she looked back at him, his expression shifted, as though he feared that she might see him in a moment of vulnerability: he had been looking at her with open wonder, which changed under her gaze to a smile of stiff amusement. Kira could guess the cause of the open wonder: Hilan had been struck by her resemblance to her mother. "Can I get you anything?" he asked.

"No, I guess not. Did Nathan tell you why I came here?"

Hilan nodded. "To help me strategize ways to defeat the ban on telecommuting."

Kira shook her head; she had thought *she* was in charge. She pursed her lips, but reminded herself that it didn't make any difference who was in charge, unless they developed mutually exclusive plans. At the moment, she had no plans at all, though she had a few ideas. "Yes," she said, "I came to discuss the ban on telecommuting."

"Great. Why don't we start with a look at the congressional votes on the original bill. That's usually a good starting point for determining who has been pressured, and who has to be pressured, to overturn the decision."

Kira nodded, her throat tight with surprise. She had wanted to recommend starting with an analysis of the vote herself, but had rejected the idea, fearing it would lead to a nasty confrontation too soon. Now, he had suggested it himself.

Hilan reached into a cabinet and withdrew a pair of flat-panel terminals, revealing for the first time a familiarity with technology. The sight and touch of the beige plastic gave Kira a feeling of reassurance; the somber wood decor of this office felt stifling and lifeless.

Hilan's voice took on a bright animation as he spoke about the men and women whose voting records scrolled down the screen. "Porter voted for it because the UAW is very strong in his district; he didn't have much choice. Shepard must have been gotten by somebody; he's a follower. We'll deal with that later. Somebody got to Burrell, too, and that's more worrisome. Burrell's no wimp—there had to be heavy pressure to get him. Besides that, he's the leader of his own caucus; he's important."

Hilan went through the whole list of votes, cataloging the senators and representatives according to their allegiances, their beliefs, and their weaknesses. They very rarely looked into the data base behind the table of votes. Hilan carried a data base in his mind almost as detailed and reliable as the data bases Daniel Wilcox kept on-line.

Finally, the scrolling list crossed the name she had feared. As Hilan skipped over it without comment, Kira punched the PAUSE button. "Wait," she said. She pointed at the name of the missing person—one of the most powerful members of Congress, who had voted for the ban: HILAN FORSTIL. "You haven't told me why *you* voted against the Institute."

Hilan looked her in the eye, then looked away, the line of his jaw set in anger at forces beyond his control. He reached into his pocket and pulled out a swiss army knife, the kind often carried by backpackers. He rubbed the smooth surface as if it somehow reassured him. Kira remembered her mother's story of Hilan and the crevasse high in the mountains and she wondered about its effect on him. He spoke quietly. "I voted against the Institute because I didn't have a choice."

"Oh, really." Kira couldn't keep the sarcasm out of her voice.

"Oh, really. The unions did an extraordinary job of keeping me in the dark until they had enough votes mustered to push the ban through despite me. They *knew* I would oppose it." He described the sequence of meetings and agreements contrived by the unions to put the plan in place while still keeping him in the dark. His description of the events was spotty. He still didn't have a perfect understanding of how they had arranged it. "But I'm fairly sure they can't do it again—at least, not the same way." He smiled wolfishly. "I've acquired a few more spies since they put the ban into effect." He shrugged. "Anyway, when they brought me an accomplished fact, I was in no position to oppose it. Since the resurgence of the unions in the last decade, they're an important force in my state as well. I can't vote against them just on impulse."

When Hilan looked back at her after this speech, Kira had the feeling of being under the scrutiny of an eagle. He countered, "As far as working against the Institute is concerned, I might ask you why you've chosen to go into business expanding and improving Wilcox-Morris's advertising campaign. I've seen some of your ads. They're very effective."

The compliment felt like a slap on the face. Kira blushed, though Hilan's question was no different from the question she had asked herself. But now, at last, she had a powerful answer. "I went to work with Wilcox-Morris to find the missing pieces in the puzzle you just described. If you've been wondering how the unions were able to work completely around you, I know the answer. They did it with the help of the tobacco companies." Kira launched into an analysis of the ban, as seen through the viewpoint of the Wilcox-Morris political machine. She had collected a vast quantity of detailed information from the Wilcox-Morris computers since that fateful night when Wilcox had confronted her uncle. She even knew the status of the investigation of her own background—they had not yet traced her connection with the Institute, because her mother's role in Zeteticism wasn't common knowledge. Jan had never stood in the limelight. Nathan, as founder and president of the Institute, had always been the focus of publicity.

With short brushstrokes, Kira painted the details of the anti-telecommuting picture that Hilan had sketched from his own sources. As she spoke, Hilan nodded as connections fell into place. Again, for just a few moments, his face lit up with wonder. "Thank you," he said as she finished. "My worries are much lighter, since you've removed these ambiguities." He frowned. "Now that we know what happened, all we have to do is figure out how to undo it." And so Hilan went over the list again. This time it was shorter. They had thrown out all the people who were not critical—all the followers. Some of the critical men could be won over with persuasion. Some could not be won at all: they believed for their own philosophical reasons in the need to cripple technology.

Others could not be won for practical reasons. The representatives from North Carolina, for example, had no choice but to follow the tobacco line, and the men from Michigan had no choice but to follow the unions. "They're puppets," Hilan explained, "and we can't cut the strings." He brightened. "I'm a puppet, too, of course, and so are the rest of the people on this list who didn't really want to vote for this ban. But we couldn't fight it because there were too many people pulling our strings. Now we have to find a way for *you* to pull our strings."

Kira laughed. "I already know how to pull your strings," she said. "I'm going to use a pressure group—a voter block of such size and power that you can't wiggle without our consent."

Hilan chuckled. "Delightful! Where will your voter block come from?"

"From the networks. I'm going to assemble the biggest conference in history—an electronic one—and we're going to show the unions, and the tobacco companies, and the politicians who's got the biggest, toughest, meanest organization in the valley!" Her eyes blazed.

Hilan sat entranced, watching her. "Kira, I intend to help you."

Kira relaxed suddenly, surprised to find she had clenched her fist. "Anyway, we have a lot of supporters available."

"Ah, but are your supporters in the right places?" They matched up the members of the Zetetic networking community with the key members of Congress.

When they were done, they had composed a plan that would give them a majority vote in Congress. Hilan shook his head. "I don't see a way of getting a two-thirds majority, and Jim Mayfield will veto our repeal in an eyeblink. He trembles every time the lobbyists come to visit." His voice grew cold and bright at the same time. "Kira, how soon can you hold your conference?"

"When do you want it?"

"The Congressional elections are a week away."

Kira looked puzzled, then realized what that could mean. "If we can form a constituency fast enough, we can overturn them."

Hilan smiled.

Kira shot up in her seat. "We can show them just how dangerous *our* lobby can be, with just a week of organizing. We'll teach Mayfield to tremble, all right." She laughed—the tense laugh of a race car driver before the opening gun. "You know, the unions are against telecommuting because they're afraid it'll make it more difficult for them to organize. Well, they're about to find out that the networks—the same systems that make telecommuting possible—make organizing *easier*."

Hilan shook his head. "Being a puppet will never be the same. Even I tremble at the thought of dangling at the end of your strings, Kira Evans."

She twitched her nose. "I promise to be gentle," she replied, rising from the table.

"Your mother would be very proud," he whispered as she departed.

January 8

To predict the future, you must first suc-
cessfully predict the past.
                    —*Zetetic Commentaries*

Black lettering blinked against white blankness. LET
ACCURACY TRIUMPH OVER VICTORY. The words
melted, then returned at the top of the wall-sized decision
duel display. For just a moment Nathan hated the words,
though he himself had penned them. He had too many
emotional attachments in this duel—attachments to the
survival of the Sling project on the one hand, and to the
survival of the Institute on the other. The beat of his own
heart outpaced the slow beat of the black letters. As more
letters appeared beneath the cautionary words, Nathan
could feel them printing, not upon the screen, but upon
his eyes, as though he himself were the display screen
upon which they would etch this duel.

Nathan slumped into the left-hand duelist's chair. Briefly,
his hands slid across the smooth-worn surfaces of trackball
and keyboard in a caressing touch. Never before had he
dueled for such high stakes; never before had the Institute
faced the danger of fading into oblivion.

The new words listed the duel topic and positions. On
the left was the position Nathan would defend: CONTINUE
THE SLING PROJECT, USING THE INSTITUTE'S OP-
ERATING CAPITAL. On the right glared the opposing
stance: STOP WORK ON THE SLING PROJECT.

As president of the Institute and the largest single stock-
holder, Nathan had the power to enforce his own opinion.
There was nothing in the Zetetic viewpoints that argued
against such unilateral action: in every decision, a single
individual ultimately makes the choice. But the very intensity of Nathan's desires bound him to the decision duel
analysis; this decision had to be the best possible. If he
concluded that the duel had produced the wrong answer,

he would disregard it—but that was the least likely possible outcome.

Duels did not always produce accurate decisions, of course. The Institute recognized three broad classes of decisions, and three broad methods of decision-making: engineering decisions, political decisions, and unresolvable decisions. Engineering decisions were made by finding the correct, or best, answer. This was the best decision-making methodology whenever possible, but often, human affairs proved too ambiguous for this wholly rational analysis.

Political decisions were made by building an answer of consensus. In difficult cases, the consensus decision might be to let one particular man make a decision, but that was a form of consensus nevertheless. Because political decision systems could generate decisions in more situations than engineering decision systems, political systems typically gained preeminence over engineering. For the most part, this arrangement worked well—except that too often, the politicians made political decisions in situations where engineering applied, usually with tragic consequences. The key question was, how do you decide whether to use engineering or politics to decide? Politicians all too often decided to use politics.

Zeteticism had recognized an important truth: the choice between politics and engineering is always an engineering decison. The decision duel technique made its most important contributions on issues that looked and tasted political, but which were actually engineering issues at heart.

Even politics, weak though it was, could fail as a decision-making system. In cases where bitter opponents could not achieve consensus, unresolvable decisions went to the last, least accurate, decision-making method: selection by force. Ultimately, any problem could be addressed by warfare. It was inefficient, but it was also effective. All one had to do was pursue the combat fiercely enough. Too often in human history, military leaders had forgotten that the decision to use force must be made politically, just as politicians had forgotten that the decision to use politics must be made through engineering.

Nathan adjusted the sound level of his earphone. As in

all well-designed engineering discussions, the primary proponents welcomed good ideas from all sources. Anyone in the Institute could participate in this duel by communicating with the duelists, who were moderators for their respective viewpoints, not stand-alone combatants. Nathan could receive recommendations verbally through the earphones, or digitally through the small displays that accompanied his keyboard.

He knew the duel had attracted a large audience. The two rows of observer chairs beneath the dueling stations had filled before his own arrival. Behind him, on an even higher tier, Nathan could sense the neutral moderator's anxiety as he counted the number of nationwide taps coming into the room. The boy had just received his duelist's certification, and he was one of the brightest and youngest graduates. Nathan hoped fervently that he would receive many third alternatives from the audience, for Nathan disliked both of the official alternatives. Of course, he disliked the opposing viewpoint even more than the viewpoint he himself defended.

Though the oversize display held his gaze, Nathan caught a movement from the corner of his eye as someone took the right-hand dueling chair. He looked to see who had been chosen to be his opposing partner. Some of the older certified Zetetic duelists had been reluctant to duel with him. On the other hand, some of the younger ones had shown an exuberant enthusiasm to oppose him—the modern equivalent of facing down a famous gunslinger.

With a small shock, Nathan saw that none of the exuberant gunslingers had gotten the chance—his dueling partner was Leslie Evans.

Les gave him a quick laugh. "Boo, Nathan."

Nathan stared, speechless, and Les continued. "Let accuracy triumph."

Nathan smiled, and nodded. They turned to the main display and started listing their assumptions, then their opening remarks.

Nathan summarized his position in the opening: The sacrifice of the Zetetic Institute could make sense if the alternative were the sacrifice of the United States. The United States was indeed in danger of sacrificing itself; it was in danger of sacrificing all of Western civilization.

This danger resulted from the rising risk of war. The Soviet Union had, in the past several years, repeatedly used violence as a successful tool in global politics. It had become confident of both its own strength and of the efficacy of war. Meanwhile, the United States had withdrawn psychologically from the world, but it had not withdrawn physically: it still had vast though ineffectual numbers of troops stationed around the world. This combination was explosive. America's nuclear Sword of Damocles was all that caused aggressive nations to move cautiously in their dealings with it. And many people, notably the Soviets, had started to believe that America dared not use its nuclear weapons: a sword so powerful that it would destroy the wielder as well as the intended victim.

Yet the U.S. had not forsaken that too-powerful sword. It had created the worst possible combination of circumstances. The people of America knew that they would have to resort to nuclear weapons in a military crisis, but no one outside the U.S. really believed the Americans would do so. Any rational analysis suggested that the United States could no longer rely on nuclear threats—it had to achieve a consistent global position without them.

The question of whether America should bring its troops home from all over the world and return to isolationism was interesting but not relevant: the Institute could not force the country to isolationism even if it was a good idea. But the Institute *could*, through the development of the Sling's Hunters, guarantee that America remained strong enough to fight a victorious war without nuclear weapons.

Leslie's response granted most of these points. He made two other observations, however. First, whereas the failure to complete the Sling *might* be important in saving America's future, failure to reinvest the Institute's funds in its own business would *certainly* destroy the Institute.

They popped open spreadsheets on both sides of the screen and projected the cost of continuing the Sling Project. The directive that had eliminated the FIREFORS program office had fortunately allowed for graduated shutdown. Currently, the Sling Project still proceeded under government funding, but that funding would end in one more week.

Nathan had weaseled the mid-January cutoff from Charles

Somerset in November, during a meeting that had left Nathan feeling sorry for the FIREFORS director. The dismantling of FIREFORS was destroying Somerset; he had seemed disoriented and lost. In semi-coherent sentences, Somerset had revealed that he had no job prospects, either government or private. He could not keep up his mortgage payments; he was selling his house. The woman whom he sometimes dated had left him permanently. Nathan had urged him to enter the Institute, to find a new orientation for his life, but Nathan doubted that Somerset had even heard his words, much less considered them.

Numbers filled the cells of the spreadsheets, and with each entry, the dusky red digits in the bottom line turned more grim. Leslie was right: full-scale development of the Sling would bankrupt the Institute within a year, despite Kira's and Hilan's repeal of the ban on telecommuting.

Nathan paused a moment and smiled at the way the Institute and the networking community had flexed their political muscles for the first time. They had held their million-person conference two days before the Congressional elections. In those last two days, the pollsters and the politicians fell, flattened by the steamroller of votes that shifted across party lines, all in districts where stubborn proponents of the ban held seats. The networking community overthrew two sure-to-win incumbents, and after the elections, the entire American political machine understood a new force had arrived. Some politicians bowed with horror, some bowed with pleasure, but all bowed.

Had that political power play failed, the Sling Project would have bankrupted the Institute in three months. It was a sobering vision.

Now Nathan described his plan for salvation of both the Sling and the Institute: they would sell the Sling System to the government after they had completed development.

Here Leslie drew up a scathing collection of counterexamples, drawing reams of data from the nationwide data bases cross-connected to the duelists' network.

In peacetime, the American military almost never accepted advanced technology from outside the DOD's own bureaucracies. His most devastating example came from the 1980s. During that decade, the Northrop Corporation had spent millions of dollars to build the F-20. The concept was that the F-20 should be operationally comparable to the F-16, yet far cheaper. Northrop had succeeded.

But Northrop had failed. For years thereafter, the Air Force had successfully fought off all arguments to buy even a handful of F-20s. Northrop, and the rest of the industrial world, had learned the lesson: never try to develop a product for the DOD unless the DOD paid for it up front.

This was a lesson the Zetetic Institute could not ignore. The United States government simply could not be trusted to buy a better idea; indeed, it could be trusted to *reject* a better idea.

The debate continued, but Nathan could not circumvent Leslie's objections. They explored the reasons why particular projects and ideas died while waiting for the bureaucracies to recognize them. They developed part of a theory of institutional blindness. But Leslie forced Nathan to reject all strategies based on victory through bureaucratic manipulation: the lesson of Northrop struck too deeply. Nathan returned to the spreadsheet windows, developing scaled-down rates of Sling development that allowed the Institute to hold steady in the face of the tobacco companies' continued guerrilla warfare. The most reasonable Sling Project plan slashed the software development team in half and left no money for ongoing hardware prototyping. It would take years, perhaps a decade, to complete the project.

Nathan felt feverish. Though he had no engineering explanation for his suspicions, he feared that the final clash between the United States and the Soviet Union would occur before the Sling could be ready. He tried to resign himself to living with that fear.

The thick gray band running like a seam down the center of the dueling screen split, as though the seam itself had a seam. The split opened into a window of reasonable size. The neutral moderator, who entered third alternatives onto the display when he received them, must have gotten a good idea from the audience.

The third alternative read, "Though the president has banned all development of smart weapons, he has not banned all regular research and development throughout the Defense Department. Many key men know how important it is to develop better methods of defending ourselves."

Nathan heard Leslie chortle with delight as the names of some of those key men rolled down the window. Following each name came a synopsis of the person's official charters, and of his private agendas. "We can sell parts of the SkyHunter development as research for recon planes. We can sell parts of the HopperHunter as studies of advanced personnel carriers. We can sell most of the HighHunter as a new pop-up satellite launch vehicle."

The third alternative continued: "Most of the men who fund these efforts will know our purpose. But they will, through every act of omission possible, conceal the real purpose from others. And even if enemies of the project find out about our activities, they will be powerless to stop us—every one of these small contracts will be perfectly legitimate in its own terms."

Nathan raised a last objection, though he was confident the creator of this third alternative could address it. "We have no one who knows how to maneuver through these political circles with the needed dexterity." Leslie made the same point on the right half of the screen.

"Of course the Institute has the right person." The response appeared on the center section.

Nathan shifted his attention to the front row of the audience, where a balding man rose suddenly. He turned to Nathan with a maniacal smile pasted across his face—a smile of defiance, of vengeance. Seeing him, Nathan returned the defiance with a smile of his own.

The man stepped around the audience, and Nathan and Leslie both rose to greet him. Nathan offered a nod of gratitude—a salute of sorts—to this newest member of the Zetetic Institute: "Welcome," he said. "Welcome to the team."

"Thank you," Charles Somerset replied with a quick, surprised laugh.

THE WARRIORS

April 18

To win a war takes billions; to lose a war takes all you've got.
                                          —Military aphorism

Nell studied President Mayfield with the professional calm and human horror of a psychologist listening to the confessions of a rapist. President Mayfield sat surrounded by the most advanced array of image projectors, monitors, and displays in the world. She could see that he refused to believe any of them. He *refused*.

CUT. Bright orange flames flare across the screen as jet fighters shriek from tree-top height in the background. Exploding ammunition supplies pound in the foreground. Through occasional gaps in the twisting smoke, the roofs of a small German town appear, oddly solid and squat in the red light of Hell.

Other cameras, computers, and panels sputtered terse messages throughout the room, communicating both the stupendous scale and meticulous detail of the slaughter. Mayfield never glanced at them. The tiny yet terrifying television screen hypnotized the president, as similar screens hypnotized millions of other men, women, and children throughout the country.

CUT. The screen sweeps to a picture of Bill Hardie, concerned yet calm. "We have an extraordinary bulletin for all our viewers. You just witnessed scenes from the sneak attack launched by the Warsaw Pact against Western Europe just minutes ago. It isn't World War III yet. It isn't Armageddon. But it could be."

Nell sat apart from the president, in a part of the room devoid of monitors. An invisible boundary separated the information-gathering area from the decision-making area of the White House Situation Room, like the boundary that separates the audience from the performer, the spectator from the athlete.

195

ZOOM OUT. A high-altitude picture settles on the screen. Brilliant thin lines overlay the photo, showing the national boundaries of Europe. "We have enhanced this image, taken from the French Spot IV satellite, to highlight the size of the attack. As you can see even from thousands of miles away, virtually the entire Soviet, Czech, and East German armies have mobilized and moved across the border into West Germany."

Flashes of terror and calm alternated in Nell's mind. She dared not panic, she knew. She could bear to see the displays and the images of war; these things were terrible but not mindshattering. But she could not bear to see the empty disbelief on Jim Mayfield's face. She looked away to regain control of her pounding heart.

ZOOM IN. The image speeds past the viewer, reaching into West Germany, expanding the view of the border area. Now, brilliant pinpoints of light all along the border fight with the artificial overlay as the brightest parts of the display. Bill drones on. "The thousands of small dots you now see in West Germany are the flashes from artillery blasts. Never in history have so many cannons fired so continuously."

Nell stared at the tiny clots of death, fighting to remember that these blinding explosions came from mere conventional explosives. She shuddered, thinking about how those points of light would blossom if the armies started using nukes.

CUT. "A Soviet spokesman stated that West German agitation had incited the East German riots. Because the Soviet Union could not get any satisfactory action from the West German government, their only recourse was to destroy the so-called 'infectious agents' themselves. The spokesman pledged that all Soviet forces would stop at the Rhine River. He further stated that Denmark had been invaded, strictly for limited, tactical purposes, and that those troops would be withdrawn as soon as the German issue was resolved."

With carefully even breathing, Nell addressed the president. "Jim. Jim, turn off the TV. We have decisions to make."

Earl Semmens sat next to Nell, as if huddling close to a

campfire. The Secretary of Defense had been excluded from this meeting—a situation that might have struck Nell as odd, except that Mayfield showed such active hostility toward the man. She had wondered earlier why she herself had been summoned. Now she understood as Mayfield followed her orders, clicking the TV off.

What else could she do to help in this situation? Jim surely expected her to recommend drastic measures. Faced with his unyielding platitudes for years, she had found herself trapped in the role of unyielding hawk. She had never succeeded in demonstrating for him the difference between a hawk and a warmonger.

Now she had her opportunity. For once, Jim would be pleasantly surprised to hear her agree with his anti-military, anti-confrontational position. No matter how hideously the Soviet forces scarred Europe, she knew as well as he did that America dared not start a nuclear war.

With a twist of pain, Mayfield whimpered, "They can't attack us. They can't."

Nell paused a moment, having difficulty accepting Mayfield's rejection of reality. "Of course they can. They are."

"We have a treaty." The president's face flickered for just a moment, from disbelief to hatred, then back.

"Jim, in the past, the Soviets have attacked Czechoslovakia, Afghanistan, and Poland—and, Jim, those places were run by their *friends*." Nell realized she sounded like the one-note warmonger again. How did Mayfield always do this to her? With a shrug, she offered counterpoint. "Of course, we did similar things in Vietnam. Treaties are political tools. We've always known that." She stressed the ending of her sentence with sudden worry: Mayfield *had* always known that treaties were tools, hadn't he?

The soft, curved lines of Mayfield's mouth straightened. "But we have a—" he stopped on a sob. "All our *treaties*. They made life better for both of us. Why have they thrown them away?"

Nell shook her head helplessly. "Germany, I guess. Jim, we're dangerous to the Soviets, even when we don't do anything. Just by existing, we create a constant threat to their empire and their ideology."

His eyes wandered. "My God, what will the polls say?"

he asked quietly. Sudden anger shattered his smooth face, like a hurtled rock shattering a windshield. "They lied to us."

Nell sighed. "Of course."

"We have to teach them not to lie."

Nell sat forward with new alertness. She had never seen or heard Mayfield quite like this; this was no time for surprising new behavior. Cautiously, she asked, "How, Jim? How should we teach them?"

"We'll nuke the mothers!"

"All-out nuclear war?" Nell shuddered in disbelief.

Mayfield looked her in the eye, then looked away. "No, of course not. We'll shoot just one, just to let them know we're serious. That'll look good."

Nell forced herself to breathe. From the corner of her eye she could see that Semmens looked as scared as she felt. "If we shoot just one, what will they do? They'll nuke us back. At least one, probably more—to show us that *they're* serious. You know that, Jim."

"We can't stand around as if we were helpless!" Mayfield fumbled at his inner jacket pocket, brought out the Gold Codes card. "Get Johnson." Johnson carried the "football"—the device used to select among the many nuclear options.

Nell sat rooted in her chair. Semmens twitched several times, then froze in numb paralysis. Nell spoke with the overly calm voice of a nurse talking a suicidal patient back from a seventh-story window ledge. "Jim. Jim, think about what you're doing."

"No!" Mayfield leaped from his chair. "Don't you see that that's what they're counting on? They expect us to think so long and hard about all the possible consequences that we'll be paralyzed with fear."

"Jim—"

"Shut up! We can't let them scare us now! We have to—" As he swept across the room, the floor slipped suddenly out from beneath him. His head thumped dully against the shiny tiled floor.

"Jim!" Nell jumped from her chair, then knelt beside the gasping president; Earl followed. "What's wrong?"

His only answer was a pair of explosive gasps as his eyes bulged from their sockets.

Through the shock, Nell realized that Mayfield had a more serious problem than a bump on the head. She remembered his periodic wince, his occasional clutch at his chest, his fear of doctors. She flew toward the door. "I'll get the doctor."

Earl rubbed Jim's head helplessly. "Jim!"

Another gasp. "Kill the mothers," Jim coughed.

Nell stopped in mid-flight. Images flashed in her mind, each too brief to capture fully—a series of flashbulbs popping with stroboscopic speed.

She remembered her first trip to Washington—a trip by bus from Bennettsville, South Carolina. It was her senior year; this was the senior-class trip. She remembered her friends' laughter as they danced through the traffic. They formed a terrifying, uncontrolled weave of high-speed cars and teenagers, running to reach the Tidal Basin amidst the monuments. She remembered how she, too, had laughed with her friends, walking beneath the trees clad in white and pink blossoms, till they reached the bottom of the white marble steps of the Jefferson Memorial. She remembered her moment's pause there, and the hallowed stillness that grew deep within her.

She remembered her sober walk to the top of those steps. She remembered standing by the statue of Jefferson himself in the center of the dome. She remembered looking up. High overhead, Jefferson's words encircled her, suffusing through her as she read.

With a nudge at her best friend, Lisa, she had pointed to the beginning of the inscription. "Isn't that a great thought?"

Lisa turned away from John, giggling. "What? Oh, yeah. But ya know, I heard he owned slaves. I'll bet he didn't even believe it when he said it."

"I'll bet he did believe it. I know I believe it," Nell replied simply.

But Lisa had already rushed off after John. Nell stood alone, turning slowly as her lips moved in a silent affirmation of Jefferson's vow: *I have sworn, upon the altar of God, eternal hostility against every form of tyranny over the mind of man.* She had felt a bond across the centuries to the man whose purpose she now shared.

The flashbulbs skipped across the years to her last conversation with a man she had once admired, a man who had been her employer for many years.

Philip had told her about the contract for the National Person Identification System for Egypt. Philip had just won the contract, the biggest job in his company's history. The success was doubly important because of a slight kink in the company's current situation: they had just lost their two other largest contracts. Egypt's ID system had saved them from bankruptcy.

Nell had studied the happy, almost carefree lines of her superior's face with resignation. "I will not work on this job," she had told him.

"What?" Philip had continued to smile, still reveling in the salvation of his company.

"I will not work on this job."

He had snapped his chair upright. "Why not?"

"Philip, it is immoral to build an ID card system for the Egyptian government. If we help them track the movements of all their citizens, you know what they'll use it for—to clamp down on every person they don't like."

Philip had been an engineer; he had an engineer's honesty. "Granted. But it will also be used for good purposes, like maintaining people's medical records so that in an emergency, they can get proper treatment, no matter where they are."

Nell shook her head. "With every invention, there are both good and bad results. But the occasional good use of this system comes nowhere near to compensating for the thousands of abuses it will allow the government to commit against its own citizens."

Philip had looked away to collect his arguments. "Nell, you've worked with us on fundamentally evil things before. You've worked on weapons of tremendous destructive power. Why are you having this sudden attack of morality?"

Nell had paused. "You know, I would not object to developing weapons for the Egyptians. Weapons can be used in two different ways: they can be used to harm a nation's citizens, but they can also be used to ward off enemies. Philip, this ID card system can really only be used for harm." She had sighed. "I'm not even sure we should have a system like this in the United States. And the Egyptian government is far more dangerous to its citizens than our government is to us."

Phil had sat quietly. Nell could see that many words came to him, but none of them quite fit.

"Philip, I'm sorry. But I took a vow many years ago." Slowly, succinctly, Nell repeated the words of Jefferson. "Philip, you're asking me to create the kind of system that I swore to destroy. You're asking me to increase the weight of the burden I'm striving to throw down. I will not do it."

The flashbulbs in Nell's mind winked out. She remembered the man dying on the floor—the man who could destroy the world; the man who now refused to think of consequences.

Nell understood that you could pay too high a price in the fight against tyranny. Why fight against tyranny, if the people you vowed to free died in the process?

Slowly, with the syrupy grace of underwater ballet, Nell turned back to the Secretary of State. "Let's get him some water first." She spoke so slowly, it felt as though she was in a movie shown from a projector that needed the speed reset.

Earl looked up at her with pale horror. He opened his mouth, but no words came as his expression transformed with understanding. A single short gasp punctuated the silence, then died. "Yes, water," he choked out.

With robotic precision, Nell stepped to the desk, retrieved the water pitcher, and went to the president's side. His face and hands had turned a purplish gray. She paused a moment, then said, "I don't think the water will help. He needs a doctor."

"I think you're right."

Nell turned slowly, then picked up speed as she ran to the door. "The president's having a heart attack! Get the doctor!"

A dozen men hurried into action. Nell crossed quietly to the place where the Gold Codes card lay on the tiled floor. She picked it up.

*   *   *

Pale blue skies, deep blue seas, and an occasional crest of white foam greeted Admiral Billingham as he gazed through his binoculars. The waters were as calm as they ever got in the north Atlantic.

He turned slowly, observing the proper placement of each ship in his fleet: the frigates in the lead, the cruisers port and starboard. Behind him, he knew, a similar pattern held, though he could not see the ships from his battle management center.

The binoculars themselves were anachronisms. He could see his forces—not only the ships fore and aft, but the aircraft as well—arrayed on the wall-sized, computerized battle board. But the battle board only gave him facts; it could not give him the feel of his fleet.

He glimpsed the fire and smoke of an F-26 Cheetah catapulting from the deck below before he returned to his battle analysis. His ship, the *Nimitz*, jerked ever so slightly as she hurled the Cheetah into the light blue sky. A chill ran through him. It was a beautiful day for a war.

The admiral still couldn't quite believe they were at war with Russia, even though his fleet had struck one of the first naval blows. An Alfa-class submarine had come clipping across SOSUS IV on a direct intercept course with his flagship. It was a foolish thing to do: the Alfas were so noisy you could track them halfway across the ocean. Clearly, the sub's commander had counted on driving so deep and fast that the American torpedoes could go neither deep enough nor fast enough to hurt him.

So Billingham had sent a pair of ancient, battered P3 patrol planes out, with half a dozen of the fast, new deep-diving Mark II homing torpedoes. The submarine became permanently quiet.

A soft bell sounded. Ensign Fletcher turned to him. "Sir, the Brits have identified a regiment of Backfire bombers coming across the gap south of the Faeroe Islands. It looks like they're coming toward us."

The admiral nodded. "Are the Brits going to take care of them?"

"They don't know if they can, sir. They're scrambling against a bomber attack on Heathrow right now."

"I see. So the question is, which attack is a diversion? Let's see what Batty recommends," he said. They turned to the battle board.

Batty was the name of the on-board battle management computer, the machine that ran everything in the room.

Over a hundred of the best software and engineering minds in the United States had dedicated years to the task of bringing Batty to life. Dozens of innovative products benefiting both civilian and military projects could have been developed by this unusually bright and energetic team; instead, all efforts had gone to molding the Battle Management System. If Batty proved ineffectual, a tremendous national resource—the minds that had created the system—would have been wasted.

But Batty had entered service as a spectacular success. It had shown itself to be one of the rare miracles of military technology. It was modern, it was efficient, it did everything it was designed to do very well indeed. It was even flexible. The developers had known from the start that no commander would accept the advice or decisions of a computer programmed by landlocked engineers. No commander would agree with any "optimal" strategy chosen by some military board of "experts."

So the designers wisely avoided that approach. Batty had started operation with a clean slate. It had learned strategy and tactics from Admiral Billingham himself. It might not be as creative as the admiral when faced with unique situations, but for the most part, it used the best ideas the Admiral had ever devised.

When Billingham first met Batty, he had wondered why anyone would bother to build such a perfect mimic. Why not just let the admiral make his own decisions? But after the second fleet exercise, Billingham understood the answer. Batty was *fast*. Batty made the decisions in seconds that Billingham would have made if he had had several hours to game out the alternatives.

So together, Batty and Billingham had outmaneuvered and outgunned the rest of the navy in exercises again and again, though the competition was getting tougher as the other carriers received Batty's sibling systems. Together, Batty and Billingham seemed invincible.

And now they had a real enemy to outgun. Enemy bombers swept toward them at the speed of sound. Fortunately, Batty worked at close to the speed of light.

Batty opened a conversation window on the battle board. Recommendations appeared. The plan called for a soft redeployment of the nine patrolling Cheetahs that formed a loose circle around the fleet, shifting six of them eastward far enough to meet the attackers. But this would not be enough of itself. Batty also recommended launching four planes to intercept and chop up the regiment before they reached this standard patrol. Batty listed out the calculations that drove this conclusion, the probabilities of kill, the radius of intercept, the radius of enemy missile launch, the amount of time the patrol would have to fight before the Backfires launched their missiles, the probability of a successful hit on the Nimitz by one of those missiles. Billingham nodded in approval. After scrambling four more fighters, it would take some time to lift additional aircraft against a second threat; but what kind of threat could arise that suddenly? Even a second regiment of Backfires passing by England couldn't get close enough fast enough to be dangerous.

The four fighters lifted off and headed toward the bombers. They were still well out of range when the Backfires mysteriously turned around and headed home. Pursuit was out of the question; the interceptors were at the edge of their range.

"Ha!" Admiral Billingham muttered. "Now the big question is, were they gun-shy? Or were they a diversion?"

Ensign Fletcher looked over at him. "What was that, sir?"

"Never mind," the admiral replied.

Another soft bell sounded, this time a warning, rather than an alert. Billingham looked up at the section of the wall Batty now lit with new information. *Admiral Billingham,* Batty explained, *recent satellite photos suggest that a regiment of Blackjack bombers has disappeared from their airfield near Murmansk. These may be the bombers that the Soviet Union recently modified for stealth missions. I recommend sending a second E2 north to search for them.*

"Yes!" Billingham yelled. "Ensign, launch that E2 immediately."

Fletcher looked up. "Yes, sir."

Billingham shook his head in amazement. The missing Blackjacks were probably not part of a sneak attack on the *Nimitz;* more likely, they were beating the hell out of some poor Norwegian target. But had they not had Batty watching with a world-girdling hookup to sensors and data, such an attack could have been very dangerous. As it was, Batty was already routing the Cheetahs back to their normal loitering positions. In minutes, the fleet would be fully rearranged to meet such a Blackjack threat.

But even as they prepped a second E2 early warning airplane, another alert went off—a harsh bell of immediate danger. The E2 circling overhead had just picked up some dim reflections. They were almost certainly reflections from the missing Russian airplanes.

How had they flown so far without being detected? The admiral couldn't believe it. There were hundreds of sensor systems on Iceland and Greenland that had a shot at them as they came through the Denmark strait. He could see on the map, even without Batty's new highlighting, that that was their probable course.

The admiral now became a spectator. The enemy was too close to be handled by human decision-making reflexes. Batty ordered more Cheetahs to veer to intercepting paths while she brought the three closest patrol fighters together for a combat run. As the additional interceptors veered, however, Batty and Billingham both knew that additional interceptors were probably wasted. The Blackjacks would be in range to launch their missiles before the extra Cheetahs could arrive.

Furthermore, this detour for the Cheetahs would consume fuel. They could not return to the carrier; they would have to ditch in the ocean. Normally, such a waste of fighters would seem insane.

But the Blackjack's missiles gained terrific accuracy when launched from closer range. Batty understood that the enemy bombers *had to* be forced to launch from the greatest possible distance. Otherwise, there would be no carrier for any Cheetahs to return to.

The attacking patrol planes came into firing range. As

the battle had moved out of Billingham's control a few minutes earlier, it moved out of Batty's control now.

The Blackjacks would fire their missiles while cruising well beyond the range of the fleet's surface-to-air missiles. Hence, only the three Cheetahs would be able to shoot at the bombers before they launched their attack. No new strategies or tactics could alter the next series of events. The whole encounter collapsed to a game one could play with dice. With cold precision, Batty printed out the results of the fight before the first shot was fired.

Number of Blackjacks: 24
Kill rate for the Cheetahs: 25%
Surviving Blackjacks: 18
Number of missiles per Blackjack: 6
Total missiles: 108
Kill rate for surface-to-air missiles against missiles: 7.5%
Surviving missiles: 100
Success rate for electronic countermeasures and decoys:40%
Missiles on-target: 60
Kill rate for point-defense guns and rockets: 45%
Missile hits: 33
Probable number of hits required to incapacitate Nimitz:12
Probable number of hits required to sink Nimitz: 21
Percent overkill used to destroy Nimitz: 57%

Admiral Billingham saw at last a serious defect in the Battle Management System computer. Batty couldn't summarize the results in human terms; it couldn't understand its own calculations.

Batty didn't realize that they would all die.

Within the hour, over five billion dollars, 40,000 man-years of human labor, and 1,000 valiant American seamen sank forever beneath the gently lapping waves.

April 22

The end of the Industrial Age saw the creation of the largest, most effective killing machine in history: the Soviet Army. The individual rationalist would necessarily run to escape. Fortunately, free men of the Industrial Age were not half so rational as they were stubborn.

—Industrial Age Societies: A Historical Perspective

Nathan looked at the president. She stood in sunlight, facing him. The bay windows to her left flooded the room with brightness that splintered as it touched her shoulder, that cascaded to the floor and returned, reflected in her hazel eyes. It struck Nathan as unnatural that the President of the United States should be beautiful. Then it struck him that nothing could be more natural.

Finally, he realized that much of her beauty was a creation of his own mind. Her silhouette stretched too long and thin. Her nose hooked just enough to please the nation's cartoonists. At this moment, as she squinted past the glare of sunlight to gaze back at Nathan, tense lines radiated from the corners of her eyes. She was not, by some objective scrutiny, beautiful.

Yet when she shook her head, loose strands of hair waved gaily, in exuberant contrast to her tightly pulled bun. And her voice, though serious, held confidence—the confidence of a woman who sees a brighter future, for she will make it brighter. "Mr. Pilstrom, the senator tells me you have a bunch of wild ideas. He thinks some of them might save Europe."

Nathan chuckled, crossing the room to avoid the sunshine's glare. "You have summarized the situation with clarity, Madam President."

Her eyes narrowed for a moment; she was not yet

accustomed to the honorific. She replied, "Hilan has told me a bit about your Sling Hunters, just enough to tantalize me. Frankly, they sound like excellent toys. The big question is: can they work in combat?"

"I don't know. But I do know that our alternatives are few and bleak."

"True enough." She gazed into the distance, as if at a field filled with corpses. "It's too late to use tactical nuclear weapons to defend Germany. We'd kill more of our own people than we'd kill of theirs. So in the absence of a miracle, we have only two choices. We can surrender Europe, or we can drop a nuke on the Soviet Union." Her eyes shifted back to Nathan. "At least if we surrender Europe, we know exactly how great the loss will be."

"Yes." The simple precision of her words pleased Nathan. Obviously, she had learned in her own ways and her own time how to filter the thousands of facts, theories, opinions, and rumors that assaulted an American president. She had extracted the fundamental points; only relevance remained when she spoke.

Nathan tried to match her. "The third alternative is a miracle—and the Sling is about the only magic box left. Let me see what rabbits I can pull out for you." Nathan inserted a videotape into the president's system and started the simulations of Hunters in action. He gave her the speech that he had once given Hilan Forstil.

Nell nodded with quick understanding from time to time. At the end she held up two fingers. "Two questions. Clearly, your Hunters qualify as a potential miracle. But are they miracle enough? Our forces are now scattered in helpless little clusters; I'm not even sure we can get the HopperHunters to the battlefield, because our logistics collapsed along with the front lines. Our people no longer know where the battlefield is. They are no longer sure where they themselves are." She crossed to the empty table by the bookshelves and sat down.

Nathan joined her. "I don't know if the Hunters are enough of a miracle. They may no longer be adequate, even assuming they perform brilliantly—and there will surely be some problems when they first go into the field. But let me point out that the Sling Project is the *kind* of miracle that can make the difference. With the Sling system, we are talking about a quantum leap—the transition from an Industrial Age system to an Information Age system. That jump is every bit as great as the jump that mankind made in going from the Agricultural Age to the Industrial Age.

"Let me draw an analogy. Suppose we could put a single Industrial Age weapon into the middle of an Agricultural Age battle. For example, suppose we dropped an M60 tank into the Battle of Thermopylae. Who would win?"

Nell wrinkled her nose. "Whoever had the tank would win."

"Exactly." Nathan pounced on her words. "Even though the Spartans were outnumbered by more than ten to one, if *they* had that one Industrial Age weapon, they would win."

He tapped the table top. "Similarly, a single Information Age weapon could decide any Industrial Age battle, even in the face of a ten-times-more-powerful enemy. What good is an army, if it does not know where to go? What good is an army, if it can no longer process enough information to make decisions? *That* is what an Information Age weapon would do to an army. That is what the Sling Project is all about." Nathan could feel his whole body pulsing with the strength of his convictions. He realized he had lost control of his enthusiasm, even as Nell gestured in mock surrender.

"I see your point," she said. "My second question is the more difficult of the two, however: can you complete the project in time?"

"I don't know," Nathan answered with dull sorrow. "We've collected the Sling team outside the Yakima Firing Range to work as fast and as hard as they can."

"Does it make sense to add more people to the team? Is there anyone—anyone in the country—whom you'd like to have with you at Yakima?"

Nathan shook his head. "No, it's too late to add people." He chuckled again and gazed at Nell with pleasure. "Madam President, I'm surprised that you're *asking* about adding people, rather than demanding it. Most politicians and businessmen don't understand how dangerous it is to add technical staff at the last minute when you're creating a new system. Adding people works so well when duplicating copies of old systems that they find it difficult to understand how harmful even the brightest added people can be."

"I've worked with engineers before," Nell replied drily. "I know they work best in small teams." Her eyes narrowed. "And I know how much effort it takes to go from a system that *almost* works to a system that *does* work."

Nathan nodded. "Exactly. So we return to the question, can we be done in time?" He took a deep breath. "How much time have we got? Good as my people are, determined and driven to succeed as they may be, I can't believe we can have something useful in less than a week." His voice shrank, fearing the answer to his next question. "Do we have a week?"

Nell shrugged. "Perhaps. Even though we've been scattered and mutilated, our men are still fighting. Jesus, they're fighters." Her eyes glistened. Nathan remembered the regular reports coming across the Atlantic of incredible stands being made by once-ordinary soldiers. "Fortunately, the Soviets are neither gods nor demons. They've made mistakes, too." Her smile might have chilled an iceberg. "At the beginning of the war, there were only a handful of railroads that could carry heavy military supplies to Germany from the Soviet Union. And their fuel came via the oil pipelines that Europeans built for them 20 years ago. Well, the railroads are wrecks now, as are the pipelines. Supplies barely trickle across the border to their troops in Germany. And their whole strategy is based on lots of supplies."

"So we have some time."

"Only a little." Nell responded sharply to the sound of relief in Nathan's voice. "Perhaps enough."

Nathan swallowed. "So you'll back the Sling Project?"

"Yes, granting one more condition." She closed her eyes, and for a moment, the lines of worry lifted from her face. Nathan stared raptly at the moment's vision of tranquility. When she opened her eyes again, they held laughter, the joy of a fond mother humoring a child. "The commanders of our armed forces aren't very happy with the idea of tossing an untried weapon into the middle of the battlefield."

"I can hardly blame them. I don't like the idea myself."

"I'm glad you see their point of view. Anyway, they're willing to go along—they're willing to grasp at any straws now—but they want the last chop on sending these things to the field."

Nathan laughed. "I'm not surprised. Madam President, the military organization is carefully designed to *prevent* men from grasping at straws. The American military has rarely achieved its victories with great strokes of brilliance. Few armies ever have. The failure of just one brilliant stroke could cost you more than a dozen brilliant strokes could gain. Cautious movements have historically kept men alive longer; and if you kept your men alive long enough, you usually won."

"I suppose so. Anyway, the major general we're sending should be helpful as well. If he were just a judge and jury, I wouldn't have let the Army foist him on you. He's a brilliant tactician, I'm told, as well as an able program manager. And he is very fair." She smiled. "He's also a skeptic about gadgetry. If the Sling passes his inspection, we'll have a winner."

Nathan laughed at the propriety of having a skeptic pass judgment on a Zetetic project. "We'll do our best to keep him entertained. I look forward to meeting him."

Nell laughed. "I suspect you're lying," she said, "but it's a gallant lie, nonetheless." She rose, offering Nathan her hand in dismissal. "I hope the next time we meet, we'll have more pleasant prospects to discuss."

A mirror hung in the hall beyond the president's office. Nathan saw his own reflection: a man with unwavering eyes, with the alertness of a sometimes swift intelligence, with a gentleness that might be construed as dignity. The man he saw might well have trouble controlling flights of fancy and impossible daydreams.

He shook his head at himself. How foolish he would have to be to fall in love with the President of the United States.

With a last shake of his whole body, his mind returned to other matters. He wondered how things were going in Yakima.

Leslie had started the day feverish with excitement. The

Sling team would come together at last, in a heroic effort to finish the Hunters, to end the war and save humanity from nuclear holocaust. At last he was free of the politicking that had wasted his time. At last he was free of the endless negotiations that had wasted his energy, his begging for small sums of money to keep the project slogging forward. Now those issues had been thrust aside, leaving Leslie with only the technical problem of building the best Hunters he knew how, in the shortest time he could manage. Certainly the technical problems formed a formidable array, but at least they were clear, understandable problems—problems of a kind he knew he could solve.

Now, three hours later, Leslie stood by the vast picture window of the airport terminal, alone and exhausted, the taste of disappointment dry on his tongue.

The passengers from Seattle disembarked in ragged groups. He recognized Juan Dante-Cortez immediately. Though they had never met in person, they had held numerous video conferences together. Leslie shuffled toward the gate, forcing himself to move, though he barely had enough enthusiasm and energy to stand. Leslie did not call to the other members of the team to come meet Juan, though they also waited in the terminal. Even without another introduction, interpersonal frictions had already made the great meeting of the Sling team a frightening failure.

Flo and Ronnie stood near the baggage conveyors, looking uncomfortably out of place. Kurt and Lila stood at another corner of the great room, within spitting distance of one another, poised with the tension of wrestlers at the beginning of a bout. Their bickering had started when Lila had arrived and Kurt had picked up her bag to carry it for her. She had made a rude comment. He had tossed his own bag at her, telling her she could carry it as well if she wished. Somehow, when the loud words ended, Kurt held both bags. Leslie wondered if they enjoyed the antagonism in some way beyond his own comprehension.

What peculiarities would Juan bring to the group?

"Hi," Juan called to him, entering the building on the tail of a gusting wind. "I'm glad to meet you at last. It's always so odd having friends that you've never met, if you know what I mean."

Leslie nodded, and opened his mouth to speak, but Juan rushed on. "Where's the rest of our team—I thought we were all arriving more or less the same time—oh, *there* they are." He had spotted Kurt and Lila in their corner. With long strides that picked up speed, Juan whirled across the room and stopped himself by throwing one arm around Lila and one arm around Kurt. "Boo," he said saucily.

Leslie expected to see Juan get punched in the stomach from both directions. Instead, Lila and Kurt stepped back uncertainly, then smiled. "Where's Ronnie?" Juan asked next. As he twisted his lanky frame around, Ronnie and Flo were already walking toward him. "Howdy," Juan said, offering a vigorous handshake to Ronnie and a gentler one for Flo. "So the gang's all here." He looked at Leslie. "We ready to go?"

Rejuvenated by Juan's energy, Leslie pointed to the Thunderbird Motel's shuttle waiting outside. "You bet."

Juan kept up a steady chatter until they boarded the shuttle. Once in motion, however, he stopped suddenly, a runner hitting the wall. He seemed totally spent, as if the extra energy he had used in his arrival had cost him far more than it might another man. By the time he stopped, however, the icy mood had broken, and the other members of the team were speaking eagerly about their plans. Besides Leslie, only Lila watched Juan with questioning concern.

As they drove through Yakima, Leslie looked around with a surprising sense of warm contentment. He had not passed through the town of Yakima in years—not since the days of Interim FAAD, a combined Army/Air Force project that had planned to use commercial equipment and that had been killed several times by government bureaucracies.

Yakima had not changed much. Sweet Evie's restaurant still offered simple yet wonderful home-cooked meals; Leslie remembered the flavor of their roast beef gravy on mashed potatoes from long ago.

The Thunderbird Motel still stood on the edge of civilization: on one side of the motel, buildings and parking lots crowded together, back to back. On the other side, a scattered handful of worn storefronts quickly yielded to barren sands.

Leslie had chosen Yakima as their meeting place for two

reasons. First, since it was far away from everything, it was a perfect place for them to wrap themselves totally around their work. Second, and more particularly, it was close to the Yakima Firing Range. The Range, a rolling sea of dunes and weeds, lay beyond the sands behind the Thunderbird. On the Range, the Sling team could test the Hunters to brutal effect.

The Thunderbird itself had not changed, either. When they arrived, Leslie took the team straight to the Tieton Room, a conference area that Leslie had commandeered for their computers. Leslie had used this same room in the same way almost twenty years earlier.

Kurt started tearing open boxes at a frenetic pace. "Did you lose something?" Lila jeered.

Kurt stopped. He looked up and explained with clipped words, "There's a continent full of men dying. As we dawdle, they die."

Awkward silence touched them all. Juan moved first, to grab a small box and throw it to Lila. "Let's do it!" he shouted with enthusiasm. He himself turned to one of the largest boxes and ripped its cover off, his thin muscles springing like wires. In a moment, everyone was hip-deep in the unpacking.

The mood lightened as empty boxes accumulated in the center of the room, and everyone felt a sense of accomplishment. Juan stopped for a moment, staring at the label on a work station he had just unpacked. "Haiku?" he asked.

Flo floated to his side. "That is mine," she explained. "Amos and I, we named our machines. Each has a different personality."

"I see." Juan turned the work station over to her to finish unpacking.

Kurt straightened for a moment; even he seemed mellower as their computers came to life. "That's a good idea. We need to name all this equipment." Lila just looked at him sarcastically. He went on, "After all, I can't imagine Lila wanting to work on the same work station I am." His voice dropped in pitch as he announced with wolfish delight, "I know how to name them."

Lila glanced up suspiciously, but continued unpacking, as did Kurt.

While others plugged in power cords and threw up screen test patterns, Leslie quietly unrolled long sheets of paper and draped them across the one bare wall that had neither doors, windows, nor blackboards. He had not brought the whole PERT chart; virtually the entire length of the corridor to his office at the Institute was a sea of green, and the green boxes of finished tasks no longer mattered.

What mattered were the angry reds and the very recent pale blues. Only a couple feet of chart remained sandwiched between the completed boxes and the final box— the box that represented the completion of the Sling. No pink boxes remained: they had all turned red. No black boxes remained: the planned end date for the entire project had also passed. But numerous blue boxes had grown amidst the red.

Blue—the transparent blue of an editing marker—represented new and unplanned tasks hastily sketched on the chart as the red failures forced the team to seek new paths to success. They seemed to take up most of the space not covered in red. In some places they replaced it, but everywhere they distorted the once straightforward sequence of steps to the end.

But both red and blue boxes would fall to the team's relentless efforts in the next week. With a momentary tingle of triumph, Leslie changed one blue box to green: the arrival of the team in Yakima was now complete.

They finished unwrapping the equipment. As Juan tossed the empty cartons into the hall, Kurt ran around the room with a labeling gun. "I'm naming the computers," he proclaimed.

Leslie could all too easily imagine the breakdown of this fragile team over who had rights to christen the equipment. He spoke quickly. "Fine. Someone else can name the HopperHunters and the SkyHunters. They'll arrive shortly."

When the label maker had finished, Leslie scanned the results. ALEXANDER, CAESAR, CHARLEMAGNE, NAPOLEON, MAO, he read the raised lettering.

Kurt explained, "I've named them for the great conquerors."

Juan laughed—the awkward laughter of someone who doesn't know what else to do. Lila glowered in silence.

Leslie sighed.

A bellboy came to the doorway. Ronnie was closest, so the man spoke to him and left. Ronnie yelled, "All right! The *real* stuff's here. Out in the parking lot."

They went around the corner, through the glass doors that opened on the desert side of the Thunderbird. Only a few cars dotted the parking lot, which was fortunate, because a very large glider consumed most of the space. Beside it, a hovercraft rested on its metal skirt.

Ronnie spoke first. "This is great! We can start real testing." He smiled at Juan. "We'll put you and your simulations out of business real soon."

Juan smiled softly. "I certainly hope so."

Lila ran her hand down the side of the hovercraft. Only a few openings for sensors and guns still needed filling before it became a bona fide HopperHunter. "I'll name the Hoppers," she said with a glance at Kurt. "I'll name them for the flowers that grow over the graves of the conquerors." She tapped the narrow head of the machine; it echoed with a tinny sound. The flimsiness of the Hopper armor reminded Leslie just how dependent the whole design was on speed and maneuver. The armor seemed puny compared to the stuff that covered the behemoths now roaming Europe. He knew how the barefoot men who first used pikes to defeat steel-clad medieval knights must have felt.

Lila continued, "I hereby christen thee Daffodil."

This time Kurt glowered at the ridiculousness of her naming convention.

Juan spoke, oblivious to the hostility exchanged. "And I'll name the SkyHunters. They qualify as birds, don't they?" He pointed to the pale blue skin that covered the Hunter's underside—a blue meant to render it less visible from the ground. "I hereby christen thee the Bluebird."

Leslie couldn't help laughing. "Caesar, Daffodil, and Bluebird. Yes, it sounds like a very American collection of machines. Now all we have to do is make them work."

They remembered the reason they had come here, and ran back to the Tieton room to start work in earnest.

April 24

Ready. Fire. Aim.
    —*Motto of Evolutionary System Engineer*

Leslie sat in one of the Tieton Room's red naugahyde chairs, his arms crossed over the long table before him. He watched Juan roll over on the floor in a darkened corner. It was noon; Juan had collapsed in that corner a couple of hours ago for his first sleep since arriving.

Juan had not yet picked up his room key, and they had been here for two days.

The rest of the team lay strewn across the room like discarded toys. Empty styro cups and bags of corn chips cluttered odd corners; they had not even taken the time to hit the cafe here in the motel. A huge coffee maker dominated the table by the door, supplied gratis by the staff of the Thunderbird. The employees of the motel did not know exactly what the team was doing. But they knew, from the glowing computer displays and overhead lights that burned all night, that the project had something to do with the battle for Europe, and that their efforts eclipsed the importance of all else in Yakima.

Lila slouched in front of the work station GENGHIS, staring numbly at the results of the latest simulation run. Kurt leaned forward above her with wide-eyed alertness. At least he seemed alert; a studious observer would have noticed that his expression never changed, that he was more a waxwork of alertness than a person.

Across the room, Flo shook her head periodically as if warding off a close-hovering cloud of gnats. Ronnie's hands trembled with the conflicting chemicals of his bloodstream: he had been running strictly on caffeine since dinner the night before.

Of the lot of them, Leslie sympathized most with Juan. Ronnie's assertion that they wouldn't need Juan's simulations much longer had proved premature. Within hours of their first live test, they had left Daffodil smoking at the bottom of a sandblown valley near Squaw Creek. After a quick survey, Leslie had determined that they could replace Daffodil more easily than they could fix her.

And now Bluebird lay in splinters against the side of the hill north of Daffodil's last resting place. Bluebird's tail fin jutted in the air in a grim caricature of a tombstone. Everyone agreed it was too soon to unpack the replacements, Hyacinth and Oriole: The software was so raw, so wild, it would destroy the Hunters as fast as a computer could load it.

So Juan's simulations became the lynchpin. The efforts of the others spun about him: each time Kurt or Ronnie or Lila threw a new fix into their software, Juan had to already have his simulations refined to test the fix. In a race where Kurt and Ronnie and Lila ran as a relay team, Juan had to run alone, yet stay forever ahead. So far, he had succeeded.

Juan rolled in agitated sleep. A streak of noontime sun, sneaking through the shuttered blinds, struck him in the eyes. He winced. Leslie hurried softly to the window, to block the light, but Juan waved him away. "Never mind," he yawned. With a long, twisting stretch, he rose to a sitting position. "It's time to get up anyway."

Leslie stamped his foot. "No, it's time for everyone to get some sleep."

Kurt objected. "We have to solve this interoperability problem."

Leslie frowned. "We'll solve it better after getting some sleep. We need clear thoughts and fresh ideas, not long hours."

Lila's voice rang out in surprising agreement with Kurt. "I for one won't be able to sleep until we figure out a solution."

"What's wrong?" Juan asked. He rose to his feet, a feverish fascination now creeping across his face.

Leslie turned to him. "We seem to have found a fundamental problem in the design of the HopperHunter system. It's a problem with the way the expert system and the sensor system interoperate."

Juan looked across the room at Kurt and Lila, as if

sharing Leslie's thought: if the expert system and the sensor system worked together the way Kurt and Lila did, they could expect the Hopper to explode. With a slow, strained smile, he asked, "What's the nitty-gritty?"

Kurt went to the white board and grabbed an eraser. As he was about to sweep a corner clean, Lila shrieked, "Don't erase that!"

Kurt jerked back, leaving a slight smudge. "Sorry," he said, in a sincere tone of apology.

Leslie almost smiled. The white board had replaced the PERT chart as the center of organization. Tasks rose and fell too quickly to be tracked on the old, butchered rolls of paper now coated with red and green and blue boxes. Today the white board contained the lists of actions, partially sorted by priority and difficulty. Interspersed with the cryptic questions and answers were equally cryptic comments, such as "DCIU 2 me too."

After careful study, Kurt picked a different part of the board to erase. Under his hurried hand two similar comments faded into oblivion: a crossed-out line, "The LKB is dead," and a newer line that was not crossed out, "Long live the LKB." LKB stood for "Last Known Bug."

Kurt listed descriptions of the interfaces between the two subsystems, with Lila making occasional comments. In looking around the room, Leslie realized everyone was watching Kurt at the board. This was the first time since arrival that they had all turned to the same question at the same time. Leslie was afraid to breathe, afraid to do anything that might break the mood: it was their first attempt to solve a problem as a team.

After a few minutes of discussion, Leslie saw the significance of the problem at a higher level. The sensor system could not make analyses of its raw information based solely on the discernible patterns. It needed some idea of the possible meanings of those patterns before it could make a definite match. It needed to understand more of the context.

The expert system understood the context. But whereas the sensor system had been designed for fast processing, the expert system had been designed for careful, meticulous processing. If the expert system got involved with the sensor analysis, the overall operation slowed down to the point where the decisions could not flow out as fast as the Hopper needed them to avoid crashing. They needed a compromise.

Leslie thought he might have an idea, but he decided to let the team try to solve it first. One by one, Ronnie, Kurt, Juan, and Lila each stepped to the board and offered possibilities. Each tentative solution was shot down. A morbid depression followed.

After a long pause, Leslie walked to the board. "How about this?" he asked, and scrawled a series of detailed modifications to the interface, using a purple marker. Meanwhile, he outlined his general idea—the overall concept of the compromise he intended. His real purpose was not to persuade them to use the detailed approach he now drew, but to get them to think about a new, higher-level approach.

Kurt shook his head. "That won't work." He explained why, and Lila nodded her head in agreement.

Leslie shrugged. "Oh, well." He stepped away from the board.

He saw Flo whisper something in Ronnie's ear. Ronnie shook his head. She waved her arm rapidly as she continued. Suddenly he brightened. "Wait a minute," he cried. "What if we modify Leslie's interface like this?" He hustled to the board and started writing, talking half incoherently as he went.

Lila took her keyboard into her lap, muttering, "Yes, yes." She started typing softly.

Kurt squinted at the board as if someone had written on it in Greek—and indeed, Ronnie had used some Greek symbols. "That might work," he concluded a few moments later.

Juan slapped his forehead. "God, this is terrible," he said. "God, this is terrific. God, what a pain this is going to be to simulate!" He strode across the room to the largest collection of displays and processor modules, in the far corner—the simulation setup. He buried himself behind the glow and hum of his machines.

Leslie smiled, though he really wanted to leap in the air and shout with victory. A movement caught his eye from the doorway. He turned to see Nathan leaning against it, framed by the light from the corridor. He must have just gotten in from D.C.

Leslie sneaked out of the room with Nathan; no one noticed his absence. "You should've joined us," Leslie said. "You were a pretty hot programmer yourself at one time, if I remember correctly."

Nathan shook his head. "I would not pit my skills against yours." He smiled maliciously. "I wouldn't want to embarrass you." They exchanged low laughter. "Besides, you clearly had everything under control. I never disturb a master at work."

Leslie pointed toward the cafe. "You hungry? I am."

"Aren't you going to hang around to make sure they all go off on the same track?"

Leslie shook his head vigorously. "In an hour or so I'll go back to force everyone to get some sleep. But I've done my part. They'll finish it. From here, it's just a matter of sweat and enthusiasm." He gave Nathan a puzzled smile. "That's the way we work with ensemble management, remember?"

"Ouch! Cut to the bone with my own words!" Ensemble management was an organizational style taught by the Institute—a style well suited to Information Age projects. "I'll buy the coffee."

"No!" Leslie exclaimed. "No more coffee." He rubbed his stomach. "I need some nutrition for a change."

"A wise choice," Nathan said. "We may need our strength. The Army arrives this afternoon, in the form of a general. General Kelvin."

"Good. He should keep you out of trouble," Leslie offered with a wicked smile.

"Yes, sir!"

Nathan heard Kurt McKenna'a voice from the hallway, accompanied by the pounding of two sets of feet approaching the Tieton Room. Kurt's voice now held the same unthinking respect that it had held during his first months at the Institute. Nathan had finally broken him of that habitual respect, though once in a while he felt a strange desire to receive that blind obedience one more time.

Of course, he knew better. In the knowledge-oriented

contexts of the Information Age, the blind obedience observed in military management never served anyone well.

Every human endeavor required a different management style. In the context of lethal battle, Zetetic ensemble management would lead to tragedy. Similarly, in high technology engineering, military organizational style could only lead to failure.

In the respectful tone of Kurt's voice, Nathan heard the fundamental driver behind generations of military research and development catastrophes. In that voice, he heard the form of his own impending conflict: the military, and no doubt the military concept of management, had just arrived in Yakima.

Kurt led the general around the corner. Stars gleamed upon his shoulders; his eyes swept the room as if he owned the place. Nathan could feel himself growing hot, just watching the man. Kurt introduced them. "General Kelvin, Nathan Pilstrom."

They did not exactly shake hands in greeting: their grips more closely resembled a wrestling match. As usual in such pointless encounters, Nathan withdrew first. "So this is the Sling Project, all neatly packed in one little room," Kelvin said, with dismissal in his voice.

"More or less," Nathan replied. "That's close enough for a first approximation, anyway."

Kelvin jerked his head, pushing the warning aside. His jaw clenched as he scanned the room. Nathan knew what he saw: stacks of computer systems strewn about, matched with the expressionless faces of programmers lost in the glow of their display screens. Juan lay curled up like a cat in the north corner, more or less obeying Leslie's earlier orders to sleep. The others had napped shortly after lunch, and they appeared more invigorated—enthusiastic zombies fresh from the grave.

Even Nathan had difficulty believing that this scene belonged in the Valkyrie's hall of heroic images. How could these men and women, some almost adolescent, shape the tools of victory? Thinking about this scene's impact on the general gave Nathan a sour moment of amusement.

Kelvin shifted his weight, preparing to step around Nathan into the room, but Nathan also shifted, blocking him. "General Kelvin, we're planning an all-hands review around five. Why don't you and I go around the corner for a cup of coffee until then?"

The general's teeth clenched tighter, then went slack. "All right."

As they struck out down the hall, Nathan tried to forestall the general's caustic remarks. "I realize that that room looks like a Kansas whirlwind hit it, but we have a good team in there."

"I've seen better," Kelvin said.

They passed the registration desk and came upon a young waitress at the entrance to the coffee shop. She seated them in a booth on the outside edge of the cafe area. According to Leslie, crowds of busy people usually hurried back and forth through the motel lobby and the restaurant, but now the Thunderbird had little business. Since the beginning of the war, the Sling team had been the only regular patrons. Part of the quiet was caused by the general decline in the nation's travel; of course, the principal cause was the Zetetic Institute's rental of the entire motel. It had seemed the least obtrusive way to ensure privacy.

Other than this unnatural quiet, you could not tell that a national emergency existed. You certainly couldn't tell that a war raged with such fury that it might destroy the planet. A few resources had become scarce: only people with military business could catch an airplane, and freeze-dried food had disappeared from the backpacking stores. But no shortages of normal foods or appliances had yet occurred; indeed, the war would end for lack of participants before such an event could take place.

The young waitress looked like she was under severe stress; Nathan suspected her boyfriend was now boarding one of the planes packed with reinforcements for Europe.

Nathan spoke to Kelvin with an ironic edge in his voice. "So you've seen better teams. I must say, you completed your evaluation with amazing speed." Nathan looked straight into the general's eyes, trying to let exactly the right amount of anger shine through.

Their eyes locked; this time Kelvin broke off the engagement first. "You're right, that wasn't entirely fair."

"Thank you," Nathan answered.

"I still can't believe this Sling of yours will make the difference." He shook his head. "Dammit, we need *tanks*, not *gadgets*." He pressed the tips of his straightened fingers to his forehead, as if he could somehow drive home a better solution to their problems. He gave up the attempt as his coffee arrived.

While Kelvin idly stirred sugar into the steaming liquid, Nathan asked, "Do you believe the only way to defeat tanks is with more tanks?"

Kelvin paused. "It's the only method that has worked so far. We've tried handheld TOW missile launchers. But if somebody kills the man guiding the missile, the missile crashes." He shuddered. "The Russians have gotten very good at killing the man." Anger entered his eyes, and he seemed suddenly to be much larger. "We lost thousands of good men trying to make that tactic work. We can't make that kind of mistake again."

Nathan nodded. "Never again. In some sense, the Russians are fighting the TOW missile with Information Age techniques. They're killing the information-processing part of the missile—the man who aims it."

Kelvin considered that for a moment. "I suppose so."

"Listen." Nathan pushed for a revelation in General Kelvin's perspective. "We both know how easy it is to prove that a project is a failure—it's as easy as proving that a project is a success. To prove failure, list the weaknesses, without mentioning any strengths. To prove success, list the strengths without mentioning any weaknesses." He brought his hand down in a chopping motion. "General, we can't afford either of those two distortions to influence our decisions here. In addition to showing you the strengths of the Sling, I am committed to exposing for you every flaw we can think of. It's a scary list. But we would be leading you, and the country, across a bridge made of tissue paper if we didn't give you that list."

Nathan pointed his hand at the general. "But we need something from you, too, for our honesty to work. You can't just look at the list of problems and shut us down.

You must help us find ways to make the system work despite the problems."

A mischievous smile crossed Kelvin's lips. He shoved the coffee aside. "Very well. Show me that it *might* work. If you show me it might work, I'll believe you."

"Excellent." Nathan felt some tension relax in his neck muscles. Kelvin's attitude was very Zetetic. At least he understood his own prejudices.

Kelvin interrogated him at length about matters that Nathan rarely had to discuss—not the flashy technology of the Hunters, but questions whose answers could make the difference between success and failure: What do the troops have to know to operate a Hopper? What will they have to feed it after a battle? How do they repair it when it breaks?

"They don't repair it, General. They throw it away when it breaks. It's disposable, like a razor blade or a paper cup."

They argued the wisdom of this philosophy—it had great strengths and great weaknesses.

When a break opened in the discussion, Nathan said, "You haven't seen any of our Hunters in action, have you? Let me show you our simulation runs." He rose.

Kelvin followed with a shake of his head. "Skip the sims. Simulations always look convincing—they're the ultimate tool for showing strengths while hiding weaknesses. I don't believe them at all."

Nathan laughed. "In earlier times, people talked about how good projects looked on paper. Now, they talk about how good they look on simulation. And a simulation can distort reality even more than paper, if abused with sufficient skill." His tone hardened. "I assure you that Juan does not build delusionary scenarios. He maintains a harshness in his sims that gets as close to reality as you can get. If he isn't sure how brutal reality is, he makes the simulation more brutal than reality could possibly be." He looked over at the general. "Still, we can do better. I'll show you live videotapes of Hunters in action. You'll see the real machines at their finest—and at their worst."

"Much better."

"We'll stop for Juan on the way up; he probably has the

best overview of the strengths and idiosyncrasies of the
system. In some sense, Juan *is* each one of the Hunters:
he creates the simulations."

Nathan stepped back into the Tieton Room, to see Juan
at a work station again, his mouth hanging wide, his eyes
locked open. Nathan inhaled sharply, afraid of the trance-
like, epileptic quality of his stare.

But Juan blinked and started typing again.

In a whisper to avoid disturbing the others, Nathan
asked him, "Are you all right?"

"Sure," Juan muttered without looking up.

"Can I disturb you to come talk with General Kelvin for
a few minutes?"

He shrugged, a weary gesture. His eyes drooped. "Why
not? I'm not doing much good here." Smoothly flicking a
sequence of power buttons, he rose to follow Nathan.

"I'm planning to show him the tapes of the live tests in
the firing range, to give him a feel of how the Hunters
really work."

Juan screwed up his face with doubt. He looked at
Kelvin. "Are you sure you want that much truth, all at
once?"

Nathan watched Kelvin's jaw work in annoyance.

Juan continued. "Well, if you want even more reality,
we're going to go play pinball," he glanced at his watch,
"in about twenty minutes."

The general stared at Juan. "You're going to play *what*?"

"We're going to play pinball." He smiled with assumed
innocence. His weariness had disappeared in the renewed
twinkling of his eyes.

Nathan ended the impasse. "That's the local name for
running a live test. If you're not too tired from your
journey, come and watch a HopperHunter go nose to nose
with a Soviet battalion. The Soviets are fakes, of course,
but the Hunter is real." He couldn't resist a smile that
mirrored Juan's. "As for why we call it pinball, you'll
understand after you've seen the battle."

When Kelvin accepted the offer, Nathan turned back to
Juan. "We'll meet you out on the Point."

He led the general out of the room, out of the Thunderbird, and into the parking lot, to an Eagle Scout four-wheel jeep.

Looking at the sad state of the jeep, Kelvin gasped, then laughed. "You *have* been at war out here."

"Yes." Nathan knew what Kelvin meant: whenever Nathan looked at the Eagle, he wondered what archaeologists would think thousands of years from now, if they found such a vehicle buried beneath the sands of Yakima.

With just a little more caked-on dirt, the Eagle would have been buried right there in the parking lot. Sand packed itself around the mirrors and the grill; the gold-brown powder smeared across the window in a frosting that would not melt or scrape away. "We've only been out here two days, and our jeeps already look like sand dunes. I suppose we could get someone to wash them, but it wouldn't make any difference." Nathan sighed. Then, laughing, he said, "We signed a statement with Avis promising that we wouldn't drive off-road. Of course, we didn't discuss *our* idea of a road, as opposed to *their* idea of a road." He slapped the roof with joy. "Any old rut qualifies as a road in the Yakima Firing Range."

"Why didn't you just buy the jeeps?" Kelvin demanded. "Money isn't a problem."

"We may have to buy them in the end." Nathan shrugged. "This seemed easier at the time. They rent jeeps at the airport; they don't sell them."

They climbed into the Eagle and closed the doors, unleashing spumes of dust. General Kelvin waved his hand to clear the air, which only served to stir the dust more thoroughly.

More of the fine powder adhered to Nathan's lungs with every breath. He could smell it—the distinctive, gritty smell of the desert. "You can't beat it," Nathan explained with the fatalism of a priest giving last rites. "The best strategy is to pretend that you like it." Keying the ignition, he brought the engine coughing to life.

Kelvin snorted.

Nathan turned right onto North First Street, heading toward I-82. They drove in silence for a time. When Kelvin spoke again, his voice seemed almost dreamy. "I'd forgotten what Yakima was like."

"So you've been here before," Nathan led him forward in the discussion.

"I think everybody in the Army comes here sooner or later." The general gazed around at the austere, rolling beauty of the desert, with the look of a man coming home.

Nathan took advantage of the general's relaxed mood to ask him about himself. Kelvin had a son in the Air Force in Germany. He knew that his son had probably died in the first hammering clashes of the war. If he was not dead, he was a prisoner. The American aircraft, superior though they were to their Soviet counterparts, had been hopelessly outnumbered. The Soviet swarm shot them down over terrain that Soviet divisions quickly overran.

They passed Range Benchmark 1944, then started up the hill that the Sling team used for observing the tests at close hand; they had dubbed it the Point. Before Nathan and Kelvin reached the top, Nathan knew about General Kelvin's frustrations with the modern Army, his occasional disagreements with his daughter, and his resigned acceptance that he would never get a third star. "Of course, if this war were to continue for a couple of years, I would surely get promoted." He shook his head. "At that price, I'd rather not."

Nathan pointed out, "If the Sling saves the day, you might yet get your three stars, and without an endless bloodbath."

They reached the Point. A van lumbered over the same ruts their jeep had used. "Here come the troops," he said, pointing at the brittle dinosaur struggling against the harsh landscape. "We bring a lot of equipment with us on these trips. Perhaps more than we can really afford."

"Leave the van here, and get duplicates of the equipment," Kelvin ordered. "In fact, put two completely outfitted vans up here, for backup. We can't waste time moving stuff around like that." He looked around. "It's not like anyone was likely to steal it out here."

"You're right. Everyone will be delighted to leave everything here."

The van bounced onto the hilltop and stalled next to the jeep. The door opened, and both Nathan and Kelvin squeezed in with the rest of the Sling team. Nathan introduced Kelvin to Lila and Ronnie; they had left Flo behind at the Thunderbird to sleep.

Juan clapped his hands. "Well, gang, let's do it," he said, squeezing himself into the controller chair. Twin monitors lit up and stereo speakers hissed. Nathan watched Kelvin watch the screen.

The new HopperHunter, Hyacinth, came to life with the whine of turbine engines. Dust clouds boiled across the screen. Juan started a team monologue. "We're watching through Hyacinth's stereoscopic cameras. Of course, the hopper's view is better than ours: its sensors run through radar and infrared, not just optical wavelengths." Juan's voice echoed oddly in the confined metal space.

On the speakers, the turbine's whine coughed; the dust cloud parted before them as the hopper surged forward. The dust cloud had been induced by Hyacinth's hovering.

Gaining speed, Hyacinth hurtled over the sagebrush, dropped with sickening suddenness into a ravine, and popped out again, all the while swiveling its camera from side to side.

It came to the base of a mountain and started straight up, with no noticeable loss of speed. Leslie spoke. "This maneuver's really hard on the engines. The power team performed a miracle, pumping her acceleration like that without blowing the compressors."

Hyacinth crested the mountain. The view opened on a valley. Vast though it was, in comparison with the limitless plains stretching beyond the next series of hills, it seemed quite tiny. Kurt commented, "From here we get a quick image of the enemy positions before going in."

The word "quick" got an odd punctuation mark from the hopper itself, for it did not slow down as it reached the lip of a precipice and plunged over. Nathan heard Kelvin gasp. Nathan felt it, too; this part of the trip always left him feeling queasy.

He wondered why no one else on this team shared his motion sickness, as Ronnie explained eagerly, "We spent almost a month fixing that leap so we wouldn't crash on the way down." Indeed, Hyacinth had landed gently on a ledge, one edge of its ground-effect skirt hanging over the side, then it plunged again, and again, in a fantastic series of hops.

Kurt spoke in the brisk but respectful voice peculiar to a soldier addressing a superior. "Sir, by coming up over the cliff in this maneuver, our view of the battlefield doesn't expose us to artillery fire." A slightly gloating expression entered his eyes. "Of course, we're pretty hard to kill even when they know exactly where we are, but why take chances?"

Hyacinth had reached the floor of the valley now. The camera jittered across the landscape as the hopper itself jumped in a staccato dance, fast, slow, left, right, a patternless modern ballet whose rhythm matched the beat of hailstones against a roof. Tanks and cannons would indeed have a very hard time lining up a shot on the unpredictable hopper.

Lila muttered, "I'm sorry the image is so hard to follow. The last time we came out here, I decided that we needed to reset the transmitted image to show an averaged view, after the second-stage image processing. But I forgot when we got back to the motel." She turned to the general with a shrug. "Next time it'll be easier to see what's happening, I promise."

Despite the bouncing of the screen, they could see the target on which the hopper now homed. A dozen troops hustled across the exposed land, occasionally turning to fire. It was easy to see which soldier was giving the orders, and Hyacinth saw it even as Nathan did. A crosshair appeared on the screen, and the image flashed bright red for a moment. Meanwhile, the speakers roared with the muffled sound of a machine gun.

Juan explained, "That was the hopper firing. Needless to say, since those are real troops, we're using blanks. Otherwise, we would have a very dead lieutenant out there."

The hopper turned to the right, away from the troops it had been approaching.

"What's wrong?" Kelvin asked. "Why isn't it finishing off that platoon?"

Nathan smiled. "For shame, General. We have no intention of wasting our limited ammunition on those men.

Didn't you notice which single person we shot? The one who gives the orders. The HopperHunter will leave those men, leaderless, to stop, or to go on in confusion to defeat. We can let them live—and we have to, because we don't carry enough ammunition to kill every soldier we see."

Hyacinth hit a ravine and, dropping into its narrow channel, accelerated in a new direction. "This is scary," Ronnie muttered. "It's a good thing my software drives Hyacinth better than Kurt drives the van."

Juan nodded his head vigorously.

When the hopper popped out again, a formation of tanks faced it.

Now they heard angry static from the speakers. Lila said, "Those are the tank radios you're hearing."

The general cleared his throat of dust, then asked humbly, "Why aren't you shooting at them yet?"

Kurt answered this one. "Two reasons. First, we haven't identified the commander yet. If we don't identify the commander soon, we'll knock a couple of the front tanks out, then listen for the new series of orders that'll let us locate him." He wrapped his knuckles against the side of the van. "There's a more fundamental reason why we can't fire yet, however. Our gun can't penetrate their frontal armor. We'll have to get in among them before we can be effective." He grinned. "Imagine telling your troops that they'd have to get in among the enemy tanks before firing." He grimaced. "I went in like that myself a couple of times. It's no fun."

True to Kurt's words, as the hopper broke past the lead tanks, the picture spun in a dizzy pirouette. The hopper fired twice— a much louder, thudding sound than the machine gun fire earlier. The screen showed kills against the first two tanks. Hyacinth spun and skittered as the speakers burst with radio activity. With a purposeful lunge, the hopper outflanked one more tank, fired, and raced away from the cluster of enemy armor.

"I take it that last one we took out was the leader," Kelvin said drily. Nathan almost betrayed his excitement— Kelvin had said *we*.

Juan scrutinized the alternate display, finely printed with scrolling data. "Yeah, we picked out the right one all right. Magic!" A general murmur of pleasure arose in the stale air of the van.

As they watched, twilight overtook the afternoon. Mottled red glares and long shadows burnished the valley. Nathan felt his own breathing take on a jerky rhythm. "Did you guys plan this test to run into sunset?"

"Sure." Juan's voice reflected the tension Nathan felt. "I've never been in a war myself, but from what I've heard, they don't go nine to five and then wait until the lights come back on."

Hyacinth now coursed along an arrow's path, straight toward a convoy of trucks. Kurt muttered, "Hit the lead." The hopper continued its unveering flight that indeed zeroed in on the lead truck. The crosshairs came up. The Hopper spun, and fired into a shadow. "Damn," Kurt muttered.

Believing itself to have completed its mission, the hopper bounced away—like a pinball, Nathan thought—toward a clump of troops on the horizon.

Nathan's ears had filtered out the incessant whine of the hopper's engine long before. But now the hum changed tune, slowly coming down the scale from soprano to baritone. As the tone dropped, so did the Hopper's speed; meanwhile, the dust cloud boiled up across the screen, as it caught up with the slowing vehicle.

Lila shook her head, her hair continuing to bounce after she had stopped. "Double damn," she muttered. "It's the dust. The engine filter's plugged full. And once we stop like this in a cloud of the stuff, it plugs my sensors, too. The dust is killing us."

Juan tried to push his chair back, but failed in the tight clutter of people and equipment. "That's one of the things we haven't any idea of how to fix: if we hover long enough, the poor thing chokes to death."

Nathan watched Kelvin's reaction to this discussion carefully: he frowned, then shrugged. "If we were fighting a war in Egypt, that would cancel the project right there. But we're fighting in Europe, in April. Do we have any similar problems with mud?" Again Nathan hid his elation: Kelvin had had two choices in the face of this apparently insurmountable obstacle. He could clutch at it as a fatal flaw, using it as a rationale to end the program. Or he could help in the search for solutions.

Juan replied, "No problems with mud to my knowledge." He raised an eyebrow. "Of course, we haven't tested it in mud the way we've tested it in dust."

The discussion continued for a while before everyone agreed to finish the analysis back at the motel. Kelvin made contributions in his own brusque way. They would no longer drive out here in vans, jeeps, or otherwise: Kelvin would commandeer helicopters for transport. A platoon of technicians would man the Point at all times, guaranteeing that the equipment was tuned and ready at a moment's notice. And above all, they would get air conditioners, with their own power generators, to keep the vans cool when they were working. He announced that last measure while wiping a thick line of perspiration from his forehead.

Nathan slid the door back and stepped into the desert. With twilight came cool air—too cool to stand in for long, but perfect for someone stepping out of a van whose cabin resembled a furnace. Though the Sling had not passed the desert test this afternoon, it had passed the political test. Nathan stood quietly, loving the simple joy of just breathing the cool, dusty air, watching the sharp orange edge of the sun put a crease in the bright blue sky.

April 29

*Filter fourth for completeness. This filter
protects from the media.*
                              —Zetetic Commentaries

Nathan and the general crossed the street to Pioneer
Pies in silence. Nathan felt famished, but his latest tense
confrontation had left him unable to appreciate even the
thought of lemon creme pie.

The silence continued as they sat down in one of the
booths and ordered steak and fries. Nathan shifted several
times on the hard boards of the bench. Although the wood
decor of the restaurant was pleasing to the eye, and the
well-varnished surfaces were pleasing to the touch, the
wooden boards were not pleasing to the human back.

Neither Nathan nor Kelvin broke the silence. Instead, a
burst of static made them look up. A television, distinctly
out of place in this rustic setting, showed them a picture
that was sure to restart their argument from an hour ago.

*FOCUS. Bill Hardie's subdued voice speaks. "Yet an-
other heroic moment occurred in Heidelberg today. Russian forces fresh from overrunning Frankfurt turned south
to destroy the fragments of the Third Armored Division."
Men and machines race across the autobahn bridge that
arches over the Neckar River.*

*PAN. To the north, clouds of smoke twist and rise from
the ground. Shells burst, spawning new smoke clouds. The
clouds and explosions seem to center on a single point, like
an unpracticed dart thrower closing in on a bull's-eye. In
the distance, dozens of giant engines of destruction slow
down as they approach that bull's-eye. Here and there
explosions appear among the attackers as well. Frequently,
when the smoke clears, only dead men and dead machines
remain.*

*ZOOM. The camera closes on the bull's-eye. A gust
of wind blows the smoke away, and a lone Abrams tank*

hugs the ground at the center of the fury, its turret shifting smoothly, its cannon periodically spitting fire. Shells pound upon it. Hardie speaks of the extraordinary toughness of the Chobham armor plate. The turret continues to spin, blithely ignoring the hellfires unleashed.

PAN. The bridge is now quiet: the Americans have completed their retreat, save the one vehicle left behind to cover their movement. That one Abrams backs slowly toward the bridge, enemy machines pressing ever closer.

FOCUS. The periodic flames from the Abrams cannon cease. One shell too many has struck it in a weakened plate. Recognizing the failure, the enemy rushes forward, firing constantly. A larger, darker cloud rises from the Abrams. It moves no longer. The dark cloud clears to reveal an empty hulk, spotlighted by a series of explosions that destroy the bridge.

FADE. "Unfortunately, individual acts of heroism may have no significance. More significant than the successful retreat across the Neckar is the French announcement of a separate peace treaty with the Soviet Union. The French armies now in Germany will return home under banners of neutrality during the next 48 hours." Bill gives a comprehensive list of the cities in Germany and Denmark that have surrendered since his last report.

Kelvin turned red while viewing the newscast. As he turned to Nathan, the pulse in his left temple throbbed visibly.

Nathan watched him with concern. "We can't deploy them yet," he said again, as if repetition would make his point fasten itself in Kelvin's mind. "Just because the Hunters passed the basic test doesn't mean they work. If you deploy now, and we find another hardware problem, we're sunk."

"And if we deploy after all our troops are dead, we're also sunk," Kelvin retorted, doggedly reiterating *his* position.

Seeing that it had become a confrontation of egos, Nathan sat back in his chair and consciously relaxed his mind and body. He concentrated on the amusing aspects of the past 48 hours; though difficult to recall, amusement was a salient feature of his situation. After all, two days ago, Kelvin had been against deploying the Sling Hunters, while Nathan had been in favor.

The pinball game on the testing range had not brought about this transformation by itself. Even discounting the problems with desert sand, the hopper had failed: it had fired at shadows rather than targets, for one thing. And every member of the team had grown silent as they had examined the detailed readouts of the battle: from the sensing, through the decision-making, through the hovering, there had been odd quirks in the hopper's behavior that left the programmers puzzled and worried. The problems seemed more numerous than the successes.

Fortunately, they would not have to wait until all the problems were fixed before they could deploy Hunters. As Nathan had explained to Kelvin the day before, once they were sure the hardware worked, they could build and ship Hunters while they continued to work on the software. As they made software improvements, they would download the new versions by satellite link: it would be no different from the way they loaded the test Hunters with new software in Yakima.

Kelvin had not merely accepted the idea of deploying the hardware before completing the software; he had ordered Leslie to start a ramp-up of all the factories involved in Sling manufacture, to prepare the production lines for peak output. They would immediately start manufacturing and stockpiling Hunter subassemblies. That way, they could run the first thousands of Hunters through production almost instantly, and they would face bottlenecks only with new parts demanded by the results of the testing.

Kelvin had gone on to ask about the software for all three Hunters. "How long do you think it will take before all the software bugs are out?"

Nathan had laughed. "It'll be *years* before *all* the bugs are out. We'll deploy before that, too."

"What about the SkyHunter and the HighHunter? Are they ready, or are you testing yet?"

"We've been alternately testing the SkyHunter and the HopperHunter on the range," Nathan had explained. "Basically, they both work, except for the kinds of problems you saw yesterday, where the Hopper started shooting at shadows. Most of the problems with target recognition are shared by both systems—fixing it in one will fix it in the other."

"What about the HighHunter?"

"The HighHunter has nastier problems. We can't run a full-up test of the HighHunter without shooting one into orbit. Then we'd have to make it dispense its Crowbars somewhere over Seattle, to make them drop here on the Range. I don't know what our chances are of surprising the Russians with the Hunters, but if we drop a HighHunter out of orbit, they'll take a *serious* interest in everything we're doing in Yakima."

Kelvin had growled—the sound of a mountain climber who has just found frayed rope in his hands. "Damn. This project is completely unclassified. I'm sure the Russians know about it."

"Actually, we're counting on it." A Zetetic observation on institutions leaped to Nathan's mind: *Organizations never know anything.* Rather, certain select individuals in organizations knew certain things. By grouping selected individuals together while dispersing others, the manipulator could dominate the organization. "Certainly, individual Soviet officers know about different aspects of the Sling. However, the Sling has never been important enough to classify. So the Russians who know about it wouldn't consider it to be important either. Our complete lack of classification may have protected us more than a Secret or even a Top Secret clearance would have. We're lost in the noise."

Kelvin had looked doubtful. "I hope you're right."

"Yeah. So do I," Nathan had responded drily. "Anyway, that chance of surprise prevents us from doing a full test of the HighHunter. We've dropped some Crowbars over the range, but I'm not comfortable with the extent of our testing. It's been far too incomplete. We'll have to be alert when the first HighHunters go into action." Kelvin had seemed satisfied at that point; they had dropped the subject.

Now, sitting in Pioneer Pies with Kelvin on one side and a terrifying newscast on the other, Nathan understood the driving force behind Kelvin's eagerness to get the Hunters to Europe. He ate slowly; a cold lump grew in his stomach.

Kelvin pressed his attack. "The Hopper flew across the twilight and hit everything it was supposed to hit. It didn't hit anything it wasn't supposed to hit. It dodged around enemy fire like a mosquito dodging a fist. Damn! And then the SkyHunter did the same thing." His eyes held a tortured combination of pleading and commanding. "The hardware's fine." He clenched his fist, his tendons vibrating, and pressed it against the wooden table as if afraid he might lose control otherwise. "We need those Hunters in Europe *now.*"

Nathan temporized. "Let's talk with the team before we do anything hasty."

After an unhappy pause, Kelvin said, "All right."

They drove back to the Thunderbird.

They asked Lila first, "Is the hardware ready to ship? Can we fix the rest of the problems in software?"

Lila pulled on her lip, twisting it in her fingers. "I don't know. I guess so. I . . . guess so. But we really ought to test it more."

They asked Kurt. "Why not?" Kurt replied. "What we've got works well enough to zap *some* of the bastards." He paused. "It wouldn't hurt to test it a bit more, though."

They asked Flo. "I believe all the equipment in the control and communications parts of the Hunters—the parts for which Ronnie and I are responsible—work adequately correctly." A pair of creases marred the soft smoothness of her forehead. "But I am sure Amos would advise against sending them yet. Even if all the separate pieces work correctly, we may be surprised when they work together at cross-purposes." She shook her head. "This is not a good idea."

They asked Ronnie. "Great. Get 'em over there. Anything that goes wrong, we'll get around it with a software kludge of one kind or another."

Finally, they asked Juan. They sat in Nathan's room, Juan stretching his long legs across the bed, toying with a microfloppy. As he spoke, he flipped the flat plastic square back and forth with ever greater agitation. As he flipped it one way, he seemed anxious; as he flipped it the other way, he seemed amused. "So here we are again, Nathan, on the verge of a beta test." Beta testing was a stage commercial vendors usually went through with software. During beta test, the vendor released the new product to a carefully selected handful of customers who understood the risks—and who knew enough to help the vendor fix the last problems. The beta customer also knew how to create his own, temporary work-arounds for outlandish problems.

But no one in the middle of a war had the time or the clarity of mind to produce novel solutions to outlandish problems. Nathan smiled back at Juan. "Yes, Juan, it's beta test time. Whom do we victimize this time?"

"No doubt the whole damn army." His head lolled, then swept sideways in a slow shake. "But not yet," he whispered desperately. "We aren't ready yet." He clenched the floppy, then tossed it aside. "Listen. I know the Hunters better than anybody else here. Kurt, Ronnie, Flo, and Lila may have developed the software, but when they test their stuff, they test it against *me*. There is not a single nuance of those machines that I don't understand as well as they do. Nathan, *it doesn't work yet*. There are too many things that nobody understands, even when it works right, the way it did yesterday."

The general spoke. "What's wrong with it?"

Juan shrugged helplessly. "If I knew what was wrong, we'd fix it. But we don't know. Christ, there's so much we don't know."

"When *will* you know?" Kelvin asked, his words forming bullets that made Nathan wince.

But Juan just smiled sadly. His shirt was open at the collar; to Nathan it seemed to leave his throat exposed. "I don't know when I'll know." The sinews in his throat rippled, and he suddenly sat erect, a judge proclaiming a verdict. "But I know I'll know when they're ready."

The general reacted, squaring his own shoulders. "We can't wait forever."

"And you won't have to." As suddenly as he had straightened, Juan coiled around the bed again. He reached into his back pocket, pulling out his credit-card-size note computer. "We may be close. Actually, I think we really are close. Maybe, if we push all the way today, we can learn everything we need to know." His right hand worked silently over the palm-size touchpad as he studied the testing schedule. "If things go well, we can pack about three days of tests in by midnight."

"And then it'll be ready?" Kelvin demanded.

"And then we'll decide whether it's ready," Juan corrected him.

They broke into two teams: Kurt, Lila, and Ronnie ran one test while Flo, Juan, and Nathan prepared the next. The tests became ever more rigorous, ever more complex, ever more ruthless—a series of gauntlets that no machine could run successfully. Indeed, that was the point: "Test to destruction," Juan explained cheerfully, "is the truest form of analysis."

They tested Hyacinth to destruction before lunch. Once too often, Hyacinth raced close to the ravine wall. A stone outcropping appeared and the hopper smashed into it, crumpling its ground-effect skirt, spinning out of control. Hyacinth bounced along until the rocks turned it to rubble.

"Hardware or software?" Kelvin demanded.

The new van, permanently emplaced at the Point, reverberated with the rumble of air conditioning—a level of cooling that kept the van so chill they had named it the Refrigerator. Now everyone twisted to hear the verdict from Ronnie and Florence. The van seemed stuffy, despite the bracing air. "Well, I guess it's software," Ronnie muttered.

Florence quietly tapped at the keyboard, pointed out a routine on the screen to Ronnie, who nodded. "That is correct," Florence agreed. Her voice matched the coolness of the van.

Juan frowned. "Why didn't we catch this software problem in the simulations?" He, too, turned to reexamine his code.

While they reworked the sims and the hopper control systems, they sent Oriole into the air.

The SkyHunter performed magnificently on one test. They set up the second test series, and it dropped all its bombs on shadows.

"Hardware or software?" Kelvin asked in a near-scream.

Lila shrugged. "I don't know. I don't know." She slumped into the chair. Nathan and Kelvin left her alone with her Oriole and Kurt's Caesar.

The wreckage of Hyacinth remained in the shallow grave of the ravine and the next hopper in the test group took its place in the gauntlet. Marigold now scurried across the plains and into combat with enemy bunkers—low, sloping bulwarks of earth and concrete. Juan, Lila, and Flo watched the patterns of fire and crossfire quietly—too quietly. So quietly that Nathan sensed a problem. He looked around the room and asked, "What's wrong?"

A sick look of exhaustion crossed Juan's features. "We fixed it, we think. But we're still not sure why our fix worked."

Kelvin started to turn purple. "You don't *know*?" He looked from side to side, then back. "What about your sim? What was wrong with it?"

Juan drew his long, elegant fingers down across his face, to pause at his throat. His hand settled there to rest, emphasizing the slow, calming rhythm of his breathing. "Nothing."

The general's eyes bugged out. "How can that be?"

No one answered. Nathan broke the deadlock. "General, let me assure you that the answers will not become any clearer if you and I stand here pressuring everybody. The worst enemy of anyone trying to find a subtle problem is anxiety. Make them anxious enough by hounding them, and they'll never find it." Nathan tapped Kelvin on the shoulder. "Besides, we haven't breathed enough dust yet today. Let's go outside and watch this run with binoculars."

With a stiff turn, Kelvin followed him out of the Refrigerator, onto the wind-swept ridge overlooking the silica mines. Nathan peered down over the valley and muttered, "Where is everything?"

At this Kelvin laughed, a short release of tension. "You'd be a terrible failure as a HopperHunter, Nathan Pilstrom. Or as a forward observer." His index finger plucked points out of the desert, commenting, "Bunker, arty, copter field, bunker . . ." His sure, precise pointing reminded Nathan of the movements of programmers, pointing and clicking on the software objects they controlled. With a touch of revelation, Nathan saw General Kelvin in a new light: he was a programmer of battlefields.

Kelvin stopped listing out objects, squinted, and held his binoculars up to look at a far corner of the valley. "And there's the hopper," he said with a lingering smile.

Nathan held up his binoculars and watched the hopper's crazy war dance across the field, leaving chaos wherever it went. It seemed somehow more ridiculous when viewed from this vantage point; before, they had always watched the action through the hopper's own cameras. But their new perspective also gave Nathan a striking view of the hopper's effectiveness. When watching through the hopper's cameras, he never saw the reactions of the men to the hopper's attacks. With the binoculars, Nathan could linger to watch the consequences. The opposing troops always stopped in confusion, melting from a tight team to a loose rabble.

Kelvin echoed his thoughts. "Ridiculous," he muttered about the Hunter, "but deadly."

Marigold completed the gauntlet with swift precision, a surgeon carefully slicing tumors from dusty flesh. But when Nathan returned to stick his head inside the Refrigerator, no one looked flush with success. "We'll see what the next round shows," Juan said with a grim, remote expression.

So Nathan and the general took one of the helicopters to the new site for SkyHunter tests. Lila had preceded them. Squinting through the tornado of sand thrown up by their landing, they could see her elation as she screwed a sensor clump back into place.

Breaking from the copter cabin, Nathan ran through the miniature sandstorm holding his breath, while tears formed in his gritty eyes.

"I've got it," she yelled in triumph over the din of the helicopter's blades and engine. "I can beat the shadows by adding some extra interpolations on near-infrared bands. All we need to do is switch a couple of our sensing fibers, to get our sensitivity up."

No applause met her explanation. "Hardware problem?" Kelvin asked with fear-filled violence.

Lila stepped back in confusion, not understanding Kelvin's harsh response. She'd expected people to be pleased that they'd found the solution.

"Well, it's partly software for the interpretation, but we'll need hardware mods as well."

Kelvin seemed frozen. Nathan took a deep breath and

smiled brightly. "I'm delighted that you've found a fix. Will your fix work with the Hoppers as well?"

Lila nodded. "Yeah, and it'll fix the problem in the Crowbars, too. Even though we haven't seen it there yet, we would have."

"Great. How long before we can get Oriole modified for the new sensors?"

"Oriole's going to fly home now. We'll be ready for more testing by evening."

So Nathan and the general shuttled back to the Refrigerator. But when their helicopter arrived, the van was empty. The Eagle Scout was gone. Kelvin spotted the Eagle down in the valley. "They're all down there looking at the Hopper that crashed—Hyacinth."

Nathan gazed through the binoculars and sagged. "That isn't Hyacinth," he said. "That's Marigold." He swallowed with disappointment. They had lost another Hopper in a ravine wreck.

Eventually, the Eagle trundled back up the mountainside. Juan sat at the wheel, the shadows under his eyes deeper than Nathan had ever seen them before.

He spoke with the exhaustion of a hospital attendant who has watched a favorite patient enter the operating room for the last time. "We know what the problem is. It's not the software at all, and there wasn't a problem with the sims. The problem is that the Hopper's hardware doesn't meet spec. Its direction control gets sloppy at high speeds."

"How long will it take to fix?" Kelvin asked.

"I don't know." Juan pointed inside the van, where Florence had already disappeared. "Flo's patching through to Cameron Corporation right now."

Long minutes later, Flo announced they would have an improved Hopper the next day. General Kelvin called them back, to discuss the importance of the Hopper to the nation, and the urgency of getting it today. But altering a fundamental feature of the design was not something that could be hastened by forceful orders from a high authority; they could no more deliver a new machine today than they could repeal the law of gravity.

They continued to test for the rest of the afternoon, but

the enthusiasm dropped as low as the safe speed for the last Hopper. No other problems appeared, but it was a pathetic group of developers that slumped in the Tieton Room that evening. No hint of hopefulness could be seen in the orange light of sunset.

Into this gloom Leslie Evans strode—and stopped, as though hitting a wall. "Good God," he exclaimed, "whose funeral is this?"

Juan answered with a pale smile, despite the dark tan of his face. "Yes, it's a funeral all right. Marigold's. And Hyacinth's."

"Yeah, I heard there was some trouble," Les said. "I happened to be at Cameron while General Kelvin was chewing them out." He smiled. "They were agitated by the importance of the problem, but they didn't know what to do about it. So I calmed them down and we held an engineering discussion. We figured out some short cuts for putting together a single quicky prototype." He shrugged. "So they gave me an improved Hopper to bring with me. Anyone interested in a little after-dinner testing?"

The gloom yielded to a few cautious gleams of hope. Juan stood up and stretched. "You know, I've always been a night person."

"Me, too," Lila agreed.

Kurt shook his head. "The firing range is a treacherous place at night. I'd better come along, too, in case we need to drive around once we get there."

"And I can drive a second jeep, if we need it," Kelvin offered with a smile. "I know my way around here, too."

By nine in the evening they had the new Hopper, Morning Glory, flying a pitch-black course. The Oriole, with new sensors in place, joined it. One by one, they ran the whole series of tests, with only the glimmer of the Yakima stars to fight by. By eleven, they had tried and passed all the tests save one. "This last one is a real cruncher," Juan explained, a mischievous glow in his eyes. "I've got magnesium strobes all over the place. If the Hunters can figure out what they're doing while getting zapped by light like *that*, they may work on a real battlefield."

Kurt objected. "There's nothing like that on a battlefield."

Juan shrugged. "True. But there are many things on a real battlefield that we can't try here. If the Hunters can deal with *this* unanticipated problem, perhaps they can deal with others."

Lila leered at Kurt. "What's wrong, Kurt? Afraid?" She nodded to Juan. "Run it. We'll pass."

She radiated such certainty that Juan coughed back a chuckle. "We shall see."

Across the velvet darkness, the starlight's twinkle retreated from shafts of seering white flashes. The flashes burst against the hillsides, splintering in blinding reflections. Stepping outside, Nathan could dimly hear the whir of Morning Glory, rising and falling in pitch with the busy variations in speed and direction. Lila stepped out to join him. "No effect," she said. "Morning Glory soaks up the data when the lights flash, and flies blind between-times." She laughed with exultation. "It works."

One by one the others joined them in the cold of a desert midnight. The flashes made one last effort to confuse the Hopper with a violent outpouring of light, then sank into the blackness.

General Kelvin looked around the group. In the faint glow from the Refrigerator's windows, Nathan could see the heady excitement on everyone's faces. Everyone was wide-eyed, despite the long day and longer night: indeed, the success tasted so sweet *because* of that long night.

Kelvin raised an eyebrow at Juan. "Well, mister, are we ready?"

Nathan watched Juan's eyelids droop into the shadows. "No, General, we're not ready." A smile twitched his lips, and his eyes popped open with furious energy—a fury directed not at the general, but rather at the universe that found so many ways to twist and destroy human endeavor. "But we shouldn't let that stop us. Tell somebody to build us a couple thousand of these things."

They arrived back at the Thunderbird at two in the morning. It was Monday, though it did not feel like the beginning of the week to anyone. No one was tired. Lila, Juan, and Kurt dragged Ronnie and Florence off to find some dancing music. Nathan, Leslie, and Kelvin turned to the next problem.

Leslie was tapping on the chair arm in Nathan's room, obviously pleased with himself.

Kelvin almost glowered as he asked, "How many days will it take to get Hunters into Europe?"

"About one," Leslie replied. His tapping fingers stopped. "You know, historically, the United States has always won its wars by use of a distinctively American form of brute force: we have won, not because of the hi-tech of our weapons, or the brilliance of our generals—with all due respect, General. We have won because of the hi-tech of our commercial industry—our ability to create huge quantities of equipment in a short time, to drown the enemy in planes and guns and tanks. How can you beat the Americans, who build things faster than you can shoot them?"

Nathan didn't know the punch line yet, but he knew the lead-in. "To beat the Americans, you have to start and finish the war so fast that they don't have time to build anything."

Leslie nodded his thanks. "Right. Stomp 'em before they can move." He looked back at Kelvin. "And that strategy would have worked back in the '80's or the '90's. There was no way we could've mobilized our industry in time to respond to a surprise attack." He leaped up from his seat, no longer able to control himself. "And today, we still can't mobilize very fast to produce the specialized, custom-built machines our Department of Defense calls weapons. There are only two foundries in the nation that can cast a tank hull. The rest were closed down by the Environmental Protection Agency ages ago, because big foundries were dirty foundries. The whole American economy developed new techniques and new products that didn't need those kinds of foundries—everyone but the military."

Leslie paced faster as he spoke; the room seemed too small to contain him. With his wide, alert eyes, his silver hair, and his tone of authority, he looked like a renowned scientist desperately trying to impart some fraction of his wisdom to slow students. "But the Sling Project and the last ten years of automation have revolutionized our ability to respond to surprise attacks. In the past decade, America has groped its way to a new form of industry. We made the change just in time."

Nathan saw the double meaning; he could see by Leslie's expression that it was intended. Nathan spoke. "Leslie's referring to just-in-time inventorying. In fully automated manufacturing, the manufacturer keeps a minimum of stock in-house. Instead, he links up through a computer network—StockNet, for most companies, another one of the networks run by the Institute—to his customers and to the companies who supply him his raw materials. As his customers' orders increase, his own orders for more parts automatically go out to his own suppliers. The whole sequence can ripple through an industrial network literally at the speed of light."

Leslie nodded. "It allows dynamic reallocation of resources on a scale that astounds even me, and I've been working with it ever since retiring from the Air Force." His eyes focused on the distance. "In about fifteen minutes, you will watch the most massive reallocation of resources in the history of the world." He strode to Nathan's room terminal. "And thanks to Nathan and the Zetetic StockNet, we will have front-row seats."

General Kelvin sat in quiet disbelief. Nathan felt some sympathy, though he had a dim idea of what would happen now. He had faith in Leslie's analysis: Garrett Technology, the tiny company that Leslie operated and that was nominally in charge of systems integration for the Sling, made most of its money by solving automated manufacturing problems.

Leslie turned from the terminal. "General, we'll need your authorization to hook into MAC." MAC, Nathan knew, was the Military Airlift Command.

Kelvin grunted. "Very well—but it'll be hard to get enough military aircraft to fly all our Hunters over there."

Leslie raised an eyebrow. "Fortunately, we don't need military aircraft. Even though commercial planes can't carry heavy military equipment, they *can* carry Hunters. We wouldn't normally involve MAC—except that MAC has commandeered every plane in the country, whether the military can use it or not."

"I see." General Kelvin sat down at the terminal and worked at it for several minutes. "What next?" he asked.

"Now we watch," Leslie replied. "Nathan rattles on

from time to time about turning our plowshares into swords. We'll see it as it happens."

The display reflected traffic on StockNet, filtered through a query that eliminated every activity not directly related to the production of parts for the Sling Project. The first hit was with Cameron Corporation, for ten thousand HopperHunters. A similar order went to Lightcraft for ten thousand SkyHunters. Another order went to Space Platforms, Inc., for a thousand HighHunters.

From there, a two-way funnel opened ever wider. Cameron ordered fans, engines, and guns. LightCraft ordered motors, optical fibers, and solar cells. Space Platforms, Inc., ordered nose cones, ceramic tail fins, and liquid oxygen tanks. Everyone ordered microprocessors and optical sensor clusters.

The funnel reached farther and wider. To build those parts, the suppliers for Cameron, LightCraft, and Space Platforms needed other things: wiring, connectors, spark plugs, tubing.

The funnel opened on a flood: Those suppliers, in turn, needed raw plastics, structural metal shapes, glass, rubber, titanium, silicon putty.

By morning light, orders for ore had been issued by refineries, to supply the foundries, to supply the small-parts manufacturers, to supply the large-parts manufacturers, to supply the subassemblers, to supply the assemblers as the originally stockpiled assemblies were consumed.

Hiccups appeared. A cutting tool company fell behind, and sent out orders for replacement parts for its lathes and milling machines. Meanwhile, the operators of the Sling network—men and women of Garrett Technologies whom Leslie has gotten out of bed to help—intervened to spill the overload onto other cutting tool plants.

A graphite-epoxy chemical stream broke down. Another laminate-mixing facility was reprogrammed; the stream continued.

As money and orders had flowed down through the nerve system of the nation, now equipment and materials— thousands of tons of it—flowed upward. This upward flow convulsed the continent in a manner that the money and orders, flying with the speed of electricity through the humming networks of cable and satellite link, had not.

The material flow required more than mere communication. This convulsion required trucks, vans, aircraft, and railroad cars, for anything that could transport an engine mount or a load of ball bearings from a factory. Another spasm of orders shot across the nation, for truck drivers and switch operators and pilots, to pump the blood back through the nation's arteries.

And the convulsion of the transport system had its own spinoffs—new requirements for fuel, for oil filters, for turbine rotors. And this had yet more spinoffs—so numerous, so pervasive, that even the StockNet computers could not track them in real time.

By lunch time, over half a billion dollars had passed through the Sling Project—from the tip of the funnel down, to touch over five million people. And tons of materials pushed upwards to the tip of the funnel—to Cameron, to LightCraft, to Space Platforms. The first dozen production Hoppers spun off the line, into a grueling—but short—quality assurance test. One was rejected.

By evening, the routes of hundreds of airplanes had been bent into an arc that soared from continent to continent. Much of this arc already stood prepared to carry men and machines of the regular Army, but now the routes changed subtly; the cargoes changed drastically.

By midnight, the first SkyHunters lifted into the skies of Germany. The first HopperHunters floated from their crates, to whir on the edge of the battle zone. By midnight, the greatest engine of creative production in human history— the American economy—had transformed itself into an instrument of war.

Of course, midnight is relative. By the time midnight swept softly into Yakima, the gray skies of Germany had already passed through the gunpowder-stained birth pains of dawn, into morning.

May 1

The purpose in conflict is not to destroy your opponent, but to disarm him.
                    —Zetetic Commentaries

Ivan stared stonily at the torn bodies of a farmer, his wife, and his two children, without thinking. They were Germans, he reminded himself.

Germans. All his life he had read about and heard about the Germans. Germans were monsters—the builders of Auschwitz and Dachau—murderers on a massive scale. Occasionally, during the lessons and the lectures and the broadcasts, he considered the anomaly that most of Germany's crimes—and all their true atrocities—had occurred over half a century earlier. But the thought always faded quickly, a delicate snowflake in the burning horror of the slaughter they had committed. Usually, Ivan wondered why the Allies hadn't simply exterminated all the Germans right after the war. It seemed justifiable to annihilate creatures that showed such a thirst for annihilation themselves.

Smoke blew past, carrying the stench of charred flesh. The farmhouse and its inhabitants had been in the center of an assault exploitation path. Before sending the tanks and the personnel carriers through, the Soviets had carpeted the route with artillery fire to kill the silly German soldiers with their silly handheld antitank missiles. In the opening days of the battle, many men had cooked to death in the armored confines of their vehicles as German and American soldiers skewered them with a plethora of rockets and missiles.

But the Russian artillerymen grew proficient at tiling the areas of advance with suppressive fires. The German foot soldiers with launchers had died. The problem had disappeared. Of course, the improved effectiveness in killing scattered soldiers had improved their effectiveness in killing farmers, too.

Ivan's jeep drove on, but he could not escape the image of the farmer's remains. Part of his mind remembered that the farmer and his family were Germans, but another part—the rational part of his mind, he now realized— whispered that they were people little different from the farmers outside of Kursk. And no part of his mind could think of German children as Germans. German children were just children.

He clenched his teeth. Mother of Russia, they were just children! How could his leaders justify this murder?

The 20th Guards Tank Army had crushed the German II Corps several days ago, but rumors said that remnants of the American VII Corps had reorganized here outside Stuttgart.

Baffled admiration shook Ivan when he thought about the Americans. Why did they fight with such ferocity? The Germans he could understand; they fought for survival. But the Americans? Why did they insist on fighting as heroes? He sighed, guilt-ridden at his own thoughts. If he felt horror at the execution of the Germans, whom he hated, how would he feel about killing Americans, whom he merely disliked? Well, they at least were combatants, not children. He shrugged.

The sound of heavy artillery grew loud, then vibrant as the earth shook with its violence. Ivan recognized a nearby ridge as the vantage point he had been told to capture.

His lonely introspection faded, and his thoughts shifted to his mission, to the troops he now commanded. He wrenched the radio handset from its socket. "Lieutenant Svetlanov, deploy your men along the left crest. Katsobashvili, center. Dig in— the rim is shallow there, and you'll take the brunt if the Americans try to outflank our armor. Krantz, you're to the right." Ivan still wasn't quite sure how he had wound up as commander of an infantry battalion. He was a scientist, dammit, not a soldier. But the casualties on the first few days had left a desperate need for officers, and he was an officer.

What he was *not* was a leader. He lacked the charisma. But as a scholar, he had a strong grasp of the theories of warfare, and he was realistic enough to recognize and be wary of situations where pragmatic experience, not theory, gave the solution.

He nodded to his jeep driver, Goga, and they bounced over the rocks and craters to the left flank of the crest, pulled up next to Svetlanov's jeep, and stepped out. With a few long strides, Ivan reached the edge of the crest, to peer out into the main battle area. The sound of artillery turned deafening here, beyond the protection of the earthen lip. Down below was a vision of Hell.

Through the gunpowder haze, Ivan could see Major Shulgin's armor charge through the valley, oblivious to the hail of Soviet shells through which they coursed. To the far, far left, a clutch of American tanks huddled behind whatever cover they could get, while to the right of Shulgin's formation, a smaller group of tanks—possibly Abrams tanks, he couldn't tell for sure—were entrenched in massive bunkers. Though the entrenched tanks were few, they would be harder to take out than the tank force at the far left.

None of the Americans paid attention to the artillery, any more than did the Russians. Save for a minuscule chance of a direct hit, neither American nor Soviet artillery posed any threat to armor; its sole purpose was to kill exposed infantrymen—men such as those Ivan now commanded. Ivan thanked the fates that the artillery pounding the battlefield was Russian, not American. He would have already died had those fires been directed at his position.

Ivan could see—and hear, on the jeep radio that his driver now cranked to full volume—Shulgin shifting his forces to crush the more distant enemy first, before sweeping around to encircle the entrenched position. Ivan pulled out his binoculars to search the center of the overall American formation. Oddly, there was no one there.

And then there was someone there. Or something. Three machines that looked like inverted cupcakes whirred forward from behind the wreckage of a small brick house. The machines moved so smoothly over the tortured pastureland, they seemed to ride on air. Focusing his binoculars, Ivan realized that they *were* riding on air. Hovercraft! He noticed that they skittered when a shell exploded nearby, but they apparently had enough armor to deflect shrapnel.

Ivan listened to the Soviet chatter. "Commander, we have three targets bearing center."

"Teymuraz, right flank, hit those targets." Six Soviet tanks peeled off to face the attacking hovercraft—the Americans were *attacking*, despite the overwhelming odds!—but even as they peeled, the odd vehicles zipped amongst the Soviet tanks. Mother of Russia—those hovercraft could fly! One of them swiveled, and the tank nearest it exploded. Ivan thought it was Teymuraz's tank, the leader of the six-tank combat group.

Shulgin didn't know what had happened yet. He had other fish in his skillet. "Anatolii, center lead," he roared. "Kiril, cover left. Hit the two M60s at—" Ivan heard the beginnings of an explosion on the receiver, then silence. The Americans had killed Shulgin!

A handful of Soviet tanks hurtled along at the forefront of the Soviet formation, moment by moment separating themselves from the main group. Had Shulgin still been there, he would have brought them back into line. But now the Americans started moving, swinging to get clear shots at the vulnerable side armor of the newly separated strays. Ivan stood up. "Bring me the radio!" he cried. Someone had to take control before things got out of hand. There were ninety Soviet tanks down there—enough to win this battle, even if they fought with no more discipline than a mob. But the casualties would be terrific without leadership.

Goga ran up, panting, with the bulky, ancient radio. Ivan thumbed the transmitter. "This is Major Ivan Vorontsov," he yelled into the handset. "Major Shulgin has been killed. I will take command." He steadied his binoculars on the leader of the strays. "Tank YZ4, stop your group. Wait for ADLT to come up on your flank."

A voice he didn't recognize came up. "Who are you?" the voice demanded.

"This is Major Vorontsov, commander of the 4-35 Infantry battalion. Obey me! Major Shulgin is dead."

There was a moment of silence, then the voice began again. "I think it's an American," the voice said. "Disregard the—" the voice ended in a sickening thump, the same sound that had accompanied Shulgin's death.

The Americans had outflanked the Soviet lead tanks. The Russians were quickly destroyed by tightly coordinated fire. Ivan had an idea. "Lieutenant Kondrashin, this is Vorontsov. Can you recognize my voice?"

The pause seemed to last a lifetime. Ivan looked at the five remaining tanks of the group Shulgin had sent to destroy the hovercraft. They had stopped in the middle of the battlefield, uncertain what to do now that their quarry had passed them. At last Kondrashin's voice spoke up. "Yes, Major Vorontsov."

"Everyone stop!" Ivan screamed. They stopped, some grudgingly, to conform with the others rather than in prompt obedience to the disembodied radio voice.

Ivan surveyed the situation—quickly, quickly, a tank that stops in the open is a dead tank—"L23Z, bear left with your group. All tanks forward at 10 miles per hour. RTY7, accelerate to 15 mph, to circle. Americans are veering left. I repeat, left." Had Ivan's comrades not taken his orders, they would already be passing to the right of the American edge. They would be taking the same beating that had already killed their eager front line.

He could already foresee the next American step: the Abrams tanks in the bunkers would come up from behind. He had to divert them. He switched his radio to the artillery net. "This is Major Vorontsov. Move your suppressive fires 1 kilometer south."

There was another long, hysterical discussion as Ivan persuaded the artillery support personnel to take his orders. At last, however, the fires moved away from the woodland to the north of the Abrams position. "Lieutenant Katsobashvili, take companies B and C down into the woods, and attack the American position," he pointed at the partly concealed tanks, "there."

"Yes, sir."

"I'm sure there are American infantry there. You will have quite a firefight before taking that position, but you must succeed."

"Yes, sir." The lieutenant hurried away. Troops began moving slowly over the crest.

Too late. The small group of Abrams tanks on Shulgin's right flank moved slowly out of their shelters, then charged with ever-increasing speed toward the rear of the Soviet tank formation. And the main group of Americans was moving again, retreating, giving the Abrams time. The Soviet formation, meanwhile, was breaking up again as it moved. The two hovercraft continued to skitter through their ranks, killing tanks seemingly at random. But those random tanks always coincidentally blocked the movements of others. Long lines of stragglers formed.

Suddenly, Ivan remembered that there had been three hovercraft at the beginning. Now there were only two. What had happened to the third one?

One of his men shouted, and started firing his Kalashnikov. Ivan tore away his binoculars and saw the third hovercraft, breezing up the hill straight toward him. "Kill that thing!" he shouted, pointing with his right arm.

An extraordinary force threw him backwards to the ground. Pain exploded through his right shoulder. The crack of a bullet's sonic boom deafened him. Goga stared down at him in horror.

Ivan lay there, numb with shock, watching his driver's face. It seemed almost amusing—that face, the wide, terrified eyes. Ivan concentrated on that face because the numbness that replaced the pain in his shoulder scared him. It made him suspect that his arm might no longer be attached there. He watched Goga's face with the greatest concentration.

Goga looked up, and his terror exploded. With a choked scream, he dived toward the jeep, sliding the last meter to get behind it. Ivan felt a blast of air behind his head. The roar of jet fans penetrated his deafened ears. A glint of metal crept up on the corner of his vision. The American hovercraft floated beside him.

Ivan's mind fragmented. One fragment screamed in pain. Another fragment panicked with the suspicion that he had lost his arm.

A third mental fragment trembled in terror of the machine that had shot him—the machine that would now kill him.

But one fragment watched the hovercraft, recording and analyzing. This fragment felt a touch of awe.

The hovercraft must be a robot; it was too small, too oddly shaped, to contain a person. It unerringly singled out those who showed initiative and destroyed them. It wasted no fire on mere soldiers, the poor lumps of meat sent to die. Goga could have come out and danced before it without fear, rather than quivering behind the futile protection of the jeep.

Out of curiosity, Ivan moved his left hand toward his grenade belt. The roar of the fans changed pitch, the hovercraft swirled, and a strange, seven-barrel gun stared at him. He recognized the weapon: it was an American ultra-high-velocity gatling gun that fired armor-piercing uranium-depleted bullets, used for killing tanks. It took Ivan a moment to notice a much smaller machine gun adjacent to the seven massive barrels; as he was still alive, that was surely the weapon that had taken his arm.

Ivan considered reaching for a grenade. Earlier in his life, he would have thought that reaching for the grenade was the brave thing to do. But he had already proved his bravery. He had proved it with the handful of words he had written above his signature in the cold lands of Siberia. He didn't need to prove himself.

He *did* have to get word of this amazing machine home. Surely it was a new, secret weapon, or he would have heard of it before. He had to find a way to counter it.

One oddity of this machine puzzled him as he lay there in a pool of blood and pain. Why did it sit over him as if watching patiently for life? Why didn't it kill him?

Lila watched the broadcast from the HopperHunter with terrified eyes. Nathan watched her and listened to her short breaths. Nathan felt the horror himself, the thickness in his mind that wanted to deny this scene any reality beyond the flat panel display. Kurt's face showed the concentration of a trapeze artist—a dynamic equilibrium of horror and hatred, both submerged beneath the overriding engineering need to diagnose the events. The others had retreated—some across the room, some within themselves.

A jet of blood spurted from the Russian's chest. Only lines of pain put expression on his dead white skin. He might once have have been a gardener, or a chess player, or a writer.

He might once have been a gentle human being.

Kurt asked the question. "Okay, what's wrong with the Hopper? Why hasn't it finished him off?"

Lila shivered. Her body turned from the violence, then her shoulders, and finally her eyes. Her attention focused on the program monitor. The computer went through its steps in slow motion—logical deductions skipping from certainty to certainty, all the certainties adding up to total uncertainty. She hissed. "It's caught in an action loop," she said in a tone as pale as the man on the screen. Her voice strengthened as she studied the problem. "I gave the concept of being 'dead' pretty broad definition in the Hopper's software. This man fits the definition most of the time, but every once in a while he moves, and that shifts the equations to conclude that he's alive. The Hopper can't decide." Her jawline tightened as she turned to look at Kurt. "I don't think we need to kill that man any more than we already have, do you?"

Kurt, still on the tightrope, thought out loud. "Can we break the action loop *without* killing him—and without broadening the definition of death even further?"

Lila coursed through the program again. "I'm doing it now."

"Good." His voice rang with cold clarity. "You're right. We don't need to kill him any more."

Lila trembled as she moved through the text on her screen, cutting, pasting, rewriting. In a minute, the boxes of text closed, and everyone turned back to the view of the pale Soviet face. The pain in his face had receded; he now looked back at the Hopper as if he could see through it—through its satellite link—to Lila and Kurt. An expression of concentration masked his pain. He, too, felt horror and hatred and a need to diagnose what had happened. It struck Nathan that the Russian's face now mirrored Kurt's.

Tomorrow, these two men would hate the things they had done. But today, they hated each other. Nathan vowed silently that some day the Institute would find a way to

prevent this twist of behavior, the twist that allowed and
perhaps even forced Premiers and Presidents to use human beings as weapons.

Lila whispered, "It's fixed." The picture whirled. With
its new definitions, the Hopper turned in search of another leader to kill.

"I can't believe we're doing this!" Lila screamed.

"What can't you believe—that we're killing them? Or
that we're letting that man on the screen live?" Kurt
mocked her. "Personally, I'd like to finish off the guy who
ordered that artillery barrage out there, and the soldier we
just saw was probably the one who did it." He turned from
her and spoke more to himself than to Lila. "But that
soldier's more useful to us alive. He's too incapacitated to
lead anymore, so he's not dangerous. And since he's dying,
it'll cost the Russians a tremendous effort to try to save
him. Better yet, if he dies despite their efforts, his death
will demoralize them, because he'll have died in *their*
hands."

Lila sat speechless, listening to this last blast of inhu-
manly cold, brutal logic. She ran from the room.

Kurt blinked his eyes slowly. "I spent some time in
Stuttgart when I was in the Army." His voice softened.
Abruptly, he grasped the dial and flicked through the
images from the Hoppers. He released the knob when the
picture focused on the ruins of a farmhouse and the charred
ruins of human beings. "I used to pass that farmhouse
every day. The man would frown—he didn't like Americans— but his daughter waved at me. She waved at all
the people who went by, smiling . . ." Fury and pain
congealed in the lines of his neck and mouth as he marched
stiffly from the room.

Ivan continued to watch his murderer as it watched
him. For no apparent reason, the machine whirled again—
how delightfully nimble it was! So graceful and precise a
destroyer!—and sped toward the troops who had moved
halfway over the ridge toward the woodland. Again, the
machine proved its precision. A spit of flame came from it,
a short burst of fire. Lieutenant Katsobashvili spun to the
ground, very dead.

Ivan rolled over and crawled toward the jeep. "Goga," he whispered to his driver, "help me into the jeep. We must get a report on this back to the general."

Goga poked his head around, then ran to assist him. He looked like he was about to throw up. Ivan almost laughed. Here was a man who had looked upon the burnt bodies of helpless children without flinching, yet couldn't stomach the sight of a one-armed comrade covered with blood.

One-armed! The thought made Ivan want to throw up, too. He refused to think about it. He rationalized that he would soon bleed to death, so the loss of his arm would not be important.

As they bounced away to the nearest hospital, Ivan looked back to see the first American soldiers come over the hill. Ivan's battalion was frozen with indecision. Most of them, like his driver, had never been in combat before. A few of them would fight and die. The rest would surrender.

The pain and the shock slammed against his rationality one more time. As Ivan slipped into unconsciousness, he had one last insight—a thrilling insight that *relaxed* him, and almost made him feel peaceful, despite his condition.

He realized that this new American weapon would not hurt any children.

The SkyHunter floated on the breeze.

Floating on the breeze meant goodness. Not floating meant endness. Not floating meant endness.

Recognition of a SAM-27 site meant more recognitions of SAM-27s. It meant float in an out-spiraling helix with radar detectors in full blossom. Recognition of three SAM-27s meant conform a template to match them and see the conformed location of the comsite. Finding the conformed location of the comsite meant match the conformation to the best nearby hill. Best and nearby meant look up pattern definitions and calculate weighted value averages.

Finding the best hill match meant float over the hill with radio detectors in full blossom. No contact meant circle float. No contact meant circle float.

No contact for many minutes meant float over the second-best hill with radio detectors in full blossom. No contact meant circle float.

Contact meant comsite positively identified. Comsite positively identified meant find the best nearby valley for a division headquarters. Best and nearby meant pattern matching with weighted averages. Finding the nearby valley meant float over the valley with infrared and optical detectors in full blossom.

Infrared patterns of human beings in frenzied action, concealed from optical vision by camouflage, meant division headquarters. Division headquarters meant float over target. Float over target meant—

Downdraft meant no float. No float meant endness. Floating on the breeze meant goodness. No float meant endness.

Safety meant altitude greater than 10,000 feet. Safety meant continue to float. No safety meant point to error block. Error block meant touch the satellite with radio transmitter in full blossom. Error block meant connect to the Thunderbird Motel in Yakima. Error block meant dump all status checkpoints to Ronnie.

Nathan's eyes jerked at the sound of the alerter beep. It took a few moments of reorientation to remember what the beep meant: another malfunction had occurred in another Hunter.

A shadow moved in the room's gloomy twilight. Ronnie stumbled out of his chair and crossed the room to lean over a glowing display of the image that Nathan recognized: an image of the ground as seen from a SkyHunter.

Nathan walked softly up behind the boy and the computer. Ronnie sighed and drooped his hand over the keyboard. The SkyHunter image slid to the side as chunks of texts, lists of definitions in Modulog style, popped out. Each Modulog definition held the meaning of another definition, of an event, or of a pattern. Nathan recognized all the words, and all the definitions. Each definition of itself seemed quite reasonable, but Nathan had no idea how reasonably they worked as a collection.

The problem with blocks of software resembled the problem with teams of people. Like the people in the team, the definitions in the program had to be molded into an organic whole. The organic whole had to make sense beyond the disparate merits of the individuals. He clenched his teeth as he thought about what this week, and this day, had done to his team of individuals.

They now played a high-speed race—the race of his team and their Hunters against the enemy killers. Creating organic wholeness took time, but they had no time. Instead, they were *transferring* organic wholeness, from the team to the programs. Every repair they made in response to a Hunter failure expended some part of the integrity of the team. As the team disintegrated, the Hunters became more complete.

Did the team have enough cohesion left to correct the Hunters? Were the Hunters still so raw and error-ridden that they would take more than Nathan's people had to give?

His voice barked as he asked Ronnie, "What is it?"

Ronnie jumped. "I don't know," he said shrilly.

Nathan shook his head. "Sorry. I didn't mean to shout like that." He dragged his chair over and sat down. The picture from the SkyHunter zigged again, a purposeful motion rattled by random twists of air currents. The craft continuously tweaked its control surfaces to capture every wisp of available lift.

Looking below the image, Nathan saw the status indicators. Despite its cleverness in using every twist of air, this SkyHunter had dropped below the safe altitude of 10,000 feet. Flying that low, the glider might well be seen from the ground, if someone looked in the right direction at the right time, despite the coloration of the Hunter's lower surfaces.

Nathan sat quietly, resisting the desire to ask more questions until Ronnie had at least finished his inspection of the situation. To reinforce his resolve, Nathan sidled his chair back and away from the work station, far enough away to remove himself from Ronnie's field of view.

Nathan watched the boy in sympathy, remembering the times when *he* had been the man on the spot—the programmer who had to fix the problem because no one else could. He remembered the annoyance of having people watch him; and smiled in sympathy with the men who had been *his* supervisors. He now understood the exquisite quality of their suffering. He also remembered how, after a few moments of getting inside the problem, he would forget their presence, as long as they were not obnoxious with their questions.

Ronnie started idly tapping on the keyboard. The image of forward motion stopped, then accelerated into reverse. Nathan realized he was running back through the sequence of events that led to the moment when the Hunter had called in its warning. He started the motion forward again.

After a few minutes, Nathan started to see a pattern. The glider seemed to be going through the same sequence of steps, covering nearly the same path, over and over again, each time at a lower altitude.

Ronnie gasped. Nathan opened his mouth, but was afraid to speak. Fortunately, Ronnie broke into a half-muttered explanation, perhaps for himself as much for Nathan. "It keeps coming around for the final overflight of the headquarters, but something distracts it. It's acting as if it has forgotten where it was and what it was doing, then goes back into the standard search pattern."

"Which part of the code has the problem?" The term "which part" was a euphemism; what Nathan really wanted to know was, is it a problem in the code that Ronnie had written? If it was, then Ronnie was the best person to try to fix it, since he understood it. If not . . .

Ronnie waved his hands helplessly. "I'm not sure whose code it is," he said, answering the real question. "It's not Lila's problem. Something is going wrong between Kurt's understanding of the tactical maneuvers and the plane's execution of those maneuvers. So it could be Kurt's stuff, or hopefully, mine." He pursed his lips. "Or it *could* be a problem with the WeatherWatcher software—the modules supplied with the glider that tell it how to fly."

Nathan nodded. A certain irony colored the hopes of a good software developer: you always hoped that the problem lay in *your own* part of the code, because if it didn't, you'd have to call somebody else to fix it. Here, their only hope of saving the SkyHunter was if the problem was

Ronnie's. If it was Kurt's, it would have to wait until morning. Kurt needed sleep before he could solve the problem, no matter how hard or long he might be willing to work.

But the third possibility was most chilling. If there was a bug in the LightCraft built-in software, they could not fix it through their satellite link. The built-in software resided in read-only memory; they could not repair it without physically opening the Hunters up and installing new chips.

A snappy staccato of typing focused Nathan's attention. The green light from the image of German forests bathed Ronnie's face, giving him the look of a man suffering from seasickness. Nathan looked closer, overcome by the suspicion that Ronnie's sickly appearance came from more than just the unnatural light.

"Ha," Ronnie grunted in a wan imitation of joy. "Got it."

"How do you feel?" Nathan asked.

The staccato of the keyboard broke for a moment. "I'll make it. I see the problem. There's a downdraft on the last leg of the approach route to the Hunter's target." The Hunter tracks very nicely until it hits the downdraft. But the downdraft is strong enough to send an interrupt to the flight control system, which needs the highest priority to maintain stability." He rolled his eyes. "By the time the flight control system ends its downdraft countermeasures, everything else has been forgotten. The sensors go back to looking for SAM sites, and it repeats. Of course, it repeats at a lower altitude because it doesn't get to correct entirely for the downdraft."

"But the flight control system must do that fairly frequently. Why haven't we seen this problem before?"

Ronnie shook his head. "It only forgets if it's in the middle of switching contexts from tactical analysis to the attack run. At that time, there are just enough things to remember that it has to forget something. Unfortunately, it forgets the wrong things." The staccato stopped. They watched a quick simulation of the revised software on the programming display, then downloaded to the SkyHunter so far away. "I wonder how many other stupid little problems like that there are," Ronnie murmured.

"At least we fixed that Hunter before any Russians saw it. I wonder how their air defense guys missed it?"

Ronnie bent over, clearly unwell. He looked quizzically at Nathan, then winced. "Are you kidding? It's midnight over there. How can they see anything at all?"

Nathan was moving to Ronnie's side even as he thought about the time zone difference. Of course! The image from the SkyHunter was an enhanced night view. It probably would have crashed before the Russians saw it.

"We need to get you to bed," Nathan said, taking Ronnie by the arm. By now, Ronnie was shivering.

Florence appeared out of nowhere. "Take this," she ordered him, a pill in one hand and a cup of water in the other. Ronnie obeyed, wobbling over to his chair. "You'll keep on getting worse until you start taking care of yourself. You know that, don't you?"

Ronnie chuckled. "Right, ma. Whatever you say."

Florence shook her head at Nathan. "I've got him," she said.

"Apparently," Nathan agreed as they headed out the door.

Infrared patterns of human beings in frenzied action, concealed from optical vision by camouflage, meant division headquarters. Division headquarters meant float over target. Float over target meant select aimpoint. Aimpoint selected meant bomb release. Bomb rack empty meant fly home.

The SkyHunter did not notice that the frenzied human activity below became even more frenzied after the bombing—even hysterical. The SkyHunter did not realize that the pre-bombing activity had been organized and purposeful, nor did it realize that the new hysterical activity had lost both organization and purpose. Kurt, however, would have understood it completely.

Soon, the regiment headquarters below the division would understand the difference also. Those regiments would understand when they stopped to await futher orders, and none issued forth.

Frozen in place, they would realize how vulnerable they were without the authority to move. Their understanding

would fade as the fearful hysteria swept their own headquarters. The hysteria would freeze ever more units across
an ever wider front. They would remain frozen for a long
time.

*The Third Shock Army will be the heroes of the next
war.*

Captain Townsend heard the words clearly, spoken in a
low, confident, sad voice. For a moment, the voice seemed
so clear it might have been real. He was back in tactical
nuke school: he craned his neck up to see Colonel Schneider, the tall American instructor, as he spoke the words.

*The British Army of the Rhine has the toughest sons of
bitches in NATO. But there aren't enough of them. And
they have the worst equipment. And the North German
Plain is completely indefensible. And the Soviet Third
Shock Army has the toughest sons of bitches in the Soviet
Union.*

Captain Townsend nodded imperceptibly to the tall
American so far away in space and time. Colonel Schneider had known what would happen.

*The Third Shock Army will have a road race amongst
themselves to see who gets to the Rhine first.*

Captain Townsend stared impassively toward the dawn.
He could not yet hear the vehicles in the road race. His
nostrils flared. But he could *feel* them, there on the horizon, shrouded in fog and smoke.

A bird chirped from somewhere in the camouflage net-
ting. The lively sound seemed unnatural in this land of the
dead. The silence that followed also seemed unnatural.
Hell should not be quiet.

The clanking of treads and the roar of diesels murmured
from far away. The members of the road race were gearing
up for full daylight speed. In an hour or so, they would
circumvent the minefields and the barricades thrown up
by British engineers in the wee hours. Then the Soviet
racers would charge across Townsend's position. *Over my
dead body,* Townsend swore to himself. He smiled for the
first time that morning, recognizing the truth in his thoughts.
His army was running out of ammunition and out of terri-

tory to fight across. They might retreat from here, but they would not find another place to make a stand.

He wondered if it was proper to thank God for Chobham armor. Too many people he had known—people he dared not think of as friends, not now—had died in their foxholes and their simple metal boxes when the Soviets launched their assault with a gray whistling rain of artillery shells. The theoreticians had counted on the foot soldiers, hidden in the brick buildings of the little towns of Germany. With shoulder-held missile launchers, they were to have countered the thousands of tons of Russian steel.

But the Russians had developed bad habits early in the game. They tended to go around the little towns when possible. They tended to pound the little towns into parking lots when necessary. The soldiers on foot disappeared. Only those clothed in Chobham armor, like Townsend, remained.

Townsend looked in all directions from his perch on the top of his tank on the top of a low rise. He saw virtually no defenders anywhere. This caused him to smile again. The defenders were few, true enough, but not so few as it appeared. The Third Shock Army would spend several unpleasant hours here before the road race resumed.

The clanking grew louder. A gray carpet separated itself from the gray dawn. The carpet crawled across the plain, spilling around the villages in fluid swirls.

German towns are separated by a distance of approximately two kilotons, Townsend heard nuclear weapons expert Colonel Schneider say. *You can't kill any tanks without killing lots and lots of people.*

The desire to live welled up in Townsend's mind, and for a moment, he yearned to throw nukes across that gray metal carpet. A sob grew and faded in his throat. With nukes, he could stop this assault, but he knew that such a defense would mean Soviet retaliation. He, Captain Townsend, would still die in the end, after condemning untold thousands of civilians to burning deaths.

A flicker in the corner of his eye made him look up and beyond his invisible army. A spattering of fireworks smeared across the sky, falling. As he watched, the sparks flickered and died. The projectiles that now advanced along the fireworks' course could not be seen, but the captain could intuit their presence, as earlier he could sense the presence of the Soviet tanks. He had never heard of an artillery or aerial bombardment quite like this before, but he understood its purpose. He visualized the graceful arc of the bombs' flight paths. They would fall on him and his troops. Even with small warheads they would do great damage.

Captain Townsend looked back wistfully at the approaching Third Shock Army. With chilling certainty he knew that the road race would cross his position unimpeded.

Blood pumped through Nathan's head in dizzying circles. He wanted to stop the rush.

He wanted to stop the world. He wanted to do anything, be anyone, go anywhere, as long as he did not have to *be here now*. He glanced across the room's occupants with wild eyes; Leslie, Florence, and Juan looked back with the same wild desire to *escape*.

The first ten HighHunters had dispensed their Crowbars over the North German Plain to break the galloping Soviet Third Shock Army. With engineering precision, the Crowbars selected and targeted themselves upon their chosen victims. But the targets were not elements of the Soviet Army. Every Crowbar hurtled now toward a vehicle that belonged to the British Army of the Rhine. The Crowbars were quite indifferent to the agony of the observers in Yakima.

"Anyone have an idea of where the problem lies?" Nathan asked with surprising calm.

Leslie displayed no more panic than did Nathan. "I'm sure it's in Lila's stuff." He turned from the work station. "I'll go get her. I hope she's recovered enough to take care of this." As he crossed the room his pace picked up, until he bore through the doorway at a dead run. Nathan looked back at the imagery from one of the Crowbars. A stolid British captain rested his arms on the turret of the tank that this Crowbar had selected for destruction. Nathan sat down at the work station, brought up the Crowbar software, and stared at the code he had no hope of fixing.

"I wish I were there," he muttered.

Juan stood at his shoulder. "Where?"

Nathan pointed at the British captain. "I wish I were there, and that they were here." He clenched his fist. "At least that would be just. This fiasco is mine."

A smile flickered across Juan's mouth. "I heard a Zetetic lecturer once. He said that 'Justice exists only to the extent that Men have the power to create it.' " Juan's eyes darkened. "Would you really trade places with those men?"

"Of course." Nathan looked away. "But I don't have the power." He looked back to see Juan staring at the screen, eyes glistening.

"Damn you," he whispered. "I hate altruists." A moment later he commented, "Lila can't fix the problem."

Nathan looked at him.

"She'll get rattled by the pressure." He reached past Nathan to pound out a terse request for the computer. When it responded, he continued, "We have not quite six minutes left to fix it."

"Can we just clear the Crowbar memories, make them miss everything and dig up the ground a bit?" Nathan asked.

Juan shrugged. "Then the Brits will die anyway, won't they? They're hopelessly outnumbered." His eyes defocussed. "I know this stuff as well as Lila does."

Nathan sat very still. "I know."

Juan's voice grew airier, more distant. "I know its response to every kind of touch." He caressed the monitor. His eyes closed, and his voice filled with authority. "Please give me the chair."

Nathan stood aside; Juan sank into the chair. He rolled close to the screen. His hands moved across the keyboard; the display changed, and kept on changing as Juan burrowed into the heart of the Hunter. The display changed faster—so fast that Nathan could not even scan the contents before they disappeared. Yet when he looked back at Juan, he had the eerie sensation that Juan had read every flashing symbol with full understanding. Nathan knew that he himself was not quite so brilliant a programmer as Juan, but nevertheless, he knew what was happening in Juan's mind as he read the sheets of computer displays. Even at the incomprehensible speed with which Juan now soared—through the Modulog meanings, and the relation diagrams, and the truth tables, and the switches in the Crowbar's programming—his speed fell far short of the speed of the computers themselves. But Juan brought something into the heart of the Crowbar that no computer had—an understanding of the *purpose* of the Crowbar and its software. At each step, on each decision, Juan now asked of himself, "Yes, this works. But does it achieve the purpose?"

Thousands of such decisions rolled across the screen; thousands of times Juan asked himself that question and produced a reluctant answer of "Yes." But sometimes the decision, having assured Juan that the program worked correctly on some larger scale, allowed him to skip across the thousands of decisions that went into that larger decision. And so he jumped and cut across the landscape of the Hunter's soul, pouncing at each stop with the same furious question: "Do you achieve your purpose?" Soon it became difficult to tell who answered the question—whether it was the soul of the Hunter, or the soul of Juan Dante-Cortez.

Nathan shook himself to break the thread of his trance. He realized that Juan would not break his connection to the computer so easily. Juan sat immobile, his breathing so shallow as to be unnoticeable, his eyes unblinking. Only his fingers moved, in tiny jerks that clicked on the keyboard.

Footsteps sounded. Nathan whirled and waved Leslie and Lila to silence. He tiptoed up to them. "Juan's trying to fix it. I think our best bet is to leave him alone." He saw Lila looking past him and taking in Juan's autistic appearance. Juan's mouth hung open now, and saliva drooled from his chin. Still the screens of the work station flickered, perhaps even faster than before.

Nathan turned to Lila. "The only thing we can do for Juan is call the hospital. He'll need the same treatment now," his voice broke, "as he did five years ago."

A burst of clicking made Nathan turn back to Juan. He saw the image from the HighHunter blur as it shifted across the German landscape. It wobbled for a moment, then locked on a new shape: the shape of a Soviet tank.

Nathan started to smile, until he heard Juan gurgling. The sound was not quite human.

Captain Townsend could not relax his back muscles as he watched the Soviet army approach. He sensed as a steady pressure the unseen bombs approaching him from the rear. That sneak attack would deprive him of this last chance to remind the enemy that Brits were not easily defeated. If only the bombs had been launched a few minutes later. . . . The Soviet tanks were close enough now that he could make out their individual features. In just a few minutes, Captain Townsend's last battle would begin.

Suddenly, he felt the release of pressure. Had his instincts failed him? He looked to the sky, expecting to be struck at any moment by the descending killers.

Instead, the sky filled with noise: not explosions, just noise. It was the sound of a thousand tiny sonic booms.

Now explosions bellowed, unmistakably the sound of tank ammunition erupting in flame. The explosions came from the *Soviet* battle line. Little sparks fell en masse and sent huge gouts of flame shooting back into the sky. Captain Townsend's eyes widened with a feeling he had not known for days: the feeling of hope.

The gray metal carpet stopped moving. Columns of vehicles blocked up behind the burning remains of the victims. The captain smiled in a way that was happy yet unpleasant. The scattered lead tanks of the Third Shock Army, the ones who sped forward ahead of the broken and dying, would be easy pickings. And the followers, now threading their way painfully through the field of wreckage, would be easier still.

Nathan stood at the doorway to the Tieton Room. It felt different; for the first time in two weeks, it was empty. He realized the extent of the ravages his small team had made on the order and neatness of the room. The red and gold chairs faced in all directions, a random scattering thrown about as by a tornado. Paper, cables, and used ribbons remained as the waste products from the computers; cups, napkins, and junk food wrappers remained as testament to the absent human beings. It looked like a war zone.

Nathan corrected himself: it *had been* a war zone. The emptiness testified to the vicious effectiveness of the combat. Not one of Nathan's soldiers had escaped unscathed; they had suffered heavy damage in the battle. He wondered whether they had won their war. Days might pass before they knew.

He shuddered. At least, in the Battle of the Thunderbird Motel, the combatants had only been wounded. The team might never work closely together as a unit again, but the individuals would go on. Most would join new teams. Hopefully, those new teams would concentrate on tools to build a new world, rather than tools to destroy an old one.

He turned out the light and headed to his room for a long sleep.

May 7

Engineering is the implementation of science; politics is the implementation of faith.

—Zetetic Commentaries

Nathan remembered her last words to him—luxurious words, terribly out of place in the nightmare they had been living: "I hope the next time we meet, we will have more pleasant matters to discuss."

How prophetic her words had been; how much they had needed her prophecy to come true. Nathan smiled at Nell Carson, seated across the table from him, and wondered whether Nell saw how much more his smile meant than just a friendly expression.

The office seemed less stark now, though nothing in the room itself had changed. Nell smiled back at him as if she, too, remembered their last meeting, as if she took equal pleasure in remembering this shared secret. Other people shared the table with them today, Hilan among them. Yet in Nathan's tunneled vision, there were just two people here, together savoring the absence of horror.

How wondrously different everything now seemed, just two weeks into the future!

"The war is far from over," a worried voice to his left complained. The voice belonged to an admiral.

Reluctantly, yielding with the stubbornness of cold taffy in warm hands, Nathan acknowledged the accuracy of the admiral's words. The war had ground to a halt—a very different thing from a war that had ended. The Soviet armies, still overwhelming in size, formed turgid lumps throughout Germany and Denmark. Some had reached the Rhine; they were now starving for supplies from the backup troops who no longer knew where they were. But malnourished as they were, they remained wholly unassailable to the pathetic remnants of NATO forces still able to move as organized units.

"He's right," an army general agreed with someone else whom Nathan had not quite heard. "We won't be able to drive them out of Germany unless Operation Steel Bridge succeeds."

Nathan blinked his eyes. Operation Steel Bridge was, very simply, having every ship the United States could lay its hands on cross the Atlantic as fast as it could. As it turned out, that meant that many of them had left at about the same time, so that a scattered crazy-quilt of ships now sailed more or less together, forming the largest fleet in the history of the world. They were also probably the least organized.

The lack of cohesion was planned. The Navy had learned its lesson on the first day of the war, when it lost eight aircraft carriers and their battle groups: *ships that sail together, sink together*. So the Steel Bridge moved at random; it would be difficult indeed to sink so many ships. Nathan asked with some surprise, "Is Operation Steel Bridge in jeopardy? Do the Russians have enough submarines to find and sink that many ships at the same time?"

The admiral smiled. "Certainly not. In fact, the Russians don't have any submarines at all anymore."

Nathan stared at the man, who stared back with growing pleasure. Nathan asked, "No submarines at all?"

The admiral shrugged. "There are a couple in drydock. But they lost everything that was at sea." His look hardened. "Maybe our aircraft carriers are obsolete, but our submarines are a damn sight better than theirs are." The smile returned. "Rather, ours are a damn sight better than theirs used to be."

Nathan shook his head. "Then how can they stop our fleet?"

The admiral rolled his eyes, growing silent.

Nell sat forward in her chair. As Nathan's eyes returned to her, she explained, "Both sides are pretty well exhausted out there. They destroyed our surface fleet; we destroyed their undersea fleet. They destroyed most of our air bases around the Atlantic basin, and shot up most of our aircraft; but now we have SkyHunters harassing *their* air bases, so they can't fly their bombers either."

Her eyes widened in frustrated amazement. "So all

that's left is our submarine fleet and their surface fleet. That would be fine, except," and now her eyes narrowed with deep worry, "for some reason, our subs can't get close to their ships without, uh, disappearing. The Russians seem to have introduced something new themselves in the last couple of weeks. Anyway, their ships seem invincible to our submarines at the moment."

She looked away. When she looked back, not only her eyes, but the eyes of all the people at the table, fell upon him. With a small twist of her head she asked, "So how would the Information Age answer this problem?"

Nathan saw himself suddenly in a new role amongst these most powerful people—that of magician, the man who plucked new methods and ideas from a mystical, supernatural world. He had joked about magic with Nell in their last meeting; since then, he had succeeded as only a magician could.

Over the long run, such a magical role would lead to catastrophe. He was no magician; no supernatural powers could be brought to bear on crises of human making. Indeed, he and Jan had designed the Zetetic educational system to guarantee skepticism about the powers of magicians, whether they be called priests or scientists or statesmen or simply experts.

Still, Nathan had to admit it was a heady experience, having the most powerful people in the world look to him for salvation. It was particularly heady, since he had a salvation waiting in his bag. And for better or worse, the form of this salvation smacked of magic. What a fantastic irony he had here, acting as a magician when his deepest principles denied the concept of magic!

Like all magic, of course, an important part of seeing the trick was state of mind. Nathan could see the answer to this problem almost without thinking, not because he was smarter than anyone else at the table, but because he had had more practice with thinking in terms of the Sling Project and the various Hunters. "Clearly, we can solve this problem by developing a SeaHunter." He pursed his lips, then nodded. "We'll build a variation of the High-Hunter. Instead of loading the missile with small Crowbars for killing tanks, we'll design a larger Crowbar—longer, maybe wider, maybe with a new shape for penetrating ship armor. I presume we know where the Russian ships are?"

Nell smiled. "Of course. Just as well as they know where *our* ships are."

Nathan smiled in response. "Then we can drop Crowbars all over them."

The eyes in the room shifted as people began murmuring among themselves about the tasks they would need to undertake to make the SeaHunter work. Nathan continued to smile at Nell. As at the beginning of the meeting, it seemed as if they were alone. With a sudden zest, Nathan walked to the bay window and looked out across the Mall. He heard Nell giving orders, questions asked and answered, the rapid motion of men who knew that the lives of other men depended on their success.

He did not hear Nell's approach. Suddenly, she was standing just to his left, sharing with him the view of the city in spring. Her voice seemed distracted. "We'll win this battle. I just hope . . ." her voice trailed off.

"You just hope that the Soviets are smart enough not to throw nukes at us. They'll face the same situation we faced when we thought about throwing nukes at them."

"Exactly." Nell turned to him. "Are you a licensed telepath, or do you just guess well?"

Nathan shook his head, resisting his desire to turn from the window, to savor her appreciation of him. "I do more guessing, though my guessing is well directed. A terribly important part of success in any age—industrial, information, or whatever—is being able to see the situation from other people's viewpoints. In the middle of a world war, a president has a very limited set of things to worry about or to hope for." At last, he turned to her. "You're chained to the position you occupy; for the moment, you dare not think thoughts other than the thoughts of a president."

It was her turn to look away. Nathan noticed the sleepless circles under her eyes as she nodded. "You're right about that. I can't afford to think about anything else."

"Nell Carson, when this war's over, I'd like to meet you. At that time, please leave the president here in the office." When she looked startled, he continued, "I predict that that will mean dinner in about a week."

She studied him thoughtfully, a chess player sizing up a fellow player, then burst into laughter. "Very well. If the war is over, dinner in about a week."

On his way out, Nathan looked in the mirror again. Again he shook his head at himself and his dreams of Nell Carson.

Ivan felt amazement that he was still alive. The past three days seemed like shadows in his memory—a feverish blur of hospitals and soldiers, screams of pain, and his own semi-coherent explanations of the importance of what he had seen. His last clear memory was of himself, mangled and bloody, bouncing down the road in a jeep while an American hovercraft executed his best officer.

Given that he was still alive, however, he understood why they had brought him to this odd little room filled with ivory figurines. Few of the bright, observant officers who had encountered the hovercraft in combat lived to tell of it, and none were in good shape. And certainly none of those normal line officers had the technological background to appreciate what they had seen. He was here to tell General Secretary Sipyagin how to fight the new American hovercraft and win the war.

Ivan sat in his wheelchair and listened. The doctor whispered to the Premier, softly, so that Ivan couldn't hear. No doubt they were discussing Ivan's arm.

Ivan chuckled inwardly at their whispered conference. Part of his mind knew, or at least was pretty sure, that he had lost his right arm. Other parts of his mind, though, could still feel that arm out there, as strong and potent as ever.

He knew better than to try to flex his fingers. And he knew better than to look. He would deal with that another time.

The General Secretary sat at the far end of the table, looking left and right, but rarely at Ivan himself. The man to the General Secretary's right, whom Ivan did not recognize, stared at Ivan with an intensity that verged on hatred. Other men filled the table, presumably Politburo and Central Committee members, but Ivan felt the power of those eyes upon him, and knew that the man next to the General Secretary would make the decisions.

Yet that man would not do the talking. One of the oldest members of the council spoke first. "Major Vorontsov, we understand you've encountered the new American weapon."

"Yes, sir." Ivan's speech came slow and fuzzy, but he tried to put some force behind it. "The hovercraft—they tell me the Americans call it a HopperHunter—is a remarkable machine. It is as graceful and precise as it is lethal." He described the way it singled out leaders and killed them. "I've made some recommendations for deceiving the machines, by having our officers act more like ordinary soldiers. We should be able to confuse the Hoppers by making it appear that there are no leaders. But I doubt that my countermeasures will be very effective. Indeed, I doubt that my recommendations will even get to the troops."

"Why not?" one of the faceless men asked.

"Who will forward the information, with half our command posts destroyed?" With exhausted admiration, Ivan contemplated the American attacks he had learned about just an hour ago. A mysterious destruction was consuming the Soviet command posts. Not coincidentally, this brutally effective elimination of Soviet generals had started the same day Ivan had encountered the first Hoppers.

No survivors could yet identify the cause of the explosions that wreaked havoc on critical Soviet headquarters. No one had seen any aircraft, nor had they heard anything that might be a Hopper. Someone had suggested they were mines, but how could even the crafty Americans plant and detonate mines with such precision?

And the destruction of the Third Shock Army from outer space was just incredible! "I have no idea how to combat the weapon that no one can see."

"They must be using Hoppers somehow to destroy our command posts. Hoppers traveling deep behind our lines."

Ivan was too weak to shake his head. He wanted to yell at the stupid creature who had spoken; instead, he whispered. "No, sir. The Hoppers use turbine engines. Advanced turbines, possibly ceramic, but turbines nonetheless. I heard them. They could not possibly carry enough fuel to travel that far. And even if they could go the distance, they could not escape detection. They might destroy the headquarters, but anyone who got out alive would know how it had happened." He licked his lips. His only idea for the cause seemed crazy, but . . . "My best thought is that our CPs are under attack from invisible airplanes. Nonmetallic, perhaps, high enough and small enough to be difficult to see. Perhaps they are using gliders so they cannot be heard."

No one laughed. Another man cleared his throat. "We had reports of such a craft before the ban on smart weapons. It is under investigation."

So, he had surmised correctly! Ivan's virtuosity here would help him in the inevitable final argument of this meeting. That final argument was one that Ivan *had* to win, although he faced the most powerful men of the Soviet Union.

Another voice asked hysterically, "Are these Hoppers invulnerable to our firepower? Why can't we destroy them?"

Ivan responded patiently. "In fact, comrades, we do have weapons that can destroy them, but those weapons are few and scattered. The Hoppers move too fast for our heavy cannons to take aim. And they are armored well enough to deflect hits from our heavy machine guns. However, I believe our older anti-aircraft guns, with 20mm or 40mm rapidfire cannon, could be very effective. But how do we get word to the troops, to the scattered few who have this equipment?"

Another man—a soldier, this one—spoke. "We must use nuclear weapons to combat this threat," he stated. "We can destroy these things with sufficient firepower. We can still win on a nuclear battlefield."

With these words the final argument, the one Ivan had feared, had begun.

No one in the room objected. Fools!

The room seemed cold, and yet Ivan could feel perspiration beading on his brow. To brush it aside, he brought up his right arm—but no arm moved to his command.

His arm! He almost screamed as the delicate balance of his mind collapsed. He'd lost his arm, he'd lost his arm—the thought twisted up in his throat, and it hurt so much he couldn't breathe.

But he could *not* deal with this now! He bit through his

lip, and the pain and the taste of blood shifted his mental
gears again.

He carefully clenched his *left* fist. He *had* to stop these
madmen, with their nuclear terrors. His eyes widened, a
feverish anger filling them. "No!" he told them. "If you
believe nuclear firepower can defeat the Americans, then
you believe a lie." He pointed at the general who had
spoken. "Where will you drop your bombs? Quickly, for
the Hoppers are moving!"

The general sat stunned for a moment, then smiled. "I
will drop them in Germany." Still no one laughed.

Ivan drove onward. "Then give me the coordinates,
General, to within a meter. That is what we need to
launch a weapon. And then you must tell me who will
issue the launch orders, with our commanders dead. The
orders must go out quickly, before the targets can move.
Otherwise, comrades, our nuclear weapons will be no more
effective than our artillery." He described the way the
artillery shells fell around the battling tanks, which remained oblivious to the massive shelling because they
never landed *on* them, only *near* them. "You could drop
thousands of bombs on Germany, you could kill millions of
farmers and children, you could destroy life all over the
planet, without stopping a single Hopper. Artillery only
works well when combined with tightly integrated reconnaissance, decision-making, and action. Even the ultimate
artillery shell, the nuclear bomb, is worthless without a
well-defined target."

The hysterical voice spoke again. "How can they be
doing this to us?" he cried. "We destroyed *their* command
and control in the first three days of war. How can they go
on fighting?"

Ivan relaxed, and smiled at the second-rate Politburo
bureaucrat who had given him his opening. "Thank you,
sir, for that question. They can fight on without orders
because they are *defenders*. It takes far less command and
control sophistication to defend your position—just shoot
at anything that shoots at you. The attacker, however,
must orchestrate every move. Without good direction, an
attacker's forces can even wind up attacking each other,
rather than the enemy." A number of faces looked up in

surprised anger, as if he had spoken of something obscene that had already happened. Had he hit home again? Were the Warsaw Pact allies deserting them? It made no difference. "This leads me to suggest the one way left that we can still achieve victory."

That certainly got their interest! He doubted they would like his suggestion, however. "To defeat the American weapons that destroy attackers, we must become defenders." He paused to let them puzzle over that for a moment. "We must advance our troops back to their permanent fortifications in East Germany and Czechoslovakia. We must make this move while we still have such superior numbers and strength that we can defend ourselves."

Retreat. He hadn't used that word, but he could see it twisting the faces around him in anger.

"Thank you for your analysis and your opinions, Major," the powerful man by the Premier said. "Now your doctors want you to rest. You are dismissed." He nodded, and someone turned his wheelchair to the door.

A sense of *deja vu* flickered through Ivan's mind. He had no regrets about his actions in this meeting. As in his study a year earlier on nuclear war, he had done his best. Perhaps this time it would make a difference.

Yurii rubbed his temples as the door closed behind Major Ivan Vorontsov.

General Ramius cleared his throat. "That man should be shot," he muttered. "It's treasonous to speak of surrender."

"He did not speak of surrender," Yevschenko responded mildly. "He spoke of retreat. He spoke as a man who has been there and knows whereof he speaks."

Pultiy, who seemed calmer now that the lowly but insightful major was gone, chimed in, "He speaks plainly, like a man who has accepted death, but who has not lost hope."

They paused. Yurii started directing the meeting toward the conclusion he had drawn, based on Vorontsov's analysis. "Major Vorontsov's greatest failing is that he speaks the truth. Unless we come up with a better alternative than any so far proposed, gentlemen, we must follow his advice. We already have a bloody future ahead of us in resubjugating the Poles." The Polish Army had started an unauthorized retreat. The trouble had begun when the Third Shock Army disappeared in a God-like barrage of fire and brimstone, just as they were about to destroy the last units of the British Army. Even Yurii felt haunted by the mystical horror of it. He sympathized with the Poles, even as he planned a hideous punishment.

General Ramius spoke again. "We could make a strategic nuclear strike. That would show the Americans that we're serious, and it would tell them to hold their positions. We would form a new national boundary based on current troop locations."

The discussion that followed paralleled discussions that had been held in the White House just weeks before. The Soviet discussion was not the same. The values important enough to affect decisions in a free society are not the values of importance in a police state.

But the conclusion was the same: nuclear missiles were too crude to operate as instruments of politics. The risks were too great.

Yurii summed up. "We could have risked it had Mayfield been alive, but Nell Carson is in charge now. She is too clever to be predictable. And being unpredictable, she is dangerous." His eyes swept the room. "Are there any other suggestions?" He paused, but not long enough to allow others to open any new discussions. "Then the major was correct. We must return to the original borders." He glanced at Sipyagin, whose labored breathing filled the silence. "And we will need to negotiate with the Americans, to make sure they don't press their advantage into our territory. In order to be credible in this endeavor, comrades, we must reshuffle the highest echelons of the government."

The General Secretary's heavy breathing stopped. "What?"

Yurii smiled without compassion. For a moment he felt an icy pleasure at the justice he would now serve on the General Secretary.

Yurii thought about the decrepit men sitting here in this decrepit room with venomous hostility. They hadn't been able to wait. For decades, the Soviet Union had waited while America's strength slowly but surely deteriorated. In just another decade, the Americans would have withdrawn from Europe completely, without any further moves on Russia's part at all. The waiting had almost been over.

But the little old men wanted to see that day of victory in their own lifetimes. They couldn't wait. They had to hurry the process just a little bit too much.

During the first heady weeks of the war, it had seemed that they had been right to finish the job quickly, and Yurii had been wrong. But the perverse American capacity for losing all the battles and still winning the war had shown through at last. Now the whole Soviet empire would pay the price for the impatience of these fools. He spoke to Sipyagin. "Sir, the American propaganda blames you for starting this war. If you remain in power, the Americans will continue to fight. They will fight to destroy *you*, believing that as long as you have power, we might try this again.

"But if we install a new leader, they can then deceive themselves into believing that our government has toppled. Our new secretary will be a peacemaker. The American news media will herald him as a savior."

An anonymous voice spoke quickly, with heavy irony. "No doubt the new General Secretary should be someone who helped the Americans sign away their defenses with numerous treaties."

Another anonymous voice snorted.

Yurii swept the room with his eyes but could not tell who had taken those shots. Whoever they were, they already realized how dangerous their outburst had been.

Yurii could identify them later. For the moment he returned his attention to Sipyagin, who was searching the room for supporters. No one volunteered. "We must ponder this carefully," Sipyagin said, stalling for time.

"Of course," Yurii conceded. "But we must ponder it quickly. We must decide before the Americans reach our Pact borders—before they work themselves into such a frenzy of victory that they fear nothing. We must hurry!" A number of logical flaws gaped in Yurii's analysis, but no one would object. Emotions now drove the decision-making process, emotions of fear and embarrassment at this terrible calamity. This pathetic roomful of almost-conquerors needed a scapegoat and a viable successor.

Sipyagin understood this as well as Yurii. Yurii continued to watch as he searched the room for alternate choices for the new leader. Yurii knew, with smug confidence, what his senile mentor would find: only one man in this room still had the youthful vitality to make a good General Secretary for the Soviet Union.

In the end, Yurii won by default. He issued orders for the Army, described the necessary propaganda for the newspapers, and adjourned the meeting.

When the last of the old guard had left, Yurii returned to his old office to contemplate the mixed tastes of his own personal victory and his country's overwhelming defeat.

If Mayfield hadn't died, the whole Soviet plan would have succeeded. Of that, Yurii was certain. If Mayfield had had a vice president as malleable as Mayfield himself, that too would have allowed Sipyagin's premature conquest of Europe to work. How had Mayfield wound up with a she-fiend for a successor?

Carson's second in command was Avery Faulke, the American Speaker of the House, a pudding of a man. *He* would have been a proper Mayfield running mate. Yuri could have used Faulke very nicely.

For a moment, Yurii dreamed of Nell Carson's death, and the succession of another pathetic creature to America's helm. He could still wrest victory from this terrible position! A simple assassination would give him triumph.

But the risks would be incredible. If the assassination failed, or if the Americans found out that he had instigated the attempt, the repercussions could destroy the whole planet. With a last lingering farewell, he put the fantasy aside. Too much reality required his immediate attention.

THE DUELISTS

May 13

May the pens of diplomats never again ruin what the people have attained with such exertion.
—General Blucher after the Battle of Waterloo

She was toying with him, Nathan realized. She played with her drink as she played with him.

At considerable cost in time and effort, Nathan had brought two Fritzbe's strawberry shortcakes from the suburbs of Reston, so they could share this unusual drink here in the private, third-story dining room of the White House. The strawberry shortcake was a deceiving alcoholic liquid with a creamy consistency and a mellow hint of amaretto blended in. Like many shortcake drinkers, Nell now swirled her straw in rhythmic patterns, mixing the pink and white layers.

Nathan continued the banter. "So you've selected the new vice president. You're honest enough to tell me that you've made the decision, but you're cruel enough not to tell me who it is, is that the situation?"

She raised her eyebrows with an innocent sip at the shortcake. "Oh, I suppose you could put it that way."

Nathan harrumphed in response. The room seemed too quiet in comparison with the hubbub of Fritzbe's, where he normally drank shortcakes. Nathan didn't really miss the hubbub too much, the collage of engineers and lawyers and teenagers that seemed like a carefully orchestrated accident. But here alone with Nell, his heart pounded loudly, and he wondered if Nell could hear it in the stillness of the room.

If Nell insisted on toying with him, he would try to reciprocate. "Very well, then, I won't tell you about the person who most recently converted to Zeteticism."

"Who is it?"

"I said I wouldn't tell you."

"I see." Nell smiled at him with an expression of mischief.

It occurred to Nathan that Nell seemed to grow younger every time they met. She no longer frowned with a look that reminded one of battered steel. Tonight, she had let her hair fall free; it was longer than he had realized. She took references to herself as "Madam President" in stride. Now that the Soviet armies had withdrawn to their old stations within the Warsaw Pact, she could afford to be graceful, not hardened. "Do you like to dance?" Nathan found himself asking.

Nell dropped her straw with a sudden laugh. "Sometimes," she said, "But not generally when I'm running a country." She raised another eyebrow. "Actually, even as president, the opportunity arises occasionally, as long as I'm not also running a world war."

"Good point. Though I suspect the dancing style at presidential functions is a bit sedate."

Nell nodded. "I'm afraid so." She paused. "So what will you be doing now that we no longer need the Zetetic Institute to save the world?"

"We're reorganizing." Nathan paused to take another cool sip of the rich strawberry, cream, and amaretto concoction. "Though the news media haven't given the Institute much credit for our victory in the Flameout, enough people have heard about us to quintuple the size of our seminars." After the SeaHunters had destroyed the Soviet fleet, and after their armies had left Germany and Denmark, the news media had given the War a name that suited its events: the Flameout. It had been a brief, fierce, and ultimately irrelevant engagement. When it was over, nothing had changed that the news media could describe as significant.

"Are there any seminars I should take?"

Nathan smiled. "I would prefer to tutor you individually."

"Hah! I'll bet."

"First, I'd teach you about best-case and worst-case event preparation. On an ordinary day, an ordinary person only prepares for the most probable future, thus leaving himself open to disaster, should the future turn out differently."

Nell sighed. In the length of her breath, Nathan could

hear a hundred arguments, a thousand discussions that might have prevented the Flameout. "I know all about the importance of preparing for different possible futures," she said. "It's more depressing than I'm ready to deal with at the moment."

Nathan shook his head. "Ah, but there's what you're missing, Nell. All those possible futures *shouldn't* be depressing. Because, in addition to preparing for the worst, you must also prepare for the best." Hardly believing what he was doing, he reached out his hand to her chin, to lift her head, to force her to look at him. "Often, the critical preparation for worst-case is to recognize the possibility. That way, if the worst occurs, you only need to deal with the problem, rather than having to deal with your shock at the same time, And that—" he felt his voice rising "—is when the sense of wonder returns."

"The sense of wonder?" Nell stared at him as though he spoke Gaelic.

"Yes, the sense of wonder that so many of us have lost." Nathan leaned forward, preparing his explanation as he had done so many times before. "Don't you see the consequences of preparing for only the most likely future? Most of the time, that most likely future will come true, and how do you react to it? 'Of course,' you say, *taking it for granted*. But if you have recognized the worst possibilities—if you have accepted them with your whole mind— then when the 'normal' future comes to pass, you can say, 'How wonderful! How special and beautiful this moment is.' "

Nell leaned back against the wooden back of her seat as Nathan leaned forward. She asked, "I guess you take your sense of wonder pretty seriously, don't you?"

Nathan retreated with a short laugh. "Yeah, I guess I do. Somehow, my sense of wonder has stayed intact throughout my life, as if it were an automatic response. Most people claim they enjoy watching sunsets. Yet, if they enjoy it so much, why do they do it so rarely? I can take pleasure in even simpler things. Every time an airplane takes off to ride on a puff of wind, every time a photograph gives us a window on a scene from the past, every time you throw a *light switch*, each one of these things is wondrous. And though we can't take time to appreciate these things every time we touch them, does that mean we should *never* take the time for appreciation?" He laughed, and held up his hands as if to cast a blessing. "Think of the universe as a supersaturated solution of wonder. Every once in a while the wonder crystallizes out in some beautiful form—in the shape of a tree, or a flower, or a skyscraper. Or in the shape of a special woman who is president." Realizing he'd said too much—indeed, he'd intentionally said too much—he brought his hands down quickly and continued. "You know, the people of America—even most of the poor—are the richest, the most comfortable, the best educated, and the most potent people ever to live on Earth. How could we acquire so many things and still not be happy? What did we fail to acquire?" He held his finger to his forehead. "We failed to acquire minds capable of appreciating our acquisitions. We failed to expand our sense of wonder."

The light struck Nell's features harshly; for a moment, she seemed pale, even meek. "I see that. You're right; I've lost many things in my life," she half-whispered.

With a shake she looked back at Nathan. "Perhaps there *are* some things to learn from the Zetetic Institute. Were you serious about wanting to tutor me? I'll make you a deal. You do the tutoring on Zeteticism, I'll tutor you on slow dancing. It would be wonderful to have someone to dance with the next time I'm forced to attend a ballroom affair."

"I'd like that very much—almost as much as I would like to know who the new vice president is."

Her laughter released her tension as much as it expressed her pleasure. "You'll know in just a few hours. Just like everyone else."

"Fiendish. I suppose I'll survive."

"Actually, you're the most likely person in the country to guess who the next vice president will be. But that's the only hint I'll give you."

"I can guess? Well, let's toast to him, whoever he is." Nathan raised his empty glass.

Nell shot him a look of mock disappointment. "A toast to *him?* Why do you think I chose a *man?*"

Nathan looked at the president with amused delight. "The women's *coup d'etat* has begun. I was afraid that once we let women into office, we'd never get them out again." He raised his glass in a toast. "To the coup. To all that's fair in love and war."

"Let us drink particularly to all that's fair in love," she replied, raising her eyebrow. "I prefer love to war, don't you?"

Nathan nodded his agreement; the lump in his throat made it impossible for him to speak.

Nathan had spent his life building families out of the friends he met along the road. Many, many people respected and admired him, but love had never quite worked out. He was too remote, somehow, peering into a distance where they couldn't, or wouldn't, quite follow.

Nell made him feel happy in ways he had never known before. His sense of wonder grew stronger.

SNAP. Bill's hands shake. He casually slides them beneath the table, to prevent the audience from seeing his weakness. He is presenting the most terrifying double-feature story in the history of journalism. He wonders whether he should discuss this material on the air or not. For mankind's sake, he must try not to create misperceptions in the minds of his viewers. The safest short-term action would be to say nothing, thus creating no misperceptions at all. Yet for mankind's sake, he must spread the information he has gathered, creating correct understandings. The only long-term safety lay in communicating only correct perceptions.

Bill digs his fingers into his thighs, and still the trembling continues. He knows he will fail.

CLICK. "Good evening, ladies and gentlemen," he tells the camera that represents over 50 million viewers. "For those of you who have not heard, an assassination attempt has been made on President Carson. Tonight we have exclusive film showing the assassin in the act. We also have an exclusive story on Soviet planning documents that suggest a possible Soviet link to the assassination attempt."

CUT. The recording of events earlier that day unfolds. A striking woman in royal blue steps gracefully across the front of a crowded room to the podium. Her silk scarf flutters ever so slightly with the speed of her motion. The room, noisy before, now breaks into cheers and clapping. She turns. She is Nell Carson, here to announce the selection of the new vice president.

WHIR. Her voice rises and falls, pauses and rushes. She speaks of the difficulty of making the decision, and the marvelous qualities of the man finally chosen. Her eyes shine, her voice sings, but not even Nell Carson can make this standard speech come to life. "—That's why I'm pleased to announce the new vice president, Hilan Forstil!"

PAN. Bill's camera, impatient with the ceremony, drifts across the audience to a stocky man—a man who might once have had glowing health, but who now has tight twists of tension across his face and a gaunt look, as if he has not slept for days. He reaches into the shadow of his pocket to retrieve a darker shadow.

ZOOM. The darker shadow now held in the man's pale hand resolves. It has the shape of a pistol.

CLICK. FLASH. CUT. The man fires twice. President Carson jerks across the stage. A dozen men move rapidly, identifying themselves by their speed and organization as Secret Service Agents.

FLASH. The gaunt man turns his pistol sideways. Looking peaceful at last, he fires once more, striking himself in the temple.

CUT. The newscast returns to Bill's somber image. Bill tells the audience what is known about Ted Muhlman, the assassin. Though Bill speaks at length, the sum of his words is, *we know almost nothing about this man.*

ZOOM. "Why did he shoot the president? We don't know. But the most terrifying suggestions come from sources outside the United States." Bill holds up the document he had received less than a day earlier, from one of his contacts in the Soviet Union. In bold red letters, the English translation of the title slashes diagonally across the cover: *A Revised Assessment of the Global Consequences of Nuclear War.*

"What does this document have to do with the attack on President Carson?" Bill riffles the pages, stopping on the final chapter, the Summary. "This document has two different Summaries. The first summary, written by the analysts who conducted the study, reflects on the logical consequences of the dangers of nuclear war." Bill takes a deep breath, a shaky pause. "However, that summary angered members of the Politburo, so it was rewritten to reflect the thinking of men in power in the Soviet Union. The man who authorized this study—and who presumably had the summary rewritten to agree with his own thinking—was Yurii Klimov, the new Soviet General Secretary."

Bill clears his throat. With the somber tone of a judge, he reads. "As this revised analysis shows, the global consequences of nuclear war remain grave, even under the most optimistic assumptions. However, this danger need not deprive the Soviet Union of opportunities to exercise its strength. Indeed, this unassailable vindication of the dangers of war can work to our advantage. We can count on the threat of global disaster to paralyze enemies—particularly enemies who already show indecisiveness. Chief among these indecisive opponents is the American President: Jim Mayfield demonstrates the archetypical set of traits we would desire to see in an American leader.

"With Mayfield in office, we can apply force with minimal restraint. Some graduation in scale is still necessary, but we see no reason not to use troops in Iran to resolve the religious tensions there. If Mayfield responds weakly to our invasion of Iran, as we are certain that he will, we may then calm the chronic East German uprisings with an invasion of West Germany. Thus we would continue the successful strategy we initiated in Afghanistan decades ago."

ZOOM. Bill looks up at the camera. "Either by coincidence or by intent, this summary describes the Soviet Union's activities for the last year. Now listen to what the summary says about Nell Carson."

SCAN. He returns to his somber recitation. "Of course, we must match our steps to the mood of the American President. If Nell Carson succeeded President Mayfield, for example, we would have to move with greater caution, due to her unpredictability." Bill licks his lips. "Other potential American leaders can be categorized easily into these two types: the indecisive and the unpredictable. We have composed such a list of American leaders here to encourage further discussion of the timing and intensity of our future geopolitical moves."

CLICK. Bill blinks slowly for the camera. His tone changes; he is done reading. He waves his hands in an impatient gesture, and synopsizes. "The 'unpredictable' men and women include both Nell Carson and Hilan Forstil. And the 'indecisive' list includes both Jim Mayfield and the Speaker Of the House, Avery Faulke. Ladies and gentlemen, until the selection of Hilan Forstil as our new vice president this afternoon, Faulke was the next man in line for the presidency."

CLOSE. CLOSE. "The men who wrote this summary believed that they could manipulate Faulke, but that they could not manipulate either President Carson or the new Acting President, Hilan Forstil. Did the Soviet Union instigate this attack on our president in the hopes of putting Faulke into power before the selection of a new vice president? It would be very dangerous for us to disregard the possibility if it is true. But it would be equally dangerous for us to believe it, if it is false."

His trembling stops. He presses on with his best Zetetic assessment of the facts, trying hard to avoid truths that might not be real.

Jet turbines hummed with their fiery power just beyond the confines of the curved metal walls of Nathan's prison. Recycled air frm the nozzle overhead blew dry and cold across his face, stealing the moisture from his throat and his eyes. He swallowed a little wetness, while his mind fell into itself. He angrily pondered the current absurdity. He sat in an airplane, performing lazy circles at 30,000 feet, while Nell lay unconscious in Walter Reed Hospital.

He blinked in the face of the air nozzle, then twisted out of its way. He joined Hilan in watching Bill Hardie on one of the monitors, moaning softly as the story built an array of evidence that the Soviet Union had ordered Nell's murder.

"That idiot!" Hilan muttered at the close of the broadcast. "What's he trying to do, start another war?" The engine hum quietly emphasized the danger. They were sailing somewhere over the middle of the United States, in case the assassination was the first step in some grander plan. Nathan focused on Hilan again, forcing himself to think of Hilan in his new role: Acting President Forstil.

Nathan shook his head. "You can tell he's trying to make a Zetetic presentation, but he still has a lot to learn. Meanwhile, even if Hardie were a perfect Zetetic commentator, he is speaking to a non-Zetetic audience. Both the speaker and the listener must know how to play their parts, or the communication will fail anyway. By the end of this broadcast, half the people in the country will think it was all a Communist plot."

Hilan shook his head. "And the worst part of it is that they may be right."

Nathan started to object, but Hilan continued. "Ted Muhlman was a Communist party member for several years, though he left over a decade ago. In the past couple of years, he's been in and out of mental institutions, suffering from grandiose fantasies. Was he Communist or was he crazy? Or perhaps a little of both? Did the KGB whisper in his ear, egging him on? And that ceramic pistol he slipped through the metal detectors—you can't pick one of those up from a Sears catalog. How did he get one?" Hilan closed his eyes. "And if the Russians really did pull this stunt, what do we do about it? Put out a contract on Klimov?"

Nathan shook his head sharply. "No! He might push the button if we did that."

Hilan threw his hands in the air helplessly. "So we just do nothing." He threw his head back into the high airplane seat. "It just doesn't pay to be a superpower."

Nathan rolled his eyes. All he could think of was Nell. All he wanted to know was that she would be all right. But these thoughts had nothing to do with the crisis they now faced. "We must keep a clear perspective on what has happened here." He started ticking off the key points. "First of all, we'll probably never know if the Soviets ordered it or not." *Nell!* his thoughts screamed. *If they did this, I want to kill them.* "Second, it almost doesn't make a difference whether they were behind the attack or not. There's a more frightening, more basic problem here: if that Revised Assessment of the Global Consequences of Nuclear War really reflects Soviet policy, the Russians are willing to risk nuclear war any time a weak man occupies the White House." *Thank God, Nell, that you were there, that you were strong!* Will you ever be there again? Will you ever be strong again? "Hilan—President Forstil—for every Nell Carson in U.S. politics, there is also a Jim Mayfield. For every Hilan Forstil, there is an Avery Faulke. If that Soviet Doctrine remains in force when another man like Mayfield becomes president, we'll go through this nightmare again. There will be more Irans, more Afghanistans, more—"

"No!" Hilan trembled. "There has to be another choice."

Nathan asked, "Is that document real?"

Hilan exhaled slowly. "As nearly as the CIA can tell. The Soviet government apparently created that doctrine." He smiled. "Of course, as I'm sure you'd point out, just because a government bureaucracy creates a document doesn't mean that particular individuals know about it. Nor does it mean that particular individuals agree with it, or that they would necessarily follow it." He quoted the Zetetic line, "*Institutions* do not *know* anything; only individuals have knowledge." He shrugged. "Unfortunately, that summary predicted recent events perfectly. And it *was* commissioned by Yurii Klimov himself, shortly after he entered the Politburo. It may not be Soviet doctrine, but it's probably Klimov's doctrine." Hilan grimaced like a trapped animal. "Jesus, he's younger than Gorbachev was when he came to power. Klimov could be in charge for decades." He pounded the arm of his chair with his fist. "And there's nothing we can do about it. There's no way to protect ourselves from Klimov, except to elect an unbroken succession of strong presidents. And we'll certainly fail to do that."

The plane bounced as it hit an air pocket. They climbed, then leveled off. Nathan felt his throat growing even drier, knowing what he would now offer. "We do have another alternative. I know another choice—an Information Age choice—that is so dangerous, so frightening," he paused, lost for words, and finally smiled, "so *incredible*, that it scares even me."

Hilan looked at him questioningly.

"We know that the HighHunter is a flexible yet reliable weapon. We built it with small Crowbars that killed tanks. Next we built it with larger Crowbars that killed ships. Now we can build a bigger one, a specially designed one, that kills hardened missile silos."

Hilan continued to stare.

"All the Russian submarines were wiped out in the war. The bomber fields are soft targets, easy to destroy. The mobile missiles on railroad cars have been tracked with near-perfection for years. Only the missiles in hardened silos are invulnerable to existing weapons—and we can destroy *those* with a new Crowbar, a SiloHunter. In principle, we can kill every Russian missile capable of reaching the United States. We can disarm them as a nuclear power."

"A preemptive first strike?"

Nathan nodded. "A *nonnuclear* preemptive first strike. No exploding warheads. There might not be any human casualties at all."

"But if something goes wrong, if they still have a few missiles afterwards, if Klimov decides to shoot them rather than lose them, we could end up with a whole planet covered with casualties."

"Yes."

The hum of engines tightened around the silence, as two frightened men stared at one another. Nathan spoke. "I wasn't necessarily recommending this as a course of action. I was pointing it out as an alternative—one that we won't have for long. The Russians are already studying the HighHunters, and the significance of the Flameout. They'll figure out the dangers of a SiloHunter, and there are a number of ways they can protect their silos, once they're alerted."

Hilan laughed—the laughter of a man on the verge of tears. "It certainly does put all our eggs in one basket, doesn't it?" He continued very softly. "But the alternative, to pray that we never have a president like Mayfield again, is like putting all your eggs into a basket with no bottom. Jesus, what an awful choice." He held his head in his hands. And then Hilan Forstil, a man who had made his life a demonstration of power and confidence, moaned like a small child. "I don't know. I don't know." He reached in his pocket and pulled out a small swiss army knife. He played with it as he spoke, more to himself than to Nathan. "You know, ever since I made that trip with Jan, I've been different. Whenever I face a crisis so difficult that I can't imagine how to cope with it, I remember that *I am a man who has climbed a MOUNTAIN*. What obstacle can challenge a man who can do such things?" He breathed deeply, and once again he was the president.

The airplane started a gentle descent. An aide appeared at Hilan's side. "Mr. President, there have been no follow-ups to the assassination. With your permission, we'll return to base."

Hilan nodded. "Very well." He smiled at Nathan. "I presume you're off to see how Nell's doing."

Nathan smiled back, despite his surprise. Had his thoughts of Nell been that obvious? "Of course. I just hope they let me in; I'm not exactly family or anything."

"They'll let you in. You'll go as my envoy."

Nathan nodded his thanks. "I have something for you as well." He fumbled for a pen and paper, wrote down a telephone number and a password. "There's going to be a decision duel tonight, an important one. One of our best students is dueling for his certification. *Join it*." He stressed the words.

Reluctantly, Hilan nodded. "I presume there's a particular reason for this?"

"Of course." Nathan smiled mischievously. "Isn't there always?"

Jessie Webler looked at the dueling screen with both pleasure and disappointment. He sat in the left-hand duelist's chair, like a chess master preparing for the world championship, suspicious that his opponent was leaving him alone during this quiet pre-game time specifically to increase his anxiety.

Such a chess-playing opponent would have smiled, for the psychological impact of the waiting was clearly taking its toll. Jessie played with the computer's trackball for a moment with rapid, exacting movements. Next he sat quite still, relaxed and unfocused. Finally, he sat as though staring into a dark shadow where monsters dwelled, while he pulled at his moustache in short jerks. His moustache had several bare patches as a consequence, exposing the chocolate-brown skin beneath.

As he shifted between relaxation, playful rolling of the trackball, and anxious tugging at his upper lip, Jessie recognized the swirl of emotions rolling within him. Sometimes, he confessed to himself, he felt the silly yet dangerous anxiety of a student taking his final exam. Jessie found this anxiety unacceptable, though understandable: it *was* his final exam. He was about to begin his certification duel. The statement he defended hung on the main screen, immutable and self-evident: NO SITUATION CAN JUSTIFY A PREEMPTIVE FIRST STRIKE AGAINST THE SOVIET UNION.

Pleasure, disappointment, and anxiety. His pleasure came from his confidence that he would win this duel. His disappointment came from his confidence that it would be an easy victory. His anxiety came from a suspicion that perhaps his immutable statement was too obvious. Perhaps the answer was so obvious as to be wrong.

The pleasure and the disappointment seemed like natural echoes of Jessie's whole life. Throughout school he had been top in his class, always enjoying his successes, yet always a little saddened by how easily they came to him. Some people accused him of arrogance, though he didn't feel arrogant inside. Other people accused him of brilliance, though he didn't feel brilliant, either. Indeed, he worried about people's definition of brilliance. Jessie made mistakes all the time. If he himself qualified as a brilliant man, despite his regular failures, what of the others? If a fellow who made mistakes as frequently as Jessie did could qualify as the cream of the human crop, did mankind really have enough smarts to survive? Pondering this question, the anxiety seemed natural to Jessie as well.

When he had first encountered the Zetetic Institute, the concept of the decision duel had staggered him with its elegance. Jessie recognized it immediately as a belated but correct response to human gullibility, derived from research performed in the '60s and '70s. In those long-ago experiments, psychologists had uncovered several critical facts, facts that no one acknowledged at the time, though they seemed obvious upon reflection.

The researchers had studied jurors in court trials. One group of jurors attended the trial in the usual way: they sat in the courtroom, watching the defendants, the accusers, the lawyers, and the judge. They watched the whites and the blacks and the men and the women, with blond hair and black hair and blue eyes and brown, wearing pinstripe suits and t-shirts, supported by lawyers both flashy and quiet. The psychologists discovered that the jurors made incorrect judgments with disturbing frequency.

So the second group of jurors did not see the trial: they heard it. They heard the voices of the defendants and the accusers and the lawyers and the judges. They heard the Southern accents and the Boston accents and the ghetto accents. They still made errors, but not so many.

So the third group of jurors did not even hear the trial: they read it. They read the transcripts of defendants and accusers and lawyers and judges. Even dull, dry transcripts did not erase all distinguishing marks from the men and women in the courtroom: the college grads and the high school dropouts *still* used different words and different expressions. And the jurors still made errors. But they made fewer errors than either of the other two groups.

When Jessie first heard about those dusty experiments and their obvious results, he wondered why America had not responded with a prompt and efficient transformation of the court system. Surely, decisions on human imprisonment were important enough to demand the most accurate possible decision-making processes!

But the court system had not changed, not even over decades of intervening time. Indeed, the results of those studies had quietly disappeared into history, remembered by almost no one. It was through this quiet human forgetfulness that Jessie encountered another of the most frightening features of the human psyche: men tend to remember facts that support the beliefs they already hold. They forget facts that contradict those beliefs.

Zetetic training recognized this flaw of human memory,

and fought to overcome it. The battle continued unrelentingly; the progress came slowly, with pain.

The rules of science had uplifted human behavior when studying repeatable, logical problems. Similarly, the rules of the decision duel had uplifted human behavior when faced with passion-filled problems. In the decision duel, only the words on the screen counted, not the race or creed of the duelist. And no disturbing fact, no tiny but fatal flaw in an argument, could be forgotten: the arrows linking the argument to the counterargument were as immutable as the quantifiable facts supporting both positions.

Motion caught his eye. He looked up, and Brad Foster leered at him.

Jessie blinked, and Brad's leer softened into a smile, though his expression did not change; only Jessie's interpretation of the smile had altered. Brad had received his certification just a few months ago, yet already he was famous. He had lost only one duel in school, when he himself had supplied his opposing partner with the critical insight that made Brad's whole argument collapse in smoke and dust. He had already established a reputation as a valuable duelist for making corporate reorganization decisions, though insufficient time had passed to assess the accuracy of his dueling analyses. Brad was the latest in the line of star duelists that included Kip Hendrix, Will Barloh, and Nathan Pilstrom.

Brad saluted him. "May accuracy triumph over victory." He spoke the duelist's creed in a monotone so perfectly without emotion that it expressed, in its perfect intensity, the depth of his commitment to his words.

Jessie's throat seemed suddenly dry; he nodded his agreement.

The work station beeped softly; Jessie jumped at the sound. It marked the beginning of the duel.

The demands of the duel moved to the forefront of his thoughts. Jessie outlined all the obvious disadvantages to a first strike. First of all, it could end all human life, particularly if the Soviets were able to launch their missiles before ours landed.

Regardless of whether the Soviets were able to shoot back or not, the resulting global effects could severely damage our nation, even with a relatively tame "surgical" preemption. What could possibly justify such a risk?

Jessie glanced at Brad again. Brad was brilliant, no doubt about it. Jessie could see it in the way Brad immersed himself in his screen, his total concentration, a pale scholar with a thatch of kinky black hair that only emphasized his ghostly complexion. Jessie felt like he was wrestling a wraith. He might find himself grabbing the words of his opponent again and again, yet he came away each time empty-handed.

Brad tossed a standard scenario up on the main screen: what if we knew beforehand that the Soviet Union was about to make a first strike against us? Would it not then make sense to try to prevent such an attack with an attack of our own?

Jessie rattled off a list of problems with this supposition. He summed up his objections by observing that, no matter how many subtle indicators flared up, we couldn't *know* a Soviet attack would occur until the attack was underway. By then it would be too late for us to make a strike that got their missiles before firing.

And shooting without that absolute certainty still entailed all the basic risks. Even if our attack succeeded, America would face the radiation and climatic consequences. Again, the risks in acting prematurely overwhelmed the risks in not acting at all. Jessie noted that this logic had surely been followed by both the American President and the Soviet General Secretary during the Flameout, and both leaders had come to Jessie's conclusion. Jessie winced as the other duelist flipped this statement to red with a polite explanation: it made no difference what decisions others had made on the matter, or how many people had shared a consensus on the matter; the question was whether or not they were right.

Despite this gaffe, Jessie's viewpoint remained unassailable. His opposing partner continued to delineate scenes and hypotheses, but all were easily countered. Once he caught Jessie off guard: what if the Soviet Union started assassinating our leaders?

Jessie felt unexpected anger, not at Brad, but at the world at large. Nell Carson was still in the hospital; she had not yet recovered consciousness. How could that kind of thing happen? What if the Russians really *had* tried to kill her? Colored with anger, an attack on the Soviet Union *did* seem justified.

But he could not write on the main screen in the color of anger; when translated to the screen, the color of anger seemed tinted with the color of foolishness. He responded, noting that a counter-assassination might be a reasonable response. But even under this provocation, they could not justify risking the whole world: no one man or woman could be worth avenging at the cost of a planet.

Brad seemed stalled, as Jessie had expected. Jessie watched Brad frown at his terminal, disturbed by his inability to budge the verdict now growing on the main screen.

The warm joy of victory washed over Jessie. He rejected it, remembering, even now, that the real victory was not in winning, but in finding the right answer. He concentrated on the hard clack of the keys, the rubbery grip of the trackball.

Brad smiled. He held his hand to his earphone and studied a corner of his screen, as though he were receiving a stunning idea from one of the members of the audience. That someone could be right there, one of the clutch of viewers in the dueling chamber, a continent away.

What novel suggestion could Brad be receiving?

Brad sat quietly for several seconds, his eyes focused on infinity. Suddenly his fingers moved, the only part of his body not bound by his concentration. Words formed on the screen. Jessie gasped as he read them.

Suppose the preemptive strike did not use nuclear weapons? Suppose that, in addition to having reasonable certainty that the Soviets would one day make a preemptive first strike of their own, America also had a nonnuclear system with which to try a preemption of that Soviet preemption?

A nonnuclear preemptive strike—what a concept! It triggered Jessie to reflect on the questions of nuclear standoff more deeply, more clearly than ever before. His mind raced with ideas that had swirled in his subconscious ever since learning the topic of his certification duel. One

particular thought stream rose above the rest, to take
flight. For the first time, he consciously considered the
problem of nuclear war from the point of view of game
theory. As his thoughts became clear, he started typing,
but he did not type new points or counterpoints into the
window defending his position. His understanding was on
a larger scale. He requested space in the neutral moderator's part of the screen. The gray bar down the middle of
the screen split, and the area of third alternatives, of new
ideas, opened wide.

The strategic nuclear problem was very similar to the
Prisoner's Dilemma, he realized. If the other prisoner
chose to betray you by firing his missiles, he went through
purgatory while you went through hell. If both prisoners
chose betrayal, your own position was approximately the
same, though at least you had the vindictive pride of
thinking you got them back.

The two-prisoner game was simpler than the global
nuclear problem, but it was a good place to start. In such a
game, the best outcome occurred if:

   1) both prisoners believed in the other's honesty, and

   2) if both played honestly, by never firing their missiles.

Given this mutual honesty, the next step was obvious:
dismantle all the missiles. After all, neither prisoner would
ever file his missiles anyway.

But mutual honesty only worked if both parties were
superrational. If either party was merely rational, the correct answer, even for the superrational player, was betrayal. Betrayal, in this variant of the Dilemma, meant an
immediate, preemptive first strike, before the opposing
partner made his *own* preemptive first strike.

What was wrong with this analysis? Jessie looked at his
conclusion in horror. Neither America nor the Soviet Union
was superrational; the right answer, then, was to attack!
Something had to be wrong with this analysis.

Something *was* wrong. The analogy to the Prisoner's
Dilemma was not perfect. The participants in the game
had a chance to make a second, follow-up decision: if the
preemptive first strike was not completely successful, the
betrayed party could betray his opposing partner later,

after assessing the betrayal. Only this risk of delayed betrayal kept the merely-rational players away from holocaust.

He had been typing his ideas as they came to him. Brad, reading Jessie's digression, also waxed philosophical, typing more fresh thoughts in the opening for third alternatives. How ironic that the two superpowers should look, from the game theory viewpoint, so much like prisoners! They were prisoners, of course, of their own weapons. The nuclear weapon itself, and the hysteria surrounding it, were the guards of the prison that held America and Russia captive. Every day these captors made men face the questions, *Today, will they strike us today? Today, must we strike them today?*

What was the purpose of the thousands of nuclear warheads in American and Soviet arsenals? Even an irrational person could understand that a hundred such warheads could destroy a national civilization. The only reason for having thousands was the danger that the opponent might try to use his warheads to destroy *your* warheads. America needed thousands because the Soviets had thousands; the Soviets needed thousands because the Americans had thousands. If each side had just a hundred apiece, the weapons would achieve the same threatening purpose, as long as the warheads were protected well enough so that the enemy couldn't destroy them.

Jessie observed that if the Soviets were superrational—if we *knew* that they were superrational—then we could initiate a slow, unilateral disarmament. The superrational Soviets would follow with their own disarmament immediately, recognizing that they no longer needed the extra missiles, and that the superrational Americans would not continue the disarmament unless the Soviets themselves came along on the journey back to sanity. They could both disarm down to the point where global catastrophe was no longer possible. They would not disarm entirely, since there were other nuclear contestants in the world, controlled by other non-superrational groups. But everyone would breathe more easily.

Brad drove back to the main point, however: if the Soviets were merely rational, if we had strong reason to fear a preemptive strike from them, if we had a nonnuclear preemptive strike option available to us, should we not use it?

Jessie looked at this new scenario with wonder. Given such a choice, he realized, his earlier decision lost its firm roots. Neither betrayal nor honesty was clearly right. The question ceased to be an engineering problem, with a clear right or wrong answer: it could only be treated as a political decision.

The colors of the main screen changed, red-lined flaws and green-lined deductions trading hues with stroboscopic speed. The new colors showed that in this nonnuclear first-strike scenario, the structure of the earlier argument collapsed. Of course, this didn't mean that a preemptive strike was right; it merely meant that a preemptive strike wasn't provably wrong.

Together, Jessie and Brad built tentative formulas for trading off right versus wrong subscenarios for undertaking a nonnuclear strike, depending on the estimated probability that the opponent was planning a strike, and the reliability of the attack systems. These new factors were no more quantifiable than the basic question, but they were more discrete, and less passion-provoking than the primary question—the question of when it might be justified to start a nuclear war.

They continued for a long time, lost in the ramifications of the possibilities they uncovered at high speed. At some time during the frenzy of analysis, a pale hand reached down and slapped the trackball, freezing both the cursor and Jessie's spinning thoughts. "Congratulations," Brad said with the same smile he had had earlier. "Welcome." They shook hands.

The duel ended in victorious accuracy: Jessie received his certification.

May 20-21

We mark the beginning of the Information Age with the implementation of the Forstil Doctrine. Many aspects of an Information Age existed before that time. But in the implementation of the Forstil Doctrine, the Information Age asserted its ascendancy. Through this Doctrine, mankind learned not that knowledge is power, but that knowledge wisely used can be superior to power.

Of course, we do not demark the Information Age with President Forstil's announcement of the Doctrine itself, but with the Night that followed.

—Bill Hardie, The Rise and Fall of the Zetetic Institute

A forest infested with termites. The American war-making machine made Yurii think of such a forest.

The Soviet Union had known the true strengths and weaknesses of the American army better than the Americans themselves. KGB spies everywhere, even in the heart of the American weapon development system, saw everything, reported every major pulse. Yet in the forest of American military development, they missed the termites.

The Americans even nurtured their termites, like the ragtag group of the Sling Project. Here were termites that could fell forests even tougher than the dense wood of the American military-industrial complex. How could even the KGB track so many termites? They couldn't, until the termites, the projects, appeared on the front pages of the American newspapers. Since the end of the so-called Flameout, Yurii had read all about the Hunters of the Sling

307

Project in the New York *Times*. Like the rest of the world, he acquired information that should have been top secret. The Americans had even supplied high-resolution photos, the very best, in the silly paper! Americans were crazy beyond comprehension.

Yurii rocked in his chair, then stopped as a squeak from the springs disturbed him. For a moment he yearned for the good old days, when General Secretary Sipyagin had ruled—correction, the days when *Citizen* Sipyagin had ruled. Yurii reminded himself that *he* was General Secretary now.

The burden weighed more heavily than he had expected. As Sipyagin's closest advisor, the job of General Secretary had looked little more difficult than advising, and it seemed to have fewer frustrations. But he realized now that this simplicity had been an illusion—an illusion only possible because the General Secretary had had no plans of his own to drive through the bureaucracy. Instead, he had had independent, vigorous advisors, such as Yurii himself, generating and herding plans through the system. If Yurii were content to let the other advisors continue their wayward performances, things would remain the same. But Yurii was most definitely not content to do so.

Even the office seemed smaller now, though it had a new, uncluttered look: the ivory figurines, the bookcases, and much of the furniture had left with Citizen Sipyagin. Barren planes of plaster and woodwork reminded visitors of the newness of the Soviet high command. Still, Yurii had enhanced the office in a technological sense: a large, flat computer display rose at an angle out of one side of the desk, and a teleconference screen coated one wall with its plain black surface. The blackness of the screen reminded Yurii of the unfathomably murky American thinking.

The video monitor across the room also made him think of the Americans, for he had seen images of the American Minuteman silos on the screen just the day before. Men had pulled back the silo covers on missile after missile: 120 in all, according to the bean counters who tracked such data. Only Americans could let all those missiles lie naked in the sunlight, exposed to nuclear destruction from Yurii's own missiles. They were even exposed to the ignoble attacks of birds, spattering their droppings across the nose cones. It seemed disrespectful to the hellish power bound within those silos.

Agonized, Yurii thrust the open-silo mystery aside, for other mysteries also blurred the future of his nation. Yurii glared at the American rocket launch reports again. The Americans continued to toss those damnable HighHunters into space at a phenomenal rate. Why? Could they be planning to destroy all of Russia's tanks and trucks, the way they destroyed her ships?

His mouth became a hard line. He could not allow that. Without her armor, Russia would become naked to the vengeful spirit of Polish, Czech, and Chinese hatred. Such a destructive move would require a nuclear retaliation. Was the new president, Forstil, so blind that he couldn't see that? Did Yurii himself have to tell the American such an obvious truth, bluntly, so that no terrible, world-engulfing error could occur? Forstil wearied him as much as the strong-willed bureaucrats in his own country. He could see no moment of calm sailing anywhere on his horizon.

Exhausting as these possibilities seemed, they did not disturb him so much as other possible explanations of the surge of American HighHunters. Yurii had reports, very reliable reports, of profoundly disquieting modifications to the HighHunter Crowbars. The reports said these missiles were larger, and even more massive, than the ones used to destroy the Soviet Navy.

For a moment, Yurii snarled as his senior military-technology analysts had snarled, staring at these reports. Why would the Americans change a weapon that already overwhelmed everything else on the planet? General Mangasarian had recommended an immediate spaceplane launch to open up one of those demon canisters and look at the new Crowbars. Yurii had rejected the idea. Hilan Forstil was every bit as unpredictable as Carson; a spaceplane assault on a HighHunter might trigger craziness, like a rain of HighHunters on Russia's spaceplane launching platforms. He could envision the effects a hundred ship-killing Crowbars would have on a delicate gantry.

Was *that* the purpose of the new HighHunter—to destroy Russia's space program by destroying her rocket launchers? To blind them by destroying their ability to launch spy satellites, so that they could no longer watch the American missile silos?

No, that made no sense either. The *old* Crowbars were perfectly capable of knocking out the satellite launchers.

More benign explanations for the new Crowbars abounded. Priorities had changed for the United States with the start of the war, and then again with the introduction of the Hunters, but now those priorities had returned to normal. Like a balloon that had deformed under the pressure of a rigid finger, the military had returned to its old shape now that the finger of war had been removed. The grand American military-industrial complex had captured the contracts to build the new HighHunters. The grand American bureaucrats were back in charge—the same ones who had "improved" their naval aircraft so much that they could barely lumber off the catapult. The new Crowbar could be just such an improvement—a new version designed to officialize the weapon with the stamp of pointlessness. Who could be sure—the new Crowbar might not even be able to kill a tank! It couldn't kill tanks as effectively, anyway: since the new Crowbar was much larger, you couldn't put enough of them into a Hunter to stop an assault.

Despite this reassuring possibility, Yurii worried that he had missed the key point someplace, though he felt close . . . With a rush of pleasure, he realized that he knew one person who *could* unravel the mystery of the American Crowbars.

He remembered the black day when the Soviet advance in Europe had ground to a halt. He remembered the crippled major who had spoken to them so boldly of that first Sling attack. That major had the gift for understanding technology and its consequences. He would look at these facts, and he would *know*—

A discreet knock at his door interrupted his train of thought. "Yes?" Yurii snapped with poorly disguised frustration. These continuous interruptions represented another flaw in the support system for the Soviet General

Secretary: how could you even complete a thought between interruptions? No wonder the old goat Sipyagin had had such trouble keeping his attention focused!

General Mangasarian leaned into the room. "Have you heard about the newest crazy American plan?"

"What?"

Swaggering into the room now that he had Yurii's puzzled interest, Mangasarian waved a video cassette in the air. "President Forstil just made a speech. Nothing new in that—but he explicitly wants *you* to see it." His voice turned exultant. "We may have won the war."

"What?!"

Mangasarian loaded the tape in the Chairman's deck. "I hope you enjoy it."

Yurii turned to watch the tape.

The image flickered for a moment, then settled on a scene Yurii had seen before. The emblem of the American Presidential Seal glared from the podium in the foreground; the muted blue wall faded into the background. Trapped between these two extremes, between the bold and the bland, stood the most powerful man in the world.

A week ago, the American President had been the second most powerful person in the world. Yurii ground his teeth in quiet fury.

The presidential face had changed so many times in the recent past—from Mayfield's face of a plastic puppet to Carson's face of a schoolteacher, and now to Forstil's face of a . . . Yurii's thought stumbled. Forstil had a look of stone, carved by lashing sea spray. An unyielding confidence lay upon him—the confidence of one who might not always win, but who always gave everything he knew how to give. And because he knew how much he had given, he had no guilt, no matter what the outcome.

This guiltless image of a president spoke. "Good morning, people of the world. I have good news today—news even better than the end of the recent war between NATO and the Warsaw Pact. Today I am here to tell you about America's plans to make the whole world safer." He paused, eyes glistening. "At least some of you have been watching us with baffled suspicion as we have called our Trident submarines into port. Even more of you have wondered about our motives as you have watched us blow back the seals on ten percent of our missiles, exposing them to the eyes of any nation with a scanning satellite."

The stony face softened with a smile that seemed to surprise the president himself. "Some of you have wondered, *What are those Americans doing this time?*" His smile held a healing joy. "Well, wonder no longer.

"We Americans have set forth on a unilateral reduction in nuclear arsenals." The camera zoomed out, to encompass both the president and a television monitor. The monitor held scenes of sabotage of such grandeur as a KGB agent might dream of in his wildest fantasies.

An American soldier stepped to the edge of a Minuteman III silo and peered into the half-light of the deep shaft. With a theatrical flourish, the soldier fondled a grenade, pulled the ring, and dropped it over the edge. A flash of light, and a short puff of smoke, announced the end of the grenade, and the end of the life of the missile now damaged beyond flight repair. Yurii's eyes bulged.

Forstil continued to speak, as though nothing unusual had happened. "As you can see, we are destroying these missiles and their silos. We will be destroying ten percent of our strategic nuclear forces every month for the next nine months, reducing our nuclear stockpiles to one tenth their current size."

The camera zoomed back in on a now-radiant president. "General Secretary Klimov, I urge you to launch a reconnaissance satellite of your own an hour from now, so you can see for yourself our sincerity and dedication to the plan of unilateral disarmament."

Yurii stared at the president with a complete loss of comprehension. Forstil's country had just won an extraordinary victory, yet now Forstil was going to throw it all away! It seemed insane—but then, Yurii remembered that Americans had thrown world domination away before, after World War II, when they had discharged over three-fourths of their men from the Army. Within a few short months of achieving total victory, they had enfeebled a military force of twelve million men down to a pathetic collection of less than two million soldiers.

Of course, at that time, the Americans had depended on a trick gadget to ensure their ascendancy: the new nuclear bomb, their precious monopoly.

Forstil continued speaking. "How can we dare to dismantle our defenses in this way? The answer is simple. In the past few weeks, we have proved an important concept. We have proved that reliance on brute power does not strengthen its holder, it weakens. The nuclear forces of both the U.S. and the Soviet Union endanger us more than they protect us. For if we were so foolish as to *use* them, even if no one lived to fire back at us, *we would still be hurting ourselves*! Just the fallout and weather changes would hurt our own citizens. Does that make sense? Of course not. It is absurd.

"Henceforth, the United States shall depend on nonnuclear, Information Age weapons to defend itself. We will retain a small nuclear force: even in the Information Age, brute force remains dangerous if not counterbalanced. But this force will be the minimum necessary. We will never need enough firepower to destroy an aggressor's civilization more than once." He paused. "Perhaps the full absurdity of our Industrial Age arsenal can be seen in the extent to which it exceeds that need. We must learn to defend ourselves with rational means, before the irrational destroys us all."

Yurii found himself gripping his chair with wild excitement, an excitement like lightning, that jerked him upright and discharged through him to the ground. So this was the purpose of the HighHunters flooding the sky! Forstil thought they could become the new trick gadget, the next-generation solution to cheap security that would replace the nuclear bomb in their thinking.

As the excitement discharged, Yurii relaxed in his chair. His worries and fears about America's Crowbars had been discharged swiftly and painlessly by the American President.

Of course, Forstil hadn't promised to destroy America's whole arsenal. America would not be at the unquestioned mercy of Yurii's missiles, but they would be so close. . . . If the Americans really did reduce their nuclear stockpile to one or two hundred missiles, a preemptive first strike became quite possible . . . no, the submarines would still pose a problem. Nevertheless, Yurii felt sure this would work to Russia's advantage.

Yurii jerked in his seat as Forstil used his name again. "We of America have now taken the first, largest step toward making our planet a safe place to live. I now ask General Secretary Klimov to join us in our casting aside of self-destroying weapons. In a few months, the Soviet Union will be the only country in the world able to bring down nuclear devastation upon Soviet land. Join us in protecting your own country." It seemed as though Forstil's eyes locked with Yurii's, despite the distance in both time and space. The weary shock of Russia's recent humiliation pressed upon Yurii with a desire to stop struggling, to do as the president suggested, to dismantle his own nuclear forces.

But that would mean throwing away a huge lever, even as it was put into his hands. Yurii grimaced. Such an abdication of advantage could not be considered.

Not all Soviet citizens would agree with his opinion. No doubt this broadcast was penetrating Soviet airspace, reaching his people despite the Army's efforts to jam it. Oh, well. The Pravda discussion of Forstil's speech would require careful editing. And perhaps it might make sense in the upcoming months to destroy a token number of Soviet missiles. They could eliminate a few obsolete weapons and thereby solidify American public opinion behind Forstil's new course. Yes, he could see considerable merit in that plan.

The tape ended. Yurii savored the victory for a moment, then reflected on his suspicions. Could this be some kind of hoax? With a quick phone call, he orbited a satellite to watch the Americans destroy their own missiles.

Two hours later, he knew without doubt the extent of the American insanity. The 120 missiles in exposed silos had been destroyed—utterly, unquestionably, and irrevocably.

It was funny how, in a quiet, darkened room, one could be crushed with a sense of terror. Hilan had lived several nights in an exact duplicate of this room in the Pentagon.

This war room where he now stood lay buried under Mount Weather, Virginia.

Though he had spent some time in that Pentagon war room, most of his mental images of this room came from trips made in dreams and nightmares—trips through thoughtworks, wherein he sweated his way across burning visions of Armageddon.

The reality now seemed inconsequential compared to those nightmares. Here, methodical discipline muffled the raw emotional undertone: the light and glare of the hot-line telecomm with Moscow lay in the Current Actions Center, behind the glass-walled control area where technicians swarmed. Here, separated from the clatter, Hilan sat at the long table with the Joint Chiefs and a variety of aides. Of course, no windows broke the walls of this quiet place buried beneath a mountain; the wall-sized display screen at the far end supplied a more relevant contact with the external world.

Hilan looked up at the display again. He did not shiver. As calm as this setting seemed, he wondered how calm he himself appeared. Any calm he might project was pure facade: He felt like a self-contained nuclear burst, the detonation surging in his body, trapped within the authority of his black pinstripe suit.

The war room would have been a dangerous place to hold this meeting before the war for Europe, now known as the Flameout. Before the Flameout, Soviet submarines cruised within six minutes of an attack on Washington—six minutes from obliterating the war room in the Pentagon. Had the subs not been destroyed already, the fragile plan Hilan would now execute could not exist.

The long table held too many faces. Hilan picked out the key ones, unconsciously. Foremost was General Hansen of the Air Force, chairman of the Joint Chiefs of Staff. He was a tall man, prone to sudden-breaking smiles, with silver hair. He had been a fighter pilot, and he still wore the ostentatious watch that was once so popular among the flyers. He sat serenely at the far end of the table.

Soft light came from the ceiling, eliminating shadows. A couple of people smoked; the ventilation drew away the smoke with brisk efficiency.

The display wall was an oversized version of the screen used by the Zetetics to hold decision duels. The technology here was more primitive, Hilan realized: the software for the display did not allow such flexible zooming and windowing. The absence of powerful software explained why they needed the entire wall for this setup. Despite the huge display, however, the commander in chief had less access to useful information than did a second-year physics student probing the atom for the first time. Plenty of information would come across that display, but little of it would be useful.

What did Hansen think of the plan they had come here to execute? Hansen might be turning purple inside, but that was submerged here. He was a soldier's soldier, calmly competent. He had objected to the plan at first as too risky. But a day's reflection, and the weight of the ideas, had made him a believer. He would never bet everything on a single turn of the wheel, he had said. But here the alternative was to bet everything on the turn of the wheel, not once, but many times—every time a weak president confronted Yurii Klimov.

General Hansen evoked in Hilan a sense of security—a delusionary feeling, to be sure. But Hilan had by now listened to too many Zetetic lectures to deny the delusionary feeling: *those who refuse to admit their own prejudices will remain forever enslaved by them.*

Hilan turned away from Hansen to look at the lower left-hand corner of the display. In that corner, photos of the Soviet Union flicked methodically from scene to scene. Over 300 SkyHunters were sending those pictures of critical targets. A checklist adjacent to the images marked off the targets as, SkyHunter by SkyHunter, they accounted for each and every one.

The photos showed the sites of deeply buried headquarters, and buildings cast with meters of reinforced concrete. They seemed impregnable. But the targets being assessed were not the buried and reinforced buildings. The targets were the thin, delicate antennae serving those mighty bunkers. The men would survive, and in a few hours, they would reestablish communication with the world. But for several precious hours, they would be blind and mute. By the time they recovered, there would be no missiles or bombers to command.

The words to begin a war seemed so simple. An Air Force captain announced: "Ready to dispense."

Hilan closed his eyes for a moment, then looked into the captain's. He held his breath, as if waiting for someone else to make the decision, knowing that no one else could.

In this last moment before sending humanity hurtling toward clear survival or clear destruction, Hilan did not think about the careful rope of logical thinking that had led him here. He had inspected it from every possible direction, examined every fiber, every mar in its surface, every kink in its depths. The rope had kinks; it could snap; the world could fall from it. But he had examined the other ropes at hand with equal care, and though the rope he had chosen *might* snap, the others were even more likely to break. The logic of the rope fibers rested in a corner of his mind, but did not command his attention.

Nor did he think of his wife in Washington, his children in New Haven, or his aunt in Cincinnati. Earlier, he had fantasized about moving them to places of safety in case the rope broke. But without the rope, no place could prove safe. If he would not risk his own family, what kind of fool would he be to risk all mankind? His family, he had decided in his earlier analysis, would be among the hostages he would hold over himself to make sure his decision was the right one. He had moved himself beneath the mountain mostly for the proximity to the hot line.

He did not think of the Zetetic Institute, or Nathan Pilstrom, who had devised this ingenious solution to the problem of thermonuclear missiles. Nathan had presented him with this dilemma. But he did not fall into the trap of laying all the blame for the future on the people who first saw that such a future was possible. Some of the blame—or some of the credit—did belong to them, but at this moment, neither blame nor credit seemed important.

He did not think of Yurii Klimov, or the possible outcomes of this evening's efforts. He had thought about the outcomes too much already, and he would need to think

about them again soon anyway. Nothing could be gained
by wrapping up his mind in a tight coil around the hideous
possibilities that *might* ensue; he would need a clear mind
to deal with whatever possibilities *did* materialize.

None of these people or events could capture his attention. Rather, a simple feeling held him, now that the
decision-making was over, and only the actions to solidify
the thought-stuff remained. It was a feeling of relief.

One way or another, the terrible uncertainty would end
by morning. The terror that had hung over his whole life,
over the lives of all the other people in America and
Russia and the rest of the world, would fade into history.
"Do it," he nodded to the officer.

They watched the display.

The HighHunter dispenser carried its own camera, and
through this viewpoint, the roomful of generals, admirals,
and presidential advisors saw a thousand tiny points of
light come to life above the Soviet night sky. The points
streaked along majestic arcs, with the grace granted by
gravity's guiding hand.

The captain who had initiated the dispensing of the
SiloHunters muttered in awe, "It's like snow—or maybe
sleet."

General Hansen, boss of the Joint Chiefs of Staff, grunted.
"A sleet of steel, falling through the night."

A murmur rose around the room. Admiral Jenson
frowned, along with General Plunket of the Army. Neither
of them liked today's mission, and Hilan agreed with their
anxiety completely.

The camera view switched to an optically amplified image, which came from a reconnaissance satellite. It focused
on the fate of a simple disc of concrete, thousands of miles
away from both the satellite and the watchers.

The full thickness of the Earth's atmosphere shimmered
above the disc, making it seem to waver, insubstantial and
anemic. Its grayish-white substance seemed more like a
ghost than an implacable enemy—something that would
swish away with the wave of a hand.

A streak of light cut the image and struck the ghost,
shattering the illusion of both. The streak disappeared as
quickly as it had come, leaving a shallow, darkened pit in

the platter, beneath a pale cloud of dusty shadows. A Crowbar had hit the silo cover.

Another streak of light cut the image, then disappeared from the far edge of the picture: a miss.

Another streak of light hurtled down, and dug a second pit into the disc's surface: a hit.

Another one missed.

Another struck, near midpoint between the other two hits. Now the whole surface of the disc disappeared under a rubble cloud that settled a moment later. The hair-thin fractures left by the first two hits, too fine to be seen even with the crystal-precise instruments of the recon satellite, now showed clearly in the chewed surface of the silo cover.

But that cover still held intact; no hole yet penetrated its full depth to the terror lurking beneath. This silo required at least two more hits to fulfill the mission—one to clear the broken shield, one to fall cleanly into the pit, to brush the monster missile with kinetic destruction. Only one more Crowbar fell toward that target, however. Helpless, Hilan watched as the last streak of light crossed, and missed.

They had allotted six shots of sleet for each silo—two to break the cover, one to break the missile, one to miss, and two more just for safety. Here three had missed, and four had been needed to break the cover. The failure was too painful to feel: the agony numbed the mind, rather than piercing it.

The room seemed silent because Hilan could no longer hear anything, beyond the pounding of his ears. His mind raced in the kind of circle he had most feared. *Destroyed,* he thought, *the whole world will be destroyed.*

The rushing sound of his own blood filled his ears. He focused his mind on his own breathing, and let his eyesight fade against the muted tones of the wood-paneled walls, cutting off his vision along with his hearing. He breathed.

After a long moment (he didn't know how long, and he dared not think about how few moments he had in which to think), he searched for alternatives to avert total destruction. Certainly, the Soviets would know that if they released their missiles at this juncture, Hilan would retaliate. Even now, a spasm launch of missiles was not in the Soviet interest. But if Hilan could not offer them an alternative—something that would satisfy the human need for revenge—they might choose a convulsive retaliation, despite their own interests.

What could he offer them? He had thought about this, along with Nathan and a dozen other men he respected, for hours on end. But none of the alternatives they had devised satisfied him. He could offer to dismantle more American missiles, and he could offer to do it faster, over the course of a couple of days, instead of months. He felt sure this would not satisfy them, however.

He could offer them a city: one free shot against a city of their choosing. He almost lost control of his panic as he thought of this. *Total destruction.* The thought cycled in his mind again. But he forced himself to examine this hideous option. He felt sure it would appease the Soviets. It was better than the destruction of all civilization. Yet when Hilan thought of the millions of innocent people, his mind rebelled. Those people were not responsible for Hilan's actions. Hilan would stand firm on simply disarming the U.S., and hope that the Soviets accepted it, before he would make an offer like that.

Of course, if the Soviets chose to undertake such an incremental punishment, by obliterating one city without Hilan's consent, what would he do? He agonized over this, and the alternatives they had collected for responding to *this* scenario, before admitting it was of secondary importance right now; he still needed to invent an adequate way to appease the Soviets. He needed a way to make sure that the Soviets knew the United States had been punished—a punishment great enough to make American presidents know never to try this stunt again, but one that did not require the murder of innocent people.

A punishment that would not harm innocent people. He faced a crisis here so difficult that he couldn't imagine a way of coping with it. Without thinking, he reached for the knife that had accompanied him up the mountain. He paused, contemplating the knife, the mountain, and the crevasse. He felt calmer.

And then he felt hopeful, for he realized that there *was* a punishment he could allow the Soviets to impose that involved no *innocent* victims. It was a third alternative, one he had thought of once before, dangling by a rope in a deep and deadly crevasse.

The strangled voice of a junior officer penetrated Hilan's meditation. "Thank God," he said. "The rest of them are getting through."

Hilan looked up to see another silo-attack sequence on the board. This time, the pattern of sleet struck with silent precision: a dead-center hit, that left visible cracks in the silo cover; a second hit, that left broken concrete rocks in its wake; a third hit that speared through the opening, to cut through the nose cone of the missile like a meat cleaver; and another hit that cleared most of the rubble from above before piercing the missile to its core in a second mortal blow. This second hit struck the fuel supply. A burst of light and fire spit back into the night from which the sleet had come, then settled to a glowing ember, deep in the shaft of what had once been a missile silo.

Hilan drew a long, shuddering breath.

General Hansen asked, with the tone of an order, "What's the ratio of kills to misses?" He leaned forward, squinting one eye at the numbers frothing in one corner of the display. "About 20 to 1?"

The officer in charge of the display nodded. "Yes, sir."

Hansen looked back at the president. "Good, but not as good as we had hoped. And not good enough, Mr. President. The Russians have over 2,000 missiles. If one in twenty survives, they still have over a hundred of them."

Hilan nodded. "Not enough to destroy the world, but enough to destroy the United States." How did this change Hilan's analysis? Certainly, it made an all-out Soviet attack even less rational from the Soviet point of view: they could not doubt, in these circumstances, that the U.S. could and would retaliate. Even so, Hilan's earlier analysis remained valid. He still needed to offer the Russians a sane way to punish the Americans.

He rose from the table with stiff precision. "I believe it is time to negotiate with Klimov." He walked past the glass control area to sit down with the hot line display system, confident that Klimov would be with him shortly.

Yurii began a painful ascent from deep slumber at the sound of mad, pounding boots. "Sir, we are under attack."

"What?" Light pounded against Yurii's closed eyelids; he winced.

And then he was in a helicopter, his robe flapping as he dressed in the dark, in the cramped space, in the screaming noise of the rotor, in the heart-tightening fear that wormed through his soggy thoughts.

As he grew older, Yurii had more trouble waking at odd hours. A moment of empathy for the retired General Secretary hovered on the edge of his mind, then vanished as his mind focused on the terror of the situation. *We are under attack.*

But Forstil had just initiated the destruction of his own missiles! Could that have been a ruse? Somehow, Hilan Forstil had seemed too sincere, in that American sort of way, to devise a trick of such scale.

Finally dressed, he set his shoulders and listened to the situation report. It was, in some bizarre sense, not as bad as he had feared. The information was fragmentary—the primary communications systems had been knocked out with superb efficiency—but apparently no nuclear weapons had been used in the attack. Just prior to the strike, the radars had noted the breakup of the new HighHunters, with the oversized Crowbars. Now that it was too late, Yurii understood the new weapon and its purpose. Ah, the accuracy of hindsight!

The briefing ended too quickly, with too few facts. Yurii retreated to the hot-line room with an army of translators, though Yurii understood English as well as many of them.

Hilan Forstil was waiting for him. The quality of the picture was uncanny; Yurii had not seen the system since the new high-resolution cameras had been installed. Forstil sat close by at a table; if Yurii focused on the oversized screen, it seemed that Hilan was with him, in Moscow, rather than half a world away.

"Greetings," the president said. "I've been expecting

you." He smiled, the sad, stern smile of a doctor who has only precarious news for his patient's family.

Yurii glared at him, a flood of anger welling up that he barely contained by his awareness of the chasm between them—a chasm large enough to swallow them both. "You have stripped me of communications. I can talk to no one but you."

Hilan looked back calmly, his face suffused with sincerity. "Really? I would like to believe you. Heaven knows we tried our best to destroy all your communication systems. However, I doubt that we succeeded. General Secretary, the Soviet Union has a *lot* of communication systems."

A feeling of near-amusement struck Yurii; in fact, the president was right. Yurii still had other assets, though coordinating them to carry out a plan remained problematic.

Forstil spoke again. "But though we failed to take away all your communications, I suspect that I know more about your current status than you do. Let me bring you up to date: your submarines are gone, all of them. Your bombers are gone as well: the handful you have in the air are under observation, and if they try to move in our direction, we will destroy them quickly, even easily."

Forstil paused, to look away at a display that was hidden from Yurii's camera. "Your intermediate-range missiles have been reduced in number along the European front, though a considerable number remain. Of course, they aren't relevant now, since they can't reach the United States. Your forces along the Chinese border remain intact."

Hilan smiled almost mischievously, knowing that these were not the critical statistics. "Your land-based missiles have taken the most severe damage. Most of them have been destroyed. But you do have about a hundred ICBMs left."

Yurii nodded. His own people could account for about 30 operational systems; something on the order of a hundred seemed reasonable. Of course, the American President could be lying. Forstil could be giving him either a high estimate or a low one, depending on his purpose. Certainly, Forstil had had more time to consider this situation. Yurii was sure the president had used that analysis time well.

Yet the man seemed so open and willing to share information. Could Yurii use that? "President Forstil, your estimate is lower than our analysis suggests. Which hundred missiles are the ones you think are still operational?"

The president leaned forward, suddenly very serious. "We can't afford to play games here, General Secretary. We have a planet to save."

For a moment, Yurii couldn't control his anger. "You have attacked the sovereign territory of the Soviet Union! We can destroy your whole civilization!"

Forstil's sorrow returned. "Yes, you can. Of course, we can destroy yours, as well." He licked his lips. "Please remember that little harm has come to your people. The United States will, of course, pay retribution to the families of the men who have lost their lives. Frankly, I don't expect that to involve many claims."

Indeed, to Yurii's knowledge, only two men had died in the attack. One had been wounded. "You have destroyed billions of dollars of investment in our defenses!"

"We will destroy a similar set of investments in our nation. We have already started, as you well know. And we were the only reason you needed all that hardware in the first place."

"Your trivial destruction of a few Minutemen is a ruse and a hoax, designed to trick us into lying still while you grasp world dominance!"

Forstil shook his head. "Yurii Klimov, you are the most astute General Secretary the Soviet Union has had in a long time. And you are the most sophisticated analyst of Americans ever to hold your office. You have studied me. I am destroying the American strategic missile force. Soon we will have no more missiles than you have today. Klimov, I have no reason to lie to you on this matter. What value would more than a hundred nuclear missiles have? What value did they ever have? Have you personally slept any better with thousands of these monsters than you did before? I can't believe it."

The open weariness of the American struck Yurii with surprise. Even more surprising, Yurii recognized the same feeling within himself—a weariness with the wrestling match he had conducted all his life, under the shadow of nuclear terror that was insane in its intensity. He looked away for a moment as he realized that, one way or another, that shadow that had haunted him would now become lighter.

A feeling of optimism followed. He began to believe that the American would destroy most of the American missile force, as surely as he had destroyed Russia's. Yurii started to tell the president that the Soviet Union had planned to follow America's lead and reduce its nuclear force, but cut off his own words. The president was right; this was not a time for games.

Still, his anger remained. His country had been attacked!

He wanted to launch a counterstrike, to destroy the American ICBM silos in return. This course of action seemed like proper justice. But he did not have enough missiles, even if he had the command and control systems to arrange it. Besides, the Americans would destroy those silos for him.

He glared at the president again. Forstil, he realized, had been studying him intently these past few moments. Yurii suddenly despised the high-resolution television system that betrayed his every movement to the American. He fought a desire to order the camera shut off, sensing that such a reduction in personal contact was the first step to oblivion. Yet oblivion seemed inevitable. What recourse did he have, but to strike back at America's cities? He *had to* respond to this attack! What else could he do, other than destroy American cities?

Hilan Forstil seemed to read his thought. "This is a personal confrontation, General Secretary, no matter how it affects the world. You must not blame the United States for the destruction of your missiles. The United States did not initiate this attack against you. I did." The president seemed to grow in presence. The sincerity in his eyes reached out, convincing. "Blame me. If you feel you must punish someone, punish me."

"Very well, President Forstil. I shall blame you." His face twisted with fury. "But how do I punish you?"

"With my hand. With yours." Now the president opened

his right hand; it contained a bright red swiss army knife. With hypnotic, casual grace, Forstil opened the blade and brought it to his own throat.

A gasp arose from somewhere off-camera. Forstil frowned at the sound, then turned back to Yurii. "Kill no innocent people, Yurii Klimov. Kill only those who are to blame. In killing them, you will get your message across most effectively. Let this nightmare end with the guilty."

Yurii stared at the knife. The steel blade flickered in the light, clean and precise in its deadly intent. It seemed so small, yet so perfectly lethal—truly, a proper mate to the surgical Hunters that had excised the Soviet arsenal. Except that *this* surgical weapon was under Yurii's control— At least, Forstil claimed that it was under Yurii's control.

Control. Control of the environment. Control of the self. No man reached the pinnacle of Soviet power without understanding control. He believed Forstil: he believed that he himself, not the American, controlled the knife.

And he wondered, did he control the knife, or did the knife control him? Yurii could not take his eyes away from it.

His eyes slid reluctantly down to the smooth plastic handle, held in a firm but easy grip. Yurii had an identical knife in his own desk. For a moment this thought gave him a sense of kinship with the president. He could feel the smooth surface sliding between his own fingers, tapping a fingernail against its unyielding strength.

Afraid of too close an empathy, he jerked up to look at the American President. And here he found a break in his rapport with the man who offered his life: Forstil looked back with steady eyes—eyes that held no trace of guilt or fear.

It provoked Yurii to another outburst. "You launched a sneak attack against us! Without discussion, without warning!" he screamed, trying to extract some admission of guilt. "Of all the people in history, you most deserve to die for starting this holocaust!"

"Yurii Klimov." The president's voice was soft, almost a whisper. "If our positions had been reversed, what would you have done?"

If he had had the chance to so cleanly neutralize America, what would he have done? The answer struck him like shards of ice flung in his face. He suddenly saw generosity in Hilan Forstil's actions.

The president was speaking again. "Frankly, it doesn't make any difference what you might have done. I am the one who did it. General Secretary, the vengeance you seek, in your belief that it is justice, is in your hands. It is yours for just the slightest motion." The knife tip pressed against yielding flesh.

Yurii had the American totally in his power. To kill this man would indeed send a potent message to anyone foolish enough to think about this stunt again. Yet, the thought continued to haunt him, *what would I have done in the same situation?*

He must have moved his head, for he saw the president's hand grip more firmly, a last tension before plunging the knife home.

Yurii leaped up. "No!" he shouted. "I will not take your miserable life."

The president's fingers relaxed, though for a long moment his expression remained the same, as if not quite believing his reprieve. Then he smiled, that same sorrowful smile. "Thank you." He looked to the side, and his smile became wider, yet also more sorrow-filled. "And now it no longer makes any difference."

Yurii looked at the president, puzzled, until Forstil explained. "A second wave of SiloHunters just struck the Soviet Union. General Secretary, your country no longer has a strategic nuclear force."

Yurii stood very still. "Will you still destroy your missiles?"

Forstil nodded. "Why not? They're pointless now anyway."

Curiosity overcame his deeper concerns. "Tell me, President Forstil, would you really have used that knife, knowing you only had to hold out for a few minutes before I was reduced to impotence?"

Again Forstil nodded. "I always keep my word, Yurii Klimov."

A new emotion struck him now that it was all over: the sense of loss—a loss that gave way to bitterness. "Well, you did not need the knife. And now, instead of death, you have earned world domination."

The president burst into laughter. It swelled, growing almost hysterical in its release of tension, then disappeared as quickly as it had risen. "So it might seem to you. And indeed, in some bizarre sense, I have great power over all the nations of the world except one. I might control the world, Yurii Klimov, but I can't control my own people. I think you'll find this leaves me with no more world control than you have." He paused reflectively. "But one thing I can assure you. Your own country, the Soviet Union, is safer now than it was just an hour ago. I'm sure you don't believe me now, but in time you will. Sleep well, General Secretary, knowing that from this night forward, sleep will be much easier for everyone." The screen darkened to black.

Yurii stared at the blank screen for a long time, wondering if the American spoke the truth. Maybe, in ways he could just begin to see, Forstil might be right.

May 23

The engineer breaks a large problem into many small problems, each of which he can solve. The bureaucrat takes many small problems and rolls them together to form a large problem that no one can solve.

—*Zetetic Commentaries*

The smell of antiseptics tainted the air.

Leslie hated illness and death. But even more, he hated hospitals, as embodiments of these disasters. He recognized the danger of this emotional reaction. In Zetetic terms—in terms stolen from the general semanticists, who had stolen it from the earlier German philosophers—it was a *reification*. It was the mapping of an idea (death) onto a real-life object (the hospital) that did not quite correspond correctly. It was a perfect example of a mental map that did not correspond to the actual terrain. Mistakes like this led inevitably to horrible fates, such as the fate that had befallen Jim Mayfield.

Even recognizing his erroneous reification, Leslie hated hospitals. It was hard to act with wisdom as great as your understanding.

Lila led the way through the hospital; a ragtag collection of software engineers followed her hasty footsteps. Leslie's eyes glistened as he reflected on the upcoming meeting of the Sling software team. He knew it would be the last one.

Partings seemed to be an inevitable defect of the Information Age. The rapidly networked project teams quickly achieved their purposes, and the fulfillment of those purposes led to an equally rapid breakup.

Leslie knew what would happen next. He had come to this point many times on projects in the past. All the team members would swear to get together in the future. All of

329

them would electronically send mail to one another at slowly lengthening intervals. None of them would know exactly when the spirit of the team had slipped away, though all would understand eventually that the spirit had indeed gone. Of the members of the Sling team, only Leslie would know that the Sling spirit had slipped away with the end of this last meeting.

But for today, for this moment of triumph, their shared accomplishment transcended the petty failings of individual human beings. Lila even smiled at Kurt as she opened the door to Juan's room; Kurt smiled back as he stepped through. Flo and Ronnie followed. Leslie entered last, so that he could quietly occupy a corner. He slipped his bag from his shoulder and smiled as he remembered the bag's contents.

Juan had trouble focusing his eyes. He squinted and blinked often, but he greeted everyone with a wiry laugh. "Good God! Is the whole town of Yakima here?"

Lila shook back her hair. "Not quite. Only all the people who had to find bugs in your software." She grasped his hand for a lingering moment. Perhaps this sliver of the team, Juan and Lila, would go on together beyond the end of the Sling.

Lila held a gift-wrapped package in her left hand. "Nathan's sorry he couldn't make it. He's with the president, waiting to hear about Nell Carson. They're operating on her again today." She held the package out to Juan. "He told me to give you this." She frowned. "He said you should practice with it."

"Sounds ominous." Juan took the package. A tremor ran across his shoulders, and he grunted, "It better not be a computer, that's all I can say."

"It's not a bomb," Kurt offered. "I listened to it carefully before I got into the car with it."

Juan unwrapped the box slowly, savoring the surprise. Suddenly it fell apart, and a wine bottle fell into his hands. Juan scrutinized the label. "Fume Blanc." Juan's grin took on Cheshire proportions. "A fine wine. It would be wasted on an alcoholic, but it's perfect for a wine taster."

An awkward silence followed for a moment. Juan asked, "So what's everybody doing now?"

After a moment's emptiness, Ronnie spoke up. "Well, you know Lightcraft Corporation—the people who make the WeatherWatcher? They want to improve the handling of their planes in mountainous areas." He glanced sidelong at Flo. "We're considering putting a bid on it."

Flo nodded. "Yes." A deep amusement surfaced around her eyes. "We may find ourselves working for my daughter."

Kurt spoke next. "And I'll probably go to work for the Institute, as an employee rather than as a subcontractor. They aren't quite sure what they'll do with me yet." He shrugged. "I'm not quite sure what I'll do with them, either. Except I'll fight the Army bureaucrats—the ones I tried to leave behind a year ago." He rolled his eyes, then turned serious. "But I have another message from Nathan." He drew an envelope from his pocket. "I'm not sure what it is, but he wanted me to read it to everybody."

He ripped the envelope apart and started reading Nathan's words. "I'm sorry I couldn't make it to today's meeting of the Sling team. But frankly, I'm not *too* sorry; I hate endings. And anyone who reflects too long on the completion of this project will miss a moment of true wonder. The end of the Sling Project is the beginning of more futures than we can imagine.

"But before we move into those beginnings, I want to discuss the meaning of our success. I'm sure some of you have asked yourselves, how long will the success we created here last?" A shudder passed through the whole group, as if everyone had indeed asked themselves this question. "If you wonder, then I want you to remember this.

"Our success has brought the human mind directly into service in the defense of ourselves and our friends. In the heart of each Hunter there dwells a small part of each of our minds. Within each Hunter small extensions of our souls watch unceasingly, protecting us from all men and nations who don't believe that freedom is important. Henceforth, those extensions of our souls will protect us for as long as such protection is necessary, for as long as men live who do not respect the rights of others. And so, for those who have given of their souls—for Lila, and Kurt, and Leslie, and Juan, and Ronnie, and Flo, and—" Kurt's voice broke, to continue in a whisper "—and for Amos, the free men of the world give their thanks."

Leslie lost the thread of the conversation. Though the message had been for everyone, Nathan had nevertheless found his way home to the source of Leslie's own disquiet. He had not thought of the Sling that way—as a permanent melding of the souls of the team. The cooperative spirit he had thought they would lose now lived within the circuits of the Hunters they had stationed around the world. The spirit had not died; it had merely faded from view. What they had created would indeed continue on, until replaced by something better. That was as it should be.

His sorrow lifted. At a lull in the conversation, he stepped forward, opening his bag. "There's an important part of the job we haven't completed yet," he said with mock sternness.

The room grew quiet as he pulled items from the bag: a steel pan, a cigarette lighter, a bottle of Jim Beam bourbon, and a folded roll of paper. He cleared his throat, taking on the tone of an announcer. "The time has come," he said quietly, "for the honorable tradition of the PERT chart burning."

Juan understood first. "Beautiful! Thanks for remembering."

With solemn care, Leslie unraveled the paper. It was a miniature of the PERT chart that had filled the hall in the Zetetic Institute. One important change had been made: green—the green of successful completion—now covered every box on every path. The pinks and reds and blues still marked all the twisting roadblocks they had met along the way—a commemoration of the pain they had shared along the path, a chapter of history rendered in wordless color. But green boxes had grown around the red, encasing every disaster in healing tones. The green had seeped all the way to the final box, the ending milestone that held the words, "SLING COMPLETE."

Leslie placed the chart in the pan and whetted it with the bourbon. Twisting one end into a wick, he lighted the alcohol and the paper. A bluish flame flickered from the obsolete chart, and smoky aroma tinged the antiseptic smell of the room.

Laughter and idle chatter grew loud. Eventually the chatter softened as, one by one, the people who had built the Sling departed. Soon only Juan, Lila, and he himself remained. He wished the two of them well and departed.

Leaving, he rejoiced at this quiet dissolution of a great team. He would have liked the Sling team to continue indefinitely, but the Institute's teachings reminded him of the consequences of that alternative: any attempt to drive a team beyond its natural life would lead to the creation of an institution. Once the culture had hardened into the rigid torpor of bureaucracy, this travesty of a team would feed upon the bright cooperative light that had created it, until the light died, leaving a cold emptiness darker than the absence of light.

Well, the future Nathan had mentioned in his note had already arrived. Leslie had a new contract with the L-5 Corporation, a chance to help build the SpaceRing. And the SpaceRing project would require a *team*. His mind filled with the questions and issues he needed to resolve before he could bring that team together.

Kira stood before the flat dullness of the apartment door and stared into the peephole. Of course, from her side of the door, she could see nothing. But she had come here planning to feign disorder and confuse the enemy; let the confusion start even now, before the door opened. Her effort to invoke confusion had worked the last time; she wondered if it would work again. With a light flick of her wrist, she raised the knocker and tapped in a bright rhythm.

She waited. Dull thuds from inside suggested the movements of a large man. When the sound stopped, she knew he had come to the peephole and that his confusion mounted with every passing moment. She smiled for him.

Bill flung the door aside. His eyes gleamed. His smile reminded Kira of an engineer who has completed the careful, painstaking analysis of what he needs to do, who can now throw himself headlong into the completion of his project.

Kira smiled in response to that engineer's smile, then stopped as she remembered that Bill was not an engineer. He always threw himself headlong, too often without making the painstaking analysis that must precede flight.

He stood with all his weight on one leg, his head tossed to the side, the tawny curls of his hair touching the door's edge. He watched her with simple pleasure.

"Let me in," she said. He did not yield. She stepped forward.

Laughing, with inseparably quick movements, his head came up, his left leg pinned the door, and he released his handhold upon it. He reached out with both arms and grasped Kira around the waist. Before she could object, he turned and carried her into the living room.

Kira twisted against the strength of his hands, a futile effort that nonetheless had the proper effect: he chose to release her. She took two steps, turned, and confronted her adversary, fully aware of the flushed heat on her face. "The last time I saw you, you looked crumpled because you'd found out what a dupe you had been. You look happier now."

"I've had what you Zetetics call a 'revelation.' After that day when you came here to destroy me, I spent a week figuring out what to do next. Now I know." A large fist smacked down against an equally large palm. "I know who to get. Daniel Wilcox is dead meat."

"I see." The thought of Bill rampaging against the tobacco industry thrilled and scared her at the same time. It thrilled her because it would save lives, but it scared her as an act of vengeance for her mother. Bill planned to attack Wilcox *only* for vengeance. She continued coolly, "So you're going to make the same kind of vicious, distorted attack on him that you made on us."

He opened his mouth to say yes, realized her purpose, and pressed his lips together. "Actually, I may not have to," he said.

"Oh? Why not?"

Uncertainty wavered in his eyes. "Daniel Wilcox seems bent on destroying himself. He's making some strange business deals." His glance turned conspiratorial. "What do you know about it?"

Kira shrugged. "I don't know anything about his plans anymore. I've retired from the agency handling Wilcox-Morris." She considered telling him about her more recent activities—the new political campaigns to protect the

Institute and the Information Age, campaigns for which she now wanted Bill's help. "I think Wilcox has found out who I am."

"Really? Well, *I* know who you are."

Kira laughed. "Really? Who am I? Is this a guessing game?"

"You're a woman with so many emotional biases about the Zetetic Institute that I'm overwhelmed by the hypocrisy of your last lecture to me."

"I see. I guess you do know who I am." She started to defend herself, then stopped. "It's possible that my emotional involvement has prejudiced my view of the Institute. I can't judge it. Can you?"

His eyes glittered. She had thrown herself open to his judgment, and now he held the power to strike at her ego.

But the same shred of intellectual honesty that in the last analysis had not allowed him to deny the facts surrounding his comet-like rise to success did not now allow him to bruise her unjustly. "Probably not."

She gave a short laugh, as if to acknowledge his weakness—a weakness she knew as a virtue. With the ease of perfect security, she threw herself onto his couch. She lay back, half-closing her eyes, her hands clasped behind her head. "You have anything to drink in this place?"

"I have scotch. I have orange juice. Which would you prefer?"

"Your choice. Whichever one *you're* having."

After a moment's pause, he muttered, "Orange juice." He went into the kitchen.

Kira chuckled at his decision not to bring out the scotch. She figured that he figured that he would need all his wits to continue this verbal duel. "Do you know Charles Somerset?" she yelled at him through the room dividers.

"He's the project manager of FIREFORS, right? Or rather, he used to be; FIREFORS no longer exists."

"Right. Well, he's come to the Institute, and we've found out that he has a rare and spectacular talent. He has a sixth sense for subliminal advertising."

"What does that mean?" Bill returned with two huge glasses. He sat down on the couch, just close enough to make Kira aware of his nearness.

"It means that he can detect, with his conscious mind, the suggestive signals that advertisers use to get at a person's subconscious." She slurped at her orange juice, making more noise than she needed to. "He says he can smell it. Yesterday he smelled it in a literal sense. He was shopping in some department store, and he could tell that something odd was happening. The shoppers were just a little too intent on their purchases. Several other Zetetics were looking around, puzzled; they could feel it, too. Well, after analyzing his sensations for a bit, Charles realized that someone had filled the store with 'new car smell.' Not too much—not enough so that people could recognize it—but enough to tingle somewhere deep inside. Charles was the only one who figured it out." She nodded. "You should come to the Institute, too. Who knows? Even you might have a talent."

Bill growled, then mumbled something.

"What?" Kira asked.

"I said, I *have* been to the Institute. I'm working on developing a Zetetic form of newscasting."

"I see. I've noticed that your newscasts seem less ridiculous lately. Of course, you have a long way to go." Kira had known before coming here that Bill was enrolled at the Institute. He had made great progress, in fits and starts. It seemed somehow inappropriate for her to compliment him, but her intellectual honesty was too great to leave it at that. "Actually, I'm delighted with some of your recent stuff. In fact, I'm worried about you—a Zetetic newscasting style would still be a ratings disaster, even though there are more Zetetic viewers every day. You'll have to be careful for a few more years, until we have a large enough group to form a significant sector of the audience."

She watched Bill shift his position, again and again, unable to suppress his drive to action. She considered his qualifications. He was smart, he was witty, he was too handsome, and he was passionate about anyone or anything with whom he got involved. In short, he had potential. The only question was, could he be trained? She would have to work on that.

The newscast that had been murmuring in the background suddenly became the focus of Bill's attention. "Yes," a military spokesman was saying, "the Hunters that helped our boys win the war were actually developed under the auspices of the Army's regular research and development system. So were the enhanced HighHunters used on the Night of Steel Sleet. Contrary to the media's distorted versions of the recent past, the Sling Project did *not* expose flaws in the Defense Department's policies—it demonstrated the health and vitality of those policies."

Bill leaped from the sofa. "Liars and fools," he screamed. "The Zetetic Institute saved your asses. The Institute is the real hero of the war." He sat down, muttering, "The Army is riddled with deadbeats. We have to get rid of them."

Kira thought about the intricacies of the facts that came closer to the truth. Yes, there were many deadbeats in the Army, and incompetents, and politicians without regard for anything but their next promotion. But there were also the thousands of men who stood and fought with their tanks, with their rifles, with their knives, and finally, with their bare hands, in the face of a seemingly invincible enemy. *Those* men were the heroes. Even the Institute could not build a machine to replace human courage.

But these points were too subtle for Bill's current frame of mind. Kira took a deep breath. His training would require long, patient hours.

Fortunately, she suspected she would enjoy it.

Daniel stepped close to the wall of glass. Outside, dark grays swirled through white clouds, hovering above trees stripped by winter. The winter had passed, but spring had not quite arrived. Daniel wondered if he would see another spring from the top floor of the Wilcox Building. In a rare gesture of fatigue, he exhaled sharply.

The warm moisture of his breath condensed on the glass. He drew his finger through the tiny droplets, leaving a trail that ended with his fingerprint. As the droplets evaporated, his fingerprint faded as well, disappearing into the past with the winter.

The Zetetic Institute had won. No one knew it yet. Not even the Zetetics themselves grasped the significance of their victory. No doubt Nathan Pilstrom could grasp what had happened easily enough. But equally without doubt, Nathan had had too many other concerns lately to take the time to deduce all the ramifications of recent events.

Daniel remembered worrying that his campaign against the Institute might make the Institute famous. He need not have worried. The men and women of the Institute had their own ways of achieving respect and prestige without him. Their fame now transcended any silly discussions of cigarettes and health. It rested with their roles as American heroes.

His nostrils flared. More condensation from his breath on the window blurred his view of the Potomac. Thinking about the latest flip-flop of the news media, he felt a sensation similar to the feeling of being jilted by a woman. He had invested so much time and creative energy into molding those news people into an effective, focused tool. For a brief time, their energies had all pointed in the same direction—in an attack on Zeteticism.

And now, with the fickleness of a woman, they had turned their energies in reverse, lavishing incredible praise upon Zetetics, imbuing the Zetetic view of life with miraculous powers.

This belief in the invincible perfection of Zetetic discipline would bring people into the anti-smoking clinics in swarms. The swarms would grow so vast that the Institute might be overwhelmed. Daniel had a moment's warm vision of an Institute growing so fast that the instructional quality deteriorated, driving the success rates down, causing yet another backlash from the fickle newspeople.

He suspected, however, that Nathan was too shrewd to make that kind of mistake. Nathan, he realized, was not interested in growth: he was interested in effectiveness. As often happened with effective people, growth came as a natural consequence.

Eventually, of course, the news media would backlash against Nathan anyway. The Institute was not perfect; its people, for all their enthusiasm and rationality, were nevertheless just people. Indeed, Daniel realized with a smile, the Institute's own philosophy militated against an image of spotless perfection. The Institute would be the first to rebut the glowing praise.

But the luster of the Institute would not wear off soon enough to help the tobacco industry. A tidal wave of smokers would kick the habit. They would convince their friends to follow them in an even greater wave. Tobacco would soon lose a major source of its profitability. The foreign sales would continue, but Daniel had little interest in riding a dying horse.

He reached into his pocket for a cigarette, thus breaking his own rule never to smoke in private. Reneging on this commitment to himself now seemed appropriate, since the very basis of the commitment would soon become irrelevant: this would be his last smoke. He lit up, in memoriam. The flavor filled his mouth and lungs.

What had gone wrong in his battle with the Institute? He worked this question over and over again in his mind. Slowly, oh so slowly, he drove to one conclusion: His loss had been inevitable with the coming of the Information Age.

He felt a bit surprised that he had not seen it coming sooner. He was the master at forecasting the future, after all. But he forgave himself. After all, the changes caused by the Information Revolution had not been readable in the nuances of life, in subtle twists of the road. Rather, the Information Age had struck everywhere with a steady, evenly applied pressure. It did not affect the road so much as it affected the very terrain upon which the road was laid. He had been so enmeshed in the change he could not see it, for he had been one of the principle users of the new information-rich terrain.

For years, every step he had taken in the defense of his industry had been based on advanced information processing. His sales projections; his political projections; his vulnerability projections; his data bases of men, women, corporations, laws, unions, and farmers; his strategies for campaigns against voters and reporters and networks—all stemmed from the central revolution. For years he had been fighting the Zetetic Institute and its forebears on their own turf, without realizing it.

Had he realized it, he would have cut and run long ago. He *never* fought on turf of his enemy's choosing, as Nathan had observed in their encounter in the Mansfield Room in the Capitol.

Taking a drag on his cigarette, he savored the long history of success he had had in fighting on his own turf. He had never argued health issues when fighting anti-smoking referenda. He had always argued on freedom or money issues—issues such as, *how much would it cost to implement the law*? In his favorite campaign, his forces had spread the word that a certain California Proposition would cost twenty million dollars to implement. The opposition had carefully analyzed his figures and found a massive error: it would only cost twenty thousand dollars.

He laughed at the memory even now, decades later. Fools! Once they started arguing about the price, the real numbers ceased to make a difference. Daniel swamped his enemies with commercial air time; people heard over and over again that the new law would cost millions. They heard it so often that in the end, the voters ridiculed the calculations made by his enemies, even though his enemies had been correct! Sweet.

But he had fought the Information Age Zetetics on their own terrain, on the terrain of information processing. This time it would be his turn to play the fool, unless he moved fast. The tight little world of the Wilcox-Morris Corporation would start crumbling in just a few months. He would have to ease his fortune out slowly, lest he cause panic. Even with care he would take a loss. He expected that his assets would drop below the magic billion-dollar threshold before the end of the affair.

But the tobacco industry would serve him well one last time, before he departed forever. Disasters could be very profitable for those who could see them coming. He would sell Wilcox-Morris stock short; that would make a tidy profit. Better yet, if he could cause a precipitous collapse in the industry, he could buy options with leverage that could get him a factor ten improvement in yield. Such a collapse could lift his worth into the multiple billions.

But the Institute would not precipitate such a fall. The Institute's focus on gradual success did not mesh with the creation of sudden catastrophes. Extra effort would have to be invested to make his vision real. He, Daniel Wilcox, would have to arrange the sudden collapse of the tobacco industry.

He would start in California, with a new series of restrictions on smoking. Once California had shown the way, he had great confidence that he could leverage his personal anti-smoking organization into the other leading states. The rest would follow on their own. With a bit of hustle, he could brutalize the Wilcox-Morris profit margins six months from now.

Daniel hummed a little cigarette commercial jingle as he turned from the window. *Change yields opportunity*, he remembered one of Nathan's little sayings. *And opportunity yields change.* Daniel could navigate the terrain of the Information Age, now that he had corrected the major flaw in his map. Profits beckoned in every direction. He had a sweet vision of one day buying up the Zetetic Institute itself. It was, after all, a corporate entity, with shares of stock for sale. What better property could he hold in a world where information was power?

On his way out the door, he paused at the trash can to toss out his cigarette stub. He reached into his pocket and pulled out his last pack of Wilcox-Morris cigarettes, running a finger over the embossed emblem that bore his name. The touch was almost a caress.

With no further hesitation, Daniel crushed the pack until shreds of weed regurgitated from it. He felt a great relief as he dumped the shreds into the trash. Smoking was a filthy habit; the world would be far better off without it.

Nathan had lived this nightmare exactly one year before. He remembered waking in the middle of the night at a chance sound, the terror of a ringing telephone, the horror of waiting. One year ago he had waited, knowing that soon the ringing telephone would end with a polite voice telling him to come to the hospital, telling him that Jan had finally escaped from the agony of dying by passing through death.

Now he waited again. This time the outcome was not quite so certain; even now the doctors were trying a radical new surgery, a technique devised during a Zetetic brainstorming conference just a month earlier. There was a chance, delicate as a snowflake, that Nell might survive. Still, the ringing of the telephone frightened him.

He waited in different surroundings. Entering the Blue Room, he joined Hilan Forstil in this vigil. Nathan hefted the small metal disk concealed in his right hand and tried to smile. Sunlight through the bay windows made it warm here; the air tasted dry.

Nathan watched as Hilan stared out the window, shifting his weight from side to side, left, right, left. "Mr. President," Nathan addressed him.

Hilan turned. His lips pursed tightly; other than that, he looked calm.

Nathan continued. "I have something for you. A medal." He opened his hand and waved the dingy metal disk, dangling from a rainbow-colored ribbon.

Hilan looked puzzled. "Tsk, Nathan. You know I can't accept gifts. It's in the Constitution."

Nathan chuckled. "I suspect they'll make an exception for this one. After all, we had to make an exception, too, to give it to you." He held out the disk. Hilan reluctantly took it. His puzzlement grew.

The disk was made of an undistinguished alloy of common metals, a gray monotone. It looked like a Boston subway token, save for two words inlaid in silver. The words "Rationality Token" flashed against the dull metal background.

Hilan flipped it over several times. "A rationality token? Just what is a rationality token?"

"It's a tradition," Nathan explained. "A Zetetic tradition that goes back before the birth of Zeteticism." He smiled. At least for a few moments, this story would take his mind off Nell and Jan. "Years and years ago, a friend of mine noticed an odd thing when he went to meetings with large groups of government bureaucrats. He would take a list of questions to each meeting, and put forth each question to the assembled body. He found that for each question, one bureaucrat in the room would have something rational and intelligent to say about the question; the rest would answer either with a magician's verbal handwaving, or with statements that were internally inconsistent, or with statements that had no apparent connection to the topic.

"Oddly, for each question, a *different* bureaucrat gave the rational response. It seemed as though a law of nature was in effect that prevented more than one bureaucrat from being rational at one time. And you could never predict beforehand which lucky bureaucrat could answer a particular question rationally.

"So my friend developed the theory of the Rationality Token. In this theory, a roomful of bureaucrats shares a single rationality token. Whoever holds the token can act intelligently, but no one else can. And the bureaucrats pass the token around, secretly, in between questions."

Hilan thought about this for a moment, then pointed at the Rationality Token disc in Nathan's hand. "If you go around handing out too many rationality tokens, you could find yourself violating this natural law."

Nathan clapped his hands. "Exactly! After sitting through these kinds of meetings for several years, my friend noticed that, scattered amongst the bureaucrats who shared tokens, there were special people. These special people were *always* rational, on all questions. My friend expanded his theory to include the notion that some people carried their own rationality tokens with them wherever they went, and as such were not bound by the laws that governed the others."

Nathan took the token in his hands, and slid the ribbon around Hilan's head so that the token dangled on his chest. "We established the decision duel to train people to such heights of rationality that they could always carry their own tokens. At the graduation ceremony we give the graduates their very own Rationality Tokens. As you can see, the token is not only useful for rationality; it is also good for a single trip on the Boston subway in case of emergency."

Hilan laughed. "But I'm not a certified decision duelist."

"No. But someone clearly displayed full rationality in a decision duel that took place the day before the Night of Steel Sleet. Someone devised an insightful third alternative—an alternative of preemptive mutual arms reduction. I would like you to hold his token for him until we find him, whoever he was."

Hilan nodded. "I see." His hand closed over the token, clenching it. "Thank you. I'm glad you think I did the right thing." Tension flowed across his features. He turned his back to Nathan, staring out the window across the south lawn of the Ellipse. Sunshine poured in, outlining Hilan as a lonely figure.

Hilan shook his head as if to toss off an evil spirit. "I remember walking past Blair House, where Ronald Reagan was staying, the day before his first inauguration. It was cold and damp, a typical Washington winter day." He turned to face Nathan, though he still looked back into the past. "The street was lined with bleachers. Scattered through the bleachers were desolate, sad people, all staring at Blair House. Those people didn't know Ronald Reagan, but they knew he would be different from Jimmy Carter. They had no rational reason for believing that Reagan's arrival would improve their individual lives, but they still stared at the house. They seemed to think that if they could just catch a glimpse of the new president, the vision could change them. Those sad, desolate people stared at the windows of Blair House with *hope*." He laughed. "And you know what? I wanted to join them."

He sighed. "They're out there now, watching for a glimpse of me. They love me without question. The gamble I played with their lives paid off, and now they believe I can do no wrong. I hope it lasts, at least long enough for me to keep my word with Klimov. I've accelerated the schedule for dismantling our missile silos. I hope that in the long run, what I've done helps the people who watch presidents from the bleachers with their sad but hopeful eyes."

Nathan nodded. "At least they know that *you* have changed their lives."

"Have I? You know, the Russians and Americans might have worked out a peaceful world without the Night of Steel Sleet. As it is, the world may be safe for democracy, but it certainly isn't safe from hate. When I initiated that Night, I *increased* the hate. The Russians hate us more now than ever before. We'll probably never know whether I made the right decision."

Nathan shrugged. "Your solution might not have been optimal," he conceded. "But at least it was *effective*. Too many of the people who have shaped the world have never even achieved that much." Nathan snorted. "I'm already annoyed when I think about the historians a hundred years from now. Some damn fool will look back on our story—the story of the birth of the Information Age—and prattle about the sweeping inevitability of our victory. Idiots!"

Hilan laughed. He moved out of the sunlight. "Certainly no Zetetic would develop or believe such an unsane view of history." His smile held just a hint of mocking amusement. "And surely the Zetetic Institute will destroy all the bureaucracies and rule the world."

"No!" Nathan was surprised by his own vehemence. He softened his tone. "At least, I hope not. I designed the Institute as a temporary structure, a scaffold, on our way to new and better Information Age organizations. Most of the good in Zetetic philosophy should be absorbed by the school system, and maybe the corporations. Zeteticism as such would then disappear, because it would be the norm. It would cease to be distinguishable from the background of normal society. If the Institute continued on indefinitely, then we would merely have created another institution. We would have failed."

Hilan waved his hand expansively. "Do you believe that only teachers can learn from you? Then what about *my* institution, Nathan? What about my bureaucracy, the United States government?"

Nathan looked into the distance. "I believe you are obsolete, Mr. President."

"Really! And who will replace me?"

Nathan shook his head. "No one will replace you, Hilan. It's the office you occupy, as head of a nation-state, that will be replaced."

"What will replace it?"

Nathan's forehead creased in concentration. "I don't know. I can't see it yet." Tears glittered in his eyes. "Perhaps Jan would have known. She often saw the future more clearly than I, though she never tried to look too far." He shrugged. "When the time comes, I'm sure someone will know. It may not be our problem. Not all the ramifications of the Information Age will settle out in our lifetimes."

"Thank heavens! We already have too much to do."

The telephone rang. The sound swept Nathan's mind with electric terror. Was this the call from the polite men from the hospital? Was it over? Was it too late?

He had never told Nell he loved her. He had been a coward, insufficiently self-assured to think of himself as a proper consort for a Madam President. Had she felt the same? Why had he waited?

Hilan's steps sounded soft as he walked across the room to pick up the obscenely ringing instrument. Hilan's tense impassivity turned to a serious frown as he listened, then changed to mischievous humor. "Thank you. We'll be right over." He hung up and headed for the door. "I think you'll want to come with me," he said over his shoulder to Nathan.

"Who was it?" Nathan's pulse pounded as he asked.

"Well, it seems my obsolescence has already caught up with me. I'm about to be evicted from the White House." He opened the door to let Nathan go through first. "It seems that Nell has just regained consciousness. They think she'll be fine."

Nathan froze. Then his eyes widened, and joyful warmth suffused his whole body. "A miracle," he said simply. It was funny, Nathan noted, that even he himself could sometimes take the goodness of the world for granted. Even he needed an occasional miracle.

He had never lost his sense of wonder, despite the loss of Jan and the jeopardy of Nell. But with Nell's return from danger, every detail of his universe shined brighter. He appreciated the air he breathed, the scent of Washington springtime, the metallic polish of the limousine that stopped for them, the texture of the leather seat, the quiet rumble of the engine, the pressure of acceleration, the glow of the green light, the blue sky, the soft clouds, the antiseptic smell of the hospital, the bright white of the walls, the cold metal of the bed rails, the warm smile on Nell's face.

He lingered there, in the wonder of Nell's smile, for a very long time.